ON THE WINDS OF QUASARS

T. A. BRUNO

10-8-21

Cover design by Daniel Schmelling
Interior artwork by Jason Michael Hall

First edition: September 2021

Soft Cover: 978-1-7346470-5-1
Hard Cover: 978-1-7346470-6-8
E-Book: 978-1-7346470-7-5

OTHER BOOKS BY T. A. BRUNO

The Song of Kamaria Series:
In the Orbit of Sirens

AUTHOR'S NOTE

The following story takes place in the far future, after humanity colonized the Sol System and lost it. It features characters from the Deaf Community who use Sol-Sign, a language based on American Sign Language, but with some liberties taken. I have had a lot of help ensuring it is as authentic as I can make it, and I hope I did it justice. Other characters speak Sol Common, sometimes with accents. Languages from Old Earth are remembered and spoken privately among families. Some readers may recall Major Pavel Volkov's Russian dialect in *In the Orbit of Sirens*.

The first chapter of this novel occurs during the events of *In the Orbit of Sirens*. Everything past chapter one takes place twenty-six years later.

I hope you enjoy your trip back to Kamaria,
—*T.A.*

To my brother Danny,
You may never read a single word in this book.
But they are all for you.

KAMARIA

- ODYSSEUS CITY
- TIMBER CHASE
- SPIRIT SONG MOUNTAIN
- AZURE VAULT (APUSTICUS)
- UNFORGOTTEN GARDEN
- STARVING SANDS (SIREN PIT)
- TANGLE MAZE (SHARP TOP)
- SUPERNAL ECHO
- EMBER-LIT FOREST
- HOWLING SHORE

THE STORY SO FAR...

All hope was lost.

The Sol System had been taken by nightmarish machines called the Undriel. One by one, each of the colonized worlds was absorbed into their dark network. The machines worked so quickly, so efficiently, that their motives were never truly discovered. Humanity fought back, but their defenses crumbled, and it became clear that the war would be lost.

A desperate escape.

The *Telemachus*, an interstellar spacecraft designed for exploration, was repurposed into a liferaft. With their backs against Jupiter, and the Undriel clawing their way across the Sol System, humanity fled across the stars.

A home abandoned.

The Undriel sunk into obscurity after the exodus. None of the surviving humans knew what had become of their old foe.

A home discovered.

Kamaria, humanity's new safe haven. It is a world of immense, raw beauty—but also of hidden dangers. The voyage from Sol to Delta Octantis took three hundred years of warp-speed travel. A forward team was sent six years before the *Telemachus* to prepare Kamaria. This crew named their first colony Odysseus.

Unwelcome guests.

Lung-lock, an airborne bacteria that permeated throughout Kamaria, paralyzed human lungs. This affliction slowly killed off many of the Odysseus colonists. A cure was on the cusp of completion, but it was missing a key component.

A new threat.

Scouts searched Kamaria for a cure to lung-lock. In their desperate search, they stumbled upon a mysterious crypt. Inside, they found the body of a creature they called the Siren. Unbeknownst to the scouts, the Siren was not as dead as she first appeared. Her phantom possessed the body of Captain Roelin Raike and wore him like a mask. The colonists had no idea of the danger lurking among them.

A stranger visits.

The native Kamarians, the Auk'nai, kept their distance from the human colonists. They were an advanced race of humanoid bird-people with a mental sensitivity to empathic wavelengths. One lone auk'nai, Mag'Ro, made contact with Dr. Eliana Veston and provided the last element needed to cure lung-lock. In exchange, she gave him a weapon, unsure what he would do with it.

A terrible tragedy.

The Siren—Nhymn, as she would later be called—used Roelin's body as a weapon. In a night of carnage, she murdered several colonists and fled in a warship named the *Astraeus*. Nhymn took Roelin as her prisoner and disappeared into the wilderness. For years, no one knew what had become of the Siren and her hostage.

The Telemachus *arrived.*

Years passed since the massacre, and time had slowly healed the colony. Odysseus had grown into a city. Humanity had gained its foothold on Kamaria. Their numbers were low, their progress steady. Relations with the auk'nai hesitantly improved.

The Siren returned.

A clue led a scout team to Nhymn's hidden location in the Sharp Top mountains, nestled deep within the Tangle Maze jungle. Upon discovering the missing *Astraeus* warship, the scouts were attacked by Nhymn. She killed half of them and took the rest hostage.

Her dark goals.

Nhymn needed to repair the *Astraeus* to find her sister, Sympha. She used a young man named Denton Castus to fix the downed ship. He did his job well, and Nhymn carried out her mission of reuniting with Sympha, taking over her body and powers. Nhymn, now more powerful than ever, vanished into the wilderness for a month. Her actions during this time were unknown.

A shade.

Denton Castus had his own secrets. In all, there had been three Sirens; Nhymn, Sympha, and Karx. Karx found Denton and tried to warn him about Nhymn, leaping into Denton's mind to vacate his own failing body. The combination of Karx and Denton resulted in a mental tether forming between them. Denton was able to walk through Karx's memories as a shade. He learned the origin of the Sirens.

Apusticus burned.

After vanishing for a month, Nhymn reappeared with devastation. The auk'nai city of Apusticus was rendered to ash by her power. Mag'Ro was killed, and the surviving auk'nai fled their destroyed city to warn the humans of her approach.

A final battle.

The auk'nai allied with the humans of Odysseus and headed off Nhymn in the Unforgotten Garden. Many died that day, both human and auk'nai. Things grew desperate as the Siren gained the advantage.

Tethers linked. Tethers snapped.

Denton Castus, Roelin Raike, and Sympha distracted Nhymn long enough so that the human and auk'nai defenses could find a way to destroy her. Roelin and Sympha were killed during the battle, but they had been successful in their task. Under Eliana's suggestion, the *Telemachus* was smashed into Nhymn. The Siren had been crushed, and the battle ended.

Sirens are immortal.

The body of Nhymn had been destroyed, but it was known she would return. Denton's previous shade walking confirmed that Sirens live on past their physical deaths. Three years after the final battle, Nhymn came back. She begged to be sent away from Kamaria, a request the people of Kamaria gleefully fulfilled. Her reasons for leaving remained a mystery.

ONE

THE CITY OF APUSTICUS burned.

The flames clawed at the stars in the night sky, flicking embers into the void above. The people who lived here were humanoid birds named the auk'nai. Their screams could be heard from kilometers off, and the unsung song they cast out traveled even farther. The world wept for the dead. A powerful being called the Siren roared with rage, towering above the ashes of the dying city. She brought destruction to the auk'nai of Apusticus, and in her wake trailed obliteration.

L'Arn hurried back to Apusticus, pushing the muscles in his wings to their limit as he careened through the night. He was one of the strongest auk'nai in the city, although he only maintained a limited presence there. L'Arn had void-black feathers, with crisscrossing slices of yellow. He wore layered sashes, the outermost a reflective gold material, with the inner layers shades of nature to ensure stealth during a hunt.

He could see the monster pounding the city into dust. The Siren stood taller than the trees themselves. A cyclone of clouds swirled above her skull-like head. A sharp horn protruded from her forehead, and two deep-pitted eye sockets dripped tar. Four arms made of wormskin and spiked with gnarled, twisted bones ended in an array of razor-sharp talons. Lightning burst from the ground around her. L'Arn had never seen anything like it before, and it shook him to his core.

An explosion. More cries. The world rocked in pain. L'Arn landed in the central district of his home city. Apusticus consisted of a series of floating platforms hanging between tall trees, with structures built atop each. Gemstones shone in the night, casting an eerie kaleidoscope of color on the destruction. His fellow auk'nai citizens took what they could and fled into the sky, exiting from openings on the residential structures. Lightning struck a fleeing female, sending her freefalling to the platform's surface with a loud, wet thud. Her blood sprayed onto L'Arn's feet and legs. Although he did not remember her face, he knew her song. All Apusticus citizens knew each other's unsung songs. He watched with widened eyes as the source of her destruction climbed onto the platform from the opposite side.

This creature was called a nezzarform. It was a constructed thing—stone and rubble clung together by electrical energy into a shape that only barely passed as a bipedal lifeform.

The nezzarform began to build up energy inside the cyclopean orifice on its face.

L'Arn's survival instincts took over. The constructed creature unleashed a bolt of lightning from its eye. L'Arn dodged but was so nearly struck that he felt static fizzle over his feathers. His hand grasped the hooked staff on his back, the daunoren staff that all auk'nai who had taken the pilgrimage to the Spirit Song Mountain wielded. Although these staffs had many uses other than combat, they were also deadly weapons in a skilled warrior's hand. As if a third arm, the staff moved like any other muscle in L'Arn's body, as natural as swinging a fist. The staff's hooked end found the nezzarform's core, then L'Arn ripped downward, forcing the stone construct to the ground. Another twirl, and a snap downward, and the staff's blunt end crashed into the back of the nezzarform's head as another blast exploded.

L'Arn was thrown from the stone creature as it burst. His skin crawled with static electricity, and his tongue itched ferociously.

<L'Arn, we cannot stay here!> A familiar voice sang the unsung song. It came to L'Arn through the half-clouded daze of the impact he suffered. He felt something shaking him.

An auk'nai with blue and white feathers was a beak-width away from L'Arn's face.

"Nock'lu?" L'Arn asked the blurry face.

"L'Arn came back just in time," Nock'lu responded and lifted L'Arn to his feet. He slammed his daunoren staff back into L'Arn's hands and repeated, "Auk'nai cannot stay here. The others are leaving. Nock'lu must help Apusticus escape." Nock'lu referred to himself in the third person, as all auk'nai did. It helped sort out who was speaking in a civilization where telepathic communication was commonplace.

"L'Arn will help Nock'lu." L'Arn grunted and twisted his daunoren staff with both hands, separating it in the middle. He pumped his left hand, and the blunt end flicked out a flat-bladed sword.

Nock'lu nodded, then flipped a device down onto his face. L'Arn had seen these peck rifles before but never trusted the things. They were repurposed technology from an alien race that had recently come to inhabit Kamaria—*humans.*

The Siren bellowed out a horrible roar, and beams of electricity blasted into the sky. The neighboring platform of the city burst into rubble and dust—songs extinguished.

Did the humans cause this? L'Arn wondered as nezzarforms began to fill the platform in front of him. "L'Arn should have stayed in the wilds," he mumbled.

Nock'lu warbled in response.

The nezzarforms divided into two modes of attack—a few rushed forward while others launched volleys of electrical bolts. Nock'lu flapped down hard against the surface of the platform, propelling himself into the smoke-filled sky and spraying particle blasts from his peck rifle. At the same time, L'Arn dashed forward, hook and sword hacking away at the approaching nezzarforms.

L'Arn's vision went red. His heart raced, and his arms were not in his own control anymore. He moved like a possessed cyclone of blades, allowing the electrical energy from dying nezzarforms to pass over his feathers, tingling the flesh underneath.

It felt *good* to fight.

———— ◆ ————

In the end, it wasn't enough to save the city of Apusticus.

After an hour of fighting, Nock'lu called to L'Arn, but the other auk'nai paid him no mind. L'Arn ripped, slashed, tore, and rendered each of the unnatural rock creatures that fell before him.

Nock'lu urged, "It is time to regroup with the others!"

L'Arn marched toward the next nezzarform and used his powerful arm to slap its head sideways. It loosed an electrical bolt, accidentally sending the beam into another group of its comrades nearby. The group burst into a rain of stone and dust as L'Arn finished off the nezzarform before him with a powerful slice, cutting straight through the rock construct's stone chest. Nock'lu landed next to L'Arn and spun him around. *<Hear Nock'lu now!>* he shouted with the unsung song.

L'Arn shoved Nock'lu, then reared his hand back with his blade in the air. He did not send it crashing down. Instead, L'Arn exhaled as if he had been under water.

"What—" L'Arn began.

"Follow," Nock'lu said, and propelled himself into the sky. L'Arn asked no further questions and took off after him. As they made their escape, L'Arn looked back on the home he barely knew. Apusticus was nothing more than fire and rubble now. The monster that had come had moved through the city as if it were a castle made of sand—generations of auk'nai history gone in mere hours.

There was no home to fly back to.

———— ◆ ————

"Our song has not been extinguished!" the young, wingless auk'nai named Talulo shouted to the crowd of Apusticus survivors. "The Daunoren still sits atop the Spirit Song Mountain. With it, auk'nai find our strength!"

L'Arn disagreed silently. He found his strength on his own, deep in the wilderness of Kamaria. The god who sat atop a mountain was still sacred to L'Arn—a force of habit—but it was not where he found courage.

It had been a day since the attack. L'Arn and Nock'lu had helped the survivors regroup, calling out in song for a gathering. The place L'Arn had chosen had everything they needed. The plants contained healing properties. Water spilled from a higher ledge into a deep pool at the base of a cliff. The insects here were fatty and ready to feed the hungry—plenty to eat, drink, and heal with.

Talulo had been dropped off by some humans. L'Arn didn't understand the aliens and therefore tried to ignore them as much as possible. He understood the wilderness, he knew its song, and he could sing along with it. L'Arn didn't need anything more than that.

"Apusticus, will you help Talulo drive back the Siren and save this world?" Talulo urged the crowd. L'Arn felt it in his mind; they all agreed. The auk'nai agreed so passionately that not even Nock'lu noticed L'Arn's dissent.

They wanted revenge.

With this rallying call to arms hitting its peak, the auk'nai began to soar off into the sky. Talulo watched them fly, lifting the daunoren staff that belonged to the previous leader of Apusticus upward. The auk'nai filled the air around him.

"Come, L'Arn. We will crush the Siren!" Nock'lu said, the thrill of battle filling him.

L'Arn looked at the ground. In honesty, since leaving the Song of Apusticus behind, L'Arn had felt freer than he had ever been. It was like his chains had been cut.

"Is L'Arn not coming?" Talulo approached, asking a question he already knew the answer to. The unsung song emitting from L'Arn had explained it already. Nock'lu's eyes widened, and his beak shook from side to side. The auk'nai could sense emotions and intentions in each other. L'Arn didn't have to say anything.

"L'Arn is coming with, yes?" Nock'lu asked, not believing the song he was hearing.

L'Arn shuffled his clawed foot against the gravel, feeling the dirt between his talons. He inhaled the fresh air through his nose and felt the cool breeze against his feathers.

"*I* will not," L'Arn said. He referred to himself in the first person. Only the *auk'gnell* did this—those without civilization, attached to the song of the wild.

"*Friend . . .*" Nock'lu whispered into L'Arn's mind.

"Come, Nock'lu. The battle needs the song of Apusticus," Talulo said aloud.

L'Arn looked away, not willing to meet his friend's unbelieving stare. Nock'lu grunted, and without another word, lifted Talulo's wingless form into the sky and sailed off to fight the Siren.

L'Arn's eyes grew wet. His lungs filled with a cackle, and he laughed so loudly his birdsong echoed off the rock walls around him. He whistled and stomped his foot. He'd had no idea how good it felt to be songless until the Siren ended Apusticus. Now that he was homeless, he could make the wilderness his home. It was the kind of logic that made sense to L'Arn and no one else—the only kind of logic that mattered.

He spread his wings and launched himself into the sky. To the west, he could see the building storm, the battle for Kamaria already underway. His brothers and sisters dotted the sky, joining the fray to help the aliens. To the east, far from here, was the Howling Shore. L'Arn had always loved the ocean, and so he set off to the east to be with his love.

L'Arn was free.

TWO

TWENTY-SIX YEARS LATER . . .

"YOU SHOULD BE GETTING close." Zephyr Gale's voice came through clear on the comm channel, as if she were standing right next to him. "Old Cyrus died around here."

Cade Castus gently drifted along the side of the S-type asteroid, his atmospheric suit separating him from the cold, dead void of space. He had dark skin and blue eyes, with short-cut ebony hair tucked inside his helmet.

Besides Zephyr's voice, Cade could only hear his own breathing, the soft hiss of oxygen whispering into his helmet, and various beeps and blips of his health readings inside the suit. His helmet had a heads-up display that showed an arcing pathway to his destination. The asteroid almost appeared to roll beneath him, for he had very little sense of movement floating in zero gravity above it.

"Ah, found him. Poor guy," Cade said as he rounded the mountainous space rock and saw the disabled prospector drone floating and sparking.

"Rest in peace, Old Cyrus," Zephyr said with a tsk-tsk.

"Oh, come on. He's a badass. Just needs a tune-up." Cade drifted toward the drone, watching it grow in size. The prospector drone was seven meters long and four meters wide but looked small compared to the asteroid and the ship it had come from. The *Maulwurf* was a mining starship built to analyze, harvest, and transport asteroids to a low Kamarian orbit for further processing. It was a bulky thing, painted an orange-yellow with black and gray accents. It was shaped like a box in the front and round on the bottom, like a fat-bellied whale. On the top, asteroid material could be pushed into a large compartment, and precious metals could be refined efficiently. It was also Cade, Zephyr, and Captain D'Rand's home away from home.

The crew lived in the ship for months during refining missions. Currently, the *Maulwurf* was tethered to the S-type asteroid with two long winch cables. This mission had been eight months of processing the asteroid for metals and volatiles.

The ship was a product of the *Infinite Aria*, a combined effort of human and auk'nai brilliance that would take both their peoples across the stars one day. The *Aria* was picking up where John Veston and the Telemachus Project had left off decades ago.

Cade adjusted his trajectory with a flick of the joystick attached to his armrest on his extravehicular activity (EVA) harness. He lifted away from the asteroid and floated freely to where Old Cyrus was drifting. As he pulled away from the rock, he could see Kamaria. The planet took up almost his entire view. The asteroid belt created an enormous radius around the planet, not visible from its surface. The *Maulwurf* worked in the ERO, the easily recoverable object zone, which also provided the best view of the planet. From here, Cade couldn't see the *Infinite Aria*. The ship was not only just partially complete, it was also rendered infinitesimally small next to the celestial objects dancing in the void around it—an insect in the heavens.

Hells of a view, Cade thought. He slowed his ascent and matched drift with Old Cyrus. The drone was a nuisance for the crew of the

Maulwurf, but to Cade, it was a friend. Due to Old Cyrus's constant malfunctions, Cade got to stretch his legs outside the ship often. He felt good in space, comfortable. Of the three-person crew, Cade was the only EVA specialist. When something went wrong on the rock, it was his job to fix it.

"How's he looking?" Zephyr asked. She had darker skin than Cade, with chartreuse-colored eyes and a blown-out afro. She wore the standard flight suit of the *Maulwurf* crew, a form-fitting one-piece suit with a zipper on the front that went from collar to crotch. It was scarlet red with accents of mustard yellow. Peeking out from Zephyr's pulled-up sleeves and around her neck above her tank top were faintly glowing tattoos that matched her eyes.

For fun, Zephyr had convinced Cade to get one on his forearm that matched hers—a canary. It was a historical homage to coal miners on ancient Earth, a place Zephyr and Cade had only been forced to read about in school. Zephyr was the refinery specialist, maintaining maximum yield for each prospector drone and strategically placing them on asteroids. Old Cyrus was a pain in her ass.

Zephyr remained on the *Maulwurf* as Cade's handler with their captain, D'Rand, the only auk'nai member of the three-person crew. D'Rand was an older bird, with a raspy voice, a dented black beak, yellow eyes, and wine-red feathers that almost blended into his suit. The captain kept his daunoren staff in a special harness next to the pilot's chair.

"I gotta open him up to see what's wrong. I'm thinking fragments again. The old guy's got bad lungs," Cade said, hooking himself to the drone and unstrapping the EVA harness so he could move more freely. From Zephyr's perspective on the ship, Cade looked like he was standing upside down on the drone, his head tipped toward the asteroid. In a perfect line at both of Cade's flanks were the other drones, each carving into the rock and extracting what they could. Small debris emitted from the top of each drone, spewing dust and harmless, pebble-sized rocks into space.

Captain D'Rand chimed in for the first time since Cade stepped out into space. "Remember, if Cyrus can't hack it, dismantle and reuse for parts. Cyrus has been a pain in D'Rand's tailfeathers long enough."

Cade sighed. He didn't want to dismantle Cyrus, but he was committed to doing his job. He walked on the hull of the drone with his magnetically sealing boots until he reached the exhaust, where the dust and debris should have been spilling out. Old Cyrus was deactivated, so there was no danger in sticking an arm inside. Cade's EVA harness followed him like a pet on a leash, drifting above his shoulders on a tether. He was correct. Chunks of rock that the cutting laser should have reduced had been sucked into the drone, causing it to malfunction.

"Yep, bad lungs," Cade whispered to himself, not using the comm. He pulled his harness closer and turned its back toward his chest to reach the tool compartment. He opened it, and inside, magnetically adhered and perfectly organized, were his tools. He grabbed a particle cutter, a stick-shaped tool that extended when he activated it. At one end of the cutter was a collider cylinder with a laser emitter that could break down the big rocks. It allowed him to poke at the debris and cut it into smaller pieces. He reached the stick into the exhaust and began shaking loose the rocks, zapping them to clear them from the machinery.

One chunk broke down and drifted close to Cade's helmet. He grabbed the fist-sized rock with his free hand and inspected it. The rock shimmered with flecks of metal and played with the light from his helmet in a way that pleased him. Cade put the rock into a loose-hanging satchel on his suit's belt, another addition to his collection, and not the first provided by Old Cyrus. Cade collected rocks on every job. He wanted to remember the celestial objects he had the privilege to walk on. Each asteroid felt like a planet, and he was the only person to ever stand on them.

"Run Cyrus quick without the laser cutter. Let's see if he coughs anything up," Cade said, unlatching his boots and getting a little distance on his tether from the exhaust.

"Activating now. Come on, old fella," Zephyr said over the comm.

Old Cyrus coughed, and a burst of dust and rocks blasted out from the drone's exhaust, silent in space. The exhaust began to whir beautifully—the obstruction had been cleared, but the job wasn't finished yet.

"We just treated a symptom so far. I want to check his cutting laser," Cade said, patting Old Cyrus on the side as he brought himself back toward the hull of the drone and stood upright on his magnetic boots.

"Drone has bad eyes too," D'Rand said. "D'Rand still thinks we should break Cyrus down for metal."

"Not on my watch," Cade said.

"Cyrus is powered down," Zephyr said. "Get him some glasses."

Cade made his way to the cutting end of the drone and pulled his tools closer. He brushed some dust away with his glove and inspected the lens on the end of the laser. It was a two-step problem. The eyes that helped the laser see kept getting dirty due to a clearing mechanism malfunction, and the laser's lens had been chipped by some rock. With a faulty lens, the laser wasn't cutting at full strength. The drone could break down rock half the size of a full-grown adult human, but the laser was designed to help cut it into an optimal shape for the refinery inside the drone.

"Well, that explains everything." Cade smiled. He grabbed some of the loose-floating rocks nearby and fed them into the side of his EVA harness. There, a replicator would break down the rocks to use as duplicating materials.

About twenty-five minutes later, Cade had printed the pieces he needed to replace the broken parts and gotten the new components installed. He slapped Cyrus on the side of the hull for good luck and pushed himself away again, using the tether to keep himself at a safe distance and steady.

"Alright, let's see if Cyrus gets to stay on the team. Boot him up," Cade said into the comm.

"Roger," Zephyr said.

Lights flashed on Old Cyrus's hull, and the laser flicked on. It looked acceptable to Cade, but he wouldn't know for sure how well it worked until the drone was cutting into the asteroid again. He reattached himself to his EVA harness and untethered from the drone. Zephyr then commanded Old Cyrus to pull itself toward the asteroid on the large winches staking it to the rock. When Cyrus's head reached the rock, it began cutting and sucking in large chunks of asteroid again. Cade watched as dust and debris spewed from the exhaust, matching the same consistency of the drones that lined the S-type asteroid around him.

Cade thrust his fists into the air in triumph and shouted, "Old Cyrus lives to prospect another day!"

Zephyr clapped from inside the ship and rotated in her chair to face D'Rand. "Looks like we aren't getting a shiny new drone after all."

"Zephyr says that like it's a good thing," D'Rand grunted. "D'Rand doesn't understand human attachment to machines."

"Honestly, we're just bored, and this gives us something to root for. Everyone loves an underdog."

"What is an *under-dog*?" D'Rand asked.

"Old Earth phrase. Not sure what it means myself." Zephyr sighed.

Sol System pets had remained in the Sol System. Dogs, cats, and other common domesticated animals were not built for deep-space interstellar travel. The stasis beds that had brought the first human colonists to Kamaria were only designed for human cargo, with some exceptions made for farm animals like cows, pigs, and sheep. When humanity narrowly escaped the Sol System, fleeing from the nightmarish machines known as the Undriel, they were sadly forced to leave their pets behind. They were wild things living in an abandoned star system now. In some ways, it might be a better life. From what they understood, the Undriel never absorbed animals.

"Heading back now," Cade said, drifting slowly back to the

Maulwurf on his EVA harness. Zephyr left her seat and floated through the ship to the locker room near the airlock. Cade came into the room and unclipped his helmet, and Zephyr helped him strip off the bulky atmospheric suit. She ran her fingers through his hair to help dissolve the helmet-hair look.

"Good job out there. D'Rand is pissed," Zephyr said with a smirk.

"He's always pissed." Cade smiled and flexed his hands, now free of the cumbersome gloves.

"Well, we have our vacation coming up in a few weeks. We won't have to see him for a whole seven days," Zephyr said with a relaxing sigh.

"It'll be nice to go back planetside. Has it really been *eight months* since we last had a gravity-leave?"

"Last time we went, I think it was summer. It's just starting to show signs of spring down there now."

"I love that time of year. Got any plans planetside?" Cade asked as he began to don his flight suit over his black T-shirt and boxer briefs. He didn't notice Zephyr admiring his physique.

"Oh, me? Uh, yeah. Family stuff. Kind of lame, actually. I usually live with my gran down there," Zephyr said.

"Family's important. It's never lame." Cade zipped up his flight suit to his sternum. "I'm doing much of the same. Hey, if we get some free time, we should hang out. Celebrate the continued life of Old Cyrus or something."

Zephyr nodded and smiled. "Yeah, I'd like—"

D'Rand interrupted them through the comm. "Cade, come see D'Rand on the bridge."

"Uh oh," Cade said under his breath.

"Wonder what that's about?" Zephyr said, but she had this air about her that made Cade think she already knew something. He floated past her and pushed himself along the halls of the *Maulwurf* to the bridge, using handrails to help him glide effortlessly through the metal ship.

Cade entered the bridge and saw D'Rand floating close to the large rectangular window, playing with his daunoren staff in the zero G. He pushed with the butt end of his staff to match Cade's orientation.

Cade saluted his captain and asked, "You needed me, sir?"

"D'Rand sent a report of your performance to *Aria* Command," Captain D'Rand said, not looking at Cade, instead favoring his staff. "Old Cyrus is reporting a higher yield due to Cade's fix. For how long? D'Rand does not know. But Command thinks Cade might be ready for promotion."

Cade smiled. "Really?"

D'Rand cooed, "Yes. Command has been looking for a new crew leader on the *Aria*. Cade would be in charge of a team working on it. No more rock wrangling. Congratulations."

Cade felt his heart race, and his smile grew wider. It was his dream to work on the *Infinite Aria*. As the grandson to John Veston, he felt like it would bring him closer to his family's legacy. The *Aria* would ferry people to other stars. They would be space explorers once again. Cade would pick up where his late grandfather had left off.

"Thank you, sir. It's an honor," Cade said.

Zephyr drifted into the room and floated to her station on Cade's left side. She smiled.

"D'Rand is sure Old Cyrus will miss Cade," D'Rand said with a cluck, "as will Zephyr and D'Rand. Admittedly."

Cade looked over to Zephyr. His smile faded, and his brows crunched in the center of his forehead. For the past six years, since Cade had started working in space, he had worked with Zephyr. She was his best friend, and he felt confident with her around. Cade felt like part of his heart was removed at the revelation that she would not be joining him on the *Aria*.

"They made the right choice. I can't think of a better crew leader," Zephyr said. He had discussed his dream to work on the *Aria* with her many times throughout their long mission stints. She knew what this meant to him, and she looked pleased to see him obtain it.

"*Maulwurf* goes back to the *Aria* when wrapped up here, but that will be Cade's departure from this team. Cade will be briefed on the *Aria* and introduced to other EVA specialists," D'Rand said. "Until then, Cade still works for *Maulwurf.* Don't let it go to the head." The auk'nai grinned and cooed, "For now, work is finished today. Get some rest. Dismissed."

"Yes, sir. Thank you, sir," Cade said with a smile.

Cade and Zephyr saluted their captain, and D'Rand floated past them to the crew quarters. The two floated on the bridge and watched the drones work on the asteroid through the rectangular glass.

"Congratulations," Zephyr said and patted Cade on his shoulder.

"Thanks," Cade said weakly.

"What's wrong? This is what you wanted, isn't it?" Zephyr asked.

"I mean, yeah. It's just going to be weird being away from you."

Zephyr laughed. "I'm no hull worker. I prefer being out here, away from stuff. I like refining and drone handling."

"It's just happening so fast."

"Well, we got a few more weeks here, and then a week planetside. So, take your time, and let it sink in." Zephyr grinned. "Crewleader Castus. Got a nice ring to it."

Cade nodded and seemed to float straighter. "Hells yeah, it does."

Beyond the drones and the tumbling asteroids, Kamaria shined like a cerulean beacon against the deepness of the void. Cade thought of his upcoming trip and how he'd tell his parents the great news.

I made it.

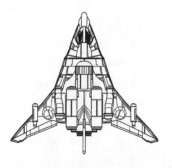

THREE

TWO DECADES HAD PASSED since the auk'nai of Apusticus and Odysseus Colony humans battled the Siren Nhymn. Many lives were lost that day. Still, after the bloodshed subsided and the battle was over, an extended harmony came to the inhabitants of Kamaria, both human and native. The refugees of Apusticus moved into Odysseus Colony and helped build a grand city by merging their technologies and cultures.

A few years after the battle, Nhymn reemerged, hiding inside the body of a creature called a nightsnare. She was an immortal being and thus would never truly stay dead. Nhymn begged to instead be sent away from the planet but would not reveal why. Happy to be rid of such a significant threat, the people of Odysseus City obliged. They put Nhymn on a spacecraft and sent her into the void, never to be seen again.

The grand valley that had been ravaged by the battle had healed over time. The wreckage of the *Telemachus* still protruded from the planet like an arrow in an apple. The interstellar spacecraft had become their hammer in the end. The ship had struck Nhymn and crashed into a molten pit of lava, fusing itself to the ground in the process. The wreck served as a reminder of humanity's reach—and also its limits.

The creatures of Kamaria had returned to the valley as well. The scientists in the observation outpost there believed that there were even more animals than before. The blue flowers that encompassed every tree and every vine drew them there with their succulence. Inert nezzarforms lay dormant in the valley surrounding the *Telemachus* wreck. Some said they could see them faintly glowing green at night, but the reports of that were inconsistent.

Beyond the high valley, nestled in the steeping mountains, lay the city of Odysseus, the home built by refugees of two impossible enemies. For the humans, it was the Undriel war machine that had driven them from the Sol System. For the auk'nai, Nhymn had brought obliteration to Apusticus. Odysseus City was a beacon of hope for survivors.

The city was an impressive sight of gleaming white skyscrapers and three floating platforms. Each of the platforms was named after beautiful gems: Ruby, Carnelian, and Amethyst. Lifts suspended in the air zipped up and down from the upper floating platforms, providing access for citizens who weren't born with functioning wings. A river ran through the city's center, with a kaleidoscope of color dancing beneath its current. Vehicles and auk'nai darted around at all times of the day and night. When the sun set, the city glowed with a soft amber hue.

Other outposts dotted the area around the city, all within easy trade distance. The most successful of these outposts bloomed into small colonies and villages of their own. Some humans even lived solitary lives in the wilderness, forging their own paths. Still, Kamaria held its secrets tightly. The Scout Program remained in full effect. Their discoveries continued to aid life for humanity and auk'nai alike on Kamaria.

———— ◆ ————

"Alright, all set," Denton said as he flipped back the welding mask. "I think it's time you get up and stretch your legs. You've been lying down long enough."

Denton Castus was now in his mid-fifties, the same age his father had been when they first arrived on Kamaria. He was beginning to look more like Michael Castus every day, with his light skin, scruffy brown beard, short messy hair, and deep-green eyes. His experiences with the Siren years ago had been permanently etched into his body—a scar on his right cheek from a knife that sliced him during freefall in a crashing spaceship, and a spiral-shaped discoloration on his chest from a nezzarform bolt.

It was a *wild* time.

Inside the Castus Machine Shop, among the high-end tools, half-built starships, and equipment in various stages of repair, a bipedal figure lay flat on a worktable. It looked carved of marble, with gray skin and a face that contained an androgynous human's visage. "Have you balanced the weight loads, Mr. Castus?" the figure asked with a smooth, synthetic voice.

"Sure did, Homer. You're all calibrated up." Denton smiled. "I don't think you'll fall over this time. Only one way to find out, though. Let's see how you do."

Homer's robotic body sat up and rotated so that their legs hung from the side of the table. Denton was proud that the movement didn't look too mechanical. It was smooth and natural. Homer placed one foot on the floor, then the other, and lifted upward to stand. The robot wobbled momentarily, then found balance.

"There you go! You'll be a real boy in no time." Denton laughed, referring to an ancient Earth story about a wooden puppet that became a human child through some sort of strange magic.

"I don't believe so," Homer said. "I am not a boy, nor am I a man or woman. I believe my person doesn't belong to any established human binary. I am simply Homer."

"Sounds good to me," Denton said with a smile. "You have a full scout kit built into your body. I can tweak anything that doesn't seem right whenever you need me to."

"Thank you," Homer said.

"We'll work on your face at some point," Denton said. Homer

still could neither blink nor open their mouth. Their face was a façade to mask the machinery underneath. When they spoke, their mouth didn't move. Instead, Homer's eyes would fluctuate in brightness. Denton added, "But hey! You can personally join us on scout missions now."

Homer was the artificial intelligence designed to ferry humanity to distant stars. They had accomplished their job years ago, and since then had been forced to learn data at the same rate as the humans who came to live on Kamaria. To an AI with unlimited learning capacity, it was dreadfully slow. Homer decided they could be of better use if they could come along on scouting missions. Having their own set of eyes, along with being part of every bioscope, drone, and cartographer's orb, would quench their thirst for data.

Tyler Castus, one of Denton's older brothers and the proud owner of the machine shop, entered the room. "Now *that's* the future!" he said and scurried over to Homer's new body. "Screw working on their gizmos and gadgets. We'll just *make* our own clients!"

Tyler had longer hair than Denton; he kept it tied back in a ponytail, but some still dangled in front of his face, with more gray hairs every day. He smiled and said, "Bravo, Dent. I'm really impressed with how he turned out!"

Denton interjected, "How *they* turned out," respecting Homer's pronoun of choice.

"Right, sorry. Homer, if you need any upgrades, feel free to come back anytime. We can add rocket launchers and all sorts of fun stuff."

"Now that you mention it . . ." Homer considered.

Denton laughed. "One step at a time here. No rocket launchers on day one." He turned to Tyler. "Thanks for letting me use your shop," he said as he toweled the grime off his hands. "You have better tools here than we got at the Scout Campus."

"Hey, it'll always be *our* shop. You're my brother—and I'll invoice you later." Tyler winked.

Homer flexed their new hand, then gripped it into a fist, testing the movements. Denton put on his old leather scout jacket and walked over to the door. "Hey, you coming?"

Homer looked up at Denton, then over their shoulder.

"Yeah, *you*." Denton elaborated, "Let's go for a walk. You ain't going to learn much in here. Trust me, I spent half my life in a shop like this."

"I take offense to that," Tyler chuckled, "but I won't deny it. You'll only get rocket science, astrophysics, and advanced calculus, *and* mechanical engineering here. It'd be a total waste of your time, Homer."

The two Castus brothers shared a laugh. Denton flicked his eyes over to Homer and noticed how much they looked like a haunted statue.

"Hmm. We have to pick Cade up from the spaceport; can't have you walking around naked as the day you were made," Denton said. He searched the shop. "Ah, here we go."

He lifted a navy-blue T-shirt with the old Castus machine shop logo and a pair of extra work pants. The clothes belonged to their oldest brother, Jason, who kept them around for occasional visits and use. Denton tossed them to Homer. "Put these on. We'll figure out shoes later."

Denton zipped up his old leather scout jacket as he exited the machine shop. The air was brisk, with the tail end of winter surrendering slowly to spring. Snowflakes gently drifted to the ground in sparse numbers. Homer didn't mind the cold; they walked into the afternoon as one would on a hot summer's day, their statuesque feet leaving prints in the thin layer of snow melting in the light of the sun.

"Hey, over there!" The grizzled voice of Denton's father, Michael Castus, a man now pushing into his early eighties, called from across the street. He sat bundled up in a blanket, sipping a hot coffee with Brynn Castus, Denton's mother, under the shop sign that read *Brynn's Fine Jewelry*.

Denton walked over, motioning Homer to follow him. A small vid-screen that used auk'nai tech floated motionlessly in the air before the elderly couple. On it was the rushcycle race happening at the track on the other side of the city.

Jason Castus had started the racetrack. For a long time, he actually raced on it, winning enough to call it a successful career. But as he grew older, Jason began to train the younger, spritelier people to race rushcycles. Their parents still watched and cheered for his team, the Arrows of Ganymede.

"Who's your friend?" Brynn asked with a smile.

"Homer wanted to join us on scouting missions." Denton gestured to the walking statue behind him, and Homer bowed. Denton wiggled his hand to say, *You don't have to do that.*

"Elly's gonna love that," Michael said, mentioning Denton's wife.

Dr. Eliana Veston—now Dr. Eliana Castus through marriage— was a woman who'd saved humanity more than once. She was among the first colonists to arrive on Kamaria in the *Odysseus* spacecraft. Eliana had negotiated with an auk'nai named Mag'Ro to secure the last elements needed to cure lung-lock, thus synthesizing the Madani Cure and saving humanity. She had done it again when she came up with the idea to slam the *Telemachus* into Nhymn, ending the battle with the Siren. Now, she was the Scout Alpha Team leader, and had been on many adventures with Denton and the Scouts over the last twenty-six years.

Michael inspected Homer much in the same way Tyler had. "Hey, speaking of your family, send those grandkids over here sometime. I feel like I haven't seen Cade in forever."

"I'm picking him up from the spaceport now. He hasn't been on gravity-leave since last summer. Said he had some good news to share but wanted to do it in person," Denton said with a proud grin.

"That's great! I remember how Cade and Nella use to play in Jason's shop. Oh, what fun it was to have little ones around again." Brynn smiled as she fondly reminisced, remembering when her own boys were so young.

Denton's soothreader pinged. It was a standard device used by almost every citizen of Odysseus City. The soothreader wrapped around the wrist like a watch and allowed data transmissions, phone calls, holographic displays, and everything the user needed for regular routine business. Denton's timer was ringing, warning him he had to leave for the spaceport if he would make it in time to pick up Cade. He clapped his hand over the soothreader and kissed his mother on the forehead. "Time to go."

Michael stood and hugged Denton. "Drive safe, Denny. And don't bring home any more ghosts, ya hear me?" He was referring to when Nhymn's brother, Karx, had hitched a ride in Denton's mind. Karx was centaur-like in shape, with two long bull horns on his flat skull head. He had shown Denton visions of the Sirens' past, although unwillingly. It turned out Karx's tether to Denton worked in both directions, and as Denton slept, he entered Karx's past. Karx was killed when Nhymn blasted Denton with a nezzarform bolt. Denton hadn't heard from his phantom friend since. He now remained a constant in-joke for the Castus family, but there was always a tiny hint of actual worry behind the laughter.

"No promises." Denton huffed a laugh, then motioned to Homer. The robot bowed once more and followed Denton to his truck.

The spaceport was on the other side of the city from the Castus Machine Shop. The skyscrapers towered around them, creating what appeared to be a tunnel of buildings over the street. Circular platforms hung in the sky, with buildings set on their flat surfaces. People, both human and auk'nai, walked about on their daily routes, lining the sidewalks. Some flew if they had wings. Denton brought the truck around a bend in the road, and between the rows of buildings, they could see the spaceport. It was a tall building with many shelves for various spacecraft.

The military used this structure to park warships and matador starfighters. There had been no enemy to fight since Nhymn, but humans would not be caught unaware again. After narrowly escaping the Undriel and only fending Nhymn off with strange, weird tricks of mental warfare, they made sure to keep an active military. Humanity was still small in numbers. It would be a few more generations before it felt less like being an endangered species. Still, the occasional space crew from the *Infinite Aria* also landed in the spaceport from time to time.

Denton parked the truck in the port lot and walked with Homer to the base of the colossal structure. It loomed over them as they approached the wide front doors. Other people waiting for loved ones to arrive from work in space crowded the area.

"Dad!" Denton heard the voice of his son and spun around. Cade was waving his arm, obscured by the crowd surrounding him. Denton smiled and worked his way toward him.

"There you are!" Denton said with a big smile and hugged his son. They separated, and Cade adjusted his luggage on his shoulder. Denton looked him over. "I hope you weren't waiting too long. I tried to get here before you."

"Nah, it wasn't a problem. We caught a good window from orbit and shaved fifteen minutes of travel time. Is Mom here too?" Cade asked.

"No, just me." Denton looked over his shoulder and waved Homer over. "Oh, and this guy. Meet Homer. Made their new body myself. Pretty cool, right?"

"Whoa, this is some pretty advanced stuff here," Cade said, and just like the other Castus men, looked Homer over with a specialist's eye. Castus folk had been mechanical engineers by legacy. Although Denton broke the mold a little by becoming a Scout, it appeared that the old ways had returned when Cade became an EVA specialist to repair drones in space.

"What did you want to tell us?" Denton asked. He grabbed one of Cade's bags and walked with him back toward the truck.

"I'll tell you when Mom and Nella are here too. They back home?" Cade asked.

"Nella is at work, and your mom got called into the campus not long ago. She'll probably be back soon." Denton said. The scout pavilion had grown into a full college campus. Denton and Eliana even taught a few classes from time to time. Denton mainly focused on Siren history and first-contact situations, where Eliana specialized in medical training and research and development. Each of them was still a full-fledged scout, exploring the still mostly mysterious planet of Kamaria to better the people living on it.

"One sec, Dad," Cade said, looking over his shoulder. Denton nodded, and Cade worked his way through the crowd to a woman about his own age. It was Cade's coworker and good friend, Zephyr Gale. Denton had seen her in the background of most of their vid-calls; she was basically part of the family already. After a moment of conversation that Denton couldn't hear, Cade gave her a hug, and they parted ways.

"Does Zephyr need a lift back home?" Denton asked.

"Nah, she has a rushcycle parked here," Cade said. They approached the truck and threw Cade's luggage in the open back.

"Hey, Homer," Denton said, "think you can squeeze in the back?"

"Of course. No problem," Homer said. They climbed into the back and tucked their knees to their chest. All three strapped their seatbelts on, and Denton started the engine.

"How has it been down here?" Cade asked, looking out the window. It was a beautiful day, and after months of living in space, it probably seemed especially fantastic to him.

"Quiet. Peaceful. You know—*boring*. Just the way I like it," Denton said with a smirk. "How about up there? You guys making good progress on the *Aria*?"

"Yeah, some big stuff happening up there." Cade nodded.

Denton's soothreader pinged with an alert from Eliana. "Oh look, it's your mom. Maybe she'll be home by the time we get—" Denton furrowed his brow as he read the message.

Incident on Spirit Song Mountain. Report to campus immediately.

"Uh oh. That doesn't seem good," Cade said.

Denton didn't want to leave Cade behind after just getting him back, and this alert sounded too important to ignore. Denton looked in the space behind his seat and saw a brand-new scout jacket lying in a mess. It was supposed to replace his worn-out jacket, but Denton liked the way his old one felt. He'd earned this jacket long ago. The new one just felt *bought*. Denton had an idea. "We have to go check this out. Hey Homer, can you hand me that jacket?" Homer handed it over, and Denton handed it to Cade. "Put this on. You'll fit right in."

"You sure it's okay?" Cade asked, manipulating the jacket in his hands. The new jackets were fully equipped with hidden survival gear—a removable hood, a fire-starting kit in the upper-right shoulder pouch, a water flask in the breast pocket, a utility knife in a sheath on the sleeve, and a rope bracelet woven into the hip pocket. The jacket was orange, white, and black, the official colors for the Scout Program.

"Yeah, no worries. This'll be fun. Like 'bring your adult kid to work' day."

They drove through the city toward the old colony gateway, a remnant of the days when humans weren't allowed outside the walls. Once the auk'nai merged societies with humans, people were free to roam the countryside. There was still some risk leaving the city, predators in the forests and hills, but the frontier experience appealed to people. They accepted the risks. Denton and Eliana had a home outside the city near the southern edge of the Timber Chase, the closest forest nearby. Past the gateway, the road led through a mostly untouched grassy field, with smatterings of melting snow pocking the landscape. Communication antennas and power lines dotted the once-empty landscape. Cade watched the grass and snow whip past. Homer sat in the back, as motionless as the luggage around them.

A scout ship flew over the truck, heading in the same direction. It was a Pilgrim-class explorer called the *Rogers*, one of the older vessels in the Scout hangar. It still held the paint job that Denton and his family had applied to it decades ago—an orange-and-red camouflage pattern that helped it blend into some of the surrounding forests. It had been built upon over the years, with a circular antenna built on top of its hull. A new nose featured a sophisticated scanner, overall upgrading everything it had been originally built with. The ship slowed to a hover, then drifted downward into their destination ahead, the Scout Campus.

Twenty years ago, this scout pavilion was a modest facility that held everything the Scout Program needed. It had consisted of two buildings, the laboratory and the quarantine facility. Now, it had grown into a large college campus, with a slew of various learning facilities and laboratories for experiments. The buildings remained short, the highest being only six stories tall. Centered between these buildings was a beautiful quad area with grassy hills tucked under the fading mounds of snow and sidewalk pathways. The outdoor hangar area housed scout ships and vehicles.

They parked the truck and exited, leaving Cade's luggage in the back. The light snow crunched beneath their feet as they walked across the quad to the Scout Program staging hall. Denton slapped his palm against the base of a Scout Program insignia statue, a triangular thing that read *Explorarent, Disce, Docere*—Explore, Learn, Teach.

Through the doors, people moved about in a hurry. It was a large room, with small workstations lining the walls and an extensive display area in its center with people standing around it.

"Whoa, pretty crazy in here," Cade said. The room was chaotic, and there was an intensity in the air. Whatever had happened on the Spirit Song Mountain must have been significant.

"Come on, let's go figure it out," Denton said. Cade and Homer followed Denton through the crowd. No one noticed Homer's strange visage. They were too focused on the data screens. Denton pushed through until he bumped into a familiar face. Fergus Reid was an older man, originally from Jupiter's moon Callisto before the Undriel pushed everyone out of the Sol System. He had been with the Scout Program since the beginning. Presently, he was sitting at a workstation and prepping the *Rogers* for launch, assigning a team.

"Oh hey, Dent," Fergus said as he moved names around. He did a double take when he noticed Homer. "Jumping nightsnares! Who is *this?*" He pointed at the robot.

"This is Homer's new mobile unit. Just finished them today. But never mind that—what's going on?" Denton asked.

Fergus shook off the shock of seeing the walking Homer unit and sighed. "Things aren't lookin' too good on the Spirit Song Mountain. We got a call not long ago sayin' there was some sort of murder. All the auk'nai are in a real mess, ya ken?" Fergus said with his thick Callisto accent.

"Oh no, is Nock'lu safe?" Denton asked. Nock'lu was the official Daunoren watcher, the role designated to observe the Daunoren on the Spirit Song Mountain and summon auk'nai citizens for pilgrimage.

"Unsure. We haven't heard from 'im," Fergus said. "He summoned a pilgrimage not long ago, and when the pilgrims arrived, he wasn't around."

"That's strange," Denton said.

"It's worse than that. I don't wannae say anythin' ere with so many people about. Elly'll tell you the rest," Fergus said.

"Know where I can find her?" Denton asked.

"She's probably already on the *Rogers*. It came back early from a scout not long ago," Fergus said, focusing on the screen he was working on.

"Thanks, we'll head over now," Denton said. He nodded to Cade and Homer, and they pushed their way back through the crowd to the outdoor shipyard.

———◆———

Hours later, Dr. Eliana Castus lowered the ramp to the scout ship named the *Rogers*. The cold mountain air blew over her thick scout jacket and scarf. Eliana was in her mid-fifties, with dark brown skin and long, thick ebony dreads. Her eyes were a burgundy hue, chosen during corrective eye surgery—wearing glasses had become more of a hassle than she cared for.

Before arriving as one of the first colonists of Kamaria, Eliana had spent years moving around. She was a child on terraformed Mars, then a young adult in Remus Orbital Academy, where she studied medicine. When the war with the Undriel began to look worse, she was moved to the *Telemachus* for a few years before finally joining the *Odysseus* mission and landing on Kamaria. She had lived on this alien world longer than any of her other homes.

Her father, Dr. John Veston, had been the *Telemachus* project leader and the original Homer AI creator. He was a visionary and an inspirational hero to the early colonists. Eliana remembered his smile and the way he would talk passionately about space travel.

Eliana also remembered watching her father's murder by a man she'd considered family—Captain Roelin Raike. Nhymn used Roelin as a puppet to stab John to death. She'd been haunted by the scene for over twenty years, and she knew it would continue until death reunited her with her father.

But she also found love in this dangerous world. Eliana had lost the family she was born with but found her own over the years. To her side was her husband, Denton, and her son Cade. Not currently present was her daughter, Nella. Nella reminded Eliana a lot of herself. She was a brilliant, beautiful young woman in her mid-twenties—and hopefully, she would have a brighter, kinder future than Eliana had experienced. The Scout team had become her family as well.

With Cade joining them this day, Eliana wished they had a better reunion than what lay ahead. Still, she was glad Cade was with them. He was a strong, smart man with a unique perspective after working in space for close to six years. Maybe his outside experience would yield some unique insight here.

Eliana turned to him and said, "Follow us."

Cade nodded and adjusted the new scout jacket he was wearing. It wasn't intended for him, but it suited him well. Denton wore the same tattered old jacket he'd earned back when Eliana had convinced him to try out for the Scout assessment. She loved him for that.

Before the ramp hit the ground, Talulo, the auk'nai pilot of the *Rogers*, pushed past the entire team and leaped from the ramp. He landed in the snow and hurried away from the ship. He would have flown, but due to an accident during the days of Nhymn, Eliana was forced to remove his wings to save his life. Talulo's pilot's license was a second chance to fly.

Sergeant Jess Combs stepped forward wearing a bulky combat suit and said, "This is going to hit him the hardest." Jess was a formidable woman. She had fought the Undriel in ground excursions as a marine. Tvashtar marines were considered the best soldiers in the Sol System, raised and trained on Jupiter's volcanic moon, Io. Her training had never worn off. Although humanity had lost Io with the rest of Sol, the name "Tvashtar" remained with the marines as a badge of honor and remembrance. Her combat suit was a heavy metallic armor set that made her into a walking tank. Under the suit, she had soft hazel eyes and light skin, and she kept her light-brown hair cut short.

"We'll be here for him," said Geologist Faye Raike. She had black hair with gray streaks of hair that covered her exotic yellow eyes and tanned complexion. She too had fought the Undriel in the past, from the cockpit of a Matador starfighter. Faye had become a self-exiled outcast after her husband was used by Nhymn to kill John Veston. After the battle with the Siren, when all things became realized, she found peace in the world again. Faye was back where she wanted to be, exploring Kamaria with a clear mind.

The ramp thudded in the snow, and the team disembarked. Eliana led the way, with Denton and Cade beside her and Jess, Faye, and the robot Homer at the back of the group. As Eliana walked with her team, they passed auk'nai pilgrims in various states of anguish. They cawed sadness and wept tears into the snow. There were hundreds of the pilgrims, each trailing a dead loved one with them up the mountain.

It was auk'nai tradition that each youth must bring a deceased member of Odysseus City to the Spirit Song Mountain and feed the corpse to the Daunoren. It was a sacred ritual, and the enormous bird they fed was revered as a living God. The auk'nai drew some of their power from the mythical bird as well. Through the Daunoren's song, the auk'nai could perform a past-tracking ritual. Eliana had seen it in action when Talulo helped track down Captain Roelin Raike's hidden location many years ago. Once the Daunoren began to feast on the dead, it was safe to enter the mines and harvest materials needed to create a daunoren staff.

Each staff was unique to the user, but most implemented a rod with a hook in some fashion. Auk'nai that were more prone to fighting would add weaponry into their staff, where the more peaceful might install something like a fishing rod or net. Eliana had seen staffs that had spears, chains, swords, and even human-tech particle rifles built into the daunoren staff's frame.

Today was different.

Humans didn't get an invite to the pilgrimage. Only those who heard the Song of the Apusticus could bask in its glory. But today, there was no song, only weeping and sadness. "Oh no," Denton whispered just loud enough to hear over the wailing of the pilgrims. Ahead, Talulo knelt in the snow, whimpering questions into the air. The crimson that dyed the snow traced its way down the mountain, past Eliana's feet.

The Daunoren had been decapitated. Its corpse lay before the pilgrims in a horrifying display of violence. Signs of a struggle were abundant, but whatever had murdered this sacred animal was nowhere to be seen.

"What could have done *that?*" Cade whispered to Eliana. He couldn't take his eyes off the gore.

"That's what we're going to figure out," Eliana said. "We should take a look around and see if we can find any clues."

"I'll help any way I can. Just let me know what I can do," Cade offered. He looked over his shoulder at the lines of pilgrims weeping. They led all the way back to the ship and beyond, each pilgrim kneeling in the snow over a dead loved one.

"Where's Nock'lu?" Jess asked. "He's supposed to be the Watcher, right?"

"Fergus said they haven't heard from him since he summoned the pilgrims," Denton said. They turned to Talulo. His eyes were wide and unblinking, his arms limply hung, his hands in the snow.

"Talulo." Eliana knelt next to her wingless friend and spoke quietly. "Hey, can you hear me?"

Talulo looked over to Eliana slowly and cooed softly and sadly. She embraced him, holding his beak and head against her chest. He eventually brought his limp hands upward around her back, returning the hug.

"We're going to figure this out," Eliana whispered. "I promise."

"Talulo knows Eliana means well," Talulo said. "Talulo thanks Eliana. But this is an auk'nai issue. Eliana needs not to sing so sorrowfully with auk'nai."

"But I will, regardless," Eliana said with a nod.

Talulo nodded in return and brought himself to his feet. He watched his fellow auk'nai, crying in tapering lines down the mountain. He felt their song in his chest, and he struggled to remain calm.

"Hey, Talulo," Denton said, "can't we past track here?"

Talulo cooed, unsure if it was still possible. Past tracking had been streamlined since the auk'nai and humans merged societies. It was an old technique that involved mixing acids, smokes, and elixir, allowing auk'nai to see into the past. It was adapted into law enforcement for human crime, which sped up court cases dramatically. The hitch was that it relied on the Daunoren to be alive. Auk'nai, like most Kamarian inhabitants besides humans, were mentally sensitive creatures that used telepathic wavelengths to do a variety of things. The auk'nai called it "the unsung song." They used it empathically, allowing them to detect lies and intentions and seek into the past for hidden truths. Other creatures used it as a trapping mechanism. A creature called a nightsnare could project an image onto its prey of something it trusted or needed, lure the victim in, then devour it. The nightsnare was a simple beast that didn't know what it was projecting, unlike the complex auk'nai, who were aware of the song and used it to its full potential.

"Without the Daunoren's song, auk'nai cannot see into the past." The voice of auk'nai leadership, Galifern, came from near the mines of the mountaintop. She was short for an auk'nai, with a flat bill and puffy orange feathers. "Galifern has attempted to see into the past and find the murderer. But Galifern only heard the Dead Song and had to stop before there was permanent damage to the mind."

"Without the Daunoren, the Song of Apusticus is no more," Talulo said, and hung his head. Eliana knelt by him once more and rubbed his shoulders.

Denton turned to Cade and whispered, "This just got a lot harder. We're going to have to solve this the old-fashioned way. You okay being here? Sorry to drag you along like this. I didn't know what we were in for."

"I just hope I can help. This is awful," Cade whispered back.

Galifern cooed and said, "Nock'lu may know, but Nock'lu has gone missing. Whatever did this to the Daunoren may have attacked the Watcher too."

Talulo's feathers rustled, and he let out a sad, low whistle.

"Let's spread out and look for clues. There have to be some answers here," Eliana said. The scouts split up and moved among the crying pilgrims to look for leads.

———— ◆ ————

Cade followed his father into the auk'nai mines to search for clues. Galifern guided them through the long tunnels carved into the mountain. The walls were lined with geodes that emitted a faint glow—laser stones. Carvings in the walls marked the history of the auk'nai who pilgrimaged here for generations. As time continued, the mine grew deeper, but tradition dictated that the tools used to harvest the minerals remain the same.

This was an ancient place.

"Nothing seems out of the ordinary here," Denton said, scanning the walls with his bioscope. "How about you, Cade? Seeing anything?"

"I don't think so," Cade said, although he could only be so sure. He had never been here before. Then again, no human had.

"I'll go on ahead with Galifern; see if you can find anything out of place in this portion of the mine," Denton suggested.

"Okay, no problem," Cade said. He watched as his father and Galifern walked around the bend, deeper into the ancient mine. Cade scanned the walls, looking for anything unusual. A number of deep-purple gems were still embedded in the walls of this part of the mine, passed up by every auk'nai pilgrim. *These gems must not be valuable enough for auk'nai to care.*

A twinkling rock on the wall caught Cade's eye. It was a deep, cloudy purple, and covered in dirt. He found it hard to believe anyone had passed up such a thing in all the years this place was carved out. Either way, it was beautiful to him.

"Find anything?" Denton asked as he and Galifern came back around the bend.

"Nah. How about you guys?" he asked.

"Nothing down here. Whatever did all this didn't come into the caves," Denton said, and joined Cade's side. Cade was admiring the gem in the wall more.

"Pretty, aren't they?" Denton asked, noticing Cade's admiration.

"You don't see stuff like this in asteroids. Although some of the C-type rocks have ice that comes off as gemlike sometimes. I usually take a little souvenir with me whenever I get to work outside the ship. It's not really about the rocks themselves. It's about the places I've been. Each asteroid is like my own little planet." Cade smiled.

"That's the Veston in you." Denton said with visible pride.

Galifern walked past the two humans. "If Denton's son wants to take one, Denton's son can. These are void stones. Songless. Like humans."

"You sure? I know this place is sacred. I don't want to offend," Cade said.

Galifern cooed her approval. Cade remembered that the auk'nai could sense intentions and empathy. She must have felt his admiration for the void stone.

"Thanks," Cade said.

"I'll be outside. Nice addition to your collection." Denton patted Cade's shoulder as he drifted away from him toward the mouth of the mine. Cade plucked the knife out of his sleeve holster and sank it into the place between the glistening stone and the wall. He pried hard, and it held firm. He pounded the handle with the base of his palm to sink the knife deeper. The stone jolted, then with another push downward, it liberated itself from its ancient place in the wall. He admired it against the light from the mouth of the cave.

How could such a beautiful gem be songless? he thought as he pocketed the stone and joined the others outside in the cold mountain air.

Homer said over the soothreader comm channel, "I believe I have found something."

————— ◆ —————

"Shit, this doesn't look good," Faye said.

On a rocky ledge below where the Daunoren was slain, Homer blew snow away with an air compressor hidden in one of their fingers, revealing a shattered daunoren staff.

"It is Nock'lu's," Talulo said with a grimace. "Talulo knows its song."

There was a hush. Even the breeze ceased for a moment.

"This doesn't mean he's—" Denton started, but shook it off.

"It only means Nock'lu doesn't have his staff," Eliana said, then thought for a moment. "Let's keep searching. Maybe he's hurt nearby."

"Talulo doesn't hear his song," Talulo said with defeat in his coos.

"Hey," Eliana reassured him in a soft, caring voice, "we'll keep looking."

Talulo and Galifern shared a glance, then walked toward the slain Daunoren to mourn. Eliana watched them leave but held the resolution on her face. She had been in their position before. After Eliana watched her father die, Roelin had vanished into the night, stealing the *Astraeus* warship during his violent escape. Her father was dead, and his murderer was gone, and Eliana was left with more questions than answers. She had given up hope, just like Talulo. Time would prove that she was wrong—four years after the murder, they'd found Roelin and the *Astraeus*. Then again, once they found him, there were only more problems.

"I want to help them," Eliana whispered as she watched the auk'nai mourn. Denton put his hand on her shoulder, and she cupped her palm over it.

"You will," Cade said. Denton and Eliana turned to their son. "You're Denton and Eliana Castus. You guys stopped a Siren. I'm sure you'll find a way to help the auk'nai."

"Thanks, Cade." Eliana smiled, but she felt defeated. She hoped Cade was right. Eliana hugged her son, then pulled away and spoke to Homer as the mourners cried for their Daunoren. "We'll let them have some time, then we should head back to the city and figure out a plan."

"Affirmative," Homer said, then broadcast that message to the human members of the team. The air filled with the songs of sorrow, and the ground glimmered with the blood of a dead god.

FOUR

THREE MONTHS EARLIER

L'ARN STEPPED AWAY FROM his hermit's nest in the forest near the shore and took in the fresh sea air. The mixture of salt and sand massaged his senses. Absolute freedom—it never got stale. He'd been living as an auk'gnell for two decades, and every day felt sweeter than the last.

They called this place the Howling Shore because the water here was stained crimson, as if a beast had been wounded in battle and was crying out as it bled to death. Waves crashed against white and black stone shores—the violence of nature, the beauty inside the chaos.

L'Arn didn't care what other people called it. He no longer had to pretend to care about anything. Life in Apusticus was the life of a shared mind. Each citizen living there had camped in L'Arn's head. It was crowded and filled with problems. They called it the Song of Apusticus, but it felt more like a riot. Out here, where the sky was filled with lesser airborne creatures of Kamaria—this was where L'Arn felt like singing. It was the Song of Kamaria that serenaded him.

How foolish Nock'lu had been for not joining him.

L'Arn had no idea how that battle of humans, auk'nai, and the

Siren ended. He'd seen enough when Apusticus was crushed into dust. The fact that he was still able to enjoy mornings like this on a world so beautiful must have meant whoever won that battle decided to mind their own business.

L'Arn grasped his daunoren staff in hand and propelled himself into the sky with his strong wings. It was a brisk morning, and although the sun was high in the bright-blue sky, the air had a chill to it. He didn't mind the cold. L'Arn kept his feathers warm with a thick sash made of dyed pelts. He had learned the techniques from an old mentor, Ilo'daro, before his pilgrimage, and ever since had made his own garments. He did such a good job, people from other auk'nai cities offered to buy L'Arn's clothing. Sometimes he took the offers, and sometimes he didn't.

The coast zigzagged underneath L'Arn as he sailed through the air. Tall orange grass grew on a cliffside here, cascading down to black stone shores below, rocked against the ruby tide. A gathering of smaller birds called vullywings joined him. L'Arn cooed politely and tickled under the beak of the closest one. They were little creatures of the sky, puffballs of feathers with four wings flapping in alternating intervals. They had short necks and long beaks used for plucking crustaceans from the sand.

The vullywing whistled and veered back toward the beach, taking its gang with it. L'Arn whistled a *good luck, friend* and veered off toward the land. Dead trees rushed underneath him. Their leaves would not return until spring.

A sound caught L'Arn's ear. He brought himself to a slow, then hovered in place, twitching his long ears to search for the source of the noise. He heard it again. Honking, well known to be created by a creature called a nurn.

L'Arn cooed with delight. He pivoted and flew over the trees, then brought himself lower to hide from his prey. It wasn't long before he found a grouping of nurn moving through the snow in a forest clearing. This part of the region was at a higher altitude and had gathered snow more abundantly. The tall pine trees emitted blue embers that drifted lazily to the ground and faded to white, mixing with the snow around it. It was called the Ember-Lit Forest for this reason.

The nurn were moving to lower ground to find food. L'Arn landed on a long branch of a dead tree and kept his eyes on the alpha nurn. It had bright-red feathers and a long, singular antler protruding from the back of its skull. It let out a loud bellow to its mates, and any of the lesser nurn who were straying from the core of the group quickly darted back inward. If L'Arn alerted the alpha, the herd would scramble. Sometimes L'Arn enjoyed the scramble, sometimes he did not.

With a twist of his hands, L'Arn separated his daunoren staff into two ends—a hook and a flat-bladed short sword. Apusticus had forgotten the old ways of the hunt, but L'Arn had not. Nock'lu had shown L'Arn the peck rifles they kept strapped to their beaks, how simple it was to aim up a shot and send out a highly charged particle of energy into your target. It was a convenient way to feed the city, but it removed the fairness from the hunt.

The hunt was a duel of minds.

L'Arn had to work very hard to maintain his stealth and silence. If he let even one claw tear at the branch underneath him or slip and rustle his feathers the wrong way, the nurn would hear him coming. They had their advantages with groundspeed and hearing range. L'Arn had the element of surprise and air superiority.

The alpha found a small outcropping of orange grass not overtaken by the snow, and began to munch, inviting the closest two females to join him with a honk. This was the moment L'Arn had waited for.

Pivot, launch, *fly.*

Silently, L'Arn flew close to the ground, hook in his left hand, sword in his right. There was no wind to sway him, and his feathers allowed the air to pass through him silently. It was as if Kamaria moved around L'Arn, instead of L'Arn moving through it.

Two nurn were targeted. The plump older male with a stubby

leg, looked up from its search of the snow with only enough time to open its mouth and not enough time to honk an alert. The other, a lean male with just enough meat on its bones, didn't even get that luxury.

L'Arn crashed into the pair with a resounding wet thud, plunging his hook and sword into each of them respectively. There was an explosion of snow, dirt, and blood as they hit the ground three meters away from the impact zone. L'Arn worked quickly to make sure the nurn didn't suffer, dispatching them both with swift movements of his blades.

Silence hung in the air as the herd processed what had happened. Then the alpha bellowed out a call of aggression. The pack honked and roared, pounding away into the forest beyond and leaving behind a dirt path in the snow.

The alpha rushed toward L'Arn, lowering its head and allowing the long antler to lead him. It stopped a few meters away from him and huffed. L'Arn lowered his hands, palms outward. He could hear the alpha's mind roaring with anger. Without the Song of Apusticus clouding his head, the world was clearer to sing to him. L'Arn mentally soothed the alpha, explaining he would hurt no more of his herd. The alpha cawed out and shook his head.

After a moment of anger, the alpha pounded its clawed foot in the snow again, huffed, then bounded off toward its herd. It had lost two of its flock, but L'Arn promised it would suffer no more.

The circle of life continued.

Warm steam seethed from the two dead nurn in the snow. L'Arn lifted them from the ground, one in each hand, and launched himself back into the sky. Carrying the dead was a technique that had to be treated with respect. They had given their lives for L'Arn to continue his own. The effort of carrying their bodies back to his nest was his payment for their sacrifice. Every time he did this, he remembered his pilgrimage, when he brought his mentor to the Spirit Song Mountain. He carried the dead back then, but it was much harder for the younger, smaller, weaker version of himself. In some ways, that weight never left him.

Once back at his hut in the trees near the shore, L'Arn wasted no time preparing his kills. His nest was built to suit these needs. It was a small hut, crafted from materials of the forest, and cemented in place with clay. It sheltered him from the rain and warmed him on winter nights—otherwise, he perched in any tree he liked. He kept a preserver in a smaller hut, the interior lined with a fungus that clung to the walls and inhaled decay-eating bacteria. It was cannibalistic for a fungus to behave this way, but beneficial for L'Arn's needs to keep his food fresh. Inside sat a large basket of various fruits and the last strips of nurn meat for the day.

Water flowed into his nest through the air, using water-honing technology L'Arn had brought with him from his Apusticus days. The liquid looked like a transparent tentacle, floating pipeless through the air from a nearby creek. A clay table was used for preparing his food. It was long enough to lay out both of the dead nurn, side by side.

L'Arn plucked the feathers of each, then began cutting away the skin. It was gruesome work, made less grim only by his skill with the knife. This was not the first nurn he had prepared, and it wouldn't be his last. By killing two, he'd ensured he would not have to kill again for some time. These could sustain him well into summer.

Twigs cracked.

L'Arn spun in the direction of the sound to see his attacker. Like his hunt earlier in the day, his attacker had been silent, waiting for the most opportune moment to strike. But they made a mistake, and L'Arn was fast.

L'Arn swung his carving knife. His wrist was caught by a large, black-feathered auk'gnell. They wore a hood, concealing their face except for their bright-orange eyes. The shape of their beak was similar to L'Arn's, which meant this auk'gnell had come from the center of the continent, near Apusticus. The Howling Shore was dotted with lone auk'gnell from all over the world, each finding their own territory and very rarely coming into contact with one another.

But this intruder had entered into L'Arn's home, and that usually meant desperation.

L'Arn pushed himself away from his attacker and noted the halberd-shaped weapon in their hands. "You came for the meat," L'Arn stated.

The enemy nodded.

"If you are hungry, you can take some. I have plenty," L'Arn offered.

"I need it all," the enemy said, and lunged, blade first.

L'Arn pushed himself to the side, fast enough to not take a mortal wound but slow enough for the blade to pass through his right wing, slicing through part of it and exposing bone. There was no time to cry out. L'Arn pulled his daunoren staff from its place against the side of his hut and twisted the handle, pulling it into the hook and sword forms.

The enemy's halberd sliced down again.

L'Arn's hooked blade fell to the floor, followed by his severed left arm.

Blood sprayed from the gaping wound on L'Arn's shoulder. The rage overtook him. L'Arn kicked out with his taloned foot, striking his enemy in the side and pushing them onto the table with the dead nurn. The enemy sprang back, swinging their halberd toward L'Arn's neck, but finding no purchase as the sword intercepted its path. A loud clang, then a scrape. L'Arn deflected the halberd and sliced across the enemy's chest, slapping blood into the dirt.

The enemy screeched. L'Arn readied another swing, but before he could connect the blade to his enemy's skull, the auk'gnell threw something into L'Arn's eyes. L'Arn shrieked as his vision began to burn away. He could feel his eyes melt into goo and smelled something akin to sulfur.

L'Arn let out a roar and blindly rushed forward, but his enemy escaped. He collapsed to his knees as the last of his strength faded. Then he fell forward into the dirt. L'Arn heard the sound of footsteps crunching gravel as his consciousness slipped away.

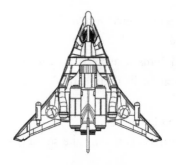

FIVE

PRESENT DAY

DENTON AND ELIANA WERE awake early. After picking up Cade from the spaceport and heading straight to the Spirit Song Mountain, they didn't get home until late at night. Nella had already been sleeping when they arrived, and Cade went directly to bed in his room. They kept it just the way he liked it for his visits every couple of months. Yesterday had been a long day, but Denton and Eliana hoped to properly welcome Cade back home this morning.

Eliana sifted through data on her soothreader while Denton cooked breakfast. The smell of cooked nurn eggs and hueginn bacon filled their home. Denton learned various Kamarian recipes from his mother over the years and enjoyed waking up early to feed his family. He slid a plate in front of Eliana, gave her a smile, and then looked past her when he heard feet shuffling against the floor.

Nella Castus walked into the room in silky, caramel-colored pajamas, stretching her arms toward the ceiling. She had smooth, dark skin like her mother; thick, ash-brown hair in long braids that went down to past her shoulders; and bright, emerald-green eyes.

Denton greeted her using Sol-Sign, the standard sign language on Kamaria. He tapped his chin with the fingers on his right hand, then lowered his hand toward her, quickly bringing it back up again like the rising sun. *"Good morning."* He smiled at her.

She signed back, *"Good morning, Dad,"* returning his warm smile with one of her own.

Eliana clapped her hands to get Nella's attention and signed, *"Did we wake you last night?"*

"No, slept like a baby."

A voice came from down the hall. "Will you all please keep it down?" Cade said with a laugh, rubbing his short-cut hair with vigor as if he had been wearing an EVA helmet. He gave his sister a quick kiss on the cheek.

Nella's eyes lit up at seeing her brother, and she gave him a tight hug. She separated herself and signed, *"You made it!"*

Cade smiled, all teeth. *"Yes. Got in yesterday."*

Nella frowned. *"You should have woken me up."*

They all said their good mornings, and Denton slid plates in front of Cade and Nella. He pinched his fingers against his thumb, bobbed his right hand, then brought it down and then back up around his left hand: *"Breakfast."*

The siblings sat at the kitchen table and began eating the meal Denton had prepared for them while Eliana sipped her coffee. Denton loved moments like this. After the days of Nhymn, there had been years of peace. He came to appreciate smaller moments like his family sitting at the same table and casually conversing, especially after Cade moved away to work in space. Moments like these were rare and beautiful.

"Sorry about yesterday," Eliana said to Cade. She deactivated her soothreader to focus on her children. "I hope it didn't spoil your trip back."

"It was sad to see the auk'nai like that," Cade said.

Nella watched their faces as they spoke. She had some skill in lip-reading, enough to understand the broad strokes of spoken conversation.

Eliana continued, "The news is just starting to reach the city about the Daunoren's death. There's more investigating to do." She spoke and used Sol-Sign simultaneously: *"Your father and I may need to leave for the night."*

"No problem," Cade said between bites, "I got a friend I want to meet up with. I'll see you guys again tomorrow."

"Zephyr?" Denton asked.

"Yeah, we were going to celebrate," Cade said with a big grin. "I got a promotion to crew leader on the *Infinite Aria*. I start after this trip." He signed alongside so everyone could know the good news.

Denton, Nella, and Eliana's eyes lit up. Denton put his hand on Cade's shoulder and shook. "There you go! Congratulations!"

"We're so proud!" Eliana said, and worked her way around the table to give him a big kiss on the forehead. "You're going to do great."

Nella clapped loudly, her smile bright and warm.

Cade touched his fingers to his lips, then pushed his hand toward Nella. *"Thank you."*

"Wait! I have something for this," Denton exclaimed, and turned to the cabinets to dig around for a bottle of Arrow Whiskey. He had stashed it away shortly after arriving on Kamaria, for fear that his brothers would hog it all. It sat, forgotten in the back of the cabinet for years. Denton pulled out the old bottle, put it on the counter, and poured four shot glasses with quick, deft movements.

"It's a little early for that, isn't it?" Cade laughed.

"It's never too early to celebrate good news." Denton handed Cade and Nella each a shot, then turned and grabbed the second round of glasses for Eliana and himself. "Cheers!" The whole family slammed back the shots and recoiled at the power of the whiskey. In unison, they let out a Ganymede holler. Nella was the loudest of the bunch.

Cade spoke and signed, *"Thanks, everyone."*

The sound of a rushcycle rumbled through the house, with muffled speaking just beyond the front door. A car was parked in the driveway next to the newly arrived rushcycle. Denton whispered,

"Quick, hide the whiskey."

The front door opened, and Brynn Castus announced the rest of the Castus family with a loud and friendly, "We're here!"

Nella smiled and ran to her grandmother, giving her a big hug. Michael Castus stepped in from behind his wife and received the next hug. He looked over to Cade. "Hey, CJ!" It was his abbreviation of Cade Johnathan, Cade's middle name.

Cade stood and walked over to his grandparents to give them both a big hug. "Grandpa, Grandma! It's good to see you again."

"Oh, it's been too long!" Brynn said as she pulled him into her embrace. "We heard you had good news and came running."

Cade's uncles, Jason and Tyler, stepped in from behind Michael and Brynn. Jason was bald, with a tuft of gray beard hanging out from under his chin and thick-rimmed glasses on the bridge of his nose. He was the oldest of the Castus brothers and the rushcycle racetrack owner in Odysseus City.

They hugged Nella and Cade on their way in. "I thought I heard a holler from outside! Almost called the fire department," Jason said with a laugh.

Nella read his lips and laughed, then gestured to herself. *"My fault."*

Tyler bumped knuckles with Nella.

After their greetings, the whole family went outside to chat and relax. Cade delivered his good news and received another loud Ganymede holler in response. He was thankful there were no neighbors to file a noise complaint. The Castus home sat on edge of the Timber Chase, alone but not too far from the city. Nella showed her grandparents and Uncle Tyler her garden. It was a lush area with plenty of vegetables and berry bushes, along with some beautiful flowers that she had curated over the years as a botanist. Since they weren't very skilled in Sol-Sign, she used her soothreader to translate her signs into spoken words. This was the way she conversed with all hearing people. The device picked up her hand gestures and spoke them aloud as she signed.

Eliana, Denton, Cade, and Uncle Jason played a game of thrust-ball in the yard, a little away from the garden. It was a popular game for casual parties, easy to play but hard to master. It involved using holographic paddles generated by each player's soothreader to slap a small flying ball toward a floating circular board. The board was like a rotating dartboard, with specific areas being more strategic to hit based on how many points the player needed. Hitting the board in the center, although it displayed accuracy, was not always the wisest choice. Ganymede folk grew up mastering thrust-ball because there wasn't much to do in the Arrow of Hope colony. It became one of the colony's major sports, almost like an Olympic event, second only to rushcycle racing.

"I wish we didn't have to leave for the investigation," Denton said as he served the ball into play. "We don't get to have the whole family here like this often. I miss days like this."

"Hopefully, we won't be gone too long, though," Eliana said, waiting for her turn to slap the orb. She watched as Cade hit the ball back toward the board, striking the area that earned three points.

"You're a lot like your dad," Jason said to Cade. "He's never been any good at thrust-ball either." He hit the ball, and it glowed red as it sailed toward the board, striking an area worth twenty points.

"Aren't we on the same team?" Cade asked with a laugh. It was true. Denton and Eliana were on the other team.

"Your Uncle Jason's trash talking doesn't pick teams," Denton said and slapped the ball toward the board. As his holographic paddle interacted with the ball, the ball's glow changed from red to green, indicating which player had hit it. It sailed back toward the board and hit the zone worth fifteen points.

Eliana watched the ball come back to Cade. "They don't play thrust-ball much up in space. When I lived on the *Telemachus*, we played a lot of soothchess. Do you guys do that on the *Maulwurf*?"

Cade hit the ball, and it turned blue. "Nah, nothing so . . . refined." His ball struck an area worth five points. Jason winced.

Cade shook his head and continued, "Me and Zephyr usually just play cards or some vid-sims to pass the time."

"Classic," Denton said.

"So, you and Zephyr are pretty close, *eh?*" Eliana grinned. Denton nudged her, and she playfully shoved him back.

"Yeah, we've been working together the whole time I've been in space," Cade said.

Jason hit the ball back, and it turned red. "I think what your mom is sayin' is, *you're close.*"

"Yeah, I mean—wait. What?" Cade flinched.

Denton hit the ball back. "So, I *happened* to notice the way you looked at Zephyr from time to time, on your vid-calls. And *maybe* I mentioned it to your mother . . ."

Eliana hit the ball and said, "And *maybe* your mother wants some dang grandkids in the future. And *maybe* your mother is wondering if she can have some fun girl time with Zephyr one of these days without making it weird." Cade laughed, and she added, "What? She seems cool. It's not often you get preapproval like this from parents. Take it as a sign."

The ball went right past Cade. Jason laughed. Cade shook his head. "Nah, it's not like that. She's just a good friend."

"Is that all?" Eliana said with a smirk.

"Yeah. Just a friend," Cade repeated.

"You said that," Denton said and put the ball into play again.

"I meant it!" Cade stated, hitting the ball back.

"I believe it," Jason said. "Me and Leese are just friends too." Leese was a professional rushcycle racer he had been dating for close to fifteen years. He winked at Cade.

Cade scoffed.

"Titanovore shit," Denton said with a laugh. "You and Leese are practically welded together!"

They all laughed and continued their game.

After some time, Michael, Brynn, Jason, and Tyler had to leave to get back to their various day jobs. They said their goodbyes and exchanged warm hugs. Brynn gave both Nella and Cade big kisses on their cheeks.

"Drive safe, y'all!" Cade shouted as his family made their way to their vehicles. Jason's rushcycle roared, and they traveled back down the road toward the city.

———◆———

An hour later, Eliana and Denton were preparing for their investigation. Eliana spoke and signed simultaneously to Cade and Nella, *"We'll be gone overnight. We have to travel to the other auk'nai regions and see if anything has affected their Daunorens. Hoping to be back tomorrow afternoon."*

"I'm going go to a rave and do drugs," Nella signed, and grinned.

Denton coughed out a surprised laugh, and Eliana gave her a faux stern look.

Cade laughed. "Hey, Dad, is it alright if I borrow that scout jacket again? I didn't think to bring a coat for later in the day. We don't really need one Up. Everything is temperature-controlled." Cade referred to his workplace as simply "Up," as did most of the people working in Kamarian orbit.

"No problem. In fact, keep it. I prefer my old jacket anyway," Denton said.

Cade put the jacket on and zipped it up to his collar. It fit well. He hugged his parents and said to everyone, "I'm heading out now. I'll see you tomorrow, yeah?"

"Need a ride? I have to take an autocar to the archive," Nella signed.

"I'm good," Cade signed back. *"I like the walk. Thanks."*

Cade hugged his sister and made his way out the door down the street.

"Alright, let's get moving," Eliana said, grabbing her things. They threw their stuff in the back of the truck. Denton and Eliana hugged Nella and said their goodbyes before entering the car. It was time to figure out what had killed the god of the mountain.

SIX

CADE INHALED THE SHARP pre-spring air as he enjoyed his walk into Odysseus City. As a kid, he had made this walk plenty of times. Stretching his legs after months in space felt great—with a bit of help from the pills he took every time he came planetside to compensate for the gravity. Cade plunged his hands into his scout jacket pockets and felt a sharp stab against his left knuckle. He stopped and pulled the purple void stone from within, realizing he'd forgotten it was still with him after the events of the day before. Cade zipped the pocket shut and made a mental note to be careful with it. Although the stone had no value to the auk'nai, it had sentimental value to Cade.

The street traced a line through a meadow of purple and orange grass with splotches of melting snow. The sky was bright blue, with only a few speckles of clouds intercepting it, and the breeze was chilled but pleasant. In the distance, creatures called meadow sailors floated above the tall grass. They were orange things that looked like balloons with long snouts. They casually gobbled up small insects and drifted among the waving sea of grass.

Ahead, the road split into a highway and a tunnel that led into the city. A transport station was just on the corner, and Cade boarded the autobus that arrived shortly after making it to the corner. It was semi-crowded, with only standing room left. Cade didn't mind. He removed a small earbud from the side of his soothreader, pushed it into his ear, and let his mind wander. The bass beat and the flow of the lyrics coming at him blended perfectly with the vibe he was getting from the streets as the buildings started to get taller around him.

Public transportation was mostly human used. Auk'nai had no need for such services, preferring to use their natural ability to fly wherever they needed to go instead. A young woman read a book on her soothreader. Two boys and their parents looked out the window and talked about their fun plans for the day. A group of teenagers huddled close to each other, playing a game on their soothreaders and cheering at their success. An old woman stared at Cade. When he noticed, he wasn't sure how long she had been or how long she'd continue to do so. He flashed her an awkward smile, and she looked out her window. The casual weirdness of public transportation was a departure from his time working in space.

The bus passed under Ruby Platform, one of the three floating platforms hovering above Odysseus City. Although the immense platform took up a large chunk of the view, it was made pleasant by technology. Each of the platforms showed the sky above through vidscreens lining its underside. It still created a shadow, but the platforms rotated throughout the day, so no one was left in permanent darkness.

Cade got off the bus and put his hood up, keeping his earbud in. This stop was on the far side of the central park area. Plant life from Sol had been placed here, an homage to life on ancient Earth, terraformed Mars, and Callisto. As Cade walked the path into the park, this area felt ironically alien to him. He'd never been to Earth, nor would he ever go there. It belonged to the Undriel now, as it had for over three hundred years. No one knew what they'd done to it, and as time went on, no one seemed to care. The grass that poked out of the patches of snow was weirdly green, and the trees were leafy and devoid of pulsing lights. A creek of rushing brownish water flowed into a still lake, where curious gold and multicolored Kamarian fish greedily attempted to fight over breadcrumbs from passers-by. Large black boulders dotted the park area, with people, both human and auk'nai, sprinkled around and among them. Cade almost tripped over a small child rushing by with a string tied to a kite. A young auk'nai girl flew near the kite in the sky, acrobatically twirling and showing off. The child's mother raced after the kid and the kite, lifting a hand to apologize for almost tripping Cade. Cade smiled and shrugged.

On the other side of the park was the old *Odysseus* landing pad, now a monument. The vessel itself had been launched into space long ago. The only passenger was the Siren Nhymn, who had begged to leave the planet. To this day, no one really understood Nhymn's reasons.

Cade had always liked coming here. It had history. Not only was it famous for being the exact spot where humanity had landed on Kamaria, but it had happened in a ship his grandfather and mother had flown on. His father would arrive six years later on the *Telemachus*. The landing pad was a large half-circle-shaped area, as wide as a football field, with a waist-high fence surrounding it. The old viewing platform and walkway were still intact at the far end. Sometimes they would hold concerts here. Rows of seats had been placed for people to watch and enjoy. Cade had been to a few shows here in the past.

"Sorry I'm late," Zephyr said. She approached Cade from behind and stepped over the bench he was sitting on to sit beside him. He removed his earbud and greeted her. Zephyr wore a rushcycle jacket with green accents and had on tight-fitting leather pants and high boots. She handed him a sandwich wrapped in glossy, oily paper. "Hungry?"

"Yeah, thanks," Cade said and took the sandwich. Zephyr unwrapped her own and began to tear into it.

"So much better than D'Rand's cooking on the *Maulwurf*," Zephyr said, and she grinned with enjoyment. Cade nodded as he chewed his sandwich. She continued, "You hear about the Daunoren?"

Cade gulped down a chunk of meat, lettuce, bread, and oil. "Yeah. I was on site with my parents yesterday."

"Ah *shit*, really? How'd you do that?" She looked him over, noticing the scout jacket for the first time. "Hey, wait, you changing jobs on me?"

Cade looked down. "What? Nah. My dad gave me this. They brought me with cuz we had to go right after he picked me up."

"Wow. How was it? Is it as bad as they say?" Her voice grew somber.

Cade looked at his sandwich and nodded. "Yeah, maybe worse."

"The auk'nai by my gran's place are all in a bad way."

"It's going to be some time before they heal from this."

Zephyr nodded. "Crazy times." They chewed in silence for a minute, then Zephyr shoved him playfully. "Let's focus on the good things, yeah? We got some celebrating to do! You're gonna be a crew leader!"

"Ah, we don't need to do anything special." Cade finished his sandwich.

"Too bad, I feel like dancing. I know a place over by where I'm staying. Want to get a few drinks?" Zephyr said with a wild look in her chartreuse eyes.

Cade froze up a little when he returned her gaze. Her eyes, face, and hair looked exotic, with lightly glittering makeup. Cade had worked closely with Zephyr for years, and they had hung out outside of work before, but today, something was different.

"Yeah, let's do that," he said.

"I'll drive. We can park at my gran's and walk to the bar." Zephyr grabbed his hand and pulled him up.

"Lead the way."

The sun started to dip down as they walked across the park to where Zephyr had her rushcycle parked. Her hoverbike was slick looking, especially when compared to Uncle Jason's bulky racing rushcycle. Zephyr's bike had smooth, curved edges and green accents along its design. There were signs of wear and tear, scuff marks, and rusted metal in spots, but overall, the bike looked well taken care of. Zephyr flicked her hand over her soothreader, and the rushcycle's engine kicked on. For a moment, bright-green lights flowed over the bike's surface, resembling the glowing tattoos on Zephyr's arms and back, currently hidden under her jacket. She approached the bike and banged her hand against a compartment on the side. A shelf with two helmets emerged, and she tossed one to Cade.

Cade put the helmet on. They mounted the bike, Zephyr in front with her hands on the controls, and Cade right behind her. "You go to Colony Town much?"

"Nah, not really. Is that where we're goin'?" Cade asked, slightly muffled by the helmet.

"Yeah, just hold on." Zephyr revved the engine, and the bike hovered off the ground. She twisted her hand, and the bike moved forward, then turned around to travel back the way she had arrived.

Zephyr sped her rushcycle through the street in the setting sun. The snow that had survived the warmth of the day rested in patches near the sidewalk, with slowly melting clumps where people had shoveled it into piles. They made their way to the outskirts of the great city, a place filled with old warehouses, cluttered streets of small shops. Apartments and family homes were everywhere. Some of this area had been built from repurposed colony domes used by the first colonists back in the early days of humanity's presence on Kamaria. The domes were more run-down now—used. Lived in. Once, they had been pristine and vital.

People called this place Colony Town.

Humans and auk'nai were tightly packed together here, even when walking down the sidewalks. When overflow colonists from the *Telemachus* joined Odysseus Colony shortly after the battle with Nhymn, they were placed in this part of the city. The surge in residency led to a quicker deterioration of the structures here, and it never fully recovered. Rough-looking auk'nai youths sat on top of buildings, most not holding a daunoren staff. The auk'nai who live in this area rarely took pilgrimage.

Zephyr pulled the bike into the driveway of a two-story house built from a colony structure's remnants. She parked it in a garage and removed her helmet. A static shield licked over Zephyr's afro, keeping her hair looking fresh and unmangled by the helmet. It was a special modification she paid extra for. Cade was a little jealous. He was always a victim of helmet hair.

She closed the garage and locked it, then gestured for Cade to walk with her to the front yard. As they came into the yard, a man wearing an old atmospheric helmet sat on his front porch and waved. "Sup … Zeph. Didn't know … ya came down. How long … you be here?" he said with a crackling, strained voice as he sucked in air between breaths.

Zephyr nodded at him. "Hey Eddie, only a coupl'a days. Say hi to Tor fer me."

Eddie lifted a hand and nodded, then proceeded to continue looking out into the street. Eddie was a buzzer, one of the rare people that the Madani Cure had failed. When humans first came to Kamaria, the bacteria in the air would cause a condition called lung-lock. Human lungs would become instantly paralyzed with even one breath, and victims would suffocate and die within a few minutes. When the Madani Cure was synthesized from minerals found in the gems that auk'nai people wore in their sashes, the pandemic had been stopped. Most of the offspring of the first colonists were automatically inoculated with the cure through birth. Still, there were rare cases where the treatment had no effect. Citizens with more money often had devices installed in their airways that neutralized the bacteria and worked around the Madani Cure's failures, but people in Colony Town didn't have credits for that. The buzzers here wore helmets like Eddie.

Zephyr led Cade through an area of closely tucked-together shops and houses until they made it to their destination. The bar was a hole-in-the-hull called Nightsnare. Zephyr walked up to a heavyset, tanned man sitting on a stool in the front, a blunder blaster strapped to his leg.

"'Sup, Zeph. Where the Hells you been?" the bouncer said as he gestured for her to walk in. "Your friend here cool?"

"Been Up too long. My friend'll be a good boy," Zephyr said and led Cade past the bouncer as he nodded. The room seemed larger than the outside implied. It was mostly dark, with laser lights flickering through the air and loud metal music blasting over some speakers. The floor was weirdly sticky on the bottom of Cade's shoes. It almost felt like walking on Old Cyrus with his magnetic boots on.

They made it to the bar, a blacklight shining on the surface, with vivid purples and greens. The auk'nai bartender was brightly lit by the light, his feathers radiant yellow and green, with his sashes an explosion of colors. The bartender's eyes pierced Cade.

"What can Yu'Olar get?" the bartender asked.

"Two Star Sirens, make 'em hot," Zephyr said with a flick of her fingers. She turned to Cade. Her chartreuse eyes and makeup were illuminated by the blacklight like twin supernovas inhaling the void. Cade found it incredibly sexy. "These are on me," she said.

Yu'Olar deftly created the shots, mixing alcohols like an alchemist creating an elixir. He flicked them across the bar with his daunoren staff's blunt end. Zephyr gestured over her soothreader and paid for the drinks. Yu'Olar cooed and went to help another patron.

"Crew leader Castus, up and at 'em," Zephyr said, holding her shot glass. It looked like swirling stars caught in an amethyst typhoon in the blacklight. They clinked the little glasses together and knocked their heads back. Zephyr smacked her lips together, and Cade let out a Ganymede holler. Zephyr laughed. "I knew you'd do that."

"Force of habit. Next one is on me." Cade tapped his forefinger on the bar.

After a few drinks, the bar's music went from heavy metal to something more synthetic and tech filled. Zephyr's eyes lit up, and she dragged Cade into the middle of the crowd. The room was tightly packed, and Cade constantly felt people bumping up against him. Zephyr began moving close to Cade, running her hands across his chest and arms. Cade felt a tickle run up his back when she put her arms around his shoulders. She was close to his face, her eyes staring deep into his own.

She bit her lip and raised her eyebrows.

Cade had never been this close to Zephyr before. Her eyes darted to his lips, then back to his soul. "You know, as a rule, I never date coworkers," Zephyr whispered, in that way only the recipient can hear in a loud club.

"Poor D'Rand," Cade said.

Zephyr laughed. She moved around him, touching him and gliding. She brought her lips close to his neck and her chest up against his. Cade felt an electrical tingle run up his arm to the back of his head.

The song ended, and another one blended into it. Zephyr smiled and pulled Cade back to the bar, where she ordered two beers. They took a seat to cool off from the heavy petting. After some chatting, Cade dropped his hand into his pocket and felt the void stone within.

"Shit. Forgot I had this," Cade said, pulling the gem from his pocket. It looked wild in the blacklight, like a thousand microscopic comets were ricocheting off its walls, trying to free themselves.

"Whoa," Zephyr said, tilting her head. She looked past the void stone to something over Cade's shoulder, and her face grew serious. "Put it away," she whispered urgently.

Cade looked over his shoulder and saw a scraggly-looking auk'nai staring directly at the stone. His yellow and blue feathers were in bad shape, with spots completely bare and covered in tattoos. Bare spots on auk'nai were typical of drug use or fighting, or sometimes both.

Cade pocketed the void stone, but it was too late. The scraggly auk'nai stood from his seat and tapped one of his taloned hands against the blunt end of some sort of daunoren baton or bat strapped to his thigh.

"Ah shit," Cade muttered as the auk'nai approached.

"'Sup, Krin'ta," Zephyr said, keeping her face firm.

"Was that what Krin'ta thinks it was?" Krin'ta asked, leaning into Cade. Cade didn't need to answer. His empathic wavelengths answered the auk'nai's question for him.

"So what?" Zephyr said.

Krin'ta snarled and spat onto the already-sticky floor. "If this human defiled the sacred mines of auk'nai Daunoren, Krin'ta will kill 'im."

Cade stood and faced Krin'ta. "Listen, man. I don't wanna fight. You can have it."

Krin'ta's irises shrank, and he exhaled a cough. "Krin'ta doesn't want a songless stone." It wasn't about the stone. It was about the act of defilement. Never mind that Cade had permission.

"Just shuck off, Krint," Zephyr said, standing next to Cade.

Yu'Olar slapped his daunoren staff against the bar between Cade and Krin'ta. "No fighting in Yu'Olar's bar. Hear?"

"We're leaving," Zephyr said, grabbing Cade's arm. Cade kept eye contact with Krin'ta, not backing down until they reached the exit. They walked out into the night, the cold air biting them. "What *is* that thing?"

"It's a gem from the Spirit Song Mountain. The auk'nai there said I could have it—said it was songless." *Like humans.* He remembered.

"Damn, I can see why Krin'ta was riled up. It's just bad timing, seeing you with that after what happened to the Daunoren. All the auk'nai here are tense," Zephyr said.

"If I knew it would make them angry, I would have never taken it. The last thing I want to do is bring more pain to them," Cade said, palming the stone in his pocket. He could hurl it into the snow, but that somehow felt more offensive than keeping it.

They walked back to her place. Snow began to lightly sprinkle in the air, probably the last of the season. Her neighbor Eddie had gone back inside. They were alone. Zephyr walked up the stoop to the door and turned to face Cade.

"I can give you a ride home in a bit if you want to come inside," Zephyr said, her eyes flicking up and down Cade's body.

He took a step up toward her. "Nah, I can get an autocab."

"It'd be no trouble," Zephyr said, quieter as Cade grew closer. Her eyes locked onto his.

"I like cabs," Cade whispered, now close enough to feel her breath on his face.

"No one likes cabs—" Zephyr said, then was stopped as Cade kissed her on the lips. She ran her hands over his chest, and he gripped her tightly against his body. Zephyr gestured over her soothreader while kissing Cade, and the front door opened behind her. She grabbed his jacket and yanked him into her house.

It was a small, aging house made of old colony dome material, plastics, metals, and faux wood. A stairway led to an upper floor, and the living room to the left of the entrance contained a small sofa, a recliner, and a vidscreen. Zephyr pressed her lips onto Cade's neck and closed the door behind him as he gripped her hips. "Upstairs." She gasped the word, then broke away from him to race to the bedroom.

Zephyr dashed into the room at the end of the hall and clicked on a small side table light, with Cade close behind. It was a small square unit with a window that started at about shin height and almost reached the ceiling. The window was newer than the home, retrofitted to open and close after the Madani Cure had been synthesized. An amber streetlight poured in through the loose-hanging curtains. Zephyr's twin-sized bed had the blankets tossed about as if she rolled like a panthasaur out of it in the morning. She turned to face him with a sexy smirk on her mischievous face. Zephyr removed her coat and pulled her shirt over her head. In the low light, the tattoos on her naked body flared with wild luminescence. Cade removed his jacket and shirt. The matching canary tattoo on his forearm shined just like hers. They embraced, pressing into each other's skin and feeling the sweat between them.

Cade kicked the door shut behind him.

———◆———

"I've wanted to do that for years," Zephyr said, exhausted.

Cade nodded. They were sweaty and naked, lying in the one-person bed, smashed together. Zephyr let her fingers slowly drift across Cade's body, admiring his muscular form. She brought her hands up to his short-cut hair and ran them through like a comb.

"Hello?" An elderly woman's voice came from downstairs.

They bolted upright. "Oh shit, I thought she was visiting my auntie's," Zephyr said.

"Who's that?" Cade asked.

"It's my gran," Zephyr said, putting a hand over her mouth to stifle her laughter.

"Is someone there?" Gran called from downstairs.

"Yeah, Gran. It's me, Zeph," Zephyr said, and began to dress while stuffing Cade's clothes into his arms.

"What's going on?" Cade asked quietly.

"You gotta go. If she sees you here, she'll freak. She's old school," Zephyr said.

"I'll just say hi. What's the big deal? We're adults," Cade said, pulling his pants up.

"Nah. Trust me. I gotta live here for the rest of the week, and I'll never hear the end of it." Zephyr quietly mocked her grandmother's voice, "That damn Zephyr bringing men home from the club, workin' on the street. I thought your mah raised you right." Zephyr opened the window and began to corral Cade toward it.

"Seriously?" Cade whispered.

"Yup!"

"Let me get my clothes on at—" Cade tried to bargain for time. Gran was working her way up the stairs.

Zephyr kissed him on the lips. "Out of time! See you later."

Cade clumsily worked his way out the window onto an old air filter pipe, his clothes bunched up against his left arm. He made it a few feet down before slipping and falling the rest of the way, landing in a wet, half-melted pile of snow with a muffled thud. He was behind the house, near the outdoor garage. A small yard with a waist-high fence surrounded him. The neighbors that faced Gran's place were outside on their deck. One whistled. Zephyr poked her head out the window to check on Cade. He winced, shook his head, and gave her a thumbs up.

Zephyr said as she turned back into her room and shut the window, "Oh, hi Gran! I thought you were—"

Cade was freezing, and he quickly worked to get his clothes back on. He made his way around the house, almost falling over as he slipped his socks and shoes on, then finally got his jacket over his arms. He rubbed his hands against his ribs, remembering an old trick he learned as a Kid Scout.

Cade walked down the block to avoid detection from Zephyr's gran before summoning an autocab to take him home. He entered his parents' house as a destination into his soothreader, and the autocab database calculated the closest automatic car to send. It gave him an estimated arrival time, and Cade couldn't help but notice how much longer it took a cab to arrive in Colony Town compared to downtown Odysseus City. He finally warmed up and shoved his hands in his jacket pockets. The void gem was still cold in his pocket, lifeless. *Songless.*

Cade's vision was shocked blue as something collided with the back of his head with brute force. He fell to the ground and saw stars as two large bird feet landed in the street in front of him. Cade pulled himself up, wincing as he struggled to see who'd hit him. It was Krin'ta, the scraggily auk'nai from the bar. He was silhouetted against a streetlight, with lazily drifting snowflakes clouding the sky around his wings.

"What the *Hells*!" Cade shouted, still trying to shake off the hit.

Krin'ta twirled his daunoren bat in his hand, a blunt thing with a club end. It only had a few glimmering gemstones, and Cade was thankful for that. "The Daunoren is dead. Human comes to Krin'ta's song and shows off stolen gem?" Krin'ta said. "Human dares defile the sacred place? Humans defile all auk'nai things."

"I didn't steal it! Galifern said I could—" Cade tried to explain.

Krin'ta rushed Cade and slammed his bat into Cade's side, knocking the wind out of him and bringing Cade to his knees. Krin'ta kicked him onto his back, then proceeded to kick him again and again. Cade couldn't react. The initial surprise impact had ruined his chance to defend himself.

There were bright lights. The automated cab that Cade had called had finally arrived. Krin'ta cawed and stomped on Cade one last time before flying off into the night. Cade lifted himself slowly, hearing beeping coming from the cab as its expiration timer began ticking down. His injuries felt like small fires all over his body. He pulled himself through the cab door and sat down.

"Do you need medical assistance?" the autocab asked. It sounded like Homer, but this was only a segmented partition of the artificial intelligence.

For a moment, Cade considered going to the hospital. He rechecked his injuries and decided he'd survive with some rest and maybe an ice pack. "Just take me home."

SEVEN

NELLA CASTUS EASED A small vividpetal flower into a hole in the dirt. When the roots discovered the soil, they reached out and pulled the plant into place firmly. Nella allowed the plant to get comfortable, then added some nutrient-rich sprinkles. The flower shined happily as she pushed the soil back into place around its stem. The vividpetals' new neighbors, vividbushes—much like the one it would grow into soon—pulsed with energy. A moment later and they were a synchronized blooming light show.

Nella used her forearm to brush some dirt off of her brow, then adjusted the gardening gloves on her hands. She signed to the flowers, *"Enjoy your new home."*

Nella's world was silent, but never devoid of beauty. She was part of the Deaf Community in Odysseus City and had plenty of friends. Conversing with hearing people was as simple as using the translation options on her wrist-mounted soothreader. The device could register her hand movements and facial expressions in Sol-Sign and convert them into spoken Sol Common. Nella found the device cumbersome, and when she conversed with hearing people, she felt like a visitor in a strange country. She had enough success with lip reading—except when chatting with auk'nai, who had impossible-to-read beaks.

Nella's family was skilled in Sol-Sign, with varying degrees of fluency. Her brother Cade could sign like a first language, having been taught since Nella was born. Nella's mother was mostly successful with Sol-Sign, and they could converse with only minor hiccups. Her father tried as best he could, but their conversations were shorter due to his low fluency in sign. The texting options on her soothreader picked up where her father's skill left off.

An elderly woman in a wheelchair pushed herself over to Nella. She had tanned skin and wrinkles gained from a life of laughter. She smiled and signed, *"Great work, they like you,"* then gestured to the flowers around them.

"They better. I just gave them VIP seats for free." Nella had graduated from the Scout Campus Academy. She earned a bachelor's degree in wildlife conservation with a focus on botany. Dr. Marie Viray had been one of her professors, and they'd become friends outside the classroom. Marie was one of the first colonists, a veteran scout, and the head chemist for the Madani Cure, back when lung-lock was a blight on the colony. Decades ago, Eliana had worked closely with Marie, and now Nella filled the spot her mother had left behind.

It was late afternoon, and the sky was starting to turn pink and orange with the slowly dimming light. Nella worked in the John Veston Kamarian Archive's garden center, named after her grandfather, whom she had never met. The gardens surrounded the cylindrical building, with particular attention made for the flowers under John's statue in the front yard area. With the dimming light, the vividpetals began to shimmer, emitting a soft teal and yellow glow.

"Jun is here." Marie Viray pointed across the garden at a young man getting out of a car. He had beige skin, black hair combed to the side, and a kind smile. He waved to Nella.

Nella lit up when she saw him. She parted with Marie and hurried over to the young man. Jun Lam was an old friend of Nella's since childhood. He was also part of the Deaf Community in

Odysseus City, and they often hung out outside of work.

She hugged Jun and signed, *"Did you get them?"*

Jun bobbed his fist and smiled with excitement. *"Yes!"* He reached into his pocket and brought out a small cloth bag. *"Gemlily seeds,"* he signed. *"It took me forever to find them. I had to dig through some scout data to figure out where they grow, then submit a retrieval request, then wait a week . . ."* Jun's hands danced as he rambled on about the process of getting the rare seeds.

He handed the bag to Nella, and she sifted through the seeds. They looked almost like small stones, with only a hint of organic plant material encompassing the shell. As the sun was setting, the seeds emitted a faint ruby glow. Nella turned toward the garden around them. Gemlilies didn't glow at night like vividpetals, but they did shimmer like rubies in the daylight. She thought ahead a season, thinking of how they would look reflecting their glimmering red light onto the archive walls in the summer. She took Jun's hand, walked him over to the front of the building, and then pointed at spots that flanked the sidewalk.

"Good spot." Jun's hands struck the words firmly to reinforce Nella's decision, and his smile was bright and warm.

"They will be beautiful here," Nella signed. *"I will plant them next time I'm here."*

Jun looked at his soothreader. *"My shift just started. See you at the party tomorrow night?"*

Nella bobbed her fist. *"Yes. I'll bring some whiskey."* She tipped her finger toward her mouth and crossed her eyes with her tongue out as she got drunk on the imaginary alcohol.

Jun laughed a quick, loud burst and nodded. They waved goodbye to each other as Jun walked into the archive. His shift as a night custodian for the archive began right as Nella's workday ended, but tomorrow they would both have the day off and could let loose at a party.

Marie wheeled up in her chair after Jun departed. She clapped her hand to get Nella's attention, then signed, *"Are you ready?"*

Nella bobbed her fist. *"Yes."*

The autocar was waiting to take them home. Most civilian vehicles in Odysseus City used a partition of Homer. It allowed for safer streets and more automation for easy living in the city. People still drove cars if they chose to; for example, Nella's Uncle Jason favored his rushcycle in manual mode. This autocar was equipped with mechanical arms that helped Marie get in and out of the vehicle easily. After Marie was sitting comfortably in the back seat, the arms pulled her wheelchair into a special compartment and stowed it away.

Nella got in the car from the other side. She flicked a hand over her soothreader, and the Homer unit lit up with a smiley face. The car began to move, heading toward the Castus home first.

Nella turned toward Marie. *"Any news from my parents?"*

Marie shook her head and signed, *"They will just be getting to the western auk'nai regions now. Probably won't hear anything until tomorrow."*

Such terrible news about the Daunoren, Nella thought. She had read more information about it throughout the day on her soothreader. Auk'nai communities were in anguish over the loss of their God. Some were lashing out at humans, blaming them for the murder. Their claims were baseless, but anger and sorrow didn't need evidence every time.

It was a short car ride back to the Castus home. Nella exited the vehicle and waved goodbye as the autocar took Marie back down the road. She opened the front door with her soothreader and walked through the living room to the kitchen.

Nella put on a pot for hot water, then went to her bedroom and removed her soothreader. The skin on her wrist where the soothreader had been felt free and comfortable. She had the whole house to herself, but after a day of gardening and maintaining the archive grounds, she was beat. She went back in the kitchen, took the pot of hot water off the stove when she saw steam propelling from its spout, and made herself some tea using some herbs and spices she had gathered herself from the wilderness just beyond her home.

It was one of her favorite hobbies, being out in the silent wild, with only the beautiful forest to occupy the senses. Mother Nature had many children: Earth, Mars, Callisto . . . but Kamaria was her favorite daughter. Nella typically brought a small guardian drone with her in case any creatures decided she might make a good meal. But the Timber Chase was a safe place. The most dangerous predator around was called a panthasaur, and it only ate fish near the river a few kilometers away.

Nella sank into a chair in the living room and turned on the vidscreen to watch some of her favorite shows. As she read the captions, sleep eventually overtook her. Nella drifted into dreams.

———————◆———————

Nella was awakened when a bright light came through the front window and shone into her eyes. *What the Hells?* she thought and lifted herself from her chair to get a better look out the window. An autocar was outside, and its headlights were shining into the living room.

She moved toward the door and looked out the peephole. No one was there. *Is someone waiting in the car?* Nella wondered. The back door to the autocar opened, and a man stumbled out. *Cade?*

Nella slid her boots on and grabbed her coat in a hurry. She flung the door open and ran to the side of the car. Cade stumbled to his knee in front of her, wincing with pain. The autocar detected that its passenger had exited, and it pulled back out of the driveway.

She knelt next to Cade and put his arm around her shoulder to help lift him up. Nella could feel Cade groaning through vibrations in her palm as she braced him to keep him from falling forward. They worked their way through the door, and she gently laid him onto the couch.

Weakly, Cade opened his eyes, squinting through his injuries. She felt a lump on the back of his head and signed, *"What happened?"* Her face was full of worry and confusion.

Cade tried to sit up but couldn't. Nella urged him to stay on his back and went to the kitchen to get some ice. She dug through the kitchen freezer and found a bag of frozen sunpears. *Close enough.* She returned to her brother's side and tucked the frozen bag of fruits under his head like a pillow. He winced again and closed his eyes.

Nella checked Cade over for more injuries. On his wrist was a cut near his soothreader. Nella removed the device and put it on the table, then remembered there was a first aid kit in the bathroom down the hall. She put a finger up to tell Cade she'd be right back, then ran down the hall, her boots tracking some mud and dampness from the light snow on the ground over the carpet.

The medicine cabinet over the toilet contained a bulky first aid kit. Aside from being Scout Leader, Nella's mother was a doctor in the medical field. They always kept an extensive first aid kit around but had never used it for anything other than light scrapes. Nella wasn't entirely sure what she'd need or even how she'd use it, but she was sure she could figure it out. If needed, she could call an ambulance after she got Cade bandaged up. She'd need to grab her soothreader from her bedroom but decided it could wait until she fixed Cade up first. *One thing at a time.*

The lights in the bathroom shut off.

The Hells? Nella thought. *Great, now the power is out? What next?*

She made her way back toward the living room, thinking she'd have to dig through the kitchen cabinets for some candles to light, when she noticed a cold draft in the air. She rounded the corner and saw that the front door was broken in, hanging off its hinges and swaying lightly. She could see snow falling outside, and some tracked into the house. Nella almost ran to the threshold to see if Cade had run off for some reason.

Her heart dropped.

Something was lurking in the darkness of the living room.

Cade lay on the couch, passed out from his injuries. Over him stood a massive auk'nai, wearing a cloak made of a material Nella was unfamiliar with. The cloak covered most of the auk'nai's body except for its black, folded wings and long, pointed ears.

Nella gasped, and it turned toward her. She dropped the first aid kit onto the floor.

Under its cloaked hood, three glowing yellow eyes shined at her. It made its way across the living room and into the kitchen in front of Nella in two paces. It said something, but Nella couldn't understand without her soothreader's translation options to sign it to her. The auk'nai razor-sharp beak was impossible to read but quite easy to fear.

The cloaked auk'nai reached forward and grabbed Nella's arm with its taloned hand. It repeated whatever statement it had before with no further effect. Nella tried to pull away, but its grip was too firm. There was something under its cloak on its left side, something substantial that the auk'nai was concealing.

Its glowing yellow eyes were made of machinery and glass, like camera lenses. They rotated and narrowed as they focused on Nella. In the darkness of the room, the brightness hurt her eyes, and she tried to look away. Her feet slipped out from under her, but she didn't fall to the floor. The auk'nai held her firmly in the air above the kitchen tile. The monster then jerked its head around toward Cade. Nella blinked the haze away from her eyes, just enough to see Cade struggling to his feet.

Cade was saying something as he attempted to maintain his balance. Whatever he said caused the monster to flick its three glowing eyes at Nella, then back to Cade.

A metal claw launched outward from under the monster's cloak and flashed across the kitchen into the living room. It grasped Cade's neck, then retracted as the auk'nai pulled both Nella and Cade toward the front door, bringing them outside into the snow.

It turned its eyes to Cade. He was fighting against the claw clasped around his neck. The monster created a blinding flash with its eyes, concussing Cade. He went slack.

Nella screamed loud enough to cause the monster to flinch. It was unhindered, though, and pulled them across the front yard, to where a metallic tube waited. Nella recognized it as a stasis pod used for keeping human bodies functioning during long periods of interstellar travel. They had been used on the starships that brought humanity to Kamaria in the past.

The monster pushed Cade inside the pod with a rough shove, then turned its attention on Nella. The three yellow eyes burned into her eye sockets. She tried to scream.

There was a flash of white light followed by darkness.

EIGHT

CADE CASTUS FELT LIKE he had been hit by a truck—a truck that was still parked on top of him. He could barely move his arms and legs, and his chest felt compressed. His vision was slowly returning to him, but the images he was getting were confusing. He was in a small, cramped place with a flickering light. It smelled like flowers, and something hairy was pushed against him.

Wait a minute.

The hairy thing crammed inside this small place was a person. *What happened last night?* Cade tried to remember. He had hazy memories of that scraggily auk'nai, Krin'ta. *He jumped me, beat me pretty bad too.* Before that, he had a fantastic night with Zephyr. *But there's something else, something foggy. Something later.*

In and out of consciousness, he remembered Nella. *A frozen bag of fruit under my head.* Cade could feel the lump on the back of his skull against whatever he was pressed against. There was something else in the haze of his memory. A large shadow—a monster. *What did it say? It asked something.*

The monster asked if we were John Veston's children.

It was a strange question. John Veston, Cade's grandfather, had been dead longer than Cade and Nella had been alive. Cade vaguely recalled telling the monster, "What? No, we're his *grandchildren.*" Then there was pressure on his neck, like a metal clamp, followed by a blinding flash.

Kidnapped. It finally made sense. *But why?*

He smelled the wildflowers again, coming from the hair that encompassed his current world. Nella always smelled like that. Working in the archive gardens covered her in sweet, natural perfume. Then it dawned on Cade.

"Nella?" Cade spit the name out in his shock. She didn't respond. *Of course, she wouldn't respond.* Cade was pressed so close to Nella he could only see her hair. His hands were pinned, so he had no way of communicating with her. But it was more than Nella not hearing him. She was unconscious. Whatever the monster had done to Cade, it had done to her too.

Mystery one solved. This person is Nella. But where are we?

Small, cramped, probably not meant for more than one person. A flickering light and a metal wall with a curve. This seemed to be some sort of tube. Cade did a mental inventory on what a large metal tube meant for one person might be and concluded it was either construction material or a stasis pod. With the cushion at his back, it was safe to assume this was a pod. He was familiar with their design. He had seen a few on the *Infinite Aria* before his first day working on the *Maulwurf.* This pod felt old, musty even. Unused, yet used. It couldn't be an *Aria* pod. It had to have come from somewhere else. Where, though? The only other options were the *Odysseus* or the *Telemachus.* Both seemed implausible. The *Odysseus* was somewhere in deep space, ferrying Nhymn around, and the *Telemachus* was a wreck.

Doesn't matter—are we flying?

The monster was taking them somewhere. From the aggressive reaction to announcing their relationship to their grandfather, Cade didn't want to find out where they were going. *I have to get us out of here.* He tried to remember what he knew about stasis pods. Stasis pods were only used for a few purposes in modern society—rich folks who wanted to live forever and take long naps to spread out their years, interstellar travel when it was possible before, and as escape pods. As an escape pod, it would have failsafes built in. Stasis pods were all pretty uniform in their construction. *So, in theory, if I just . . .*

Cade pushed his right arm against the wall and felt an armrest. Good—he was lying in the actual chair. He must have been shoved into this can first, with Nella crammed in after him. Cade stretched his arm to its limit and reached with his fingers for the end of the armrest, where a small latch should be. His fingertips found it, and with some force, he pulled the latch upward.

The lid of the bed creaked, then ripped away from the main tube. Cade grabbed Nella tightly, almost losing her as the air pressure outside tried to tear her away from him. The snow was drifting through the night air, chilling Cade instantly. Each snowflake whipped by at high speed, creating sharp white lines. Treetops lining the lower extremities of Cade's vision confirmed they were flying. He looked up, past Nella, and saw the monster above them.

It was an auk'nai, and a big one at that. Its wings were more extensive than most auk'nai Cade had encountered. *That's not Krin'ta*, Cade realized, which made this more confusing. Each wing flap was measured and even. It was as if the stasis pod it was carrying weighed nothing at all. A metal tether trailed out under its strange cloak and attached itself to their pod with a viselike claw hand.

The monster auk'nai turned its attention on Cade, noticing the pod lid had been removed. Cade saw its three glowing yellow eyes shining brighter in the night sky. The auk'nai began to retract the metal hand, pulling the stasis bed closer to its body. Cade acted quickly. He shifted Nella in his hand, keeping a tight grip on her limp body, and searched blindly for a compartment on the sidewall. He found it, cracked it open, and managed to work a flare gun into his hand.

Cade acted before thinking. He pointed the flare gun at the monster above them and fired. There was a white-hot flash of light, and then the world tumbled around them. He could hear the beast shrieking, and as the stasis pod dropped, he could see the monster burning as it fell with them.

The impact hit them like a massive sledgehammer. The pod rolled, then began to slide on its backside. Sticks, snow, and rocks made their way into the open pod, but Cade held his sister tight to keep her from being flung away. For a moment, Cade saw the monster's claw reach toward the open hatch, fire flicking out from its feathers. The pod rolled, and the claw vanished beneath his view. Cade's gut sank as they free-fell once more. Another impact, and this time the stasis bed ceased all movement.

Cade was dizzy. The world was still spinning as if the stasis pod was tumbling further and further. They were vertical—the pod had thankfully landed bottom down. He crushed his eyelids together until the need to vomit subsided. A blue light seemed to fill the pod, and in his daze, Cade was unsure of its source.

Once he regained his composure, Cade's attention snapped to Nella. Her eyes were slowly starting to open, and she began to groan. He maneuvered them both out of the damaged pod with a series of pushes and grunts. He laid Nella in the snow and waved into her half-open eyes, then signed, *"We need to move. Not safe."*

Nella's eyes opened wider as the situation revealed itself to her. She recovered, and Cade took in his surroundings. They were among tall trees in the snow, in the foothills of a large, pointed mountain. Pulses of blue light licked up the trunks of the tall trees, brushing through their blue pine needles and flickering like embers back to the ground. Some of the light embers danced across Cade's nose, but there was no heat to their touch. The blue embers of light mixed with the heavy snowfall that silently graced the hillside.

Too much snow, Cade thought. *It's supposed to be the end of winter. A light dusting would have been expected, but this is damn near a blizzard. Maybe we're north of the city? No, these blue embers . . .* Cade recognized the trees as part of a place called the Ember-Lit Forest. *That monster must have taken us across the damn continent!* He wasn't sure what he should do. *Maybe wait for rescue?*

Another shrill birdcall echoed from the cliffside above them, where the stasis pod had slipped off into its second freefall prior. Cade saw fire coming from the ledge, and in the flames was the silhouette of the monster that had brought them to this place.

Cade knelt in front of Nella and sat her upright. He signed, *"We have to go. Now."*

Nella held a hand to her head and nodded. Cade put her arm over his shoulders and hurried her deeper into the Ember-Lit Forest, away from the stasis pod. Behind them, the monster auk'nai shrieked out again.

———————◆———————

After an hour of scrambling through the Ember-Lit Forest, Nella Castus fell to her knees. Nothing made sense, and she needed time to collect herself. Cade leaned against a tree, lit by the slow pulse of light that moved up its trunk. He was keeping his eye on where they had come from. *Is something chasing us?* she wondered.

Nella was cold and tired and hurt. Her right arm felt tense, and it hurt to move it. She shivered under her jacket and felt every spot she had banged against the pod during their fall. Cade came to her side and signed, *"Are you hurt?"*

"I'll be fine," Nella signed. *"What is out there?"* Her arm hurt as she asked. Her eyes were wide, and her attention darted between Cade and the forest around them.

"Monster," Cade signed, putting both hands up like claws facing Nella and opening his mouth like a fierce animal.

Nella remembered their kidnapper. It had three yellow eyes— auk'nai didn't have *three* eyes. And that metal arm; she had never seen anything like that before. The way it moved was so unnatural.

Nella shivered again. *"We need shelter. Need fire."*

Cade frowned and paced back and forth.

"We can't run all night." Nella's brow was raised, and her mouth slightly open in pleading.

Cade nodded. Then his eyes darted around the area. They were deep in the Ember-Lit Forest, surrounded by the ember trees and uneven rock terraces. Cade held a finger up, then scrambled to a higher terrace. He was gone for a few moments, but it was long enough for Nella to feel her skin crawl. She felt small and weak. Her lack of hearing had never stopped her from accomplishing her goals, but right now, it added to her terror. She was lost in the wilderness, being chased by a monster, and had to rely only on what she could see to save herself. Nella wished she had her guardian drone with her.

Something caught her eye between the trees. It was a hulking thing, too big to be the monster that had kidnapped them, but a monster all the same. The beast was tall, lurching itself through the snow on four long legs covered in white, matted fur. It had a long snout with small, sharp teeth that lined it from its front all the way back to its ears in a grin. Its head was drooped toward the snow on a long neck covered in strands of hair. Its eyes seemed to glow pale blue in the night, looking hazy, like those of a dead thing. As it lifted one of its long legs to take another step, it revealed a paw with sharp claws at the end.

To Nella, the creature was silent, which made it all the more terrifying. The beast closed its wide grin and looked at her, showing curiosity. It stared with those dead-looking eyes, unblinking.

Nella grabbed a heavy stick and clutched it in two hands. The creature opened its mouth again, sniffed the air, and then took a cautious step toward her. Nella lifted her stick to give the beast a warning, hoping to ward it off. It grinned and planted its foot forward, then took another step closer. Nella let out a quick, loud shout, and the beast flinched but didn't flee.

She was done warning. Nella reared back and hurled the long stick at the creature. The beast dodged the missile and bounded around in a circle, then retreated deeper into the forest. This surprised Nella. She thought for sure the thing might take advantage and rush her. She jumped out of her skin when Cade slid down from the upper ledge in front of her.

"Are you okay?" His face was full of worry and regret as he signed. He looked in the direction the creature went. *"I think that was a putoripard."* He spelled out the name of the beast. *"I remember from Kid Scouts."*

Nella nodded, then pounded her fist against his chest. She

signed, *"Don't leave me like that."*

Cade nodded. *"I'm sorry."*

"We need to stay in each other's line of sight," Nella signed.

Cade nodded again. *"I found a cave,"* he signed, then pointed downhill.

The cave wasn't deep, but it had enough interior space to keep them out of the cold wind and snow. Laser stones, geodes that resonated energy, lined the interior walls, generating a small amount of heat. Nella remembered her father telling her they could be used to power a spaceship if she ever found herself hypothetically stranded in the wilderness. She wanted to laugh, because she was *literally* stranded in the wilderness, but wouldn't you know it—no spaceship.

"Feeling better?" Cade asked.

Nella bobbed her fist.

"I will watch for the monster. You sleep now."

The putoripard had been scary, but the monster Cade implied was the auk'nai with the metal arm. *What a mess this is*, Nella thought. Cade leaned against the mouth of the cave and kept an eye on the trees. Nella curled up on the ground next to a laser stone and allowed sleep to overtake her.

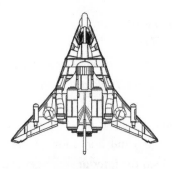

NINE

ON THE WESTERN REACHES of the continent, Eliana and Denton Castus watched a line of pilgrim auk'nai pull the bodies of their dead up a mountain path. Although the ritual was similar to that of the auk'nai of Apusticus, this place was unfamiliar. Here, the climate was warmer, spring was in full effect, and the flowers were blooming. The blue-green grass lined the pathway the pilgrims traveled to the Daunoren that lived at the peak.

The auk'nai of this western region had long, thin beaks, and mostly white feathers with black sashes. Since the union between humans and auk'nai two decades prior, the scouts had explored many new regions of the continent and met with different auk'nai and auk'gnell. To the south, the auk'nai were flightless, with featherless heads and bright-blue and red skin. Their beaks were adorned with hornlike protrusions. Northern auk'nai had flat faces with small beaks and large, dark eyes. There were more scattered loner auk'gnell of various races to the east, but the scarce natives had short, sharp beaks, red and white feathers, and exotic head dressings.

Talulo walked toward Eliana and Denton, shaking his head. "Talulo asked the Watcher here about anything suspicious. Watcher said all was normal. Only the Song of Apusticus has been ended. Talulo warned the Watcher to be alert."

"So, the slaying was an isolated event," Denton stated.

"Seems that way," Eliana said, "but whatever killed our Daunoren isn't anything like what we've seen before. Homer analyzed the body and discovered the blade had to have been incredibly sharp. It was a unique weapon that took down ours."

"Elly!" Faye Raike shouted to them from the *Rogers*'s access ramp. "We have a situation. It's about Cade and Nella."

Eliana and Denton exchanged a look of worry and confusion, then hurried toward the ship. Inside the *Rogers*'s locker room was a vid screen featuring a distraught Marie Viray. She seemed to be inside the Castus home.

"What's going on?" Denton asked. He could feel his pulse quickening. His neck tensed up.

"I don't know for sure," Marie said. She was clearly flustered. "Nella didn't come to work this morning. I started to get nervous when she wasn't answering her soothreader, so I came to check up on her—"

"Oh no," Eliana gasped. Behind Marie, the front door of their home was hanging off its hinges. Snow and mud had been dragged into the house. There were tracks of dirt kicked around and a small, mysterious crater in the yard.

"She's not here," Marie said. "And Cade isn't answering his calls either."

"We're on our way," Eliana said. She gripped Denton's jacket tightly and looked him in the eyes. He was speechless. Denton hoped it was a misunderstanding. There had to be an explanation for whatever was going on.

The *Rogers* took off immediately.

— ◆ —

Hours later, Denton and Eliana pulled up into their driveway in their truck. They exited and hurried toward the front door. Eliana stopped when she saw the broken threshold to their home and the drag marks on the carpet. Marie Viray, Jess Combs, and Homer's robotic body were inside, searching for clues.

"I've already contacted the authorities," Marie said when Eliana entered. "They will be here soon."

Denton froze as he entered the living room. He was surprised there wasn't more chaos, just some ripped-up carpet, a broken door, and dirt tracks. The table had been knocked over and pushed. But even with the lack of destruction, it was enough to know something had come into the home.

Faye Raike entered in behind Denton and Eliana and gasped. She and Eliana shared a concerned look. Eliana began to frantically search the house for Nella and Cade. Denton tried to remain calm, but he felt paralyzed. His arms felt like his bones and muscles were replaced with air, and he couldn't move anything except his eyes. He thought his heart stopped. Then, he had an idea.

"Homer." Denton snapped his fingers toward the robot. "Can you get any data from the street cameras leading up to the house?"

"I'm sorry to say I cannot," Homer said with their soothing synthetic voice.

"What?" Denton spat the question, angry there wasn't a better response.

"Last night, when we believe this incident occurred, there was a wave of electrical disturbances. I noticed a pattern in the power outages." Homer gestured in front of themself. A map of the city appeared in a blue glow. "You can see—the outages created a path around the city before coming to your home."

Everyone watched the map as it traced a yellow pathway, entering the city from the east and bouncing around to different locations until it ended up vanishing around the Castus home. For a minute, it seemed like that was where the trail ended, but then it reappeared and exited the city to the east once more.

"What the Hells can do that?" Eliana asked.

"I am unsure," Homer said. "No creatures documented on Kamaria can disrupt our electronics like this."

"You don't think—" Faye began to ask.

"Another Siren?" Denton cut her off. "They have unique powers. I can see one having the ability to do something like this."

"Shit," Jess Combs grunted.

"We don't know anything yet. Let's not go jumping straight to Sirens," Eliana warned.

A buzzing came from near the couch. Faye pushed the knocked-over table to the side and found a soothreader on the carpet. She examined it, and it buzzed once more.

"That's Cade's," Denton said. He moved over to Faye and took the soothreader. With a few gestures, he brought up the notification—a text from Zephyr.

I had a great time last night. Sorry about the window.

"Maybe Zephyr knows something about what happened," Denton suggested. He flicked over the soothreader and called Zephyr. After a moment, the image of Zephyr appeared over the device. She was wearing a loose-fitting tank top and looked shocked when she realized it wasn't Cade on the other end of the call. She almost hung up. "Wait, wait, wait! I'm Cade's dad! I need your help," Denton urged.

"Mr. Castus?" Zephyr asked. She looked at how distraught his face was. "What's going on?"

"We think . . ." Denton began. He struggled to say it, but he had to bring it out into reality. "We think something might have happened to Cade and Nella."

"Oh no," Zephyr whispered.

Eliana moved over to Denton's side and asked, "Were you with Cade last night? Do you know where he might be now?"

"Yeah, I was with him. Uh—we went to the club to celebrate his promotion. He came back here after for a bit, but then he had to go. I didn't see him after that."

"Is there anything else you can think of? Anything at all?" Eliana asked.

"Listen, I really want to help, but I can't think of anything," Zephyr admitted.

Denton and Eliana looked at each other with deep despair in their eyes.

"Hey," Zephyr said, "how about I do some searching around here? Maybe something will come up. If I find anything, I'll let you know."

"Thank you. Here's our information," Eliana said, and gestured over her own soothreader, tossing their contact info to Zephyr through the network.

"I'll do my best. I hope they're okay. If anything happened to Ca—" She cut herself off. Her brow furrowed, and she looked away from the camera and blinked away a tear. Denton could tell she cared for Cade.

"If we all work together, I know we'll find them," Denton said. He held Eliana tighter and rubbed her shoulder.

"Thanks. Okay, I'll start searching. Talk to you later," Zephyr said.

They ended the call. Eliana sat on the couch and held her face in her palms. She took deep breaths. Once she gathered her strength, she said, "Okay. What do we have to work with?"

"Homer, can you bring up that map again?" Denton asked. "The power outage one."

Homer displayed the map once more in front of their chest. Denton studied it further, tilting his head. He brought his hands up and gestured in front of the map, taking control of it. Denton pulled out and followed the path to the east, where it vanished. "So, this anomaly came here from the east, then went back this way . . ." he said quietly, mostly to himself. Denton thought for a moment, then added, "There's an outpost east of the city. Near the *Telemachus* wreck."

"Yes, the trajectory here would line up with the Telemachus Outpost," Homer confirmed. They brought up a different map that showed a small outpost near the *Telemachus* crash site. Decades ago, the Siren had been smashed into the ground by the interstellar spacecraft like a bug under a hammer. The wreck still stood upright in the valley, like a needle halfway thrust into an apple. "This outpost has been experiencing satellite trouble due to a seismic event that occurred in the region a month prior," Homer explained. "But yesterday, hours before we believe this event occurred, they experienced the same residual phenomenon we have in the city. It was faint as if the phenomena was nearby and not close enough to cause a full outage."

"And it is east. Albeit also more south than I expected," Faye added.

"It's also where Nhymn and Sympha's shared remains are," Denton said. Everyone eyed him with cold stares. He put his hands up in defense. "I'm just saying! Couldn't Nhymn have come back somehow?"

The room grew silent at the possibility.

"We're going to have to see for ourselves. Everyone pack up. We don't know how long we'll be searching, so prepare for a long trip," Eliana said. "We can't burn any more time."

TEN

THREE MONTHS AGO

L'ARN HEARD THE SOUND of waves lapping against stone, of water dripping from high up onto a flat rock, of seabirds cawing over the ocean. He opened his eyes and was surprised to see that his vision had been restored. The acid his attacker had thrown at his face had not permanently blinded him. He inhaled the fresh sea air and coughed. Somehow, he had survived the vicious attack he suffered at his nest.

He looked around. Somehow, his eyes worked better than they had before. Everything was in such incredible detail, even sharper than usual for an auk'gnell. Ruby-red waves lapped against wet, black boulders. L'Arn was inside a cave outlet on the Howling Shore, though he was not near his nest.

With a sharp inhale, L'Arn reached for his left arm with his right claw and was shocked to find it was there. He had not lost it, although he vividly remembered having it sliced off by his attacker. The sight of his limp arm dropping to the ground would never leave his memory. He sat up, looked at his hands, and then inspected the area where his arm should have been severed by the shoulder. Perfectly healed, as if nothing had ever happened.

"Welcome back," a raspy voice said in Sol Common, the human language. L'Arn searched the interior of the cave for the source of the voice and found nothing. He spoke again. "Come outside. I have food ready for you."

Although the voice claimed it was outside the cave, L'Arn felt like its source was standing next to him. Confused, L'Arn followed the voice's instructions and walked out of the cave onto a flat rock outcrop.

The sea rolled against the rocks here, casting refreshing mist into the air. The waves were stained red from the abundance of algae under the water's surface. The sky was dark and overcast but not threatening rain. L'Arn guessed it might be close to sunset from the yellow-orange hue that peaked around the corners of the masses of clouds.

"It's good to see you on your feet, friend."

A human male sat next to a modest fire. He was bald, with a bushy white beard and lightly tanned skin. He wore a loose-fitting white T-shirt that went past his waist, along with beige pants that ended at the middle of his shins. The man looked at L'Arn. He had an orange tint to his left eye, and his right eye looked like a solid ball of black marble.

"Come and sit," the man said. "Let's get to know each other."

L'Arn looked around, unsure if he could trust this stranger.

"Oh, what am I thinking. You probably don't understand me, do you?" The man poked the fire. "Finally get some company around here, and I can't even have a conversation."

"I understand you," L'Arn said.

The man looked up, his eyes wide as a smile crept onto his face, "You do? I mean, you can speak Sol Common? I'll be damned!"

"Everyone from Apusticus can speak your language," L'Arn said. "Humans are too stupid to learn our language."

"Humans are stupid. Boy, don't I know it." The man laughed

to himself. "Apusticus?" He scratched his head. "Never heard of it. Is that what you call that hut of yours?"

"No, it is the city L'Arn—" L'Arn stopped himself, slipping into the auk'nai way of speaking in the third person for the first time in two decades. "Where *I* came from. A city in the center of the continent."

"L'Arn, is that your name?" the man asked.

L'Arn nodded.

"Well, friend. You can call me Auden," he said and held out a hand. L'Arn looked at the hand and didn't know what to do. In fact, L'Arn couldn't hear Auden's song at all. He had limited experience with humans, but he remembered listening to their intentions through their unsung songs. Auden was silent. The only song he sang was in his words and actions.

Auden waved his hand away, giving up on the gesture. "Ah, that's okay, we'll get there." He poked the fire with a metal stick, then pulled a small fish from its roasting position. "Here, eat this. You have to be starving."

L'Arn sat next to Auden and accepted the fish. He thrust his beak into its center and began to strip away the skin.

"Eat all you like. I'll get more if you're still hungry. Plenty of fish in the sea, as they say." Auden smiled. He let L'Arn eat a little more before asking, "So, you know other humans?"

"No," L'Arn said as he gobbled down the remainder of the fish, "but they came to my city from time to time. Our leader, Mag'Ro, taught us your ways and your language."

"Humans in the center of the continent." Auden smiled. "What are the odds . . ."

L'Arn's stomach growled, and he wanted to ask for more fish but couldn't ignore Auden's statement. "Are you not with the humans from the central continent?"

"No, can't say I am. I didn't even know they were here." Auden laughed. "I haven't seen humans in a long time."

"I thought you all came to Kamaria together," L'Arn said.

"Kamaria?" Auden asked. "Is that what you call this planet?"

"It's the human word for it. We call it—" L'Arn let out a birdcall that was both beautiful and loud.

"I like that more." Auden smiled and poked the fire.

"Where are you from?" L'Arn asked.

"The same place the others were from, just came at a different time." Auden stood up and put his hands on his hips. "You still hungry, friend?"

"Yes."

"Okay, let me go snag another fish," Auden said and casually walked over to the rock edge. L'Arn expected Auden to get a tool to help him fish, maybe something like a peck rifle—humans always took the easy route when it came to hunting. They were the reason Apusticus forgot the ways of nature.

Auden stepped onto the water, and to L'Arn's amazement, he didn't sink. The human walked across the surface of the waves, calming them as he moved away from the shoreline. He moved with casual grace, as if he were shopping for gems in the city marketplace. Auden knelt down, put his hand under the surface, and stood up with a fish the size of his arm in his hand. The fish didn't struggle. Its gills heaved in and out.

Auden came back to the fire and strapped the fish to the roasting spit, cooking it without protest. He sat back in his previous position and sighed, then asked, "You ever hear of a man named John Veston?"

L'Arn was still shocked by the strange power Auden had just displayed and didn't know what to say.

"You alright?" Auden asked. He looked out over the water, then back to L'Arn, "What, that? Anyone can do that."

"I cannot," L'Arn said.

"Sure, you can. I can help you." Auden smiled. "Like I helped you with your wounds."

L'Arn looked at his left hand and flexed his claw. "You healed me?"

"Believe me, buddy, you were a challenge. When I found you, you weren't all in one piece." Auden laughed. "I never met something like you before, but I'm damn good at my job."

L'Arn cooed his appreciation.

"Don't thank me yet," Auden said and looked into the fire. "If I understood your people better, I could fix a whole lot more of your problems."

"Problems?" L'Arn asked.

"I can show you how to do what I can do," Auden said.

L'Arn laughed and eyed the fish. Auden put his hand up. "One minute, friend. Tell me, do you know Dr. John Veston."

L'Arn thought for a moment. The name sounded familiar—there was something special concerning it. He thought back to all the humans he had seen those years past when he had joined Mag'Ro and the others for their early meetings with the alien species. He remembered them wearing shells of some sort and that they couldn't breathe the Kamarian air or they would die. There were many humans in the valley with the river, but only a few would meet with them. Yes, there had been a John Veston among them. He remembered two of them were Vestons—John and a younger one, Eliana.

"There were two Vestons. But where they are now, I do not know," L'Arn answered. "I only saw humans a few times."

"So, John is here." Auden smiled, then mumbled to himself, "The other one . . . maybe his daughter?"

"Is he a friend?" L'Arn asked.

"Yes—well, actually no. We were friends once, but we had a misunderstanding."

"It is like myself and Apusticus. Different minds, different songs." L'Arn looked into the fire. Auden handed him the cooked fish.

"I think you and I are going to get along," Auden said.

L'Arn cooed and gobbled down the fish with delight.

ELEVEN

PRESENT DAY

CADE CASTUS THOUGHT BACK on what he learned as a Kid Scout. It was a program run by Fergus Reid to teach aspiring youths the ways of Kamaria. There were some fun times when his father would join along on camping trips out in the Timber Chase. Back then, Cade wanted to be just like his parents. He wanted to be a scout. As Cade grew older, his aspirations looked to the stars above instead of the planet below.

Never in his life did Cade imagine he'd have to use those old skills in such a dangerous situation, but here he was. The simple things he'd learned could be strategies to keep him and his sister alive. Although the putoripard beast from the night before was relatively harmless, it might have seized the opportunity to attack Nella if it thought she was vulnerable enough. Sometimes the element of surprise was all that was needed to make a beast go from harmless to dangerous.

The sun rose in the Ember-Lit Forest, casting long shadows of light from the tall, piney, ember-emitting trees. The pulsing glow they gave off at night dimmed at dawn, but the snow still continued to fall. Nella was sleeping, and Cade was shivering. He was cold and hungry, but not thirsty. Kid Scouts had taught him that munching on the abundant snow wouldn't rehydrate him. His body would have to work harder to melt the snow, which would only make him more dehydrated. Instead, Cade melted the snow and drank the pre-warmed fresh water.

It was a simple trick. The small cave they stayed the night in was lined with laser stones emitting a small amount of residual heat. It wasn't enough to burn skin, but plenty to melt snow. Cade found an indent in the rocks to act as a basin, filled it with snow, and plunked a fist-sized laser stone inside, watching the residual heat melt everything in the basin. The stone, once fully submerged in water, lost its electrical charge. After a few minutes, the water was pure and drinkable. Hells, it even tasted better than a lot of the purified water he'd drunk on the *Maulwurf.* This water tasted natural, with minerals that helped his hurt body heal.

Cade took inventory of what they had to work with. They both lacked their soothreaders. Cade was unsure what had happened to his. The last time he checked, he had one, but the night of their kidnapping was confusing. There were blurry memories of Nella removing it due to a cut he got from Krin'ta stomping him. Didn't matter much. It was gone, regardless of how it happened.

There were no human settlements that he knew of on this side of the continent. Although humans had spread out from Odysseus City after the days of Nhymn, they still remained within trading distance of the city. If there were any humans this far out, Cade had no idea where to find them. They'd be off the grid.

Luckily, the scout jacket Cade had received as a gift from his father had plenty of assets.

In the years that followed the Days of Nhymn, the Scout Program had gone through some adjustments. One such modification was the standard-issue jacket. In the past, it had been a way to help the auk'nai view humans as a team. Now it functioned as a sort of a wearable field kit. In the interior chest pocket was a flask, which Cade filled with some of the water in his basin. The forearm of his left sleeve concealed a knife, which wasn't a great weapon but was better than nothing. In the side pocket was a bracelet that could be loosened to make a long rope. Cade fastened it around his wrist to replace his lost soothreader. His shoulder's right pad held a fire-starting tool—a magnesium kit he could scrape to generate a spark. He could have used it to keep warm overnight but was afraid a fire might lead their pursuer directly to them. Cade was wearing the jacket's removable hood.

The flare gun he grabbed from the stasis pod still had one shot left. It was a mechanical thing, using a cartridge instead of a collider cylinder. Collider tech wouldn't produce a flare anyway, only quick bolts of charged particles. The flare wouldn't work if no one was around to see it, but it could be used as a deterrent. He remembered seeing the monster auk'nai burning as they fell from the sky.

They had the essential tools they would need, but Cade wished he had a bioscope. With a bioscope, he could ping Homer by scanning a living creature or plant. Even if that didn't work in this location, he could, at the very least, know what was edible or poisonous. A collider pistol would be fantastic too.

He felt the void stone in his pocket. The souvenir seemed to have caused him more problems than he could ever have anticipated. Cade considered throwing it into the snow but then felt like it might somehow come in handy, maybe as a weapon. Better to keep it. The stone wasn't taking up much room anyway.

Nella stirred. She woke up and looked around frantically until she saw her brother. He approached her and handed her the flask of water.

Nella signed, *"Thank you,"* and took a sip, then handed the flask back to him. *"What do we do now?"*

"Monster auk'nai might still be out there. We can't stay here," Cade signed. *"What do you have on you? What can we use?"*

Nella searched herself. She was still wearing the clothes she'd had on when she dragged Cade back into their house. A winter jacket, boots, loose-fitting pants, and a long-sleeve shirt. She rummaged through her pockets and found some gloves and a beanie. She put both on right away. Nella went back into her pocket and slowly pulled forward a little cloth bag. She shook two seeds out of the bag into her gloved hand and eyed them with a distant, empty stare.

"I don't think we can make a garden here," Cade signed, and shrugged.

Nella dropped the seeds back into the cloth bag and tucked it back into her pocket. She patted around her body for more tools but came up with nothing. She wasn't wearing a scout jacket, and she had no training in this sort of thing.

Cade smiled and clapped his hands. *"You know advanced botany! You're like a walking bioscope."*

Nella was confused.

"We won't starve. You will know what we should and should not eat."

Nella realized what he meant and nodded. *"Hope it helps."*

"It will. Are you ready to leave?" Cade asked.

Nella bobbed her fist and weakly stood. She winced and held her arm. Cade went to help her, but she signed, *"I'm fine. Bruised."* Nella looked outside, and her brow furrowed. She looked at Cade. *"Where are we going?"*

Cade looked out of the cave into the Ember-Lit Forest. The sun had come up enough to reveal the dense pines, but it all looked like a maze to him. He didn't know this area well, just where it was on a map. They needed to get off the mountain and head toward civilization, to the west. Cade signed to Nella, *"We keep heading downhill. There should be a valley below. It could lead to warmer climates."*

Nella nodded. *"Can I lead? The monster might sneak up behind me."* She waggled her hand in front of her ear.

"If it got me while I'm behind you, you'd never know. We can walk

together," Cade signed. *"That way, we can keep each other safe."*

Nella understood and nodded. They exited the cave and searched the area like nurn watching out for a dray'va. Nella tapped her forefinger against her ear, asking Cade, *"Do you hear anything?"*

Cade shook his head.

Slowly, they stepped out into the sunlight. The breeze was inviting, and the slow dance of embers and snow was relaxing. Still, they both knew a monster lurked somewhere behind this peaceful façade. Side by side, they walked down the slope through the snow.

⸻ ◆ ⸻

They continued walking well into the afternoon. The mountainside was a steady decline, and the farther down into the valley they traveled, the warmer the weather became. The trees thinned out, and flowers were blooming in the warm afternoon sunlight. Nella removed her gloves and hat and stuffed them back into her pocket. Cade lowered his jacket's hood. Had they not been pursued by a monster auk'nai, the hike would have been pleasant so far.

They came to a cliff ledge that overlooked the greater valley below. The grass was tall and a vibrant yellow. It swayed in the breeze, giving the impression of an ocean with gentle waves. A series of waterfalls emptied into the meadow below, creating rainbows. A mixed herd of herbivores grazed in the fields, munching on the various flowers that grew there. They recognized nurn, with their feathered bodies, four legs, and trunks grasped at the wild grass. A parade of arcophants joined them, bulky creatures with thick bodies and long necks. They used their horns to cut fruits from high trees to eat.

"Dead end," Nella signed, and sighed.

Cade shook his head and unraveled the bracelet on his arm. As it loosened, it revealed a long, strong rope. When he finished, they had ten meters of line, which would get them close enough to the ground below that they would only have to drop a couple meters into the grass.

Cade found a sturdy tree near the ledge and tied it around the side. Nella saw the knot he made and scoffed.

"What?" Cade shrugged.

Nella pushed him out of the way and tugged on the rope, watching it fall into her arms with little effort. Cade said aloud, "Oh, wow." Nella wrapped the rope around the tree once more, tied an advanced knot, and then gave it a hard pull four times. The knot remained firm.

She gestured to the rope, then signed, *"All yours."*

"You want me to go first?" Cade asked.

Nella bobbed her fist in affirmation, then signed, *"We know it is safe up here. We don't know if it's safe down there."*

"Comforting," Cade mumbled to himself. He grabbed the rope and lowered himself onto the ledge. His gut sank when he looked down. The line was free-hanging for more than half of the distance. Cade had seen extreme heights from outer space, but in zero gravity, it never felt like he'd fall *down*. He'd also been tethered to his EVA harness in those situations, giving him a life raft if he were to drift too far from anything. This was gravity reminding Cade to take it seriously.

"You got this." Nella smiled. She thrust her forefinger and pinky upward, her thumb jutting to the side. It was Sol-Sign for *"I love you,"* but it was also had general use as a sign of encouragement for care, love, support, and now rallying her brother to climb down a cliff.

"Oh, shut up," Cade said out loud. Nella read his lips and laughed. With a heavy sigh, Cade began to lower himself. Pressing his feet against the rock wall felt comforting, although Cade wished for a magnetic seal. As he came down, the distance of a potential fall shortened, and by the time he got to the free-hanging part of the climb, it wasn't scary anymore. He scaled down the rope, then dropped the last section. He misjudged precisely how far the last drop would be thanks to the tall grass and landed on his ass with a loud thud. Creatures skittered away. It reminded him of the fall he'd taken from Zephyr's window the night before.

"Not so bad," Cade said to himself again, then took a look around for anything dangerous. When he determined it was all clear, he looked up to tell Nella it was safe. He caught himself before he tried to shout to her, and instead jerked the rope three times. Within a minute, Nella was on her way down the line.

She looked like a pro in comparison. She hopped away from the wall and allowed herself to slide, anchoring the rope around her waist. Cade laughed at how easy she made it look. Then his eyes widened.

In the sky above Nella, he saw a shadow with large wings circling. *Did the monster auk'nai catch up already?* Cade thought as his body crawled with goosebumps.

Nella landed next to Cade and used the *I love you!* hand gesture again, this time with a big grin. Cade waggled his hands in front of her and pointed up. She saw the shadow circling above. They were out in the open, perfect prey.

Nella tapped Cade on the shoulder and pointed toward the long grass of the valley, near the herd of grazing animals. They could conceal themselves if they kept low and moved slowly. Cade led the way, hunching over himself as he moved toward the herd. Eventually, they were close enough to the herd that Cade could hear their honking and grunting. It was possible that these creatures had never seen humans before—which meant there was no way to know how they would react. Cade looked into the sky and discovered the shadow had vanished. *Did it leave?*

Nella gasped.

Cade pivoted and looked back toward the cliff wall.

The dark shape was flying low to the grass, approaching rapidly. It made no sound. Cade scrambled and grabbed Nella's arm, pulling her deeper into the valley toward the herd. The animals became alert, and all at once, the world was rumbling with the chaos of a stampede. Honking, roaring, and the sound of immense pounding feet filled the air. The dark shape grew closer, hovering just above the tall grass.

Nella shoved Cade into the grass as the monster auk'nai sailed into them, knocking Nella away from Cade in the process.

"Nella!" Cade shouted and scrambled to his feet. He searched for her, almost forgetting the stampede around him. He saw the auk'nai crash into the side of a nurn and tumble into the grass only twenty meters away. The stomping of a huge arcophant came from behind Cade, and he turned with just enough time to leap out of the way of the massive beast as it rushed past him.

"Nella!" Cade called out fruitlessly. She wouldn't be able to hear him, but impulse begged him to try. Cade bumped into something with his shins and fell down into the tall grass.

It was Nella. She turned toward him with her eyes wide and sweat beading on her brow. Cade held her close as the world around them rumbled.

The herd had moved on, but something else followed. Cade heard the grass rustling only a meter away. He peeked over the top to see scales and spikes parting the grass in two lines.

"Dray'va," Cade whispered to himself, remembering his father's stories. Nella's eyes went wide as she read his lips. These large reptilian carnivores had powerful arms with an array of razor-sharp claws at the end and a maw filled with knifelike teeth. Spikes protruded from the backs of their skulls, giving the appearance that they were built for speed. Dray'va hunted in duos, often tricking their prey into ambushes. The dray'va on the left had violet scales, while the one on the right was pink-rose colored.

The dark form of the auk'nai recovered from its sloppy impact with the nurn and turned to see the dray'va rushing. The auk'nai tried to fly off, but its wing had been damaged. It barely had time to brace itself for the incoming dray'va attack.

Cade laughed. These predators might be helpful, after all. If they killed the monster auk'nai, then the rest of this journey home might be more comfortable. They could slink away while the reptiles devoured their captor.

Nella nudged Cade and pointed toward an outcropping of trees.

Cade nodded, and they quietly worked their way through the grass. There was a loud birdcall and the roar of the dray'va. Cade peeked over the grass again to watch the brawl and gasped. Nella saw his face and tugged his shoulder. When he looked at her, she signed, *"What's up?"*

"That is not the monster," Cade signed, then looked back at the auk'nai.

The auk'nai that fought the duo of dray'vas had white and gray feathers and a flat face, with large black eyes and a small beak. It wore a dark-green cloak and twirled a long, halberd-shaped daunoren staff.

Nella realized it too. She had seen the monster very clearly before the kidnapping. Their monster had three yellow eyes and a long, sharp beak. This auk'nai had come from the northern reaches of Kamaria.

The auk'nai smashed its halberd's blunt end into the rose-colored dray'va, then spun the blade deftly, slicing a wound into the violet dray'va. It let out a shrill birdcall as it attacked, which caused each reptile to shake their long snouts as if hit with a concussion grenade.

Rose slapped the auk'nai with its powerful spiked tail, and the violet one pounced. Grass flung upward, and the halberd spun wildly as the grounded auk'nai fought off the attackers.

Nella stood and patted her hands against her chest, shouting exceptionally loudly. The rose dray'va looked over, and Cade jerked Nella back into the grass.

"What are you doing?" Cade's hands struck his words with firm movements, his eyebrows up and his mouth frowning, tight-lipped.

"They will kill it. We have to help the auk'nai," Nella signed back.

The distraction was enough for the auk'nai to take advantage. It thrust the blade of its halberd into the distracted rose-scaled dray'va's chest with a wet thud. As the creature screeched in agony, the auk'nai spun and grabbed the violet one. They rolled until it was pinned under the auk'nai's weight. The white-feathered auk'nai then drove its short beak into the violet beast's eye. Blood sprayed, and there was a loud howl. The auk'nai hopped backward away from the violet one, then pulled the halberd out of the rose dray'va and kicked outward with its strong legs. The second dray'va was not killed, but its injury was enough to drive it off limping. The beasts roared, then scrambled back into the tall grass, away from the auk'nai.

The auk'nai let out a long birdcall into the air, signifying its victory, then slumped onto its knees. Its wings had been torn up, and blood oozed out of deep scratches on its body.

"Let's help it," Nella signed, and walked toward the wounded auk'nai.

Cade tried to protest, but Nella wasn't facing him. He gave in and joined her side. His muscles tensed as they approached the mysterious auk'nai. Cade had now had two bad encounters with auk'nai this week—Krin'ta and their monster—and was not enthusiastic about a third.

"Come no closer," the auk'nai shouted. "Humans? I have not seen humans in my song before." The voice was gruff, yet feminine. She slumped back to one knee and grunted.

"You speak Sol Common?" Cade asked with a smile. He noticed she had said *"I"* and understood that she was an auk'gnell, not an auk'nai. Which also meant there was probably no auk'nai city for kilometers.

"Yes," the auk'gnell grunted as it pulled some glass vials from its satchel tucked in its green sashes, "I was a trader with the Song of Apusticus. I made it my business to know the human language."

"My name is Cade, and this is my sister, Nella. We are lost."

"Very lost." The auk'gnell cooed out a laugh. "Apusticus and the human song are far from here. You are almost near the Howling Shore."

Nella tugged at Cade's shirt, and Cade translated into Sol-Sign as the auk'gnell spoke. She could read Cade's lips, but having never encountered an auk'gnell from the North with such a small, flat beak, Nella had no way of reading her speech. When Cade mentioned they were close to the Howling Shore, Nella's eyes widened, and she coughed in surprise.

The auk'gnell looked them both up and down, then tended to its wounds by smearing various slimes on the damaged areas. "I am Hrun'dah. You two have ruined my hunt."

"We're very sorry," Cade said. "We were chased by an auk'nai, or maybe an auk'gnell—I don't know, we didn't ask it. Hells, we thought you were it when you swooped in."

"Another auk'gnell? In my song?" Hrun'dah asked. Nella nodded after the translation came through Cade. Hrun'dah peered at them. "Is this from the fireball last night? In the sky?"

"Yep, that was probably us," Cade said.

"I knew it was no star stone," Hrun'dah said and wrapped her wounds with sashes. She stretched her wing and winced, letting out a weak caw.

"Did the dray'va break your wings?" Cade asked.

"They will heal, in time," Hrun'dah said and tucked them behind her back. She stood and leaned on her halberd. She looked at the two lost humans and said, "You have saved me. I *thank you*, as the humans say." Hrun'dah looked to her side and pointed at the dead nurn. "If you are hungry, we can share this nurn together."

Before Cade could finish translating, Nella was nodding furiously.

"Come with me. If you are being pursued, then we must get away from the open sky," Hrun'dah said. "Tell me more of this auk'gnell who intrudes on my song." Hrun'dah lifted the dead nurn over her shoulder and used her halberd as a walking stick. The three walked toward the outcropping of trees together under the bright-blue sky.

———◆———

After a short hike through the grassy fields, the three travelers came upon a dirt hut carved into a hill. Hrun'dah hopped up onto the top of the hill with the dead nurn in hand and opened a latch made of wood. She hopped down into the hole, then poked her head back up and said, "Come in. I will start cooking."

Cade and Nella looked at each other, feeling a little like children being lured into a witch's house in an ancient folk tale. If Hrun'dah was indeed tricking them, they would be at her mercy inside the grassy hut. But if she was a friend, her support would mean some safety from the monster that pursued them. Cade checked his left sleeve holster, making sure his knife was accessible if it was a trap. He nodded to Nella, and she nodded back. They climbed up the hill and followed Hrun'dah into her hut.

"Close the door. We don't want any creatures following us in here," Hrun'dah said from beyond a small tunnel. Cade flicked his hand toward the hatch, and Nella closed the door behind them. They made their way into the main chamber of the grassy hut.

It was comfortable, with laser stones providing soft, warm light and root systems carved into shelves and furniture. There was a perch in the corner near a small hole that let in the fresh air, and a flat stone slab that acted as a table and meal-preparation area. Hrun'dah was busy carving up the nurn she had killed earlier in the day. A fire crackled in a stone pit behind her, with a spit ready to roast their dinner.

"This is your home?" Cade asked. He was surprised by how tall the room was. He assumed Hrun'dah could perform a low hop and not hit her head on the dirt ceiling.

"One of them. I have a few nests in this song," Hrun'dah said.

Nella signed, *"It's lovely."*

Cade translated, and Hrun'dah cooed her thanks. "This nest belonged to another auk'gnell. The last time I saw spoke with him, he wasn't doing well. He was a good auk'gnell, not like your monster."

"Was?" Cade asked.

Hrun'dah gestured to the halberd daunoren staff leaning against the wall. "I found his body. He had been almost cut in half by something. He joined the Song of the Dead shortly before I found him."

"I'm sorry to hear that," Cade said. "Did you take him to a Daunoren?"

Hrun'dah flayed the nurn cleanly, allowing the blood to drip into a large glass jar. After she had skinned the animal, she put the carcass over the fire. The smell of cooking meat filled the air, and Cade's mouth watered. He quickly realized how long it had been since he had eaten last. *The sandwich Zephyr gave me.* He felt his heart ache when he thought of that night.

"Auk'gnell do not obey a Daunoren," Hrun'dah said, eyeing the jar of blood she extracted from the nurn. "The dead are absorbed back into the planet. Kamaria repurposes all things. I took his weapon to continue his memory, and because I could use it."

Cade translated everything to Nella in Sol-Sign. She had been looking at their faces, and although she could make out a good chunk of what Cade was saying from his lips, Hrun'dah's beak was hard to read. It was short and flat, and it barely moved as she spoke. Nella worked with the context she gained from reading Cade's lips and observing his translation.

"You need to get back to your human city, far to the northwest, correct?" Hrun'dah asked, watching the meat sizzle. She brought the jar filled with blood to the other side of the room and opened a hatch. A table with vials and beakers and other scientific equipment slid out from the wall. Hrun'dah put the jar over a flame and began to concoct some sort of elixir.

"Yes, we were taken by this thing. It looked like an auk'gnell, but it had something wrong with it. It had three eyes, and they were glowing," Cade said, remembering the brief haunting sight of the thing that had taken him and his sister when he saw it through the open lid of the stasis pod. Nella nodded, remembering the horrible monster as well.

"Three-eyed auk'gnell in my song," Hrun'dah cooed. "Never seen anything like that before. Seen all kinds of creatures too." She paused, then asked, "What do you think it wants with you?"

Cade translated Hrun'dah's question, and Nella raised her eyebrows and shrugged. He thought back on the night before; it had something to do with their grandfather. Cade remembered telling the thing—in his injured stupor—that they were John Veston's grandkids.

"We're the grandchildren of someone significant. The leader of the project that brought humanity to Kamaria." Cade looked down at his feet. "But he's been dead since before we were born. We never even met him. I don't see why an auk'gnell would want anything to do with him."

"Someone significant, you say," Hrun'dah cooed. "You know, us auk'gnell can hear the Song of Kamaria louder than any of the auk'nai living in the songs of the cities. When you approached me in the field, I heard your unsung songs so loudly, I thought more beasts would come to see what it was. You two are special, maybe more special than you know. Maybe your monster knows it too."

Cade translated to Nella, and then they shared a look of confusion.

"It will be a long walk for you back to your city. These eastern lands are wild. The closest song was Apusticus, and even that is silent now." Hrun'dah passed a chunk of meat to Nella. She snatched it before Cade could translate entirely and began chomping away with a grin on her face.

"Do you think you could help us?" Cade asked. "I don't think I have anything I could—" He remembered the void stone in his pocket. "Wait, can I pay you?"

Nella caught that, reading Cade's lips. She cocked an eyebrow and wondered exactly what he was talking about. She knew the auk'nai didn't need money, and an auk'gnell would need it even less.

"*Pay* me?" Hrun'dah asked. "What do you have as payment?"

Cade dug the stone out of his pocket and showed it to Hrun'dah. "I know it's songless, so maybe this isn't enough. But—"

"That stone is *not* songless," Hrun'dah said quietly as she eyed the purple gemstone.

"Really? I was told it was like humans. The leader of the auk'nai said I could have it because it had no value to the pilgrims of the Spirit Song Mountain." Cade looked the gem over with curiosity.

Nella had not seen it before, and she eyed it with intense fascination.

Hrun'dah cooed, "No. The auk'nai just don't hear the Song of Kamaria like we do. If you got that from the Spirit Song Mountain, you received it from an ancient font."

"Whoa," Cade said. "What's that mean?"

Hrun'dah couldn't take her large eyes off the stone. "The song that stone sings is one of an era of life. It has seen every pilgrim that entered the caves to build daunoren staffs. It even holds the song of my old friend within it," Hrun'dah said. She pointed to the daunoren staff she had taken from the auk'gnell she shared this land with. "The places we go remember us, even if we don't remember them in return. One could listen to that stone's song for ages and never grow tired."

Cade observed the stone again. Galifern had given her this thing because she found it empty and useless. She'd even said it was "like humans." Cade couldn't get that out of his head. Now, Hrun'dah was saying the stone had immense value, history, and even insight. Cade had always thought the auk'nai had a deep connection with Kamaria, but apparently, there were ways to go even deeper. The Song of Kamaria had many meanings.

Cade twirled the stone in his hand and held it out toward Hrun'dah. "So, what do you say? I give you this ancient song for a guided trip back to Odysseus City for two."

Nella looked from Cade's lips to the stone, then to Hrun'dah.

Hrun'dah considered the offer. "I would find that stone's song quite beautiful. And it would help me understand my old friend better. But you are being pursued." Hrun'dah chomped at some meat. "That seems like a risk."

Cade thought for a moment of how he could sweeten the pot. He eyed Hrun'dah and asked, "Have you ever been *Up* before? Outside the planet's atmosphere—outer space, I mean."

"What?" Hrun'dah asked.

Nella caught enough of that and smiled at her brother's cleverness.

"My boss, D'Rand, tells me that the work we do yields rocks with strange songs. He's an auk'nai of Odysseus. So if he thinks asteroids give off strange songs, I wonder what you'd think of them," Cade said.

Hrun'dah looked at the void stone and blinked. "How would I get rocks from outer space?"

"I collect little souvenirs whenever I go EVA—outside the spaceship, I mean. I have a whole bunch of samples. I could have them sent down from my room on the *Maulwurf*."

Hrun'dah considered the offer. "I want to help you. But there is still the risk."

"You can read my thoughts a little, right? You know if I'm lying, I mean."

Hrun'dah cooed a confirmation.

"Well, our monster might not be so tough anymore. When we crashed the other night, I shot it with this flare gun." Cade took the gun out of his pocket. "It burned it up pretty good. After watching you take on those two dray'va earlier, I bet an injured monster won't be too much of an issue for you."

Hrun'dah cocked her head sideways and warbled, "You speak true."

"Sound like a deal?" Cade asked.

Nella was impressed with her brother's negotiating. She had never seen him in a situation like this before, but he worked through it well. She eyed Hrun'dah, seeing if Cade had managed to seal the deal.

"I will help you. But you keep your stone until we get you home," Hrun'dah said. "I will not accept payment until you get back home safe."

Cade smiled and slapped his knee, and Nella saw his enthusiasm. In unison, they both let out a loud Ganymede holler. They laughed, Hrun'dah included, amused by the weird human display. Cade apologized. "Sorry. Force of habit."

"I know a fast path," Hrun'dah said. "I cannot carry you, and my wings need time to heal. I can speed up the process with these." Hrun'dah finished making her nurn blood elixirs, a few vials of liquid, each a different color. She continued, "We can make our way to the Supernal Echo, the lake just beyond the mountain pass to the west of this nest. There is a river we can follow through the forest."

"Over-the-river-and-through-the-woods," Cade sang while signing, remembering an old rhyme his mother used from time to time. Nella snickered.

"No, we walk next to the river through the woods. Not over it. You understand this, yes?" Hrun'dah asked.

"Yeah—yes, of course. Sorry," Cade said, a little embarrassed. Seeing her brother change his tone, Nella sobered herself and nodded. They spent some time eating and chatting in the small grassy hut, enjoying the company of their new friend.

In the morning, they would begin the journey home.

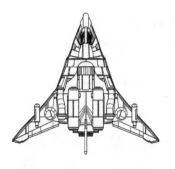

TWELVE

THE SUN WAS SETTING in the great valley nestled in the mountains. The auk'nai translation for this place was the Unforgotten Garden. It had always been a healthy ecosystem, with a variety of life that kept it wild and beautiful. When the humans brought the hammer down on Nhymn, the ground burst open, and the land was forever altered.

Life had returned to this garden, but it was different now. The *Telemachus*'s wreckage remained upright in the valley, with a massive skeletal monster's arm clutching to its side for eternity. Wild birds and other animals crawled out from their nests to hunt in the night. Glowing stones and plant life began to pulse their energy into the night. Clouds were rolling in over the mountains. It would rain soon.

Denton sat with Eliana in the passenger seating of the *Rogers*. They had wept privately, their team allowing them time to process this new trauma without interruption. Their minds were swirling with anxious thoughts. Hope was still bubbling from within, and determination was strong and fierce as a dray'va, but these were mixed with dread. What had come to their home and taken Cade and Nella? For what purpose? This wasn't random. This was organized.

According to Homer, an electrical anomaly came into Odysseus City from the east and left the same way. It also affected Telemachus

Outpost—the research station was dedicated to observing the valley's changes after the battle with the Siren years ago. The anomaly was their most substantial lead, but it was wrapped in so many questions.

Mysteries intertwined within more mysteries.

"Approaching the outpost now. The sky is getting chopped. Please buckle up for landing," Talulo said over the comm from the pilot seat.

One by one, the team entered the passenger cabin and took their seats. These were Denton and Eliana's friends, and their allies in the hunt to find Cade and Nella.

Faye Raike—an ex-Matador-class pilot who had lost her husband years ago to the Siren's possession—knew how hopeless Denton and Eliana felt. Marie Viray was one of the last people to see Nella before she mysteriously disappeared. Sergeant Jess Combs, equipped in full Tvashtar Marine combat gear, would protect them from anything dangerous. Homer, the robotic automaton, would be useful in searching for clues. Talulo, the flightless auk'nai, had become a skilled pilot and replaced Rocco Gainax aboard the *Rogers* after his retirement.

Telemachus Outpost looked like a grouping of tall, straight, metal mushrooms. It consisted of three thin towers lined with windows. A wide cylindrical area on top had a viewing platform. Against the setting sun, their silhouette blended in with the countryside, with only the amber lights from their windows betraying their natural aesthetic.

Talulo landed the *Rogers* on the small landing pad area near the base of the mushroom-shaped buildings. The comm pinged the ship. "Who's come knocking at this hour?" An elderly male voice came from the speaker, mixed with fuzzy static.

"Hey George." Marie used her soothreader access to ping the outpost. She spoke into the comm channel. "There's been a situation back in the city. We've been trying to contact you because we have a lead that involves your outpost. You haven't responded, so we thought we'd just drop by."

George Tanaka, former leader of the Scout Program after the death of John Veston, chuckled into the speaker. "Marie, it's good to hear your voice. Sorry, we've been having technical difficulties here lately."

"We know," Marie said. "That's part of the reason we're here."

"Right, right," George said. "One . . . second . . . Let me get the door open for you."

Eliana and Denton exited the *Rogers* and led the rest of the team toward the central tower's front door. It opened before they could fully approach, revealing George Tanaka. He was an elderly man of with warm beige skin, dark-gray hair, and wrinkles gained from a life of optimism and grand achievements. He wore a jacket with unique straps around his shoulders that used auk'nai antigrav tech to keep his posture straight.

"Ah, my friends," George said with his arms out, "it has been too long. What brings you to my little outpost today?"

Eliana walked into his embrace and gave the old man a hug, then stepped back and said, "It's urgent, George. Nella and Cade have gone missing, maybe kidnapped. We think whatever may have taken them also came this way."

George's face went sober, and he looked Eliana in the eyes. "Then there is no time to lose." He nodded. "Let's see what we can discover. Follow me." He waved them forward into the outpost. Inside, a small squad of Tvashtar marines sat around a table, eating and playing a holographic tactics game. They saw Sergeant Combs enter, stood, and saluted.

"At ease," Jess said. The soldiers nodded, sat back down, and returned to their game.

Eliana brought George up to speed. By the time they made it to the research floor, he was fully informed. They walked into a vast room with warm amber lighting and various computer terminals with data readouts. Windows lined the walls, giving the room a 360-degree view of the valley. A light rain began to tap quietly against the glass, and the last of the fading pink and yellow sunlight was slowly engulfed by the dark clouds in the sky.

George sat down at a console that overlooked the wreckage. He scooted his chair closer to the computer and spoke. "Homer, brin—"

"Yes?" the Homer android answered from behind George and startled him.

"Not you! Well—" George said. "Well, sort of you. Who do I talk to in this scenario?"

"I am downloading all the data from the previous nights." Homer answered George's question by skipping to the next part. "Normally, I would be able to do this from Odysseus City, but whatever disrupted your communications here blocked me from remote access."

"We've been having comm issues long before the other night," George said with a sigh. "I feel like we only get incoming calls when the sky is clear and the moons are full. Which is nearly never because it rains so much here."

"Find anything?" Eliana asked Homer. She dug her fingernails into her palms. Denton gently reached over and took her hand in his, giving her a reassuring squeeze. She looked into Denton's eyes, and at once, he recognized this version of his wife. He had seen her like this over twenty years ago when she was lost in a sea of questions about her father's murder. This new fear was more profound, somehow more alive than the previous shadows that haunted Eliana. The answers dictated the fate of their children.

"Interesting," Homer said. "As George said, systems here were malfunctioning before our anomaly occurred, but the anomaly's presence pushed them into an overload pattern. What I have found is that this system failure doesn't coincide with what is happening inside the *Telemachus* wreckage."

"Are you saying . . ." George seemed to lose his train of thought. "Wait, what are you saying?"

"The anomaly activated something inside the *Telemachus* wreckage," Homer said. "What it is for certain, I cannot say. There is too much anomalous interference. But if we can get inside, we can know more."

Faye shook her head. "Wait, so this thing that shuts off everything it comes across, somehow turned something on?"

Homer nodded.

"There's still functioning equipment inside that thing?" Faye asked, thrusting her hand toward the shadowed *Telemachus* wreckage silhouetted against the dark clouds. The drizzle had escalated into a light rain.

George said, "Not much, but some things on board were designed for incredible stress."

"That's a little more than *incredible*," Jess muttered.

Eliana asked, "Does this mean Nella and Cade might be in there?"

Everyone in the room turned to each other. There was a possibility Nella and Cade could be inside the *Telemachus* wreck. Maybe whatever took them was using it as a hideout. Or possibly a nest.

"We'll have to go into the *Telemachus* and see for ourselves," said Denton.

"Uh, well," George coughed, "I believe the ship has new residents. Creatures of the valley had made themselves at home in the nooks and crannies of the wreckage. It's a bad neighborhood, to say the least. The flowers all over the hull are normally seen deep within auk'nai mines. When we cracked open the valley to stop Nhymn, we might have brought some new things to the surface. Whatever may have taken Cade and Nella might be just one of many dangers inside."

Eliana looked at the team. Denton gripped her hand tighter. Faye and Jess nodded, Homer blinked, and Marie sighed. The elderly botanist looked at George and smiled. "Guess us old folks are stuck here. Never thought we'd be partners again, *did'ja* Georgie?"

"Never thought, but always hoped." George smiled back. "We have kits and other equipment if you need them. Bring Lance Corporal Ghanem and Private Simmons too. They've done a few perimeter checks on the wreck. They might know a good way in."

"How soon can they be ready? If Nella and Cade are inside—" Denton began.

"They are ready right now," Sergeant Jess Combs interrupted. "They're Tvashtar Marines. Just say the word, and we go."

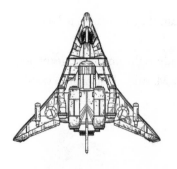

THIRTEEN

THE *Telemachus* LOOMED IN the darkness of the valley, with the speckled lights of luminescent plant life making the old shipwreck seem alive in the night. The rain was coming down steadily. Denton drove the *Tiger* rover as close as he could to the crash site. It was a sturdy vehicle that Denton helped construct. The *Tiger* was designed for uneven terrain and housed a full package of scanning equipment similar to a Pilgrim-class explorer.

Denton parked the rover as close as possible to the wreckage, blocked by a wall of inert nezzarforms. These were Nhymn's army years ago, stone constructs pulled up from the planet itself. After Nhymn was defeated, the nezzarforms reverted to a null state. They looked like an army of statues, and each felt like they could wake up at any moment.

The team got out of the *Tiger* and stepped into the rain.

Sergeant Jess Combs was in command of the two Tvashtar marines George had loaned out for this mission. Lance Corporal Rafa Ghanem was a young man in his thirties with tanned skin, a bald head, and a bushy black beard. Private Ken Simmons was even younger than Rafa, in his mid-twenties with pale skin, short blond hair, and a frame like a muscular arcophant. Each of the marines was equipped with a full kit, including a combat suit, assault rifle, and sidearm. Ken Simmons also had a device adhered to the gauntlet of his suit called a doorbuster.

Denton, Eliana, Faye, and Homer made up the rest of the ground team, with Talulo acting as a backup recon from inside the *Rogers*. George and Marie were providing insight from the Telemachus Outpost across the valley.

"It's just this way," Rafa Ghanem said. "Watch your step. The ground is very uneven here."The marines had shoulder-mounted lights on their combat suits illuminating the way. The rest of the team used the flashlights mounted on their collider pistols, except for Homer, who emitted a bright light from their chest.

They moved through rows of inert nezzarform statues. The last time most people got close to these stone constructs, it was a fight for their lives.

"Sir, permission to, *uh*—speak freely," Private Ken Simmons asked Jess.

Jess looked over her shoulder and nodded.

"You got close to these things in the battle, right? I mean—when they were alive and fighting for the Siren." Ken stumbled over his words as he gestured to the inert nezzarforms. For such a large and imposing figure, he had a soft voice.

Jess sighed and eyed the nezzarform she passed by, remembering that day and the dear friends she had lost.

"She was there," Rafa Ghanem answered for her. "You pulled my brother up from the ground, Sergeant Combs. Farnham would have been crushed without your help. You saved his life, sir. I'm honored to help you today. It's the least I can do."

Jess nodded her appreciation to Rafa.

Rafa smiled and nodded back.

The team made it past the last row of nezzarform statues and were soon within a few meters of the *Telemachus* hull. The ground near the wreck was like hardened ripples of water, where molten lava had cooled against the ship's hull, fusing it to the planet. There was no clear line where the ground stopped and the ship started. Before the *Telemachus* was used as a hammer, humanity's defense forces had attempted to use the ship's large particle cannon—or LPC—against the Siren. Nhymn had dodged the shot. The LPC lanced Kamaria instead and burned a hole in the Unforgotten Garden so deep, a pit of molten lava formed. When the hammer came down, the lava acted as sort of a catcher's mitt, absorbing some of the impact. There were significant gaps in the hull where explosions and ruptures occurred during the crash. After two decades of waiting, these holes had been filled with plants and animals.

The *Telemachus* almost looked like it was breathing with the amount of life thriving in its twisted metal skeleton. The flowers that lined its structure were beautiful, but they originated deep underground. Denton wondered what other things the impact had brought to the surface.

He remembered the first time he had seen the *Telemachus*. It was bursting through Jupiter's outer atmosphere during their harrowing escape from the Sol System. He was young then, crammed in their family's small ship, the *Lelantos*, with his brothers and parents. The *Telemachus* had been a beautiful piece of machinery back then. Now it was just another marker in a cemetery of statues.

Denton asked Homer, "How are you holding up? Is the anomaly messin' with your functions?"

"It is not. I can see clearly now that we are closer to the site. Whatever caused the outages must not be here any longer," Homer said. "I am picking up energy signatures coming from the admiral's quarters." Homer pulled up a holographic blueprint of the *Telemachus* and highlighted where the admiral's quarters were located. They tilted the diagram to match the same angle as the upthrust wreck. A blip of light on the back end of the hull's upper portion pulsed in and out.

"We're in luck," Rafa said. "I know of a ladder that will get us very close."

"Rafa, come on. You don't mean—" Ken said.

"Yes. We take the arm up," Rafa said, and pointed to the skeletal arm of the Siren that still clung to the *Telemachus* hull in a viselike death grip. It had been picked apart by carrion birds and other scavenging creatures, leaving only a crackled spiderweb of cartilage and long bones. As time passed, the bones began to look more like stone.

"Whatever took Nella and Cade may have done the same thing," Eliana said and walked toward the skeletal arm. She began to climb before the others could analyze the situation. They followed her example.

The higher the team traveled, the more the wind buffeted against them. The glowing blue plants gave them enough light to see without trouble, combined with the moons peeking through the rain clouds. Although the dampness made everything slick, the webbed cartilage was safe enough to climb.

They passed a lemurbat nest. The small bidpedal creatures had slick purple skin, large ears, and four orange eyes. Among the six curious lemurbats in the nest, the glint of their eyes made them look like a much larger crowd. When Homer's robotic body moved past the nest, the lemurbats scurried deeper into their hole.

Large Kamarian birds called welkinhawks scattered from various portals inside the ship's broken hull as the team neared the top of their climb. They were now over a hundred meters from the valley floor and peering over the slanted top of the wreck. With the ship on a heavy tilt, about sixty degrees off-axis, the team needed to brace themselves to avoid tumbling down the deck.

Ken pulled himself onto the deck and helped the others find their footing. Eliana kept her feet braced against any notches in the broken hull she could find. Denton was close behind her. One by one, they each made their way across, taking careful steps. Homer magnetically sealed their feet to the hull and walked as if they were taking a stroll through a garden. They surpassed the others easily and shone their bright light ahead.

The rainwater started to rush down the deck as the team worked their way across. Rafa looked past Homer and pointed to the massive structure ahead. "Just over that way, we'll cut a hole and make our way in," Rafa shouted to the team. "I'm not sure what's in there. We've never been this high up before."

It was the command structure of the *Telemachus*. The entire spacecraft was designed like an old-Earth aircraft carrier. The bottom was long and curved, and the top was flat except for the command structure protruding from it like a nail sticking out of a plank of wood.

Eliana had lived on this ship before the *Odysseus* mission sent her to Kamaria. She didn't need a map to the admiral's quarters, because it had only been down the hall from her own room. The *Telemachus* Project staff lived close by in the same hall. Eliana felt like she was coming back home to a haunted house.

The front end of the structure had glowing vines and flowers pouring out of it. The entire command bridge must have burst during the crash, and the plants pushed outward from the breach. Eliana thought of Nella. She would love to see these rare underground-dwelling flowers shimmering with light above ground in the moonlight. Eliana had taken Nella to the Telemachus Valley a few times, but never after dark. They'd never even approached the wreck.

"Talulo," Eliana said into the comm channel on her soothreader, "can you use the *Rogers* to scan the area we are heading to for life signatures?"

The *Rogers* drifted toward the team and shined a spotlight, causing more creatures to scatter. There was a low hum as the scanner went to work while the team finished their journey across the hull.

"Scanners show something large inside," Talulo said through the comm channel. "Be very careful."

Eliana looked back at Denton, and they exchanged identical worried glances. Rain washed against them, chilling their spines. Finally, they approached the place where Rafa had said they could enter. Homer got into position and clamped against the hull. The robot's eyes began to glow, and they turned to the team and said,

"You may want to look away. This will be very bright."

A white-hot light shot out from Homer's eye and began slicing through the hull. Molten metal dripped from the worksite, harmlessly past Homer's legs, and rolled down the deck with the rain. Homer finished, and their eyes faded back to their normal brightness. The robot repositioned themself higher on the tilted surface and kicked the square area they'd carved out hard with their foot a few times until it gave way and flew into the ship. Dust and dirt blew out of the new hole as air and rain entered the sealed compartment for the first time.

"Excuse me, Homer," Ken Simmons said with his soft voice. He jumped into the ship with his assault rifle aimed and ready for anything. Ken pivoted, scanning each corner of the slanted metal hallway he had entered. "Clear down here!" he shouted up.

"We're going in," Eliana said to Talulo through her soothreader.

"Talulo will make sure nothing follows you in. Stay safe," Talulo said over the comm as Eliana dropped into the hole and brought out her collider pistol. One by one, the team disappeared from the *Rogers*'s spotlight.

Eliana vividly remembered her days living on the *Telemachus*. As they carefully maneuvered their way through the broken ship, she reminisced. She had walked these halls in her younger years, sometimes with her father, but often alone. The sixty-degree slant to the ship didn't do much to deter her nostalgia. In the decayed, haunted halls of her youth, Eliana could almost sense her father's ghost walking with her now.

Piping on the walls of the hallway helped the team move through the tilted world. Eliana shifted herself sideways and held the wall for support. She envied Homer as they walked effortlessly down into the metal hallway. The light the robot cast filled the entirety of the space ahead. It highlighted burst pipes, cracked and crunched floors, bent paneling, and plant life with softly glowing blue flowers and thorned vines. The wind outside caused the ship to creak and whine as if they were disturbing an old dragon's slumber.

Private Ken Simmons moved around Homer to reach the door at the end of the hallway first. He held his hand up to tell the team to stop moving, then turned to them and said, "Please wait one—I gotta do the—just stay put, folks." The bulky young marine clapped a hand onto his left forearm, and a device shifted outward and rotated over his hand. He balled his left hand into a fist, and electrical energy began to glow on the knuckle-mounted device. Ken pulled back and punched forward into the door. On impact, the electrical energy exploded, and the old broken door burst into the next room away from its threshold and crashed against the opposite wall.

Ken laughed and shook his hand, allowing the doorbuster device to fold itself back into his suit's forearm. From somewhere in the ship, there was a shriek and a growl. Ken pulled his assault rifle up and carefully stepped into the next room.

"Eyes open, everyone," Sergeant Jess Combs urged the team.

Denton nudged his way into the next room, watching as dark shapes scattered into various holes in the walls as the light spilled in. The team followed Homer.

Eliana recognized this room as the Operations Hub, or as the others called it often, the War Room. It was a meeting place to sort out plans. She remembered discussing the *Odysseus* mission here with her father and the others. Even though a devastating war had engulfed the Sol System, the mood during those meetings was inspiring and hopeful. They were going to save humanity and start a better life orbiting a distant star. There was no talk of lung-lock, or Sirens, or kidnapped people. They weren't going to be victims. They were going to be space explorers. They had no idea that the Undriel would win the war five years after the *Odysseus* launched for Kamaria.

Eliana's memories drifted even farther back, to the first time she had stepped into the War Room, years before the war. The command structure was still being built on Mars while the rest of the *Telemachus* was made in high orbit—long before the ship was sent to Jupiter to keep it safe from the clutches of the Undriel. There were still large openings in the hull back then, with some excellent views of the terraformed Martian landscape surrounding the horizon. Her father was so excited to show her what they were building. Eliana ran her hand against the wall and remembered that day—not a fond memory at all.

The seeds of annihilation had been sown right here, in this room.

It was the day Dr. Nouls was fired from the *Telemachus* project. That man had always creeped Eliana out. His views about where artificial intelligence could take humanity were more frightening than inspiring. Dr. Nouls insisted that artificial intelligence on its own would either usurp humanity or never achieve true consciousness. He had been experimenting with augmenting brain functions via a technological device called a crown. John Veston wasn't interested, and the two had a heated argument. Dr. Nouls argued that humanity would transcend its current state and become something greater. John stated that it would destroy what made humans *human* and create some sort of false living state. Both arguments were valid, but Dr. Nouls offered a version of the future where humanity became ghosts inside of machines. Without coming to an agreement, John fired Dr. Nouls right in front of Eliana.

Dr. Nouls would later take his crown-tech to a system-renowned visionary trillionaire named Tibor Undriel. The Undriel war machine would be born from that partnership. How the crown-tech evolved into the nightmarish machines that overtook the Sol System was still a mystery to the survivors living on Kamaria. As pervasive as the Undriel were, they remained an enigma.

Eliana moved toward the next doorway. She grabbed part of the wall and felt a slickness slither its way away from her hand. In her shock, she pushed herself from the wall and lost her footing on the tilted floor. Eliana slid and rolled toward the next door but was stopped when Denton grabbed the back of her jacket. She braced herself against the floor and looked up to see something moving on the ceiling. The plants and flowers were undulating, and there was a sprinkle of thick fluid as thorns began to emerge from the vines that slithered around.

"Are you okay?" Denton asked. Eliana looked toward him to say she was alright but noticed a thin vine inching its way toward his neck. She pulled him down into herself as the vine lashed into the space where his throat had been.

"Watch the vines!" Eliana shouted. Faye turned in time to see a vine whip itself against her bicep and tear it open. She screamed and pulled at the assaulting plant, but it had gripped her firmly. Rafa was quick and cut the vine off with a slash of his combat knife. More vines began to slither around the room. Glowing orbs revealed themselves in the opposite wall in a diamond pattern. A bulbous form pulled itself free from the network of thorns and flowers.

It was a bipedal thing with slick, oil-black skin covered in writhing vines and glowing blue eyes as if a person had been swallowed up by a rose bush. Some of the vines that protruded from the monster slithered through the floor and wormed their way around the room. The vine-figure let out a low, gurgling growl. Droplets of water scattered as vines sprinted through the ceiling and walls.

"Open fire!" Jess shouted. The marines shot at the vine-figure, and it moved. The thing seemed to slither around, almost as if it were made of liquid. In an instant, it had made its way to Ken and began to wrap him with its thorns. The marines stopped firing, as to not shoot Ken.

Denton acted before thinking. He leaped from his place on the slanted floor and allowed gravity to smash him into the vine-figure. He missed as it slithered away, but in the process, it let go of Ken. The young marine lost his footing and toppled through the room, landing next to Denton against the far wall.

Jess flicked her fist, and a rotating saw blade emerged from her gauntleted knuckles. She slammed it into the wall and began cutting at the vines. The vine-figure shrieked, just as it had when the door was thrust into the room previously. It bounded across the room and began slashing at Jess, pounding her to the slanted floor with an array of thorned tentacles.

"Sarge!" Rafa shouted and used the jump-jet on his combat suit to launch himself into the monster. This time he struck the vine-figure, but it caught him and enveloped his body. He screamed as the thorns ripped through his suit, finding the spaces between his armor plating to rip and tear at.

Ken slapped his left forearm and brought out his doorbuster again. He charged, then punched the wall. The vines began to burst as the electricity surged through them. The monster shrieked as it was reduced from the shock. The network of plants in the room started to shrivel and slump onto the floor. When they had all slumped away, only a slick, black bipedal form remained. It had thin arms and long fingers. Eyes lined the middle of the beast, and there was no neck or head, just a torso with arms and slender legs. Small gaps on the monster opened and closed, like the gills of a fish suffocating on land. It crunched into itself and started to move, but slowly.

There was a loud bang, followed by three more shots. The vine-figure's shriek was cut short by the last shot, and it slumped to the ground and rolled into the edge of the slanted room. Eliana's collider pistol whirred to a stop as she ended the vine-figure. She watched the creature shrivel up and die. When Eliana was satisfied it was finished, she moved her way toward Rafa.

"Who's hurt?" Eliana asked as she inspected him. The marine was cut up, and his leg had a large gash. Eliana pulled her medical kit off her back and started working on Rafa's wounds.

"I'll be okay," Jess said as she got to her feet. Her face had taken a few lashes, and parts of her suit had deep cuts.

"I'm okay here, uh—" Ken said with a little laugh. He turned to Denton. "Thanks, Mr. Castus. I was sure that thing was gonna—well I didn't know for sure, I just—well you know, I—"

"No problem," Denton said, rubbing his shoulder. He'd bruised it badly when he crashed into the wall.

"Elly, can you toss me a suture foam?" Faye said, holding the wound on her arm. Eliana fished the fat syringe out of her kit and tossed it to Faye. She pulled off the tip, placed the needle on her wound, and pushed the plunger. The foam emitting from the syringe expanded until it completely filled the gash in Faye's arm, then rapidly retracted, folding the wound shut.

"Much better," Faye sighed. "I thought gardening was supposed to be relaxing."

Homer said, "I believe that was one of the new inhabitants."

"Did it cause the anomaly?" Denton asked.

"No," Homer confirmed. The robot walked on the slant effortlessly, compensating for the angle with internal mechanisms. Homer's eyes flashed blue as they scanned the dead monster. "Biosignatures indicate this was a young creature. There may be larger ones ahead."

"Big brothers. Great," Denton muttered.

George Tanaka's voice came from Homer's mouth. "That coincides with things we have witnessed over time. Some of the plant life on the outside of the ship has moved in unnatural ways. I don't believe the vines were doing it on their own, but creatures like that monster you just saw can manipulate them."

Marie's voice came through Homer's mouth next. "They may have come from deep within the planet. Many things in this valley were brought up from the depths of Kamaria after the *Telemachus* crash. Not sure if that helps."

"I hate this ship," Rafa grunted. He brought himself to a sitting position and nodded to Eliana. She packed up her medical kit and quickly looked over the rest of the team to make sure she hadn't forgotten anyone's injuries.

"We don't have far to go," Eliana said. "Just into the next hall and to the left. Admiral's quarters are at the end."

"I'll stay back here with Rafa," Faye said. "We can make sure nothing sneaks up behind us. We'll shout if we see anything."

"Stay alert," Jess said. "And make sure that thing doesn't get back up." She pointed at the recently dispatched vine-figure. Jess had fought creatures in the past that refused to stay dead. It never hurt to be careful.

"Are we ready, everyone? I can—you know what, I'm just gonna do it," Ken said, and punched open the next door with his doorbuster. The panel sailed into the next hallway and crashed against the floor.

Eliana stepped into the four-way hallway and stood in the center, grasping at the pipes on the ceiling to keep her balance. Behind her was the room Faye and Rafa were securing. To her left were the admiral's quarters and her old bedroom; to her right was a mess of jagged metal and broken piping blocking their path. In front of Eliana was the pathway to the bridge. Deep scratch marks at her feet trailed from the admiral's office, moved around the corner, and into the bridge. There were shriveled-up vines on the floor.

"I think this confirms our anomaly was here," Eliana said, pointing at the evidence.

Jess stepped forward and looked at the scratch marks on the floor leading to the bridge. She turned to Ken and said, "Go with the others to the admiral's quarters. I'll make sure nothing comes out of the bridge." She eyed the dead vines in the mess of debris. She could see the scattered moonlight shining on the old broken command stations through the open bridge door.

"Yes, sir," Ken said and turned to Denton, Eliana, and Homer. "If you will all just follow me—I'm your guide—or Sherpa, or—"

"Lead the way, please," Eliana said.

"Can do," Ken said.

Eliana, Denton, Homer, and Ken traversed across the tilted ship down the hallway to the admiral's quarters. More deep scratches traced the hallway walls. Some of the scratches were in the shape and pattern of claws, but one was a solid line, much like a blade. Eliana traced one of the scratches toward her old bedroom door.

She remembered how it had been when she was almost thirty years younger. It had been a comfortable space, with soft lighting to study, a vid-window with a view of the swirling layers of Jupiter, and a twin-sized bed with burgundy sheets. It had a bathroom with a stand-up shower, which was always a relaxing break during intense study sessions. It was her sanctuary.

Now, the door was stuck in a half-open position. The interior of the room was filled with glowing plants. Eliana shuddered at the thought of a vine-figure inhabiting her old bedroom, like a ghost in a haunted house. As long as they didn't go inside, the creature would not bother them—or so she hoped.

"You see this mark on the wall?" Denton said, snapping Eliana's attention away from her old room. He continued, "It looks like a blade cut through it. I'm not talking about a particle saw. I'm saying a metal blade."

"Yeah, I think you're right," Eliana said.

Homer's eyes glowed blue as they scanned the cut on the wall. They said, "This cut matches the same blade density and sharpness that decapitated the Daunoren."

"I didn't even consider that," Denton said. "Is it possible these events are connected then? Whatever killed the Daunoren also took Nella and Cade?"

Eliana nodded, considering. "It might be connected. But *why*?"

Homer said, "Perhaps further investigation will yield answers." They pointed down the hallway to the admiral's quarters. The team shuffled their way over.

Light seeped into the hallway from inside the room. The hydraulic door was stuck in a loop, jolting back and forth but remaining mostly open and safe to pass through. Ken entered the room first, his assault rifle drawn. "It's clear. There are vines in here, but not as many as in the other room. I—I mean there could be, but—it's entirely possible there's, uhh . . ."

"Maybe the lights in here are scaring them out," Denton suggested.

Eliana put a hand on the marine's shoulder. "We won't take long. Just keep an eye open for anything moving."

"Roger that," Ken said.

Eliana, Denton, and Homer entered the admiral's quarters. Eliana felt deflated, yet also relieved to discover her children were not here. She wanted this to be over. She wanted to find them here, huddled up and alive. But at least their absence shown that they weren't trapped in this nightmarish place with the vine-figures. It was a hit, but Eliana's hope and determination didn't fade.

The admiral's quarters had been Hugo Marin's private suite. The kind fleet admiral had passed away peacefully of old age only a few years ago. It still felt strange rifling through his old, discarded things. The space was nicer than most, with a full kitchen, bathroom, loft area with a vidscreen, and a separate bedroom. During the crash, everything had been thrown toward the right wall. The admiral had always been fond of ancient paperback books. His collection of old-Earth literature was scattered on the floor and the wall. This collection would be worth a fortune.

"Homer, is the energy source still in here?" Denton asked, keeping his eyes out for any moving vines. Homer moved around the rooms, scanning the walls and countertops with their flashlight-blue eyes. They angled the light toward the bed, deeper into the room.

"I believe it is over there," Homer said.

Eliana was closest. She traversed her way over debris and broken floor until she was at the foot of the bed. The sheets and other bedding had been thrown off during the crash. A mattress lay against the wall and floor on the right side. Eliana pushed the mattress upward. Underneath was a concave area, cylindrical in shape, a little bigger than her. It was where the emergency stasis pod should be, but it was nowhere to be found. Next to the empty stasis pod slot was a small, puck-shaped device emitting a low hum.

"There's something here. I think it's somehow powering the room." Eliana placed her hand on the puck and felt like she had run sandpaper over her fingers. She gasped and retracted her hand. The device was spinning so fast that it appeared to not be moving at all.

Homer came to her side and scanned the object. "Interesting. This is a modified collider cylinder. It's generating enough energy to power this room on its own. I will run a full sweep of its contents." A flat, blue beam of light lanced from Homer's eyes and fluttered over the mysterious puck.

"What? A small collider cylinder like that can't power a whole room. How the Hells is that possible?" Denton asked.

"I am unsure. This is beyond human understanding of particle-collider technology. And it is more sophisticated than the auk'nai version they reverse-engineered from us."

"It's not—" Eliana said but couldn't finish.

Homer said it instead. "It does resemble Undriel technology more than anything, but even this is more complex than the designs we reverse-engineered from them."

A silence followed.

"Could it actually be an Undriel device?" Denton asked.

"I am unsure. Our long-range satellite data has not picked up anything coming into the Delta Octantis system. This collider technology is different from known Undriel collider cylinders," Homer said. "There are still too many unknown factors to determine."

"Now I really wish this was a new Siren," Denton said.

There was a loud bang, followed by the sound of an electrical discharge. Denton, Eliana, and Homer turned to see Ken Simmons with his fist against the wall. Thorned vines on the wall began to shrivel and die, but no vine-figure emerged.

"Ah-ha! I got it—did you see? No blob guy sneaking up on us this time!" Ken looked sheepishly at the others. "Did you find what you were looking—"

The ground shook, and there was a low-pitched groan throughout the ship. Dust jumped from ledges, and everyone held tightly to anything within reach to maintain their balance.

Marie's voice came through Homer's mouth. "Did you do something? We're getting weird readings over here."

The voice then flicked over to Talulo. "Something is moving on the outside of the *Telemachus!* The plants are—"

"Get over here *now!*" Jess called from the hallway.

Eliana looked around for something she could use to pick up the hyper-fast spinning puck but couldn't find anything useful.

"Leave it!" Denton shouted and pushed her toward the hallway door.

"I have completed a full, detailed scan of the object. We may—" Homer began.

"*We may* get the Hells out of here!" Denton shoved Homer too.

Eliana, Homer, Denton, and Ken moved through the admiral's quarters as fast as possible, stumbling and shifting on their way out. Jess was shooting her assault rifle toward the War Room down the hall, where the four paths converged. At the same time, Rafa and Faye hurried past her toward the bridge.

"Get to the bridge. We're blocked off over here!" Jess shouted.

They moved down the hallway, with Eliana leading the way and Ken trailing behind in the rear. When Eliana made it past her old bedroom, a thorned vine lashed outward and clapped itself onto Denton's shoulder. Ken grabbed the vine and pulled it away from Denton, but it tangled itself around his arm. More vines launched from the bedroom and wrapped themselves around Ken. He charged a punch with his doorbuster, but he couldn't move his arms to use it. The vines pulled Ken closer to the bedroom door. Denton shot into the tangle of vines, hoping to free the private.

A huge, oil-black hand with long fingers came out of the bedroom and clapped itself against the threshold of the bedroom door. A thousand blue eyes peered from inside the room, filling the doorway with a dim glow. Denton and Eliana shot at the monster in the door, but it didn't seem to care. Even as some of the eyeballs exploded from the blasts of their guns, it pulled Ken into the room. He screamed as the thorned vines ripped him apart and swallowed him in the doorway.

"No!" Denton shouted.

"Get over here!" Jess called between shots. Vines came at Jess, and she held them off with her assault rifle and knuckle sawblade. Eliana, Denton, and Homer made it to the hallway's intersection and saw the monster she battled. It was similar to the one in the bedroom, and it reached for Jess with long, black fingers but much larger in scale. Six of the ghastly hands were coming from the War Room, grasping for human flesh. Behind the reaching hands was a swirling array of eyeballs, darkness, and thorned vines.

Jess continued her assault on the monster, moving backward and allowing gravity to slide her toward the bridge. The team had made it onto the bridge. It was moonlit from outside, and a large hole in the windscreen let in the fresh air. The *Roger*'s spotlight spilled into the room through the opening.

"Where's Ken?" Rafa asked as he helped Jess assault the monster with his rifle. Denton shook his head and let out a few shots from his pistol. The creature slowly made its way into the room, despite the number of injuries it was receiving.

"We need to get out of here," Faye shouted.

"Talulo is here," Talulo shouted. "Team will need to jump!"

Outside the breach in the windscreen, the *Rogers* pivoted and lowered its access ramp. Faye and Eliana moved toward the hole in the windshield and looked down. With the wreck's angle, they could see all the way to the valley floor, a hundred-meter drop. The *Rogers* hovered in place as close as it could to the *Telemachus*, but still five meters out.

"There's no way we can make that jump," Faye said.

"Yes, we *can!*" Rafa shouted. He grabbed Eliana and Faye around their waists, then activated the jump-jet on his combat suit. They propelled over the open air toward the back of the ship and landed with a crash.

"Sarge! Get your ass in here," said Rafa.

Jess, Denton, and Homer slid down through the room, using the slant to their advantage. They reached the edge of the breach, and Jess grabbed onto Denton and Homer, activating her jump-jet and launching them across the gap. Long, dark hands uncoiled from within the ship and lunged for them.

They landed inside the *Rogers*, nearly crashing into Faye and Eliana in the process. Jess and Rafa sprayed particle blasts at the creature's hands with their assault rifles.

"Go, Talulo!" Denton shouted.

The dark hands grabbed onto the ship's tail as the access ramp raised. Everyone inside felt a jerk as the monster caught the *Rogers*.

"Hold on!" Talulo shouted over the intercom.

As the monster began pulling the *Rogers* into the *Telemachus*, Talulo hit the ultra-thrust. Fire propelled from the engine thrusters and roasted the hands that grabbed the ship, boiling and melting away at the creature. It let go, and the *Rogers* lobbed itself into the air, then stalled.

They went into freefall as Talulo worked to correct the *Rogers*. It tumbled through the sky, activating thrusters all over its hull to find stability. Talulo was all over the controls in the pilot seat, moving through them as fast as he could to keep the ship airborne.

Meters before smashing into the ground, the *Rogers* slowed its descent and kept itself upright. It didn't entirely stop the fall, and smashed into the ground on its underbelly, bouncing off the smooth rocky surface below and breaking a few nezzarform statues. The *Rogers* skidded to a stop, and the engines turned off. Smoke drifted from the hull and thrusters, and there were a few pops and crackles as the ship settled in its unnatural landing position.

High above, the monster roared into the night, then slunk back into the old, haunted shipwreck to await more prey.

Talulo came into the cargo bay in a hurry. "Is everyone alright?"

Eliana, Denton, Jess, Faye, and Rafa checked themselves. Homer ran a diagnostic on their android frame. Faye nodded. Denton coughed and went to Eliana's side. Jess stood and walked over to Rafa, who was still on his knees in his combat suit.

"That thing *killed* Simmons," Rafa said quietly.

"He saved our lives," Eliana said.

Rafa stood and looked at the floor. "Sir, permission to exit?" he asked Jess.

Jess nodded. Rafa left the cargo bay without saying another word.

Faye approached Denton and Eliana. "What happened in the

admiral's quarters? Did you find anything? Any sign of Nella and Cade?"

"Let's get back to Telemachus Outpost, and we'll figure out what we know," Eliana said.

———— ◆ ————

Talulo, Jess, and Denton stayed behind to fix the *Rogers*. Eliana, Homer, Faye, and Rafa took the *Tiger* rover back to Telemachus Outpost. After a short ride, they were inside and reunited with Marie and George.

"It's good to see you safe," Marie said, embracing Eliana from her wheelchair as they walked in.

"Rafa, I'm so sorry about Ken," George said. "I will contact his family—"

"No, sir," Rafa said. "I will call them. Ken was a good friend. It wouldn't be right if they didn't hear it from me."

"I understand. Please let me know if there is anything I can do. Take some time for yourself," George said.

Rafa nodded, then left the room. They took a moment of silence in respect of Private Ken Simmons.

"Was it worth it?" Faye asked weakly.

Eliana sighed. "We found a strange device powering the admiral's room. It has a resemblance to Undriel technology."

"*Undriel* technology? That can't be right," George said. "Can we see it, Homer?"

"We were unable to take the object," Eliana said.

Homer created a holographic image of the puck in front of their chest. "I was only able to take scan data."

"It'll have to do," George said. "I expect going back to retrieve the object is impossible."

"Correct," Faye said curtly.

Outside the window, the *Rogers* lifted away from the ground and made its approach to the outpost. Beyond the *Rogers* loomed the *Telemachus* wreck, and the glowing plants that were once considered beautiful, now holding back a menace. The rain gently continued to fall.

"The admiral's stasis pod had been removed," Eliana continued.

"Why on Mars would anyone do that?" Marie asked. "It was there during the impact. Hugo had never used it. He was retrieved in the lifeboat after the battle with the Siren."

"Whatever took it dragged it from the admiral's quarters and out through the breach in the front of the bridge. We don't know what could have done this, but it does give us a heading," Eliana said. "Homer can ping the admiral's pod and figure out where it went. It might lead us to Nella and Cade."

Homer added, "There is also a possibility that this anomaly is responsible for the death of the Daunoren. Deep cuts in the hallways match the same blade width and sharpness necessary to decapitate the Daunoren. It isn't solid evidence, but there is not much that can do both. We still are unsure exactly what that would be."

"So, what is next?" George asked.

"We ping the admiral's stasis pod and go to it," Eliana said, "and pray that we find Cade and Nella there."

FOURTEEN

CADE WAS RUNNING. HE was surrounded by glowing statues, each staring down at him from tall perches. Their cyclopean eyes shimmered with blue electricity. He looked over his shoulder and saw the monster auk'gnell rushing toward him like a world-encompassing shadow. Its wings were spread, and its metal claw stretched toward him from across an impossible distance. Cade slipped and fell to the stone ground. He tried to push himself up, but his strength failed him. It was as if he were glued in place.

Four skeletal hooves entered his vision. Some immense beast stomped toward Cade, stopping in front of his face. Cade tried to look up, but the invisible thing that kept him pinned to the ground prevented him from seeing the beast before him.

<*GET UP.*> A voice boomed loudly into his mind.

Suddenly, Cade was flipped onto his back. The monster auk'gnell's shadow looming over him. Its three yellow, glowing eyes beat down, inching closer to Cade's face.

<*GET UP!*> the voice said again.

———————◆———————

Cade sat straight up.

Cold sweat on his dampened brow, his breaths were shallow and hurried. Hrun'dah cocked her head, looming over him. Finally, Cade realized it was only a nightmare, and that he was safe inside Hrun'dah's nest. He took a deep breath.

"Get up," Hrun'dah said. The veil of the nightmare lifted, and Cade's mind began to forget about the dream world he'd just emerged from. His eyes darted around the room, and panic gripped him once more.

"Where's Nella?" he asked.

Hrun'dah cooed and stepped to the side. Nella entered the nest through the tunnel. She was carrying various flowers and herbs, and she had a smile on her gentle face. Nella plopped the pile of plants on the stone slab and signed to Cade, *"We let you sleep in. Are you well rested?"*

Cade sighed with relief and signed back, *"Yeah, I think so,"* with a weak bob of his fist and the dazed expression of a dreamer. He stood and stretched. Hrun'dah and Nella began to create something with the plants. Cade looked over their shoulders and asked, "What's going on?"

"We are making tea," Hrun'dah said.

"You were foraging with Nella? Do you know Sol-Sign?"

"I do not know the hand-language Nella uses, but I can hear her unsung song," Hrun'dah said as she ground one of the flowers into a powder. "Perhaps by the end of our journey, I will be able to use her language as well. Comparing the unsung song to the human languages is how Mag'Ro learned to speak with the early colonists of Kamaria."

Nella and Hrun'dah added their ingredients to a boiling pot of fresh mountain water. Within a few minutes, everyone was drinking tea out of clay jars. Cade had never been much of a tea drinker in the past, but this made him see the appeal. The warm vapor that rose from the tea cleared his nostrils and sinuses and had a deep, natural smell to it. When it had cooled enough, he sipped at its surface and tasted the sweet, honey-flavored mixture of wildflowers and herbs.

Cade felt a warmth wash over him as he drank the fresh tea, and soon he was energized and ready for the journey ahead.

When they were ready, Hrun'dah, Nella, and Cade emerged from the nest and looked into the mountain valley. The tall, yellow grass reached toward the pink and blue dawn sky. There were only a few pockets of clouds, and the stars were beginning to wink out one by one. A thin fog hung over the grass as the early sun started to burn away the morning dew. The scent of wildflowers, moisture, and the mountain air was everywhere. The herd of animals from the day before was missing.

"If we head to the west, we will find a river at the end of this valley," Hrun'dah said. "The river will lead us to the Supernal Echo and closer to your human home. But we have a long walk ahead of us."

"What is the Supernal Echo?" Cade asked.

Hrun'dah's face lit up, and her feathers seemed to wiggle in joy. "A beautiful lake, with water so still, it acts as a mirror to the stars above. This time of year, it is especially gorgeous. And luckily, it is also our fastest way to the human song."

Cade turned to Nella and translated Hrun'dah's words into Sol-Sign. Nella bobbed her fist in acknowledgment. Her face was pressed with determination and a little bit of the mischievous confidence she was known for. Cade was beginning to wonder if Nella was enjoying this kidnapping. He was starting to wonder if he was enjoying it too. There was something special about being out in the wilderness, dangers or not. He should have been more scared, but strangely enough, Cade felt only a faint nostalgia. As if he had been out in the wild before and was returning home after a long trip away. It was more than just being in space for months. It was something more profound. His heart felt stronger out here.

They started their journey, following a game trail that Hrun'dah had carved out from years of observing the creatures of this valley. The soft crunch of the ground beneath their feet was the loudest thing they could hear in the early morning. Hrun'dah led the way,

Nella walked behind her, and Cade took up the back of their pack. Cade looked over his shoulder repeatedly, thinking he might see the monster auk'gnell swooping in.

"Do not worry," Hrun'dah said, sensing Cade's unsung song. "If your monster is invading, I will know it."

"How would you know?" Cade asked, curious.

"I suppose humans would not understand. It is not even common among auk'gnell," Hrun'dah said, allowing her talon to drift along the tips of the tall, yellow grass as she spoke with the tone of a whispering lover. "I am from the North, a place of ice and snow. The auk'nai and auk'gnell who live there can sense the heartbeat of a ruemowse from a plain away. We are a people of deep listeners. The Song of Kamaria loves to play for us." Hrun'dah took in a deep breath, and her eyes closed as she cooed.

Then Hrun'dah's eyes snapped open, and her head spun all the way around toward Cade and Nella. A trumpetlike sound blurted out from a small outcropping of trees they had just passed. Hrun'dah tilted her head and listened for the sound again, and when it whined out, she nodded and said, "Follow." She hopped over both Cade and Nella to walk through the grass toward the trees.

Nella was confused, and Cade didn't really know what to tell her. He signed, *"Follow me,"* his thumbs up, one behind the other, and pushed his trailing hand toward his leading hand. His eyebrows raised in confusion.

Through the bushes and leaves, they found a baby arcophant. The strange creature had a bulky, fat body and a long neck with a cute, round head and big eyes. It had the bump of a horn on its forehead. The clumsy baby whined and shrank away from them as they approached.

Hrun'dah cooed and put her hands out, palms up. She let out a peaceful birdsong and gently swayed her head. The baby arcophant seemed to ease up and timidly approach Hrun'dah. When it got close enough, the auk'gnell reached out and stroked the baby's ears, and the arcophant hooted softly.

"Where's the rest of its herd?" Cade asked, scanning the tree line.

Hrun'dah responded as she patted the baby on its bumped head, "You scared it off yesterday when you messed up my hunt. This little one must have been separated from her family during the stampede. I'm surprised predators haven't found her yet."

The arcophant would have been a vulnerable target. Cade thought that being with it was a risk. He looked for a stick to use as a weapon just in case anything tried to sneak up on them and remembered the knife in his sleeve. He readied to bring the blade into his hand in case danger came running.

Nella got close to the baby arcophant and gestured toward its head, asking if she could pet it too. Hrun'dah cooed and nodded, and Nella stroked the arcophant's head with a big smile on her face. The baby scooted closer to her and tooted happily.

"Predators will come to eat her if we don't lead her back to her family," Hrun'dah said.

"Do you think we should risk it?" Cade asked. "If predators will be all over this arcophant, it's dangerous to take her along. Isn't it?"

Hrun'dah turned her head all the way around on her shoulders, listening to the Song of Kamaria. Her ears twitched, and her head rotated to hone in on the herd's mental wavelengths. She hooted and said, "Your disturbance in my Song caused this problem. So, we must work to correct the wrongness. Let us bring the baby back to her family. The herd moved toward the river, and that is where we are heading. It will waste no time."

Cade screwed up his face and conceded, "I guess we did cause this." He watched Nella feed the baby some leaves from a nearby tree. Cade remembered a time when his father had brought him to a place where arcophants and nurn grazed. It was one of his favorite childhood memories. Cade even used to have a stuffed arcophant he kept with him in his bed. It scared the monsters away for him when he was only three or so.

The baby arcophant seemed to enjoy Nella's attention and honked joyfully as it gobbled up the leaves she was offering. She turned to Cade and signed, *"She must have been starving. She's too short to reach the leaves here."*

Cade sighed and gave in. *"Let's take her back to her family."*

Hrun'dah cooed and walked over to the baby arcophant. She swayed her head and let out a low, calming bird song. The arcophant perked up and began to follow her. Nella walked near the baby and continued to feed her leaves. Cade unsheathed the knife from his sleeve holster and kept his attention on the tall grass surrounding them.

The four walked through the mountain valley as the sun drifted higher into the sky. Small birds tweeted their morning songs, and bugs buzzed and fluttered about. The arcophant continued to honk and blurt happily as Nella strung her along with a feast of leaves.

"Hey Hrun'dah," Cade broke the silence between them, "won't these animals get scared when they see you? You hunt them often, right?"

Hrun'dah said, "Yes, I hunt them, but they also hunt other things. When I take my kill, I do it fast and out of sight. Even the nurn we ate yesterday was left behind in the stampede. In return, I help the animals of this valley. I grind elixirs to heal wounded creatures. I build shelters and bring water to dry areas. I cultivate this song not just for myself but for everything living within it. This allows us to continue to sing together."

This sounded very different from what Cade had experienced in Odysseus City. In the urban sprawl of white towers and floating platforms, people were less likely to help their neighbors. They coexisted, sure, but it wasn't a *song* to Cade. It was just mutual survival, an unwritten contract to not kill or steal from each other. It wasn't unusual for people to break the contract either. Cheaters came in many forms: thugs, murderers, politicians. If there was something to exploit for personal gain, it was often used. Cade enjoyed his visits during his gravity-leaves, but he was always happy to return to space.

It was quiet in orbit.

It was quiet out here too.

Can people from a different star ever learn to listen to the tune of this world? Cade wondered. He thought of the void stone in his pocket, the once-thought-songless thing. Turned out it wasn't songless, yet it was still "like humans," as Galifern had said.

"What interesting songs you both have," Hrun'dah cooed. She had been listening to their mental wavelengths. "There are sounds that are new and curious, but there are also older tunes in there. It is as if each of you sings two songs at the same time. In all my years, I don't think I have heard anything like it. Perhaps I need to speak with humans more. Are you all this surprising?"

Two songs? For each of us? Cade thought. "I'm not so sure. Humans can't hear the unsung songs. Maybe there are lots of people who have two. Sounds kind of hectic to me."

"Not in the slightest," Hrun'dah said. "The blend creates something new, something unheard before. I regret not meeting more humans sooner. Introduce me to some when we make it to your city."

"It's refreshing to be around an auk'gnell who doesn't want to kill us. Lately, there's been some tension in Odysseus," Cade said.

"The Daunoren of the Spirit Song Mountain has been killed," Hrun'dah said with a coo.

"Yeah." Cade cocked his head. "How did you—"

"A sadness so deep casts a wave in all directions."

Cade nodded. "Yeah . . ." They walked for a moment in silence. Hrun'dah's daunoren staff plodded against the ground with each step, the halberd's blade reflecting glints of sunlight. Cade asked, "Do you think the auk'nai would have been better off if we never arrived?"

"What have you done?" Hrun'dah asked.

"No, not us specifically. I mean *all humans,* in general."

"That does not answer my question. Are you *all humans*? Do your actions repeat through your people? If one man murders another, do you also become a murderer? If a woman paints a masterpiece, have you also done so?" Hrun'dah said.

"Well . . . no," Cade said. Ahead of them, Nella played with the arcophant, laughing as it honked and stomped its feet with joy. They didn't have a care in the world, despite the dangers that might be lurking around them. This was a moment of peace, pure and joyous. Cade slid the knife back into the sheath on his jacket sleeve.

"As far as I am concerned—for I too, do not speak for all auk'gnell," Hrun'dah said, "you are here, whether we like it or not. What happens now falls only on the ones responsible and not on those with similar songs."

Cade nodded and took in a deep breath of the fresh mountain air.

Hrun'dah added, "And with songs like you two, I am happy you are here. I would not want to live in a universe so empty to only contain us auk'gnell and auk'nai." She cooed.

Cade smiled. "I'm glad to have met you too."

"Although, you did ruin my hunt yesterday," Hrun'dah grunted.

"Is that a joke?" Cade smiled as Hrun'dah hooted. "Wow, a joke. I'm shocked."

The arcophant interrupted their conversation and began to trumpet with joy and hop around, pounding its heavy feet into the dirt. Ahead, the baby's herd was grazing in the tall grass near where the mountains started to come together and form a canyon.

Nella signed to the baby arcophant, *"Your family is waiting."*

The arcophant tooted and began to lumber forward through the tall grass, honking with delight. Hrun'dah, Cade, and Nella watched her walk away from them. Hrun'dah cooed and said, "That one will grow to lead the herd one day. It is a good thing to see her returned home."

The baby danced with its siblings and accepted neck-hugs from its immense parents. The herd looked toward Hrun'dah, Cade, and Nella in appreciation. Hrun'dah rotated her palms toward the herd and swayed her head, cooing a birdsong. They trumpeted to her and stomped their front feet into the grass. Hrun'dah turned and said,

"They will permit us to pass through them peacefully."

They walked through the herd of arcophants. Each of the large animals bowed and accepted some petting from Nella. The babies tooted and followed them, stumbling over each other and bumping their long necks together as they tried to get close to the strangers. The baby they had saved was waiting at the end of the herd with her parents, and a forested canyon with a river flowing downhill was just beyond them.

Nella patted the baby's little head and hugged its long neck, saying her goodbyes before the long journey ahead. The parents bent forward and nuzzled against the strangers one by one. Cade felt the warmth of their large heads, their faces encompassing his entire torso. He almost fell over as they enthusiastically nuzzled against him. This wild animal was so powerful, yet so gentle. When the parents brought their heads back to full height, they loomed over the group. The herd trumpeted in unison as if waving goodbye. Nella could feel the vibrations of the arcophants' call and tensed up with giddy excitement. She waved goodbye and blew them a kiss. Hrun'dah cooed them a song. Cade smiled and nodded, then followed the others toward the river.

"The song continues," Hrun'dah said to Cade. She led the way into the canyon forest along the river. Cade smiled. He felt the same warm rush come over him as he did when drinking the tea a few hours earlier. Bringing the infant home had invigorated him in an unfamiliar way, even though it could have been dangerous.

Some things were worth the risk.

FIFTEEN

ONE WEEK EARLIER

L'ARN HAD NEVER FELT better. Not even in his younger years had he felt as vigorous as he had after his near-death experience. His eyes had a sharper vision, and his strength was a match for ten auk'gnell. Whatever his new friend Auden had done to him made him feel invincible.

L'Arn had been back to his nest on the shoreline many times since the day he awoke in Auden's cave. Still, he felt drawn to the strange human in a way he'd never felt connected to the auk'nai of Apusticus. He found himself leaving his nest often to fly south along the shore to sit next to a campfire and share stories with the mysterious man with the black marble eye. L'Arn answered many questions and didn't notice that he knew almost nothing about Auden.

On this day, L'Arn was flying south along the Howling Shore when he found Auden walking along the beach not far from his cave. The man waved to him, and L'Arn brought himself down to the sand next to his friend. They walked together as the rose-hued water lapped against their feet, and the sea air filled their nostrils.

"I see your injuries aren't giving you any trouble," Auden said. He was focused on the red sea.

"Yes, it is as if nothing happened," L'Arn said. "What magic have you done to me?"

"Magic?" Auden laughed. "My friend, I would never do something so crude to you as *magic*. That is fairy tale stuff. What I did to you was *work* and nothing more."

"You are very skilled," L'Arn said.

"I am," Auden agreed with a smile. They walked farther in silence. Then Auden stopped and sighed. "My friend, I must admit. I have failed you."

L'Arn cocked his head, allowing his ears to droop.

"I promised I would fix all your problems. Yet, here you are, imperfect."

"I feel incredible. What do you mean? I have no problems."

"Tell me, can you stay under water for a hundred years? Or even just one hour?" Auden asked. L'Arn thought about it and shook his head. Auden asked another question. "Can you go months without feeding?"

L'Arn shook his head.

"Can you fly to the stars and not miss the air? Or walk through a desert and not feel thirst?"

"No."

"Then you are not yet perfect," Auden stated flatly. "But that is my failure, not yours."

"What do you mean?" L'Arn asked.

"You are the first of your kind to be my friend. I don't know enough about what makes you work on the inside to correct your faults. If I was able to perform an autopsy to learn the auk'gnell better, then I could make you perfect."

"I am happy already, though. What else would I need?" L'Arn asked.

"If you think you are happy with such problems, I envy you.

But you do not understand happiness. Happiness is never having to worry when your next meal will arrive. Or never having to breach the surface of the ocean to suck in oxygen. Or watching the stars twirl all night and never having to worry about sleep. As long as you live, you will know death is coming, wearing a mask that it only removes at the very end. You are living in a world of limitations, and it kills me to see you suffer that way. Nature should bow to you, not the other way around." Auden looked at his feet. "I also need your help, but I would not ask you for a thing until I helped you first."

"You have already helped me. What can I help you with?" L'Arn asked.

"Let me make you perfect first. I would not feel right asking anything of you until then. It would be like asking a sick dog to build a cabin," Auden said.

"What is a *dog*?" L'Arn asked.

Auden laughed. "I have an idea—would you hear it?"

L'Arn nodded.

"You have mentioned the Daunoren pilgrimage. Where you made your sword," Auden said and pointed to the sword L'Arn kept strung to his belt. He had never recovered the hooked end of his two-piece daunoren staff. It had gone missing after the attack by the desperate auk'gnell with the halberd.

"What of the Daunoren?" L'Arn asked.

"The auk'nai bring their dead on the pilgrimage to feed to the sacred bird. The dead could be so much more useful, though, don't you think?" Auden asked.

"The dead sustain their God. Most would consider that the best use of a body."

"Yes and become the shit it leaves behind. It is a foul thing for a body to endure," Auden said. L'Arn had given up the ways of the auk'nai when he became an auk'gnell, but the Daunoren was still sacred to him. This was the first time Auden had offended him.

"If you could go to the mountain and take one of the bodies, I could do an autopsy and learn how to fix you," Auden said.

"I . . ." L'Arn began. "I cannot do that. To steal from the Daunoren is . . ."

"Is what? *Blasphemous?* Heresy? Criminal?" Auden asked. "I thought you were free of the Song of Apusticus. Such things would not apply to a free *auk'gnell*."

"I do not wish to hurt those who still know the Song," L'Arn said.

"You cannot hurt the dead, my friend. And the Daunoren will have plenty to eat. You said it yourself—the beast gorges for months on the bodies left on the mountain. Surely it won't notice one has gone missing. By the time it feels hunger again, another pilgrimage will come along. A victimless crime, with so much to gain."

L'Arn thought about the proposal for a moment, then shook his head, "There is a Watcher on the mountain at all times. He would not let me take a body."

"One Watcher? Please, L'Arn, that will not be an issue. You are a silent hunter. Stealth is your ally. If it is some sort of technology you worry about, I can help you with that," Auden said with a grin full of teeth.

"You want me to sneak past the Watcher and take one body from the Daunoren, and that is all?" L'Arn asked.

"If you bring an intact body back to me, I can fix you," Auden said. "Then you can repay me when you are perfect—and not a moment sooner."

L'Arn considered the idea further. There was something about Auden he found irresistible to deny. What he was asking went against L'Arn's spirituality, but at the same time, he understood that no one would be harmed in the process. L'Arn hadn't left the Song of Apusticus because he was angry. He just wanted to be free.

Auden offered pure freedom. A magical release that meant L'Arn would not have to kill to survive. Freedom that could be spread to others, like the desperate auk'gnell that attempted to murder L'Arn just for a meal. Auden had been a good friend so far, and he'd saved L'Arn's life.

L'Arn flexed his left arm and felt the raw power within it. It felt good—amazing, in fact. Auden could make L'Arn into something more than auk'nai or auk'gnell. He could become like a Daunoren himself.

All he had to do was take a dead body off of a mountain.

"I will do it,' L'Arn said.

Auden laughed and clapped L'Arn on the shoulder near his wing. "I knew you'd see reason! Come with me. I'll give you some things you can use."

The two friends walked down the beach toward Auden's cave.

———◆———

L'Arn sailed through the sky on his way to the Spirit Song Mountain. He had been flying for two days, only stopping for short periods to eat and rest. Auden gave him some equipment, a strange black cloak with technology woven into it, a headset to communicate over long distances, and a harness to carry the body back.

L'Arn had not traveled this far west in decades. Nostalgia overtook him as he flew over lands he used to hunt and trade. He had run into many auk'gnell over his younger years and always felt envy for their lifestyle. Now he had become one, and still sought to become something more.

He soared over the ruins of the city of Apusticus, his old home. It was a dark place now, retaken by Kamaria. In the past, he would fly over the city and admire the kaleidoscope of lights that would twinkle in the azure-colored trees. It was like looking through blue glass at a beautiful gem. That was how L'Arn admired his city—not from within it, always from outside.

Now the city was a mass of rubble covered in the plant growth of decades. L'Arn didn't know what had been done to the city after the night of the Siren attack. Perhaps some survivors still lived in the rubble, more auk'gnell now than auk'nai. It was a haunted place, but it sang no song. Even the Song of the Dead had taken its tune elsewhere.

L'Arn flew past Apusticus and continued his long journey. The sun would rise soon; the sky began to glow with the predawn light. He looked into the valley below him, the Unforgotten Garden. He peered through the clouds and paused. L'Arn brought himself to a maintained hover as he looked down at a large shipwreck below. A human thing—like a mountain itself—was stuck in the ground with a skeletal claw holding it in place.

"Now *that's* something," Auden said into L'Arn's ear. L'Arn was startled by the voice, unsure if he had said anything to announce what he was observing.

"That's the *Telemachus.* I've only seen it once," Auden said. "Did the humans crash it into the planet?"

"I am unsure when this happened," L'Arn said. "How can you—"

"Out of all the things I can do, you think *seeing what you see* is special?"

L'Arn felt foolish.

"Let's remember this ship is here. We'll come back later. For now, continue your journey," Auden said.

L'Arn gave a mighty flap of his wings and propelled himself to the north.

A few hours later, L'Arn arrived at the Spirit Song Mountain. The sun came up, and dark clouds filled the sky. A terrible storm was on its way, and snow was already starting to fall. This was a good combination for L'Arn's mission. The Daunoren would be nesting to stay warm, and the Watcher would be confined to a perch instead of patrolling the mountain. The snow would conceal L'Arn's tracks after he left.

L'Arn knew approaching the peak the same way that pilgrims did was a dead giveaway. The Watcher's perch faced that side of the mountain. He would be seen instantly. Instead, L'Arn climbed partway up the back side of the peak, remaining as silent as possible. Climbing came easier than L'Arn anticipated. His strong left arm— mysteriously charmed by Auden—lifted him effortlessly up the rocks.

He made it to the top and peered over the ridge. The Watcher's perch was sheltered in a tall outpost. A light was on, and smoke was drifting from a chimney. The Daunoren was nowhere to be seen. This was a good sign. Perhaps he could commit this sin without the watchful eye of his old God as a witness. L'Arn lifted himself over the ridge and stayed close to the rocks.

"Any of the bodies will do, as long as it is a complete thing," Auden said into L'Arn's ear. L'Arn sneaked past the cave opening, where the pilgrims would go to build their daunoren staffs as the deceased were devoured. He moved over more rocks until he was near the trail of the dead. With another pilgrimage happening soon, there were not many bodies left on the mountain. L'Arn saw four neatly wrapped figures in the snow, the clothes around them covered in warm laser stones to keep the snow from burying them.

L'Arn moved over to the closest body, keeping an eye on the Watcher's perch. He knelt next to the covered corpse and was about to strap it to the harness when he heard Auden say, "Check it first."

"I thought you said any of them will do?" L'Arn said.

"Just check it first. It needs to be a *whole* thing, not some rotten, moldy shit."

The disrespect was offensive, but L'Arn obeyed. He pulled back the face covering and revealed a marble-eyed dead auk'nai female. The month of snow and decay had not been kind to the body, mummifying it. L'Arn put the cloth over the face once more and was about to strap it to the harness again.

"It won't work," Auden said. "If they are all like that, this won't work."

"What?" L'Arn seethed. Had he come all this way for nothing?

There was a shrill cackling behind him. L'Arn turned and saw an enormous bird with wings the size of warships and a beak as long as he was tall. It was the Daunoren, and it was arching back its head to strike.

L'Arn rolled to the side as the beak slammed down into the corpse he was standing over. The Daunoren pulled its head back once more and turned toward L'Arn, unsatisfied with the dead when it had a fresh morsel so close. L'Arn tried to reason with it with his unsung song, the way he did with alpha nurn and other forest creatures. But this bird was the epitome of the Song of Apusticus, the living thing the Song emitted from. L'Arn had abandoned it long ago, and thus, this God did not recognize him. The Daunoren leaped toward L'Arn and thrust out a taloned claw.

L'Arn didn't feel himself move, but in a heartbeat, he had slid sideways away from the bird, cutting a pathway in the snow. The Daunoren shrieked loudly with aggravation. L'Arn tried to leave. He flapped his wings and leaped into the sky. The Daunoren caught him in its giant beak and slammed him back into the snow. L'Arn rolled onto his back and looked up at the sacred bird. It reared its head back.

L'Arn had not noticed a change, but *something* happened.

Instantly, he was standing on his feet, his sword in his hand, and blood was everywhere. The Daunoren lay on its back, its head cut clean off and lying in the snow with its tongue loosely hanging from its beak. L'Arn was breathing heavily, and steam was spilling away from his left arm. He felt power surging through the arm, hot and pounding but painless.

"L'Arn!" a voice shouted. L'Arn turned to see a familiar old friend.

Nock'lu stood in the snow, his daunoren staff in hand and his sashes swaying in the building snowstorm wind.

"What has L'Arn done?" Nock'lu demanded to know.

L'Arn turned back to the dead Daunoren, then looked at his bloody sword. There was something different about his blade. Auk'nai knew everything about their daunoren staffs. They built them from scratch and added to them over time. Each was like an autobiography for the user. But L'Arn did not recognize the sword in his hand. It was not the one he had built as part of his two-piece daunoren hook. This sword was long, slick, and black metal, with a heated edge that glowed red hot. L'Arn turned toward Nock'lu.

Instinctually, L'Arn somehow knew how to handle this strange new blade. The sword changed shape, flattening into a short blade. It was as if the weapon were an extension of his mind and not something he held in his hands.

"What has L'Arn become?" Nock'lu asked, his face twisted in horror. "This Song is a wrongness."

"Let me leave," L'Arn said. "I do not want to hurt you."

"L'Arn has killed the Daunoren. Nock'lu will not let L'Arn leave!" the Watcher shouted and launched himself forward with a mighty flap of his wings.

L'Arn deflected the attack and pushed Nock'lu away. They hovered above the ground, flapping their mighty wings and beating up plumes of snowdrift. L'Arn felt his heart pounding, the bloodlust beginning to overtake him again. Everything was confusing, yet somehow, entirely in sync.

Nock'lu launched again. L'Arn vaulted upward into the air above the attack, pivoted, then brought his fist down on his friend. Nock'lu slammed into the ground, shifted, and countered. L'Arn dodged, then grabbed the sharp hook of Nock'lu's daunoren staff with his bare left hand.

The blade should have cut through his hand without a problem, yet L'Arn felt no pain. There was a surge of energy, and L'Arn crunched the blade in his hand as if it were nothing. He kicked Nock'lu in the chest, separating Watcher from weapon. Nock'lu slapped against the ground near the Daunoren's still-bleeding corpse. L'Arn cracked the remaining portion of the staff in half and tossed the pieces over the side of the mountain. L'Arn landed in the snow and seethed steam.

"L'Arn, *don't*—" Nock'lu pleaded, but L'Arn could hear nothing. He could only see red.

L'Arn did not step forward. Instead, Nock'lu seemed to be pulled violently toward him. In a heartbeat, the Watcher was in front of L'Arn. Nock'lu struggled to breathe as his friend choked him. L'Arn gripped tighter, the rage overtaking him until there was a crunch.

Nock'lu slumped in his hand.

The rage simmered, and L'Arn finally saw what he had done. The Daunoren lay decapitated in the snow, blood still gushing from its neck, and his old friend stared up at him with dead eyes. The Song of the Dead began to fill the air. It was a low-toned thing, natural yet unnatural at the same time. L'Arn struggled to catch his breath, and steam boiled off his body as if he were on fire. The snow began to fall harder as the storm came to a head.

"Nock'lu . . ." L'Arn whispered into the twisted, dead face of his friend.

"That one will work," Auden said in L'Arn's ear. "Bring him back to me."

L'Arn wanted to scream. He wanted to break Auden into a million pieces and then break those pieces. He wanted to hurl himself from the mountain and explode on the rocks below. At the sound of Auden's voice, he felt his body work against him.

He could do none of those things.

Unwillingly, he obeyed.

SIXTEEN

PRESENT DAY

IT WAS THE SECOND day of Zephyr Gale's investigation into Cade and Nella's disappearance. She started with the last places she had been with Cade. They had gone dancing at the Nightsnare club in Colony Town, not far from Gran's house.

In the afternoon, Zephyr parked her rushcycle in the club's parking lot and tucked her helmet into the compartment on its side. The club was closed, but Yu'Olar, the auk'nai owner of the Nightsnare, lived on its second floor. He should be around. Zephyr walked up to the door and gave it a knock.

The door opened, and the bouncer greeted her, filling the door with his massive frame. "Sup, Zeph. We don't open for a few—"

"I need some help. Is Yu'Olar here?" Zephyr interrupted him.

"Let Zephyr in." The voice came from the bar beyond the bouncer. The bouncer nodded and let her in, shutting the door behind Zephyr. The Nightsnare was a different world in the daytime when compared to its after-dark façade. It was a musty place with brick walls and a thin layer of grime everywhere. Yu'Olar drank tea that smelled like fresh gemlilies, even from a distance.

"Zephyr needs Yu'Olar's help?" Yu'Olar asked. The auk'nai bartender was wearing a brightly colored blue and pink sash, with sparkling jewels sewn within. He looked like a completely different bird in the daylight.

"Yeah. You remember the guy I was with the other night? Tall, dark, handsome—you know."

"Yu'Olar thinks none of those things about the man you brought here. But Yu'Olar remembers the song of whom you speak." The auk'nai bartender sipped his tea.

"Do you remember anything weird from that night?"

"Zephyr and the man left after Krin'ta wanted to fight," Yu'Olar said, understanding precisely what Zephyr meant by "anything weird" by reading her mental wavelengths.

That's right! Zephyr thought back. Cade had some sort of special stone with him. A void thing from the Spirit Song Mountain. Krin'ta took offense to seeing a human with it and got in Cade's face. To avoid a fight, Zephyr had suggested they leave.

"Krin'ta, that's right . . ." Zephyr was putting the events together.

Yu'Olar continued, "Krin'ta stayed here for some time after. Looked angry. Yu'Olar kicked Krin'ta out when Krin'ta couldn't pay the tab. Started scaring human customers. Flew off."

"Any idea where he went after that?" Zephyr asked. Her first good lead. She wasn't sure how Nella would be involved with Krin'ta's malice, but maybe she'd figure that out later.

Yu'Olar cawed and shook his beak.

"Shit," Zephyr mumbled.

The bouncer piped up from behind her, "Krint is fixing up his bike at the Chopyard. Had an issue the other night, I hear. Maybe he's still there."

"Thanks. I'll go take a look," Zephyr said.

"Be careful," Yu'Olar said as he sipped his tea. "Krin'ta has been saying scary things about humans since our Daunoren was murdered. Others might be agreeing." The bartender wasn't clear if he was one of the auk'nai agreeing with Krin'ta's statements or not.

Zephyr nodded and thanked them for the help. They said their goodbyes, and she got back on her rushcycle to make her way to the

Chopyard on the other side of Colony Town.

Zephyr sped down the street and conjured up some theories of what may have happened. *Maybe Krin'ta followed him home or found him on a bus, or something like that.* Krin'ta was known for violence. If that scraggily auk'nai did something to Cade—it was too much to think. Zephyr needed to see Cade again. The night they spent together was like a breath of fresh air after a long time under water.

She remembered when Cade first joined the crew of the *Maulwurf*. Zephyr herself had only done one job previously, and Cade was replacing the other EVA specialist on the ship. He was young then, but brilliant for his age. Cade may have even been one of the youngest EVA specialists on the *Aria*, but Zephyr never verified it. He was respectful to D'Rand. Zephyr thought Cade would be an all-work-no-play kind of guy, but once D'Rand left the bridge, she saw the real side of him. The funny, charismatic, clever Cade that she grew to—if she was honest with herself—love. The way he used to talk about his desire to work on the *Infinite Aria* as a pickup to his grandfather's dream was inspiring. She knew he could do it well. Zephyr even submitted some paperwork to recommend Cade for a role as a crew leader.

She parked her rushcycle outside a dome that used to be a botanical garden, now called the Chopyard. It was a junkyard chop shop for many illegal vehicles used in the nighttime street races. Inside, glowing plants clung to the ceiling, sucking in smokey air. The lobby was small and dimly lit, with a steel door just beyond a counter concealing the hills and valleys of scrap metal. Eddie the buzzer leaned over the counter at the front desk, flipping through videos on a ramshackle soothreader device he'd cobbled together himself.

"Sup, Eddie," Zephyr said.

"Zeph? The Hells . . . you doing around here?" Eddie asked, sucking in air through his helmet between words. The buzzer was Gran's neighbor and had been around for most of her life.

"I'm lookin' for someone," Zephyr said. "Know where Krin'ta has been?"

"Krin . . . Ta. Yeah, he's 'round . . . What you needin' . . . him for?" Eddie asked.

"Just want to chat about the race tonight."

"Heh . . . Sure . . ." The buzzer grunted and hit a button on the counter in front of him. The steel door behind him shuddered, then opened. Zephyr nodded to Eddie and walked into the back garage. "Just be careful . . . in here. Got it?"

It was a vast, dark room. The glass dome roof was blackened with paint and sheet metal. Amber lights lit various work areas, and junk lay everywhere between, separating the workstations like twisted metal cubicles. Some rushcycles were suspended in midair with auk'nai hover technology. Zephyr walked through the labyrinth of scrap metal, asking the people she knew where Krin'ta was and avoiding the bone-chilling gazes of the people she knew to avoid. Her tattoos glowed under her jacket as she walked between dimly lit workstations.

"Heard you were lookin' fer Krin'ta," Krin'ta himself shouted to Zephyr from a work area she had nearly walked past. The scraggly auk'nai looked up at her from the guts of a floating rushcycle he was stripping for parts. Something he'd won in a race.

"Yeah, where have you been?" Zephyr asked.

"What?" Krin'ta said. "Krin'ta was visiting the Daunoren memorial. Get outta Krin'ta's worksong. Don't want to see humans."

"Not leaving until I get some answers." Zephyr stood tall, approaching the scraggily auk'nai. Krin'ta's eyes darted to his daunoren bat, just out of arm's reach.

"Yeah? What questions does Zephyr have?" the mean auk'nai grumbled.

"You remember the guy I was with the other night?"

Krin'ta grunted.

"Did you do something to him?" Zephyr asked.

Krin'ta grunted again and slid himself under the rushcycle he was stripping. He wrenched at some parts in the guts of the bike. Zephyr kicked the auk'nai device that kept the bike hovering in the air, and it dropped onto Krin'ta's chest, pinning the scraggily auk'nai to the ground.

Krin'ta swore in auk'nai and scrambled like a pinned panthasaur. His eyes went wild, and he tried to claw his way out from under the bike. Zephyr put a boot to his neck and asked her question again. "Did you do something to Cade?"

"Krin'ta did!" A young man scrambled over the heap of junk from the scrap cubicle next door. He was a skinny human with light skin and red hair, wearing dirty brown clothes and covered in oil smatterings. He had a Callisto accent. Although he looked too young to have been born on Callisto, he may have been raised by people who lived there.

"Shut up, Goero!" Krin'ta hissed.

Goero laughed and spat on the ground near Krin'ta. "Auk'nai don't lie, but boy, do they brag. Ole Krinty here was bragging about bruisin' a fella the other day."

"What do you mean?" Zephyr got angry and pressed her boot harder against Krin'ta's throat.

"Whacked him good, he says. Threatened to whack me a few times with that bat o' his. I reckon someone's taking the Daunoren's death poorly. Aye, mate?" Goero said.

Zephyr pulled her boot back and knelt next to Krin'ta's head. "Talk. Where'd you take him? What did you do with his sister?"

"What?" Krin'ta's eyes widened and darted between Zephyr and Goero. "Krin'ta didn't take the man anywhere. Krin'ta jumped him and left when the car came."

"Liar!" Zephyr seethed the word through her teeth.

Goero laughed and lifted a finger. "Nah, auk'nai can't lie. He never said nothin' about taking your boy anywhere. Nothin' about a girl neither."

Zephyr gritted her teeth together.

"Plus, Krin'ta was racing later that night. Bastard almost won too, if it wasn't fer the weirdness," Goero said and spit on the floor again.

"Weirdness?" Zephyr asked. She stood up, then looked back down at Krin'ta, making sure he didn't try anything.

"Yeah. Mighty weirdness happened. We was racing through Central City, and *bam!* Everyone's rushcycle just stopped," Goero said.

"The Hells?" Zephyr said to herself. She sighed. It seemed that Krin'ta had seen Cade and even attacked him, but something else took him and Nella. Still, this weirdness Goero described felt fishy. But how could it be connected? Maybe it wasn't.

Zephyr kicked the auk'nai device on the rushcycle and let the bike lift off of Krin'ta. The auk'nai seethed with anger, and Goero jumped back over his scrap pile and skittered away before Krin'ta could vent violence over him.

"Listen, Krint," Zephyr said and ran a hand through her afro, "I'm really sorry about what happened to the Daunoren. I know it's sacred to you, and I can't imagine what you're going through right now."

Krin'ta's eyes remained red hot with anger. Zephyr's attempts to come to a middle ground may have pushed the battle lines farther.

"You hurt my friend. I just want to find Cade and make sure he's okay."

"Krin'ta knows nothing. Zephyr's man got in a car and left," Krin'ta said.

"Alright. I guess that's all I'm getting," Zephyr said with a sigh.

Krin'ta flapped his wings and propelled himself from the floor, his daunoren bat clutched in his fist. Zephyr didn't see when he grabbed it, but that didn't matter now. She fell backward in surprise, just managing to dodge Krin'ta as he sailed over her by luck alone. Quickly, she scrambled back to her feet and grabbed a long metal pipe from the scrap heap to her side.

"Humans killed our Daunoren!" Krin'ta shouted. He looked as though he'd launch again.

Thinking fast, Zephyr whipped the metal pipe as hard as she could and flung it directly into the scraggily auk'nai's head. The pipe struck him right between the eyes, and he fell backward into a pile of junk.

Zephyr didn't wait around for Krin'ta to recover. She took off running for the entrance. Over her shoulder, she saw Goero hop back into Krin'ta's scrap cubicle and begin stealing his salvage. Criminals of opportunity were plenty here.

She waved to Eddie as she ran out through the lobby to her rushcycle. Zephyr mounted the bike, slammed her helmet on, and took off down the street to get some distance. She drove for a bit until she ended up outside Colony Town, on a hill that overlooked the city. Zephyr stopped the bike and got off to catch her breath.

"Shit." Zephyr spat the word. "Dammit, Cade, what happened to you?"

The city in the distance looked like an anthill, with vehicles and people flying and scurrying about. There were a few clouds in the calm spring sky. From here, she could only hear the soft breeze as it brushed against her.

Zephyr let herself drop to the grass on the side of her bike as she thought about what could have happened. *A car picked up Cade, perhaps the kidnapper? Maybe Nella was already inside at that point.* Now that Krin'ta had officially become the last person to see Cade—but not kidnap him—this car was the only lead she had. Zephyr decided it was worth mentioning to Cade's parents. She flicked her hand over her soothreader and called them up.

Denton Castus answered the call, with Eliana close by in the video. They looked a little dirty, like they'd been digging around in a graveyard for clues. "Hey, Zephyr. Any news?"

"I got a lead, but I don't know how to pursue it. Apparently, Cade had been attacked by an auk'nai named Krin'ta. Krin'ta admitted he attacked him but has a solid alibi for not kidnapping him. He mentioned a car picked Cade up. Any way we can figure out more about the car?" Zephyr informed them.

"Homer went through Cade's soothreader for clues," Eliana said. She looked tired, and at the mention that Cade was attacked, she shrank away. Currently, she couldn't bring herself to look into the camera when she spoke. "Cade got in an Autocar and was delivered to the home."

"Damn," Zephyr said. *Another dead end.*

"Thank you for looking into it, though," Eliana said dejectedly.

"Wait. Someone also mentioned something weird that happened, but I'm not sure if it's connected. Might be reaching at straws at this point," Zephyr said. "They said that a rushcycle race had been interrupted when all the power to their bikes shut off. Somewhere in Central City. Does that mean anything to anyone? It's all I got." *Please be something.*

"We're aware of some sort of electrical anomaly that passed through the city. It's connected. Here, let me send you a map," Denton said, and flicked his hand over his soothreader. A map appeared, showing a yellow line darting through the city. "We're tracking down a lead of where Cade may have been taken to, but we still don't know why this happened, or if it will happen again."

Zephyr eyed the map, tracing the anomaly and matching its timeline. She went to about the time Gran got home, when she had to kick Cade out through the window. Zephyr's heart sank, knowing he had been attacked shortly afterward. She'd let him get hurt. Zephyr would never forgive herself for that.

The anomaly traveled over to the John Veston Kamarian Archive for a bit. It hovered there for a suspiciously long time. After the delay, it traveled to the south, passing over Central City. "That must be when the rushcycle race was affected," Zephyr said to herself. It went to the Castus family home for another delayed moment before exiting the city to the east.

"It only stops twice," Zephyr mumbled.

"What's that?" Denton said. "Did you find something?"

"Maybe—just something strange. The anomaly only stops twice during this whole event. Once at your house, and once at the archive."

"You're right," Eliana said.

"I'll go take a look at the archive. Maybe I'll find something we can use." Zephyr said, "I'll let you know what I come across."

Denton and Eliana looked at each other and nodded, then looked at the camera on the soothreader. "Thank you, Zephyr. We appreciate all the help. Stay safe out there."

They said their goodbyes, and the call ended.

Zephyr put her helmet back on and revved her rushcycle. It lifted off the ground, and she sped off toward the archive.

SEVENTEEN

HRUN'DAH LED CADE AND Nella through the mountain canyon toward the Supernal Echo. The river babbled next to them on their right, and their path was growing more expansive, accommodating a thin forest. The trees' trunks were stark white, the leaves a mixture of orange and red with vibrant blue flowers poking through and spewing pollen into the sky. The river shimmered with various colors as it flowed in the same direction they walked. Cade remembered that there were fish under the river's surface, nearly invisibly thin, that reflected colors based on which fins they were moving. They were called river dancers, if he remembered Kid Scouts correctly.

Cade thought of his parents. He missed them, as he was sure Nella did too. He had not seen them in months, and then this vacation had been cut short. The visit back home had been strange from the very start, with the death of the Daunoren and now the kidnapping. *Are we the only ones who were kidnapped?* Cade wondered. *Are there more people who didn't break free from the monster? Taken to Hells-knows-where?* It was still unclear what their monster wanted with them. Even more frightening, it was hard to tell if the monster was still tracking them. It felt like a week had passed since they'd crashed in the Ember-Lit Forest, but in reality, it had only been about two days.

His last moments with Zephyr felt like a lifetime away, like remembering a dream. He missed her too, maybe even more than he missed his parents. That night was just the beginning of a new kind of relationship. He had feelings he'd pushed into the depths of his heart for years, putting work over love.

Cade remembered the moment he started to have feelings for Zephyr. They had been playing cards in the crew quarters of the *Maulwurf* and stayed up too late chatting and drinking a fridge full of beer. They didn't have to worry about rationing, because the ship was already returning to the *Aria* with a full cargo. They'd restock before the next prospecting mission. Cade loved to watch her laugh, her smile so bright and full of a mixture of joy and mischief.

Hopefully, with Hrun'dah's help, they would return to Odysseus City and put this whole event behind them. Then Cade could go back up to the *Aria* and start his new job as a crew leader. No monster could chase him up there. He craved the safety of the stars—safety in the most hostile environment known to man.

Cade sighed and looked at the ground as he hiked next to Nella and Hrun'dah. He translated a conversation between the two, converting Sol Common to Sol-Sign and reverse. He had done this plenty of times in his childhood for his little sister and was grateful to help. He felt like he was talking more than everyone, even though he was just using their words. Cade could tell that Hrun'dah was already starting to pick up on Nella's Sol-Sign, mixing her intentions and empathic wavelengths with the gestures she was making.

Nella was always good at making friends.

Hrun'dah hooted, "If we are lucky ones, we will have this kind of weather the whole journey." Cade translated it to Sol-Sign for Nella.

"It is beautiful today," Nella signed. Cade passed it back to Hrun'dah in Sol Common.

"This is why I love being auk'gnell. The walls and platforms of a city are lovely, but nothing sounds sweeter than the Song of Kamaria."

"Were you born in a city?" Nella asked.

"I was not. Like many born in the northern parts of the world, I was born in the ashes at the feet of a volcano. My mother nested my egg in a tunnel near the lava runoffs, and it incubated me. It kept my egg warm in the harsh winter. I had not seen a city until I was much older."

Cade interjected with his own question. "Did you grow up without parents?"

Hrun'dah shook her beak and cawed. "No. In the North, we find our parents after we hatch. We learn to walk and fly on our own, then listen for their song."

Deep listeners come from the North. Cade remembered what Hrun'dah had said.

Hrun'dah cooed, "My mother said she knew I had hatched because a bright star had flown overhead, larger than anything she had ever seen."

Nella asked, *"Was the star the* Telemachus *crashing?"*

Hrun'dah cawed something like laughter. "No, no. You think I am so young? Auk'gnell sing a long song. I have seen many things, and I was already very old when I saw humans come to Kamaria. I am very old still, and I imagine I will continue to be very old for a long time."

"What are we talking, like, upper fifties?" Cade asked.

Hrun'dah had to stop walking to warble a laugh this time. When she regained her composure, she thought for a moment, then said, "In your human standard, I would be about two hundred and seventy-three."

Cade's eyes widened, and when he translated it to Nella, her eyes widened too.

Nella signed, *"You don't look a day over two hundred."* She closed her eyes and smiled.

Hrun'dah laughed again.

Cade felt something clamp against his foot.

Before he could look down to see what had grabbed him, Cade

was dragged backward through the forest. Rocks, grass, and dirt scraped against him as he was mercilessly pulled through the woods. Suddenly, Cade was upside down, staring at three glowing yellow eyes.

The monster auk'gnell had caught up to them at last.

It was holding Cade effortlessly with its mechanical arm. A flat-bladed sword was grasped in its other claw, its edge a hot red glow. Sparks flicked from its technology-enhanced cloak, and waves of electrical energy pulsed from the damage it sustained from the crash the other night. Cade wanted to scream but had become paralyzed by fear.

There was a shrill birdcall, and then Cade felt an impact on his neck and shoulders as he was dropped to the ground. The monster dodged Hrun'dah's thrown halberd, but in doing so dropped Cade. He looked up at the monster, its focus on Nella and Hrun'dah. Hrun'dah was tethered to her halberd by a long metal cable, and with a firm yank, her weapon returned to her at high speed.

The monster was struck by the halberd's backswing, blood spraying from its back as the blade ripped through its unique cloak, narrowly missing its wing. Cade scrambled away from the auk'gnell. Hrun'dah caught her halberd and prepared for another strike.

Nella shouted loudly, beckoning Cade to come to her. When he reached her, Nella grabbed his hand and pulled him away from the two auk'gnell. They ran along the river as fast as they could while Hrun'dah stayed behind to protect them.

———◆———

<I have seen that blade before.> The monster spoke to Hrun'dah's mind directly through the unsung song.

<There are not many who can sneak up on me in my own song. What sort of monster are you?> Hrun'dah replied mentally. Although she could hear the monster's unsung song, she winced at its sound. It was an unnatural thing, perverted by something strange, half-dead almost. *<I knew the one who held this weapon. He is dead now,>*

Hrun'dah said. <*You and I have no conflict. Leave us.*>

<*I need the humans. Allow me to take them, and I will—NOT—WILL—NOT!*> the monster's unsung song became fragmented—robotic. It jerked its head sideways, and its eyes shined brighter. A spark launched from its face. Hrun'dah used this glitch to her advantage. She flapped her injured wings as hard as she could and propelled herself into the monster. It recovered from its glitch, but not fast enough to prevent Hrun'dah's attack.

Hrun'dah pivoted in midair and drop-kicked the monster, launching it into the river. She fell to her knees in pain, the wounds on her wings reopened from the effort. Hrun'dah looked up to see the monster flailing in the river, forced to rush with the current downriver to the west. She had temporarily bought them some time. If they were lucky, the monster would drown in the river. If they were unlucky, the monster would be waiting for them at the lake they were walking toward.

———— ◆ ————

Nella ran in with blind fear, like a nurn fleeing from a dray'va. No one could tell her when to stop. She'd just run until her legs gave out. She held her brother's hand firmly and moved as quickly as she could through the hilly forest, following the river. They were heading toward a lake, her panicked mind just focused on finding it.

She tripped over a loose tree root and tumbled downhill. Cade fell beside her, and they rolled until they were stopped by a fat tree trunk in a flat, open area. Nella didn't notice she was crying until she saw the tears hit the grass under her face. She looked up to find Cade and felt the panic sting her when he wasn't in front of her. She pivoted and found him lying on his back behind her. For a moment, she thought she may have gone too far and stranded herself in her silent world, unable to know if the monster was approaching or not. Nella repositioned herself over Cade and shook him.

Cade blinked the dizziness away and signed, *"Are you okay?"*

"I'm fine. We need to run away." Nella put her right pointer

finger between the forefingers on her left hand, then flung it away. Her mouth pushed out a puff of air, and her eyebrows rose in panic.

Cade nodded and brought himself to his knees. Then he quickly jerked Nella down behind the tree. Nella tugged his hand, urging him to start running. He pointed, and Nella looked toward the river, where she saw the monster flailing in the water. It launched its mechanical hand outward and caught a tree, then pulled itself from the river on the opposite side. Sparks flung from under its cloak, and it flinched in pain. The monster jerked its head upward in alert. Nella held her breath as she watched it shift its beak robotically around, searching for them.

Another flinch and spark, and the monster stumbled off into the woods away from Nella and Cade. They waited longer to make sure it didn't return.

Nella felt the vibration of something thud against the ground. Cade was looking over her shoulder. Nella turned to see Hrun'dah standing behind her. Her wounds had been reopened, and the tall auk'gnell was applying new bandages to help them heal faster.

"I bought us some time," Cade translated from Hrun'dah. *"But we must hurry to the lake."*

Nella nodded. She tugged Cade's jacket sleeve and signed, *"Are you okay?"*

Cade shifted the ankle that the monster had grabbed, testing it. He sighed, then searched their immediate surroundings. His brow furrowed, and he looked determined about something. Cade hobbled over to the fat tree and found a long stick. He plunked it down and nodded, satisfied with his new walking stick. Then he jerked his head downstream toward the lake.

Nella walked with Cade and Hrun'dah through the downward sloping forest. She noticed the tone had changed. Before the monster's attack, they had been joking and casually discussing the world. Now they didn't say anything—a different kind of silence to Nella. This was the silence of caution and fear.

Cade removed the knife from his jacket sleeve sheath and asked

Hrun'dah for something. She reached into the sashes on her hip, pulled out some loose cloth, and handed it to him. He took it and wrapped the knife tightly to the walking stick's end, creating a sharp spear. Cade turned to Nella and nodded.

Nella smiled, wishing she had a way to help. Hrun'dah reached into her satchel and dug around for a moment, then pulled out a strange device. It was an auk'gnell gadget that looked like a bracelet with an oval-shaped compartment at the top. Hrun'dah equipped the bracelet to Nella's right hand. The auk'gnell demonstrated, bringing her flat palm from her chest down to her hip in a whiplike movement. Nella looked at the device, then followed her example. When her hand reached her hip, the oval-shaped compartment rotated and uncoiled into a sharp, thin blade the length of her forearm.

"Skinning blade," Cade translated from Hrun'dah. *"It is not much but could be used as a defense in a bad situation."* Hrun'dah pointed at her wrist, showing Nella a small button on the side of the bracelet. When Nella pressed it, the blade coiled itself back into its oval shape. She thought of the monster auk'gnell that pursued them.

This blade might not be enough.

———— ◆ ————

The three travelers continued their journey through the forest, following the river. After two hours of hiking downhill and checking over their shoulders for monsters, Cade could see the water through the trees. The Supernal Echo.

He was confused. There was no distinct line where the forest ended and the lake began. It was as if the trees were growing in the water. When they got closer to the lake's rim, though, it was clear where the forest stopped and where the colossal timbermen parade began.

Cade had seen archive footage of colossal timbermen, the walking forests. Each creature had long, spindly tree-trunk legs joining together in a central body high above the treetops. They were classified as plant life, but their ability to roam the countryside made them more complicated than that. Among their branchlike legs, other forest creatures found shelter. Lemurbats were a frequent rider on the timbermen express, raising their young in the moving trees' hollows.

Hundreds of timbermen paraded through the lake. Their enormous legs moved through the water, soaking up as much as they could hold in their bodies for their long migration. The lake rested in the basin of a circle of mountains, emptying on the opposite side through some canyons. Waterfalls spilled from high ledges on the surrounding cliffs, making the entire basin look like an enormous fountain. Birds circled overhead, some diving into the water to gobble up fish, others resting on the branches of the timbermen.

"We are not too late," Hrun'dah said to Cade. "If we ride these timbermen, they will take us closer to your human city. It will be a long ride, but faster than you can swim it."

"How do we get on them?" Cade asked. Nella had her eyes on the beautiful sight before them and didn't need a translation during this moment of awe.

"Normally, I would fly, but that won't be an option for any of us," Hrun'dah said, unfolding her damaged wing and wincing. "Instead, we swim to a leg and climb up. Think you can do it?"

"We'll have to," Cade said. He translated the plan to Nella.

"Go now," Hrun'dah said, her eyes fixed on the tree line.

The monster auk'gnell emerged from the forest on the other side of the river. Here, where the river emptied into the lake, the water was calmer. The monster moved across the water. Its head flicked, and sparks ejected. Smoke seethed out of open ports in the mechanical arm, and the sword in its other hand kept morphing into different shapes and lengths.

Cade shook his head. "No, I'll help you fight it. I got you into this mess."

Nella surprised them both when she approached Hrun'dah's side and flicked out her bracelet blade.

"Despite you, I could not permit this monster to remain here. I have sensed enough of its song to know it caused the death of my friend." She gripped her daunoren halberd tightly. "It is an abomination and must be destroyed."

Cade jabbed his makeshift spear into the sand, feeling just a little inadequate in comparison. He said, "If we can kill it here, the journey will be safer." Nella adjusted the skinning blade on her wrist bracelet. She too would not abandon Hrun'dah.

Hrun'dah cooed. She understood she couldn't convince the humans to leave, and she admired their courage. "If this thing gets the upper hand, you two must run."

The monster cleared the river and stood on the bank, motionless except for the smoke emitting from it.

"Spread out," Hrun'dah said. Cade translated to Nella, and they separated from Hrun'dah, Cade going right, Nella going left. They moved slowly, keeping their eyes on the monster.

"I—I—I have seen—*seen*—that blade be-*be*-before," the monster said out loud this time, a mechanical sound hanging behind its voice.

"You have said that, monster," Hrun'dah shouted.

The monster slowly tilted its beak toward Nella, then toward Cade. It looked down at the sand and spread its wings, revealing a mess of burnt feathers and ravaged skin.

"Last chance. Crawl back to whatever depths you came from." Hrun'dah tried one more time to stop a fight before it started.

"I will—*will*—will not—*will* hurt—you." The monster twitched.

Cade was done waiting. He rushed forward, limping as fast as he could, with his makeshift spear pointed at the monster. He let out a battle cry as he charged.

The mechanical claw ejected from the monster and sailed through the air at Cade. Although Cade's charge was sloppy, it had been calculated. He had seen the retractable claw in action too many times to allow it to catch him off guard once more. He leaped to the side, narrowly dodging the claw as it came toward him. He crashed to the sand and scrambled to his feet.

The claw reached its maximum distance and smashed into a tree, knocking the mighty pine on its side and collapsing it into the forest. Hrun'dah took advantage of the moment. She hurled her halberd at the monster, allowing the tether connected to her wrist to uncoil.

The monster slapped the halberd away with its morphing sword, then caught the tether with its clawed foot. Before it could yank the tether and knock Hrun'dah off balance, she detached the leash and continued her approach. When she got close, the monster blasted her with a bright flash from its three mechanical eyes. Hrun'dah stumbled into the sand and let out a shriek.

Nella made her move. She ran toward the monster with her bracelet blade arched back and ready to swing. Cade joined her in a two-front assault, rushing from the other side with his spear. The monster kept its eyes on Nella and retracted its mechanical claw while pivoting.

The claw smashed into Cade, knocking him sideways into the calm river water. The monster swung its morphing sword at Nella. She deftly dropped, sliding like a baseball player going toward home plate. The blade passed over her head in a downward arc and slapped the sand where she had been. Nella's foot crashed into the monster's leg, and using the momentum, she sprang up into the monster's side blade first. The auk'gnell skinning blade sank into the monster's cloak.

Nella thought this was a killing blow but was shocked to see the monster still standing, despite the long blade in its torso. More steam spilled into the air around the beast, and it began to growl. Nella tried to get away, but the monster grabbed her with the mechanical claw. It threw her across the sand, ejecting her blade from its torso with a torrent of blood.

Cade rose from the water and hurled his makeshift spear. The knife tied to the end of the walking stick slammed into the monster's back under its right wing. The monster auk'gnell turned to face

Cade, the spear stuck in place under its wing as it pivoted. Cade's eyes went wide. Now he was defenseless. He had been aiming for the monster's head.

The monster roared. Smoke and steam flew out of it like an old train racing toward a station. "Run!" Hrun'dah shouted. She grabbed her halberd's tether off the ground and yanked it hard. The halberd returned to her, and she leaped into the air.

The monster moved unnaturally.

Its sword morphed, parrying the halberd. Hrun'dah locked blades with the monster and pressed it. "Run *now!*" Hrun'dah shouted again. They separated blades with a loud clang of metal and continued their fight. Halberd crashed against morphing black and red metal. Hrun'dah ducked under the monster's attempt to backhand her with its mechanical arm, then hopped over its shifting blade as it came across with a follow-up attack.

Unarmed and having failed their joined attack, Cade knew there was nothing they could do. Hrun'dah was the best equipped to fight the monster. He rushed to Nella's side and pulled her to her feet. They made their way into the lake and began to swim for the timbermen parade. The cold water surrounded them, and they swam with all the speed they could muster to the closest timberman.

Hrun'dah stabbed forward with her halberd, just missing the monster's head. The nightmare auk'gnell grabbed the halberd's staff with its metal fist and bashed Hrun'dah with the hilt of its sword. Hrun'dah was pushed away from the monster, disarmed.

Hrun'dah looked up in time to see the metal claw crash into her face. The monster slammed her into the sand, almost knocking her unconscious. It released Hrun'dah's face, her beak broken and blood seeping through multiple lacerations in her head.

"I will—not—*will*—stop—you," the monster roared as smoke spilled from its cloak and arm.

Hrun'dah's eyes widened as the sword morphed into a blunt, hammer-shaped object. She shrieked as the hammer came down on her head with an unnatural speed, like a piston. It brought the hammer down again and again until her shrieking stopped. Hrun'dah became silent.

The monster retracted its morphing blade and slung it into a holster. It stood over Hrun'dah's corpse and caught its breath. It was quiet on the beach. The monster twitched, pivoted, and yanked the spear from its back. It then hurriedly searched the beach for the humans, having lost them in the battle.

Cade saw it happen from the side of the timberman's leg. The monster had slain their friend and protector. Hrun'dah's body lay in the sand of the shore.

Nella focused on the climb, working her way to the top, unaware of what had just happened to their friend. The monster roared with anger, having lost its quarry again. It moved back to Hrun'dah's body and began digging around in her sashes for clues.

Cade made it to the top of the timberman, the last in the parade. Nella panted and cried. She turned to Cade and signed, *"Hrun'dah?"*

Cade shook his head, tears dripping from his eyes. Nella sank into herself and began to cry. He nudged her with his hand, and she allowed herself to be pulled into his embrace. She heaved with tears, struggling to keep herself from flailing in despair. Cade cried as well, as he held his sister in his arms. The timbermen made it across the lake and stepped down a cliff ledge into a larger body of water.

They entered the Supernal Echo lake as the sun fell behind the horizon. The stars reflected off the glassy expanse of the still water, like a mirror. It was more beautiful than Hrun'dah had described— it was like floating in space.

The timbermen marched under the stars as the two lost humans wept for their friend.

part 3
ANTHEM
of the
UMBRA

EIGHTEEN

FIVE DAYS EARLIER

L'ARN FLEW BACK TO the eastern shore. When he stopped to rest, he sat across the fire from his murdered friend, Nock'lu. The corpse was his only companion. L'Arn looked into Nock'lu's lifeless eyes and listened to the Song of the Dead. The Daunoren had listened to this same song for months as it devoured lost loved ones in a ritualistic feast. Auk'nai of Apusticus could not hear this song, but the auk'gnell of the wild knew it all too well.

It was a low-tone hum. Slow and even. Haunting. Nock'lu's eyes remained open, staring into L'Arn's soul. L'Arn stared back until the campfire faded, and the stars revealed themselves in the night sky. In the low light, he half expected his friend to stand up and move toward him. It was somehow more eerie that he didn't. An attack would have meant his friend was not dead.

L'Arn did not sleep.

The following day, L'Arn made it to the shore. Auden had a fire going near his cave, the smoke signaling L'Arn. When he landed, Auden emerged from the cave with his arms outstretched and exclaimed, "You're back!"

L'Arn dropped the body on the black rocks and pulled his sword out, holding the blade toward Auden. The man with the black marble eye put his hands together and smiled. When L'Arn didn't lower the sword, Auden's smile faded into a frown.

"I can assure you, that will not work on me," Auden said. He stepped forward and pushed the sword to the side as he knelt next to Nock'lu's body. "Yes, this one will do nicely. Bring him over to the cave. I have a spot ready for him."

"What have you done to me?" L'Arn asked.

Auden turned and raised one eyebrow at the question. His eye looked up and down L'Arn's body. He sighed and said, "I fixed you. But not completely. You still aren't perfect."

"*What* have you done to me?" L'Arn repeated with a raised voice and stepped forward, pounding his clawed foot on the stone.

Auden shook his head, then flicked his hand toward L'Arn. "If you really want me to lower the veil, I'll do it. Take a look for yourself."

As Auden waved his hand, everything changed.

L'Arn noticed the campfire on the shore first. It had been made of sticks and tinder, a roaring red fire. Now it was some sort of light with a metal base. Heat spewed from the top of it, warping the air around it. He raised his hand toward his face and felt metal over his eyes, three cylindrical tubes with lenses on the ends. When L'Arn pulled his hand away, he felt the lenses adjust to sharpen his vision.

L'Arn lifted his left arm and screamed.

Where his arm had been was now a piece of machinery. It moved like an arm, but that was where the similarities ended. Open compartments vented steam and heat, and smoke rose from gaps in the metal panels. His hand was a sizeable viselike metal claw.

"It's rude to ask a magician to reveal his trick," Auden said.

L'Arn looked up from his augmented hand and saw *something* standing before him. It was not the man with the black marble eye, but instead, a machine made of dark metal wearing a cloak. The parts that peeked out from the cloak looked like a robotic insect. Auden's head was crablike in shape, with sharp metal teeth and a glowing white eye. Auden's body was lean, like a mactabalis wasp, thin but powerful and menacing. Smoke seeped through open panels from under the cloak, much like L'Arn's arm.

L'Arn wanted to scream, but as Auden flicked his hand once more, the illusion faded. The campfire made of sticks roared with fire on the shore, his arm had feathers and a hand, and the man with the black marble eye stood before him.

"Pick up the body and bring it to the cave," Auden said.

L'Arn's body obeyed, even though his mind wanted to fly off and never return. It was a strange sort of magic that overtook his body, as if machinery in his bones was carrying out his actions beyond L'Arn's control. Auden had turned L'Arn into his puppet.

Inside Auden's cave was a flat piece of stone. L'Arn placed Nock'lu's body on it, his dead eyes staring up at the ceiling. He had no idea what was real anymore. Now that he knew his vision had been compromised, it began to flicker between reality and lies. In one instant, Auden would be a man, and in another, a machine. It hurt his mind to comprehend the shifting reality, so he looked toward the wall. It morphed from cave rock to metal, but it was easier to comprehend than Auden.

"This was the Daunoren Watcher, correct?" Auden asked.

L'Arn grumbled a coo.

"An important role. Surely others will wonder where he has gone off to. And since you killed their big precious bird, I'm sure they will waste no time tracking us down," Auden said as he put his hands—metal claws—over the body of Nock'lu.

"I was not seen," L'Arn whispered.

"You can't know that. The humans I remember were very clever, very insightful. We have to speed up our plans."

"Our *plans*?" L'Arn asked, wincing like an injured lemurbat.

"Yes. I told you before you left. I needed to ask you a favor. I wanted to wait until you were perfect, but you were clumsy, and we don't have that option any longer."

L'Arn looked at the floor.

"Can you see the lights in the water?" Auden asked.

L'Arn looked out into the rolling waves and allowed his augmented eyes to adjust. He did see it, twinkling lights under the surface like stars had fallen from the sky.

"Those are my friends. We have been here for a very long time, and I need your help freeing them. They are trapped under the water, you see," Auden said, stepping to L'Arn's side and watching the waves roll over the underwater stars. "We never meant to come here. We had important work to do elsewhere, but an unforeseen interdiction caused our ship to come to this world. It happened so fast we couldn't course correct, and we crashed into the water. I managed to make my way out, but my friends are trapped. The ship isn't responding. There's a machine casting out a pulse that is keeping everyone offline."

"Can you not fix it with your magic?" L'Arn hissed.

"I tried to fix it, but I can't get close to the damn thing. I risk shutting myself off every time I try. I do not possess the tools needed to bring the ship back online and free my friends." Auden clapped a hand on L'Arn's shoulder. It felt both like a soft human hand and a metal claw. "That's where you come in."

"I do not know how to raise your ship," L'Arn said flatly.

"Of course you don't. You didn't even know your arm was metal." Auden chuckled. "No, I need you to fetch. Like a good dog."

L'Arn still wasn't sure what a dog was, but he was beginning to understand that it might have been a creature that served Auden in the past. Auden continued as he walked back to the rock slab to inspect Nock'lu. "I cannot leave the ship, but you can."

"Why can't you leave the ship?" L'Arn asked.

Auden sneered at L'Arn, then sighed and said, "I can't until it is powered back on. But this is beside the point—*you* can leave the ship."

L'Arn cocked his head. He didn't need the unsung song to tell him that Auden was lying about not being able to leave the ship. *What is the real reason?* L'Arn wondered.

"Remember how I asked you about John Veston?" Auden asked.

L'Arn remembered that first encounter with Auden. He had asked about the man John Veston after walking on water and delivering a fish to their campfire. L'Arn did not know the fate of the man.

"I want you to find him and bring him here. He built something that works like the machine in my ship. He'd know how to shut it off so I can free my friends. If anyone knows how to help us, he would." Auden stepped forward and put both his hands—claws on L'Arn's shoulders. As L'Arn looked into his eye, the man flickered from human to robot. "You will go to the *Telemachus*, that big ship that crashed in the valley. I want you to get something that will help you bring him here. Then go to the human colony and search for Dr. John Veston."

Auden grabbed L'Arn's mechanical arm and opened a hatch near his bicep. He slipped in three puck-shaped devices, then sealed the hatch. "I will tell you when to use these. Now go. There is no time to waste. The humans may be on to us already."

L'Arn didn't want to go. He wanted to leap into the sky and fly as far to the west as he could, to get away from the confusing man-thing with the black marble eye. He wanted to strike Auden with his sword, cut him in half as quickly as he had cut off the head of the Daunoren.

L'Arn did none of those things.

L'Arn cooed.

"Good doggy," Auden said and clapped. He turned back to the body of Nock'lu. "While you're gone, I will learn what I can from this specimen you brought me. I will make you perfect, my friend. I promise. Only a little longer now."

L'Arn took to the sky.

NINETEEN

PRESENT DAY

ZEPHYR NAVIGATED A CITY of unrest on her rushcycle, searching for clues to Cade and Nella's disappearance. Throughout Odysseus City, the auk'nai who once praised the Daunoren of the Spirit Song Mountain were gathering. Some had the idea that humans were behind the murder of their sacred deity. The logic was connected to the events with the Siren over two decades prior. Before humanity arrived, the auk'nai had their city of Apusticus, their God of the mountain, and their traditions fully intact. Now that they had lost their home and their Daunoren, they feared what they would lose next.

Zephyr piloted around crowds of auk'nai who were shouting for answers. She was a Kamarian-born human and knew no other life beyond this planet and living on the *Maulwurf* in orbit. Zephyr's parents and Gran were the interstellar voyagers from a distant star, fleeing an impossible enemy made of metal. But arriving on Kamaria had been to the detriment of the natives living here. The auk'nai had lost so much. *Did humans cause this?*

Some would say yes. If humans had never arrived, Captain Roelin Raike would never have been possessed by Nhymn, and the Siren would never have found her sister Sympha. Apusticus would still be standing. It was still unknown what killed the Daunoren, but humanity had a bad track record.

Others would argue that humans did not directly cause the events that led to the destruction of Apusticus and the eventual death of the Daunoren. The place where Roelin had become possessed by Nhymn was called Ahn'ah'rahn'eem. This place caused madness within any auk'nai who ventured into the territory. The thing was, auk'nai still ventured into the territory regardless, although not in great numbers. It would have been only a matter of time before an auk'nai ventured far enough into Ahn'ah'rahn'eem and stumbled upon Nhymn.

An auk'nai possessed by the Siren would have been even more immediately devastating. Roelin was confined to his downed warship, the *Astraeus*, during most of his possession with Nhymn. An auk'nai would have flown directly to Sympha. Although Nhymn claimed to be looking out for the best interest of Kamaria, she had a violent mind, and the rule she offered was a controlled thing. The auk'nai would have become enslaved, and they would have had no *Telemachus* to slam down into the Siren to stop her. In a way, humans saved the auk'nai from total enslavement and annihilation.

This planet was doomed for change, with or without humanity. Sometimes it's what happens after the devastation that matters most. Some trees grow after forest fires and still bear fruit.

Zephyr's rushcycle came to a halt in front of the John Veston Kamarian Archive. She took her helmet off, placed it on the seat, and then double-checked the map data Denton and Eliana gave her. The anomalous data blackout had pinged this area along with others but stuck around here longer than anywhere else, including the Castus home. Now that Krin'ta had an alibi, this was her only lead.

She dismounted her rushcycle and walked toward the building. Zephyr had only been here a handful of times in her youth, usually for a school field trip. She'd gravitated toward the Archive's chemistry and geology wings back then, triggering her admiration for asteroid refining. Rocks seemed like null, useless things to most people. To Zephyr, each one was a key just waiting to be forged.

As she walked through the garden toward the Archive's big double doors, nothing seemed out of the ordinary. The statue of John Veston was the way it always was, standing tall before the entrance and surrounded by flowers. The flowers flanked each side of the doors and wrapped around the cylindrical building. Some would glow at night, and others would sparkle in the sun.

Zephyr entered the front door into the mostly empty building. Only a few people roamed the halls, quietly learning about the world outside the city. Her footsteps were the loudest things on Kamaria. Her jewelry jingled, and her boots clapped against the floor. Embarrassed, she moved toward a dark corner. Her tattoos glowed in the shadows. Zephyr sighed, feeling utterly exposed.

A man was cleaning a statue of an auk'nai leader in the room near Zephyr's corner. He was a young man with beige skin and short black hair. Zephyr's loud shoes and jewelry didn't seem to bother him. He simply minded his own business—keeping the Archive clean for visitors. *This guy could have been working here when the anomaly passed through,* Zephyr thought. She decided he might be worth asking. "Hey, excuse me?"

The man didn't answer. Zephyr was sure she had spoken loud enough and was a little embarrassed to try again. "Excuse me, sir?" she asked.

In the silent hall of the archive, Zephyr heard the man's soothreader vibrate. A small arrow of light shone on its display, pointing directly at her. The man turned and smiled. He stepped away from the statue he was cleaning and put his hands to his ears, indicating that he was Deaf. When he used Sol-Sign, his soothreader detected his arms, hands, and face. A synthetic voice projected from it. *"Can I help you?"*

"Uh. You might be able to. But I'm not really here for the Archive," Zephyr said. The top half of a blue holographic man appeared above Jun's soothreader and began signing what Zephyr was saying. "My friend got—well, he was taken. Him and his sister." She fumbled with the words.

The man watched the hologram convert her speech into Sol-Sign, and his eyes lit up. He signed, *"Are you talking about Nella Castus and her brother Cade?"*

"Yeah, actually. How did you know?" Zephyr asked.

"Nella is my best friend," the man explained. *"I was the last one to see her the night she went missing. I miss her so much."* The voice on his soothreader reflected his pain, but the man's face was even more telling. He looked tired; he might not have been sleeping well.

"Looks like we both lost someone we cared about," Zephyr said quietly. "I'm Zephyr Gale. I was with Cade the night they went missing. I've been working with Denton and Eliana Castus to find them. They are out in the wilderness somewhere, tracking them down."

"My name is Jun Lam." He bowed. *"Is there a way I can help? I feel so useless dusting off these statues while Nella is out there."*

Zephyr was hesitant to ask her questions. So far, she had done her investigation without leaving her comfort zone too much. Asking questions around Colony Town was easy. She was talking to people she had grown up with. Questioning Krin'ta felt more natural than talking to City-side people. Still, she needed help.

"Yeah, maybe. Did anything weird happen that night? Here, specifically. I've been tracking this anomaly, and it—" Zephyr asked.

Jun grunted and clapped, interrupting her. *"The weird blackout."*

"Yes!" She felt like she was getting somewhere.

"Yes, I was here when it happened. Very strange. I had started my shift a little bit before," Jun signed. His face tightened as he thought back on the night.

"What was strange about it?" Zephyr asked.

"I'll show you." Jun put his thumbs up, one behind the other, and pushed his trailing hand toward his leading hand. *"Follow me."*

As they walked, Jun signed and his soothreader spoke Sol Common so he didn't have to face Zephyr when conversing. *"All of the lights shut off. Even my soothreader shut off."* Jun stopped at the entrance to a display room. *"Except this room."*

Zephyr stepped into the Colony History wing of the Archive. When the Archive had first been erected, this room was dedicated to Silence Day. Over twenty years ago, Captain Roelin Raike had become possessed by the Siren named Nhymn and was forced to carry out a horrible massacre. Over forty human colonists were killed. The room was later converted into a display of the first years of human colonization. Only the corner of the room was dedicated to Silence Day now, featuring a memorial to John Veston and the others who were lost that day. Some of the old colony dome models looked strange to Zephyr. She had just been inside one of them earlier, and it didn't look as new and clean as it did in miniature form.

"All the lights were on in here," Jun signed. *"And there's one more thing."*

"What else?" Zephyr asked.

Jun's hand looked like he was holding an imaginary gun sideways as he brought it up to his face, then pushed the sign toward Zephyr. *"Watch."* He made a few gestures over his soothreader. The lights in the hallway outside the room faded off and on.

"Hey, what's going on?" someone asked from the hallway, unnerved by the fading lights. The patron's speech was picked up on Jun's soothreader. The avatar that converted the speech to Sol-Sign was green instead of blue to identify a second speaker.

"Sorry! Just fixing a light!" Jun signed as his cheeks flushed red. The robotic voice was louder automatically, adjusting based on the range it was converting for. He turned to Zephyr and signed, *"My soothreader allows me to control all the lights in the archive. This room hasn't been responding to my commands since the night of the blackout. I assumed something tripped in the colliders. But maybe it's more than that."*

"That is weird," Zephyr said. "Mind if I take a look around?"

"Of course. Let me know if you see anything."

Zephyr wandered the room. She walked past the models of the interstellar ships that brought humanity to Kamaria, the *Telemachus* and *Odysseus. What it must have been like to be in a stasis bed for three hundred years, only to wake up as if one night had gone by?*

Cade's mom, Eliana Castus, was holographically hovering in the display about the cure for lung-lock, along with a team of the other early Scouts. The deadly bacteria that crept into the colony through any tiny opening and suffocated its victims—cured by auk'nai intervention through a deal Eliana made with Mag'Ro. She was a hero and may have saved humanity from a slow-drip death from the air Zephyr breathed freely. Sadly, it didn't cure everyone, as her buzzer neighbor Eddie would attest to.

Zephyr made it to the corner dedicated to Silence Day. On the walls were the names of those killed in the massacre, and a vid screen flashing each one, with quotes from John Veston playing over somber music.

"We will no longer be a one-star race," the voice of John Veston said. "We will become space explorers. A shared life in the cosmos."

Zephyr thought she heard a humming coming from the voice as it spoke. It was distracting, and it felt like a mistake. "Hey, Jun?" Zephyr clapped her hands, as she had seen Jun do earlier. He turned to her, and she asked, "Is this thing broken?"

"Is something wrong with it?" Jun signed as he walked over.

"I hear a whistling—or humming."

Jun flicked his hand over his soothreader, and it brought up a wave-sign graph that detected noise for him. As he moved his soothreader toward the display, the wave signature jumped and held. Jun nodded and looked at Zephyr, then signed, *"Odd."*

Zephyr's eyes darted around the display, looking for anything out of place. Since the room wouldn't respond to an external command, they couldn't shut off the exhibition's sound and listen for the hum. They had to work around it. She could hear it best when John Veston's speech paused for effect.

"With Homer's help, we will find our place in the heavens," John said, then paused for effect before continuing. "We will carve our own paths in the void."

Zephyr used that pause to hone in on the obscure humming. There was a pedestal to the side that had a bust of Captain Roelin Raike hovering above it. The events with the Siren were described in the text below. The Siren was the true murderer that horrible night of the massacre. Roelin was credited with stopping Nhymn, with help from Denton and Eliana, in a story that Zephyr had never really believed. People entering alien minds and tethers and so on seemed too fantastical to be true. She had met Eliana and Denton; they seemed like ordinary people to her. The soldiers who fought in that battle believed it, though.

Jun approached the pedestal and put his palm against it to feel the vibrations. His face lit up, and he looked back to Zephyr with his eyebrows raised. The humming was coming from the pedestal.

"Bingo," Zephyr said. She checked both sides and didn't notice anything at first. When she looked toward the bottom, she saw that the pedestal wasn't flush with the wall. It had been pulled away and slightly rotated. "Can we move it?"

"Yes, let's move it," Jun signed. It was a heavy and required both of them to slide it farther from the wall. The side that faced the wall was indented from the rest of the pedestal's flat rectangle shape. A receiver tapped into the room's energy wirelessly, synced with the collider cylinders that ran the whole archive. But there was something else—a solid black puck-shaped object. It was shaking ever so slightly and emitting a hum. When Zephyr reach out to touch it, she felt her fingertips burn.

"That damn thing is *spinnin*!" Zephyr exclaimed.

"What is it?" Jun signed.

"I have no idea. Do you remember anything else that night?"

Jun thought to himself for a moment. He began to retrace his steps. *"I gave Nella her seeds, we chatted, and she left. I started my shift. Cleaned the Biology and Geology wings. Then the lights went off."* His hands were moving fluidly as he remembered; his face was focused. *"I tried to get them back on, but even rebooting the collider cylinders in the power room didn't work. I went outside to enjoy the night air until the power came on. I walked out the front door and sat on the steps. It was dark. Even darker with all the lights off. So I didn't notice him at first—"*

"Notice who?" Zephyr asked.

"In front of the statue of Dr. Veston was an auk'nai. He was wearing an odd cloak and seemed to be holding something big. He was standing in the way, so I couldn't see whatever it was. I tried to ask if he needed help, but my soothreader shut off when the power went out. When I approached, he flew off with the big object."

"How big? Like a gun?" Zephyr asked.

"It was about as big as a rushcycle," Jun signed.

"Nah, that can't be right."

"Kid Scout's honor!" Jun signed, and pointed to the Scout Patrol mission patch on the wall.

"So, we have a weird-lookin' puck thing and a mysterious auk'nai with a big object." Zephyr ran a hand through her afro. "This is the best evidence I've found, honestly."

"Really?" Jun signed. His face was a little dejected.

Zephyr nodded and sighed. "Well, thanks, Jun. I'll let Eliana and Denton know. Maybe they can put it all together."

"Call me if you need me," Jun signed and flicked his soothreader information over to Zephyr's. *"I want to help."*

"I will. Take care."

Jun gave a bow and went back to work tending to the archives.

Zephyr exited the archive to make a call.

TWENTY

DENTON CASTUS SAT ALONE in the *Rogers* spacecraft's cargo bay, the *Tiger* rover his only company. The team had pinged the admiral's missing stasis pod and were on their way to its location in the eastern mountain range. George and Marie had stayed behind at Telemachus Outpost to keep an eye on the old wreck, in case the anomaly decided to return.

Somehow, the murder of the Daunoren of the Spirit Song Mountain, the disappearance of Nella and Cade, the rolling blackout in Odysseus City, and the missing admiral's pod were all tied together with a single thread. The potential Undriel device found in the *Telemachus* wreck was a bad omen, a nightmare long forgotten that found itself in the real world once again. Denton hoped it was something brought over from the Sol System by accident. Just an old device used by an old enemy, and nothing more. But he knew better than to lie to himself.

Denton thought of the young marine who'd died while they were exploring the wreck. Private Simmons was close to the same age as Cade. *Is it fair to ask others to risk their lives for the lives of my children?* Denton wondered. This investigation was becoming more perilous, and the stakes were getting higher and higher. What had begun as a murder investigation had now evolved into humanity's fate once again resting on the edge of a knife. To Kamaria, this investigation meant everything. To Denton, the only thing that mattered was finding his children.

I kept wishing for Cade to come back down planetside and live close by again. Now I wish he'd stayed in space, where he'd be safe. Denton wrestled with himself.

"Hey." Eliana entered the room while Denton was in deep thought. "I just heard from Zephyr. She found another one of those strange pucks in the Kamarian Archive."

"The Undriel cylinders?" Denton asked.

"Looks that way," Eliana said. "But we don't know for sure they are tied to the Undriel."

"What else could it be?" Denton asked. "Think about it. If the auk'nai made it, we would have data about it. Homer was just as shocked as we were when we found it. We can't just ignore the possibility and hope it never comes true."

Eliana didn't say anything.

"They must have finally found us," Denton said. "There's no other explanation."

"We were so careful, though. There were contingencies upon contingencies in place."

"We thought the same thing about Nhymn. Roelin took every precaution. There was no way he could become contaminated through his suit, and yet . . ."

"But we *understand* the Undriel. We had no idea what the Siren was or how it could cheat death." Eliana shook her head.

"Do we really, though? If we understood them, they probably wouldn't have driven us out of the Sol System. I was there for the last of it, and what I saw was an impossible enemy. You think putting distance between them and us was enough? You don't think they still had tricks we didn't know about?"

"I—" Eliana started, then groaned. "I don't know! I have no idea what the Undriel are capable of. It's a huge universe—the odds of them finding us here on Kamaria in our lifetime would be a trillion to zero point zero *zero* one!"

"Well, here is that 'zero zero one' now, looking us right in the face . . . We avoided our Armageddon only to bring it across the stars with us." Denton paraphrased something he'd heard Nhymn say. A silence in the cargo bay followed.

Eliana churned the possibilities until it frustrated her. "I just want to get Nella and Cade back; screw everything else," she said with her head buried in her hands.

Denton shifted over to the crate she was on and rubbed her back. "I want them back too. God, I hope they're alright. Nella is probably so scared."

"At least Cade is with her," Eliana said, accepting Denton's embrace and laying her head on his chest. "Why are *our* kids missing?" she asked. "Why not anyone else?"

"I don't know," Denton said. Most people planetside didn't know Cade well, and Nella lived a peaceful, quiet life as a botanist. There had not been any particular reason Denton could see to single them out. The anomaly clearly made its way to the Castus family home with a purpose in mind. After arriving, it had left the area entirely. "Whatever did this singled Nella out. Cade might have just been in the wrong place at the wrong time. But Nella was for sure—"

"Whatever took them didn't know we weren't home," Eliana said. "Maybe *we* were the targets."

Denton let that sink in. It made the most sense. The anomaly came to their home, and the kids were just a convenient target. If they had been home at the time, maybe the kids would have been spared. Denton felt his heart drop a few centimeters, and a lump blocked the back of his throat. It should have been him.

"Oh, God. I should have been there." Denton started to breathe heavily, and his eyes darted blankly around the room. Tears began to overflow, threatening to spill out onto the cargo bay floor.

"Hey, hey," Eliana said. She brushed his cheek gently. "Denny, you've got to stay strong. If you don't stay strong, I don't know how I will make it."

Denton took a few deep breaths and tried to regain his composure. It was hard these past few days. Ever since the kidnapping, he had been a wreck whenever he was left alone. He had cried so much in private, and he was quick to panic. Eliana was in a similar state. They both looked ragged and worn out. If they could just find Nella and Cade and make everything better again—they couldn't rest until they were back safely with them. "I've never been as strong as you." Denton sighed. "I'll do my best. We aren't going home until we find Nella and Cade. I promise."

I will not fail to find them.

"We're going to find them. It may seem impossible, but we *will*," Eliana stated, then kissed his cheek and gave him a hug. She clung to him tightly, as if she had been slipping off a cliff and needed him to catch her.

"*Rogers* has arrived at admiral pod location in the Ember-Lit Forest. Talulo cannot bring the ship any closer. Team will have to go on foot," Talulo said over the ship's comm channel.

Eliana released Denton and brought her soothreader closer to her face. "Thanks, Talulo. We'll get ready."

———◆———

Within fifteen minutes, the team was on the ground and making their way uphill through the snowy forest. Sergeant Jess Combs led the way in her combat suit, the admiral's pod pinging her soothreader and providing direction. Eliana, Denton, Homer, and Faye followed behind her, all but Homer carrying particle rifles.

"Keep your eyes open. If Nella and Cade stayed with the pod, they could still be close by," Faye said. Homer's eyes were glowing blue as they scanned the perimeter, looking for signs of the missing people.

"The pod should be just ahead," Jess said. She used the jump-jet on her suit to vault up onto a rock ledge, then held her hand down and lifted each of the team members up, one at a time.

Tucked in the trees near a tall rock wall was the admiral's stasis pod, thrust halfway down into the snow. It was covered in a fluffy white blanket, and glowing blue embers twinkled against it before fading out. Eliana and Denton scrambled toward it while the others kept their eyes on the surroundings.

Denton reached inside, plunging his hands into the snow that had filled the pod over time. If they were still inside, maybe it wasn't too late. Maybe hypothermia hadn't set in. Maybe the embers from the trees were enough to keep them alive.

He found nothing but snow inside the damaged pod.

"They aren't here." Denton sighed with a mixture of frustration and sadness and some relief. Eliana looked slapped by the words. Every time they made it to where the kids might be, it led them somewhere else.

Faye stepped forward. "Maybe we can track them from here."

"I'll see if I can get the databox working on this thing," Denton said. "These old pods have a little camera on the inside. They're also made from old war tech, so the anomaly shouldn't have affected it too badly. Maybe we can use that." He waved over to Homer. "Come give me a hand with this."

"Anything I can do to help," Homer said. They approached the pod and began to melt the snow using a heater concealed in their wrist. Homer then opened their chest compartment filled with tools. Denton pulled out a screw thimble and particle saw and began working on the databox. As the man and the robot got busy fixing the stasis pod, Eliana grew restless. The blue embers from the pine trees mixed with the gently falling snow, creating a haze that obscured her vision. She wished for a bright, sunny day, but fate clearly didn't give a lemurbat shit about wishes. Eliana looked at the cliff wall behind the stasis pod and noticed that some of the trees above looked dead and broken.

"Can we get up there?" Eliana asked Jess.

Jess Combs checked the cliff, then nodded. "I'll drop a rope down for you. One minute." The Tvashtar marine activated her jump-jet and launched herself onto the rock wall, then used strategically timed spurts of energy to help her scale it to the top.

Once there, she lowered a rope.

Eliana climbed up with a little more effort than it used to take her. She made it to the top, where Jess pulled her up to steady her. The trees had been bashed in and perhaps even set ablaze. Although snow covered the ground, Eliana could still imagine the path the stasis pod must have taken. It fell from the sky, smashed into the trees on this higher ledge, then tumbled into its landing position below. But there was something else.

Something was humming and clicking.

"Do you hear that?" Eliana asked.

Jess lifted her chin and listened, then nodded.

"It sounds like the device we found in the *Telemachus*," Eliana said. She walked closer to where the pod must have impacted the ground and brushed the snow away. Sure enough, there was another black puck, but this time it was sputtering with some sort of mechanical failure. "Jess, come look."

The sergeant looked over Eliana's shoulder.

"Can you pick it up? The last one—" Eliana said, then wiggled her hand.

Jess picked up the device. Her gauntleted hand was unaffected by the speed of the spinning apparatus. It attempted to jerk itself away from her hand with every sputter. After a few tugs, the device freed itself and tumbled into the snow. Jess reached into a satchel on the right thigh of her suit and retrieved a cloth bag. She emptied it, and a paperback novel slipped out into her free hand. The title was in ancient pre-Sol Common Russian. Eliana couldn't read it, but she recognized the book. It had belonged to an old friend, Major Pavel Volkov. The major had died in the battle against Nhymn long ago, and since that day, Jess had taken care of his prized book.

Jess gently tucked the book into a compartment on her other thigh, grabbed the puck-shaped device, and plunged it into the cloth bag. The puck tried to jump out but was unsuccessful. It looked as if they had stuffed a small animal into the sack.

"So that's three of these strange collider cylinders now. I'm surprised we didn't find one at the Daunoren site," Eliana said.

"Hey, we got the databox working!" Denton shouted from below.

Eliana was about to turn and head back down the rope when something else caught her eye. Something else had been revealed in the snow near where the puck had fallen out of Jess's hand. Eliana knelt and brushed some snow away, then pulled a few feathers from the site. They were black with flecks of yellow, and definitely auk'nai or auk'gnell based on their size and shape.

"You guys coming?" Denton shouted.

"Be right there," Eliana called back. She scanned the area quickly for more clues but couldn't spot anything else, then nodded to Jess. They made their way back down to join the others near the empty pod.

Eliana came to Denton's side. They exchanged eye contact, unsure if they wanted to see what the video had shown. Homer was tapped into its feed and displaying the footage holographically in front of their chest.

"Are you ready?" Homer asked.

"Show us," Eliana said.

"The databox of the pod only records the fifteen minutes surrounding a catastrophic impact. Here is what it recorded," Homer said, then allowed the video to play.

The video had no audio, and the image was hazy from anomalous interference but still watchable. At first, the view had been blocked by Cade's hair. He shifted and revealed Nella smushed against him. The camera was located above the chair of the pod and to the right. Cade got his bearings and looked around. After a few moments of this, he reached down and pulled the emergency pod latch, blowing the lid off the front of the pod.

Eliana jolted, and Denton gasped. They both thought Cade may have accidentally gotten Nella thrown away from the pod, but he grabbed her and held her tightly. Denton squeezed Eliana's hand. This was the first time they had seen their children since before the kidnapping.

Cade looked up, and his eyes went wide. He seemed horrified. Eliana began to tear up. Seeing her son with such horror on his face was unbearable. No parent ever wants to see their children scared out of their minds. Eliana wanted to reach into the video and pull them to safety.

Cade's expressions shifted. Eliana had seen this look before, but in Denton's eyes. The grip of determination had found her son, and he took action against whatever horror was looming outside the pod door. Cade reached into the compartment that concealed a flare gun, aimed it out the door, and fired.

The video exploded with stark whiteness for a heartbeat. When the camera adjusted, the world outside the pod was swirling. Cade and Nella were pressed against the seat until—*wham*—impact. There was a brief moment where everything looked weightless as the pod bounced off the ground. For the first time, Eliana and Denton got a glimpse of the monster that had taken their children.

It was on fire.

The monster moved past the open pod door, attempting to reach in. It was the taloned hand of an auk'nai or auk'gnell, but behind it, behind the fire and snow filling the video screen, there were three bright yellow glowing eyes.

As fast as the moment had come, it vanished. The pod tumbled off the cliff into the snow below and ceased movement. For what felt like eons, Cade and Nella didn't move. Denton held his breath, and Eliana couldn't feel her heart beating. Then, Cade stirred.

"What the Hells?" Faye whispered, but the others saw it too and couldn't find words.

Cade's eyes were glowing bright blue as he pulled Nella from the pod and laid her in the snow just outside of view. Shortly after that, the video cut itself off.

Denton and Eliana stood silently for a minute after the video ended.

Jess nodded. "They made it out of the pod. That's a good sign."

"Cade's eyes were glowing," Eliana mumbled.

"Homer, is there a chance that was some sort of technical glitch?" Denton asked.

"It is possible, but unlikely. I believe Eliana's assessment is correct," Homer stated mechanically.

"What is going on?" Eliana whispered. "Is it the Undriel, or a Siren? What is happening? His eyes were *glowing blue!*"

Jess lifted the cloth bag they had placed the jumping puck in, displaying the sporadic movements to the rest of the team. "Maybe this has some answers."

"What is that?" Denton asked as the bag tried to free itself from Jess's hand.

Eliana answered, "It's another one of those Undriel devices—or so we think. It's damaged, though."

"If I could take a look at it, maybe I can discover its origins," Homer said.

"It's all yours. But if this thing finds a way to get in your head, I'm putting you down," Jess said flatly. She handed the jumping bag over to the android. They held it steadily and scanned it with their eyes.

"No need, Sergeant. Since the first puck's discovery, I have taken precautions against potential Undriel influence. In the case of a network invasion, I will shut down and erase my data cores," Homer said. "I will work with George and Marie to analyze this device and compare it to the functioning cylinder we found before. If we can find its source, we may be able to find the kidnapper."

"We should keep looking in this area for Nella and Cade," Denton suggested. "They might still be around here somewhere."

Eliana nodded. "Yes, although I'm unsure. We didn't find that auk'nai's body. If that thing was still chasing Nella and Cade, they could have gone anywhere." She thought for a moment. "Homer, can you get back to the *Rogers* on your own while we search? Take these feathers with you and ask Talulo if he can get anything out of them."

Eliana handed the feathers she discovered over to Homer. They nodded, then said, "I will ping Talulo our location now. He can also provide light as the sun sets." Homer stepped backward, and their eyes flashed red as the ping was sent to the ship. Within minutes, the *Rogers* was hovering above the tall ember-lit pines, its searchlights illuminating the increasingly darkening forest. It couldn't land, but it could hover in place above the trees.

Homer activated the auk'nai device implanted in their legs and began to silently levitate toward the ship until they were able to step onto the lowered access platform.

"Alright, everyone, spread out. Let's find Nella and Cade," Eliana said. Denton, Faye, and Jess each picked a direction and walked. They searched into the night as the embers drifted from the trees and mixed with the snow. Each snowflake worked to hide the trail of the missing people.

TWENTY-ONE

NELLA CASTUS LOOKED OVER the edge of the colossal timbermen and down into the water below. The Supernal Echo was a mirror lake. The stars and thin clouds that lined the sky above reflected off the water below, blending seamlessly. It was like walking through the heavens. Hrun'dah had loved it here. But Hrun'dah was gone now, slain by the nightmare that pursued Cade and Nella.

Cade had kept to himself, watching their wake and making sure the monster auk'gnell had not followed them. Hrun'dah's body remained on the beach. The silence was filled with thoughts of their lost friend.

The monster was unstoppable.

Hrun'dah, Nella, and Cade had attacked it all at once, and it swatted each of them like flies. Hrun'dah was the mightiest of them all, and she fell to the monster's raw power. She died so that Nella and Cade could live, even though she barely knew them. They owed Hrun'dah a debt too deep to pay.

They would stay on the timberman until they reached the other side of the Supernal Echo. Nella was unsure how long the parade would take to get there or if the monster had followed them. She looked across the twilight surface of the lake, but darkness obscured her vision, and no land was in sight. It was as if they were crossing a calm ocean.

The parade of walking trees guzzled up water as they marched. The energy granted to them created pulsing green lights that traced up their legs and dissipated in their central bodies. The green glow reflected off the water below, illuminating large fish swimming near the timbermen's legs, which were gobbling up anything that dropped off.

Something caught Nella's eye. Cade had his back to her, and a faint blue glow was reflecting off the timberman as if he were holding a light she couldn't see. She thought maybe it was some bioluminescent thing in the timberman, but the color was wrong. She reached toward Cade's shoulder, and he turned, startled. The light had vanished.

"What's wrong?" Cade signed, his pinky and thumb stretched outward from his curled fist, then tapped against his chin. Nella saw the sadness in his eyes as he asked. He had just come home to visit before starting a new life as a crew leader on the *Infinite Aria*, and then all this happened. She wished Cade hadn't gotten tangled in this mess, but she was glad he was here. Nella shuddered at the thought of being out in the wilderness this long alone.

Nella wasn't sure what to sign, so she shook her head. "Are you alright?"

Cade looked down, his eyes tired. He sighed and signed back, "I'm sad about Hrun'dah. It's my fault she's dead. I made the deal with her to bring us home."

"I'm sad too." Nella sighed.

Cade looked straight up at the stars. There wasn't a cloud in the sky, and the universe was open to them. A shooting star zipped by. Nella tapped Cade on the shoulder to get his attention again. "Why do you think we are here?"

Cade misunderstood. "Philosophically?"

Nella tapped her two forefingers against her thumb. "No. Why did the monster take us?"

Cade said, "Oh," out loud, then signed, *"It asked us about Grandpa before it took us."*

Nella's face scrunched together, and she reiterated, *"Grandpa? What does Grandpa Mike have anything—"*

Cade shook his arms from side to side. *"Grandpa John."*

That was strange. They had never met their Grandpa John. *"What did it ask?"*

"It asked if we were John Veston's children," Cade signed. *"I told it we were his grandkids."*

"So, it was looking for Mom?" Nella cocked her head sideways. *"But it took us anyway? Why would it do that?"*

Cade shrugged. They pondered the situation for a moment longer, but no answers came. Nella sighed and shook her head. *"What a mess."*

Cade clapped and got her attention. *"I'm sorry you got wrapped up in this. Maybe if I didn't answer the monster, we wouldn't—"*

Nella shook her arms this time and cut Cade off. *"No. This is not your fault. You shouldn't even be here. You were doing fine in space, and now you're caught in this net with me. I wish you didn't have to be."*

Cade took a deep breath. *"If it had to happen, I'm glad I am here with you. I wouldn't have it any other way. We will make it back home. I promise."*

Nella looked Cade in the eyes and noticed the faint blue glow coming from his irises. She wasn't sure if it was some sort of residual light from the stars or not, but it haunted her nonetheless. She seemed to understand something beyond his words. It was almost like the unsung song the auk'nai talked about.

Ever since they had been taken, Nella had felt a growing sensation inside her body. It was as if the danger of the wilderness brought out something hidden deep within, awakened by the same blinding light the monster used to knock her out. Throughout their journey, this warm feeling in her chest had begun to spread, and she could feel the sensation in her fingers and toes. Nella couldn't explain it. The light in Cade's eyes seemed to imply he had the same energy inside of him too. She could understand his unsung song, the unique tune that Hrun'dah had described.

Cade blinked, and the light faded. *"This is our stop,"* he signed, and then pointed. Nella looked back out over the water in the direction he indicated. Land peeked out from the darkness as the colossal timberman marched forward. The walking trees in front of them began to step onto the shore and parade north into the forest.

They climbed down the long leg of the timberman. Cade made it onto the ground first and helped Nella dismount right before the timberman's leg lifted to move forward. They waved goodbye to their ride.

Nella tapped Cade on the shoulder and signed, *"Is your leg okay?"*

He jiggled his leg and tested it, putting his weight on his ankle. The time on the timberman seemed to help heal his injury, but it wasn't perfect. He wiggled his hand, indicating that it'd be good enough.

Cade knelt down and pulled the flask out of his jacket compartment, dipping it in the water. He took a long drink, then offered it to Nella to do the same. They spent a few moments admiring the Supernal Echo. Without the timbermen parade on its surface, it looked like staring out into the edge of the universe.

Nella took a sip from the water flask and thought about Hrun'dah.

When they were ready, they filled the flask once more and set off on their way.

The two lost humans walked into the dark forest. Laser stones in the grass dotted their way, and veins of pulsing light running up the trees gave them enough illumination to walk without stumbling in the night.

They walked side by side, the agreed-upon way to journey for the safety of them both. The forest began to thin, revealing a cliffside. Beyond the ledge of the cliff, the forest tapered off into desert and plateaus. Rock archways and canyons lined the horizon, and plates of a mirrorlike rock reflected the stars on the ground. The dunes were crimson colored, looking as if blood was spilled onto the world, staining it forever.

Auk'nai called this place the Starving Sands.

"This is where the underground palace is," Cade signed. *"Where Mom and Dad first encountered the Siren years ago. We are on the eastern end of that valley."* Cade looked out over the expansive plateaus, nodded, then signed, *"If we head northwest, we'll reach the jungle. Then beyond that is where Apusticus used to be."*

Nella faded into hopelessness. *"That's so far away."*

Cade's smile morphed into sheer determination. *"We got this,"* he signed, then stuck his forefinger, pinky, and thumb out to make the *"I love you"* symbol with his hand. Nella smiled and mirrored his sign of endearment. Cade looked along the cliff ledge, then pointed. *"Look, we can scale that archway down into the valley below."*

The stone arch protruded from the side of the cliff they were standing on, then gently sloped to the dunes below. She nodded and followed Cade.

They scaled the rock archway with little difficulty. The air became dry and warm the lower they traversed. Once in the valley below, Nella looked up at the mountain range they were leaving behind. They'd had a hard time before, but she'd grown comfortable in the hills and cliffs of the region they were leaving. The Starving Sands ahead of them was full of new mysteries and monsters. She wanted to slump to her knees and cry. But she remembered what Cade had said on the back of the timberman: *"We will make it back home. I promise."* His eyes were glowing blue when he said it, and a wave of reassurance flowed over her. Nella summoned her courage and followed her brother.

We got this.

————◆————

Hours passed as they hiked through the desert valley under the twilight.

Cade felt a pain in his stomach, and suddenly walking all night wasn't going to work. He was hungry, and he knew Nella might be too. They hadn't had an authentic meal since they met Hrun'dah. He wished their auk'gnell friend was here. She'd know how to catch food.

He tapped Nella on the shoulder, then signed, *"We should rest for the night."*

Nella nodded.

"We need to find food," Cade signed. *"I can make a trap."*

Nella shook her head. *"No need. Just make a fire."*

Cade looked at her. Nella knew something she wasn't telling him. *"Make a fire. I will be right back,"* Nella reiterated.

Cade wasn't sure if he should let his sister wander off, but she seemed to have a handle on whatever she was doing. He listened to her suggestion and began gathering dry sticks and rocks to make a little fire pit.

He kept his eye on her as he prepared their fire. Nella didn't walk too far away, heading to an outcropping of rocks within eyesight. She plucked some things from a dead-looking tree, moved to a different tree, and reached to collect more.

Cade finished preparing his tinder and used the firestarter from his scout jacket's shoulder pocket to light it. It crackled and glowed, adding heat to the warm night. Nella returned to their campfire with an armful of strange prickly fruits with bulbous ends and softly glowing fronds. She put them down next to the fire and smiled. *"Sunpears. Edible if we heat them. They will drip out the toxins. Just make sure to spit out the seeds."*

Cade smiled. Within a few minutes, they were roasting the desert sunpears over the fire, watching them sizzle and pop as the toxins boiled out from under the prickly skin. When they were ready to eat, the fronds uncurled and emitted a slight squeaking sound.

Cade carefully pulled them from the fire and placed them on a flat rock. Nella used her gloves to pull them apart. Inside was a meaty-looking fruit with small seeds sticking up from tiny strands of fiber. Nella collected the seeds and pocketed them.

"A memento for this journey," she signed.

Cade smiled, then rubbed his hands together. After cooling, they began to eat the sunpears. The fruits tasted sweet and bitter simultaneously and had a crunchy texture to them, like eating thick snow. They spat the seeds out into the dirt nearby as they munched. After hiking so far without eating, it tasted like the best thing Cade had ever eaten. With their stomachs full, Cade and Nella grew tired. It wasn't long before they drifted into sleep next to their campfire.

———————◆———————

Cade awakened.

The sun was just starting to rise, revealing the crimson sand and plateaus in greater detail now. Something was moving nearby. Cade sprang upright to see if the monster auk'gnell had caught up with them. He suddenly felt like an idiot not staying up to watch over them. Something bumped against him from behind, and Cade whirled to see what had approached.

It was a strange creature, four-legged like a nurn, but larger. It had a long snout with short fur, and its dark-red and brown coat was patterned to blend in with the rocks around them. The beast stood two and a half meters tall, waving a long, thin tail with a tuft of fur at the end. It stomped its two-toed hoofed foot against the dusty rock near Cade's lying position. The creature grunted as it snacked on the remains of the sunpears.

They call these creatures loamalons. They were peaceful beasts that roamed various biomes of Kamaria. They were known to have mild personalities and could be aloof or very social. This loamalon may have never seen humans before and clearly held no fear of Cade and Nella.

Cade nudged his sister. She slowly awakened, then jumped as she noticed the loamalon. They slowly moved away from the creature, hiding behind a boulder to watch the beast eat the rest of the sunpears.

The loamalon grunted and looked toward them, then began to move forward, plodding carefully. Nella scrambled around as Cade kept his eye on the approaching beast, wishing Nella would stop making so much noise. Although the creature was peaceful, that didn't mean that it wouldn't trample them if it became startled or confused. Nella found another sunpear next to their hiding position and lobbed the fruit over the boulder. The prickly fruit crashed onto the ground in front of the loamalon. The beast let out a combination of whinny and purr, then began to eat the fruit raw. It had large, flat teeth to bypass the fruit's prickles, and its stomach must not have minded the natural toxins that came from eating the fruit unheated. When it had finished, it grunted as if asking for more.

Cade began to form a crazy idea. He turned to Nella and signed, *"We should try and ride this thing."*

Nella shook her head.

Cade nodded.

As the two argued, the loamalon's snout moved around the boulder and nuzzled into Nella's shoulder.

"See, it wants us to," Cade signed.

The beast was persistent. It nuzzled its snout against Nella and purred. Nella sighed, then signed, *"Okay, I'll collect more fruit. You make a saddle."*

Cade clapped a hand against his knee and scurried away to find supplies.

As the sun rose higher, the heat came with it. Cade was sweating and removed his scout jacket. It was the first time he'd taken it off in days, and it felt great. His canary tattoo on his forearm glowed against his dark skin in the hot desert sun. He smiled when he discovered a secondary use for the jacket. Cade scavenged the area and managed to find enough fibrous plants to strip to make some ropes.

With everything ready, he approached Nella and the loamalon. The creature stood close to a meter taller than his sister. It lowered its head and smushed its wet nose into her hand as it gobbled up the fruit. Cade approached it from the side and showed Nella what he had in mind.

The scout jacket his father gave him had been converted into a makeshift saddle; the torso area would be the seat, and the sleeves would serve as a flap. Cade wove the fibrous plant ropes into the jacket so that he could secure it to the loamalon. A secondary rope would act as the reins, and Cade had used some pieces of stray bark he found lying in the sand to act as a bit.

Now, how to ride it? Cade had seen a few old movies with his dad that had people riding something called a horse on ancient Earth, but none had explained how to tame one.

I might be able to get the saddle onto it without it noticing too much, but the reins will be trouble. At least he had the advantage of surprise.

Cade tucked the saddle under his armpit and signed, *"Keep feeding it."*

Nella nodded and got another fruit ready. The loamalon chomped away at it, grunting and purring with delight. Cade gently placed the makeshift saddle on its back, and it turned to face him. For a moment, he thought it might kick him. Instead, the loamalon gave him a silly look of drunk appreciation and coughed. Cade exhaled as it turned to face Nella once more. He secured his jacket to the beast by tying the two intertwined ropes together on its underbelly.

Now comes the hard part.

Cade shook off his nerves as if getting ready to play basketball in front of an audience. He stretched and exhaled deeply, psyching himself up. The loamalon looked at him. Cade thought it chuckled, but it snorted and coughed again. He held up three fingers and let them drop in succession, *"Three . . . two . . . one . . ."*

Cade leaped onto the loamalon's back and slung the bit into its open mouth. The beast jumped backward in surprise, then began to shake as it tried to throw him off. Cade held on, grabbing tufts of fur on its neck for added grip. The loamalon growled and hopped around sporadically. It misjudged one hop and fell on its ass, scrambled, then flung itself in a circle. It roared, then darted toward a rock formation. Cade thought it might crash headfirst into the rock, but instead, the loamalon leaped into the air, catching itself on the rock, then springboarded off. It landed and began to rush across the red sand.

Cade gripped it tighter. He felt like his arms might give out from the strain. When he had reached his limit and his grip began to fail, the beast stopped. Cade didn't realize he was screaming until it got quiet.

The loamalon settled and purred once more.

Cade looked toward Nella. Her eyes were glowing bright emerald green, unlike anything he had ever seen before. When the loamalon had calmed, Nella looked toward Cade, and her eyes had returned to their normal state.

"What the fu—" Cade began to mutter out loud.

"You did it," Nella signed with a big smile on her face.

The loamalon turned to look at Cade out of the corner of its eye, then grunted. Nella took her jacket off and bundled the fruit together inside, wrapping it all up like a satchel. When she was ready, she reached her hand up to Cade.

He pulled her up. Cade wasn't sure what to make of Nella's eye trick. *Did I see that right?* He was being thrown around by an alien creature; maybe it had jumbled his perception. Cade decided he'd ask her later. For now, he had to focus on keeping the loamalon under control.

Now that they were both on the loamalon's back, Cade wasn't entirely sure what to do. He used his heel and tapped the sides of the creature's torso and said, "Yip," because he had seen it in an old cowboy film his dad made him watch, but nothing happened.

Nella raised her hand so that Cade could see it. She wiggled her fingers in the air for a moment, then she slapped the loamalon's butt hard. The beast roared and sprinted forward. Nella held on tightly to Cade as he pulled on the reins. He quickly began to figure out how to guide the loamalon left and right by pulling the reins the right way and leaning with his body. After a few minutes, he noticed his seating on the beast's back affected its movements. If he leaned back with the reins tightly in his hand, the creature began to slow down, even stop. If he shook them and leaned forward, it began to saunter ahead. He imagined that if Nella slapped it on the butt again, it would go full sprint.

After a few hours of trial and error, he began to get the hang of riding the loamalon, and they had made decent progress across the dry desert plains. Nella was continually feeding the creature, encouraging it to stay with them. It purred with delight as more time passed. After the travelers ventured deep into the vastness of the desert terrain, they came across a strange sight.

Cade and Nella dismounted the loamalon and tied it loosely to a dead tree. The beast did not seem to mind the rest and laid down, folding its hooves in front of itself like a nurn as it waited in the shade. They were about a half kilometer away from a deep pit, with floating boulders slowly rotating in midair. It reminded Cade of some of the asteroids he had worked on in the past, but seeing it here planetside didn't make any sense. It was as if someone had shut the gravity off in this one particular area. There was no strange sensation, or sound, or anything other than the rocks that defied physics. *What the Hells is this place?* Cade wondered. Nella climbed up a boulder to observe the anomaly while Cade made sure their new friend was comfortable.

"You need a name," Cade said to the loamalon, petting its neck with newfound affection. It purred as if agreeing. He remembered old holograms of loamalons in the archives; males had a long, wild mane, while females were sleek like this one. *What would Grandpa John name you?* Cade wondered. John Veston had used the ancient author Homer's *Odyssey* and *Iliad* for his naming conventions. The *Telemachus* and *Odysseus*, and even Homer the artificial intelligence, were products of that theme. Cade had read through the old book on his soothreader for a class project in his youth, skimming most of it for the exciting parts with the mythical monsters. He remembered the name Penelope, wife of the hero Odysseus and mother to Telemachus.

"It's a big name for you. Do you think you can handle it?" Cade whispered to the loamalon. "You look strong enough to me. Okay, Penelope it is. Thank you for helping us find our way home. We promise to feed you and keep you—" Cade wanted to promise to keep Penelope safe, but he knew that the monster auk'gnell could still be following them. He couldn't save Hrun'dah. *Will I let you down too?* He exhaled and said, "We promise to keep you as comfortable as possible if you stick with us."

Penelope purred.

Cade looked at Nella and noticed her eyes were glowing green again, this time with a wildfire intensity. There was no mistaking this now. He had been unsure what he saw the first time, but this was as clear as the floating boulders before them. Cade gave Penelope some fruit to eat and climbed up the boulder next to Nella. She was in some sort of trance state, her eyes so green they seemed to not contain pupils. Cade tapped her shoulder, but she didn't react.

"Shit, Nella?" Cade asked with panic in his voice, knowing she wouldn't hear him.

Cade remembered where he had seen this place before. This was the emergence hole of the Siren Nhymn. Inside the pit would be an underground palace made of alabaster stone. It was where Nhymn's sister, Sympha, had made her home for centuries. This place had been lost for decades. When scouts returned to this area after Denton and Eliana tried to warn Odysseus Command about the Siren, the sand and rocks had concealed the pit. Apparently, something had revealed it once more. *Why now?*

Nella began to smile with her mouth open.

Cade wanted to ask her what was happening, but he knew that asking out loud wouldn't work, and signing right now wouldn't help unless she was looking at him.

The ground under his feet began to rumble. Cade fought to keep his balance. Penelope perked her head up and twitched her ears.

Nella lifted her arms to her sides and watched the anomalous rocks twirl faster.

The rumbling stopped, and for a moment, it was quiet again. The floating rocks dropped back into the pit as if they suddenly remembered how gravity worked. Cade looked around to see if anything else had changed and realized even the slight breeze had ceased. It was eerily quiet, and his skin flecked with bumps.

"Nella?" Cade asked out loud, knowing it was futile, but he had to try something.

Nella clapped her hands together.

With an enormous bang, the pit erupted violently. Rocks and sand spewed into the air as if from a volcano. Cade fell backward at the sight of it, and Penelope whinnied and barked in fear. The debris from the explosions rained down from the sky, peppering them with small chunks of rock and sand, while more massive boulders collided with the ground ahead of them. Nella stood through it all, her arms raised. A beam of red light exploded from the pit, sending a wave across the desert. The light passed through Cade and Nella, seeping into their bodies and pulsing through their cores. The light passed over Penelope but not through her the same way it had the siblings. As fast as it came, it vanished. Suddenly it was a quiet, clear day in the desert again.

Nella dropped to her knees. Cade caught her before she could fall sideways off the boulder. "Hells!" Cade coughed the word. Loose debris still hung weightless in the air above the pit, like shards of broken planet. Cade felt the energy inside of him. It felt good—like his blood had gulped up a refreshing glass of ice-cold water on a hot summer day.

What do I do now? Cade wondered, looking down at his sister's unconscious body.

<GET UP.> A deep voice that was not his own echoed in Cade's mind.

Before Cade had time to question where the voice had come from, a red light began to radiate from inside the pit. Cade felt drawn to it, overcome with an odd sense of nostalgia and purpose. The pit called to him on a level he couldn't fully explain. It felt natural, yet was like nothing he had ever experienced, like remembering a dream he'd never had before. He carefully carried Nella over to Penelope, laid her on her back on a flat rock, and walked toward the glowing pit.

As he walked through the floating debris, Cade tapped a floating rock and watched it drift away from his hand. This was like fixing Old Cyrus back on the *Maulwurf*, except at a much larger and more unpredictable scale. As he got closer to the edge of the pit, he felt a tingling sensation run through his body, like someone had pressed ice cubes against his skin.

Cade peered into the pit.

Deep down, the planet was moving. It looked like the inside of a blender, rotating and shining with red energy. He jumped back as an electrical arc licked up from the bottom. A pulse of energy spread upward and out into the sky above, knocking away more loose debris.

Cade decided he had seen enough, worried that the pit might explode again while he was close to it. He hurried back over to Nella and quickly prepared Penelope to leave.

"Let's rest somewhere else. What do you think?" Cade asked the loamalon.

Penelope grunted in agreement.

He laid Nella carefully on Penelope's back, and within a few minutes, they were dashing across the plateaus once more. A canyon came into view, with a river flowing into it. Cade used it as a guide, keeping it on Penelope's right side. A large cliff wall with waterfalls lining its expanse was at the end of the vast canyon, with a jungle atop the upper ledge. Beyond that was the hook-shaped mountain called the Sharp Top. It would be a long journey yet, but there was hope they would see Odysseus City again with Penelope carrying them.

Cade looked over his shoulder. The glow from the pit faded as they got farther away, and the debris succumbed to gravity once more. Whatever that place was, it liked having Nella around.

TWENTY-TWO

A FEW NIGHTS EARLIER

L'ARN WAS ON HIS way to start a cascade of events that would change the planet forever. He arrived at the crashed human ship in the Unforgotten Garden as the sun was setting. The interstellar ship would have looked haunted had L'Arn not been a monster himself.

Strange vines grew on the outside of the ship. L'Arn had been an auk'nai tracker for decades, and after that, a wild auk'gnell living on the frontiers of Kamaria. He had encountered many variations of plant life, but these vines were new to him. An opening where the vines had been spilling out near the top of the ship gave him access to the broken interior.

"Follow my instructions, and follow them precisely," Auden said into L'Arn's ear.

L'Arn felt no need to answer the voice, nor did he want to. He was obeying, but he didn't understand why. His body did what Auden demanded despite his mind's protesting, a slave to a mysterious master. L'Arn had murdered his friend Nock'lu—*and for what?* L'Arn wondered who else he would have to kill for Auden before he could be made "perfect."

"Move forward, and make a right when you get in the hallway," Auden instructed.

L'Arn obeyed.

The ship was slanted heavily, but it didn't affect the auk'gnell monster. L'Arn used his metallic arm and sword to move through the ship. There was a fluidity to his movements as he grappled and swung through the metal plating of the hallways and broken terminals.

He moved around the corner and saw vines slithering out of an open door in the center of the hallway. Although there was no light inside the ship, L'Arn could see through the darkness with his augmented eyes. The vines approached L'Arn with a careful, measured pace.

"Go through the door at the end of the hallway," Auden said.

L'Arn moved, but as he passed the curious vines, they snatched his leg. L'Arn slashed the vines with his sword, cutting deep gashes in the wall with the backswing. A shriek came from the open door, and a massive, oil-slick hand reached toward him. L'Arn dodged, then slashed again. Another scream filled the hallway as some of the hand's fingers dropped to the floor. It recoiled back into the room, bringing its vines with it.

He moved toward the room at the end of the hall and pried the door open. It was dark inside, and contents from shelves and cabinets had been tossed during the crash. Items were cluttering toward the front of the room due to the slant in the ground.

"Toward the back of the room will be a bed," Auden said.

"What is a bed?" L'Arn asked. Auk'nai and auk'gnell used perches for sleeping. L'Arn was aware of humans, but he had never watched them go to sleep.

"Ugh, *stupid thing*. There will be a flat surface humans use for sleeping. Move to it."

L'Arn gracefully swung about the room until he was near the object Auden had described. There were two flat surfaces, one fixed to the slanted floor, another softer and thrown against a wall.

"Remember the devices I gave you? Take one out now," Auden said.

L'Arn reached into the hatch on his metal bicep and retrieved one of the puck-shaped devices. He turned it over in his hand, inspecting it. It was smooth and perfectly cylindrical. There were no buttons on the device, and it all appeared to be one solid piece of metal.

"Attach that to the floor next to the bed. It will bring power to this room," Auden said.

L'Arn pushed the puck onto the floor, and it clung tightly. There was a barely audible humming noise, and within a heartbeat, the lights had clicked on. Music began to play, something twangy, from a strange alien instrument. He had never heard human music before. L'Arn found it lacking when compared to the intricate Song of Kamaria.

"Let me do a few things," Auden said. L'Arn's mechanical arm pivoted involuntarily, and a long rod protruded from the underside of his wrist. The arm plunged the rod into the smooth surface of the puck, like slipping into a still pond. After a few moments of computerized micromovements, a panel on the floor opened and revealed a large metallic tube.

"I want you to remove that. We can carry John in it safely so he can help my friends."

L'Arn grabbed a handle on the tube's exterior and yanked it free without much effort. His augmentations allowed him to carry the weight of the pod without trouble. With pod in hand, L'Arn made his way back into the hall and out into the starlight. The creeping vine creatures did not disturb him, scared of what he might do if they tried.

Hours later, L'Arn arrived at the city of Odysseus. The sun had fully set, and the night was just beginning. The city was an alien place but had some familiar elements. Lights danced upon auk'nai-designed floating platforms accompanied the human skyscrapers. Strange vehicles moved like little skittering bugs. Humans and auk'nai littered the sidewalks.

Auden whispered in L'Arn's ear, "We need to find Dr. John Veston. To do that, we will need to search the city. Keep to the shadows, and stay out of sight."

L'Arn started with the eastern side of the city, landing on the top of a two-story building as quietly as he could. It felt like hunting nurn. It felt good. He moved silently across the rooftop, noticing the lights around him flicker and shut off. Wherever L'Arn went, darkness followed.

"Your cloak will conceal you from surveillance equipment and other sensors. As long as you don't run into any damn Tvashtar marines, they won't be able to detect you. Don't stay in one place too long," Auden said.

L'Arn looked at the strange cloak Auden had given him. It was buzzing at a low frequency. Something inside the metallic scales adorning the cloth worked hard to deactivate the area's lights and cameras. The effect spread in a large enough radius that it would be hard to pinpoint L'Arn's exact location in the rolling blackout he was causing.

"Maybe we can find a database. I'll let you know if I see one," Auden said.

L'Arn kept low and used the sides of buildings. He swung through the skyscrapers like a lemurbat in an urban jungle, flapping his wings only when he needed to clear large gaps. Even with the awkwardly large stasis pod, his movements were silent and snakelike. As he approached potential areas of interest, Auden would read the signs on the buildings and consider if they were worth searching.

"Wait, *there*!" Auden said. L'Arn's head involuntarily jerked in the direction Auden was implying. It was a three-story cylindrical building with flowers glowing all around it. "That's *him*! That's John Veston. It's been a long time, old *pal*."

The statue that stood outside the building had the visage of their target. John Veston was a tall man with a strong jawline and glasses. The figure held a familiar planet in one hand—Kamaria, L'Arn could tell from the shape of the land masses on its curved surface—and a separate alien planet in his other hand—*the human place, Earth?*

"Our answers might be inside. Let's take a closer look when the coast is clear," Auden said. L'Arn watched as some humans talked outside. A younger female with dark skin and long ebony hair and a young man with beige skin and short black hair were making hand signals at each other. An elderly woman in a wheelchair planted flowers and peeked over at them with a smile. After some time, the two women left in a vehicle, and the young man went inside the building. L'Arn waited for some time to make sure no one else entered.

Eventually, Auden gave the order. "Time to move."

L'Arn let himself glide down to the front of the building. As he landed, the lights inside the building flickered and died. L'Arn placed the large metal tube down near the statue and observed his target's visage closer. A small plaque at the base of the statue read, *Dedicated to the memory of Dr. Jonathan Veston, who brought us the stars.*

"Shit. This makes me think our friend John has perished somehow. Maybe he died in the *Telemachus* crash? Let's go inside and see if we can figure this out," Auden said.

L'Arn hid the stasis pod in a bush and moved inside. He remembered that the young man with short black hair was still around. With the pod gone, his movements became even more fluid. L'Arn slunk through dark hallways, using his enhanced night vision to search for anything of interest. Statues of animals were posed behind glass walls, and paintings displayed various elements of Kamarian life. L'Arn felt a fondness for the wilderness paintings and how he missed his life before Auden had come into it. He wished he had died when the desperate auk'gnell had attacked him in his nest.

The man with the short black hair walked through the halls, fumbling around in the darkness for a way to turn the lights back on. L'Arn moved around him easily enough. He made his way past the man and farther along the pitch-black corridor. "Wait, go back!" Auden hissed in his ear.

L'Arn moved back down the hallway, watching the young man

move away from the target room before entering. Inside, large model ships were on display. Immediately, L'Arn recognized the model that replicated the shipwreck he had just rummaged through. He stepped inside and concealed himself near a pedestal. L'Arn looked around, unsure of what made this room stand out among the others.

"Time for another booster. Grab another device from your kit. Make sure to hide it this time. We don't want any humans to know we were ever here," Auden said.

L'Arn reached into the bicep hatch of his mechanical arm and brought out another puck. He poked his head out into the hallway one last time to make sure the young man wasn't around. When the lights came on, he'd be exposed. L'Arn knew he had to make this quick.

He found a pedestal near the back corner of the room and moved it aside, placing the puck on the back. A heartbeat later, the lights flickered on. L'Arn jumped when the ghost of a man appeared floating above the pedestal where he had placed the puck. For a moment, he thought he had been discovered. The holographic man was displayed from the chest up. He looked dignified yet stern, with eyes that could make a mountain kneel. Below his holographic image read the words, *Captain Roelin Raike.*

"Not our guy," Auden said. "I'm going to download all the data from this building. You need to remain concealed until I finish. If you were perfect, the way I wanted you to be for this task, this would take no time at all. But in your imperfect state, we need to wait, like animals."

L'Arn heard footsteps approaching. The lights had attracted the young man to the room. L'Arn darted behind the closest display he could find—a model of how the colony appeared when humans had first landed on Kamaria.

The young man walked into the room, scratching the back of his head. He looked down at his soothreader and watched it reactivate as he came closer to L'Arn's concealed booster. He made some hand gestures, and his soothreader asked out loud in a synthetic voice, *"Hello? Is someone there?"*

He was answered by the displays as they began to activate their audio narrations. The young man's soothreader erupted with various holographic people, each a different color of the rainbow, making hand gestures the way he had. The man jolted in shock, then laughed. He made a gesture over his soothreader and saw the holographic people fade away. He shook his head and looked at his soothreader, flicking his hand over it and watching the outside hallway. His back was turned to L'Arn.

"Maybe we should kill him," Auden said.

L'Arn looked down and noticed his sword was already in his hand. He didn't remember reaching for the blade. It had just appeared.

The young man looked toward the ceiling lights, visible confusion plastered across his face. L'Arn gripped the sword tighter. Just as he was about to dispatch the unsuspecting victim, the young man walked out of the room.

L'Arn sighed.

A few moments later, Auden said, "Alright, I got a heading. Our friend John is no longer the target. We're going to have to improvise. Get back outside, and we'll consider our options."

L'Arn began to move to the pedestal with Captain Roelin Raike when Auden stopped him. "Leave the puck. I can siphon more data. Just make sure it's hidden." He moved the pedestal back against the wall, leaving only a little room to allow the puck to spin freely. Shortly after, L'Arn slithered outside and retrieved the stasis pod. He stood before the statue of John and listened to Auden's report.

Auden said, "So, John *is* dead. His daughter still lives on the planet, and not far from here. She might know how to help my friends just as well as her dad. It's a long shot, but it's all we got. I did some digging. Eliana married some *nobody* named Denton Castus, and they had two kids. So, we're now looking for Dr. Eliana *Castus.*"

"Her name changed?" L'Arn asked.

"Yes, it's a weird human thing. A side effect of marriage sometimes. I traced her work profile to a home on the outskirts of the city. That's our next move. Fly south, past the buildings, and toward the forest. A road will lead us to her home."

L'Arn nodded.

There was a shuffling of feet on the path behind him.

L'Arn's skin went cold. He grabbed the pod and vaulted into the sky as quickly as he could. He looked back briefly to see the young man had almost reached out and touched him. How that person could move as silently as an auk'gnell hunter, L'Arn was unsure.

"Idiot!" Auden shouted into his ear. "You left a witness. You better hope he didn't see too much, or else the humans will be on to us!"

L'Arn felt cold, but he wasn't sure why. *What was it Auden was so afraid of? Why was it so important that the humans didn't find him?* L'Arn had seen humans plenty of times in the early days when he still belonged to the Song of Apusticus. They didn't look like conquerors to him. If anything, the robotic form of Auden looked more dangerous than any human he had ever seen.

Why are you so afraid?

———————◆———————

It didn't take long to find the Castus home outside the city. L'Arn hoped to enter the house and find sleeping humans on those weird bed-things he had seen earlier on the *Telemachus*, but a vehicle pulled up. No one exited the vehicle at first, and it began to pulse with light and sound, like a timer ticking down. Eventually, a man pulled himself out of the back door of the car with great effort. A woman came out of the house and approached him, just as the man slumped down to one knee.

"I think that's Eliana Castus. Don't fuck this up," Auden said.

The humans retreated back inside. After a moment, L'Arn made his move. He had to act quickly, unsure if the young man at the previous site had alerted anyone. This home was secluded enough. He could deal with anyone inside and get away before any problems arose.

L'Arn coasted to the front yard of the home and slammed the pod upright in the ground. He moved toward the front door without stopping and used his metallic arm to push it open with ease, breaking the locks and knocking the frame loose. It was a quick movement that produced a lot of noise.

"Getting sloppy, L'Arn," Auden said in his ear.

L'Arn wanted to silence Auden but didn't waste the energy. He looked around. The lights had shut off as he entered. A half-conscious male was lying on the couch near the front door, moaning and covering his eyes with his arm—the man from the vehicle.

Injured? Drunk? He was unsure.

"Are you John Veston's child?" L'Arn asked.

"What? Who the—" the man mumbled, his injuries pushing him near a blackout. "Who—who are you?"

Auden said, "Not *Eliana*. But I could have told you that."

L'Arn heard a gasp and turned. The woman dropped a first aid kit, her eyes wide in horror. L'Arn moved toward her, like a lobersnake seeking a ruemouse. He asked again, "Are you John Veston's child?"

"We're his grandkids," the man weakly said, struggling to sit up on the couch. "Wait, what's going on?" He began to stand.

L'Arn didn't realize he was holding the woman above the ground, her feet dangling in the air. The situation was deteriorating quickly. If Auden thought John's daughter was a good fit, why not two of his grandkids?

"I'll take what we can get. We're out of time," Auden said.

L'Arn rotated and deployed his mechanical claw at the injured man. The claw hit him in the neck and clamped down. He retracted the tether and brought the man closer, then dragged the grandchildren outside into the snow toward the pod.

Will they both fit? L'Arn wondered.

"Take one and kill the other. I vote for the woman," Auden said.

L'Arn thought about it. If he twisted his hand the right way, he could dispatch the injured man and stuff the woman into the pod without a problem. His mind flashed to Nock'lu, remembering how it felt to kill his friend.

"I'm taking both," L'Arn said.

"Have it your way. Might I suggest this little trick? It worked well on humans in the past." Against L'Arn's will, his mechanical arm brought the injured man close to his face, and then there was a bright flash. The man went slack in his grip. Auden said, "Stuff him in."

L'Arn shoved the unconscious man into the pod, then turned to the woman. She screamed in horror, so loud it made L'Arn flinch. He flashed her with his augmented eyes and held her as she went slack in his hand. L'Arn pushed her into the pod, glad to see he had just enough room to close the door around them without crushing the humans.

"They better be worth it," Auden said. "Get back here, and we'll see if they can help us."

———— • ————

The night air brushed against L'Arn's feathers as he flew back across the continent to the eastern shores. L'Arn allowed the pod to dangle away from his body, using his mechanical arm's metal claw as a tow rope. With the grandchildren of Dr. John Veston locked away inside the stolen stasis pod, L'Arn's mission had been semi-successful. It was up to the humans locked in the tube to do their part now. As far as L'Arn was concerned, he had finished the job. He wanted his freedom back, and he didn't give a damn about Auden's lust for perfection.

Snow began to fill L'Arn's vision. The Ember-Lit Forest trees below him added their blue flakes of wild light to the hazy night. Usually, L'Arn would land and rest until morning, but he had a mission to complete.

There was a loud bang. L'Arn looked down to see the metal pod's lid fly off into the night and crash to the snow below. It looked like one of the hostages might fall out through the opening, but she was pulled back inside. The injured man seemed to have shaken off Auden's flash trick and was now working against L'Arn.

Before L'Arn could pull the pod close and reach inside, a bright light filled his vision. He felt something hit his chest so hard it pushed all the air out of his lungs. He couldn't fly, and they began to freefall into the Ember-Lit Forest below. L'Arn felt his feathers start to smolder and saw flames bursting over him. He shrieked in pain, silenced only for a moment as he collided with the ground next to the metal pod. An explosion of snow and dirt blew into the air with the impact.

L'Arn's mechanical arm had taken most of the impact, and he recovered enough to sit up. He saw the pod rolling toward him. L'Arn tried desperately to reach into the pod with his unaltered arm and grab the woman inside, ignoring the man altogether, but he wasn't fast enough. Before L'Arn's hand could reach her, the pod had rolled over his body and fell off the ledge to his side.

L'Arn felt pain everywhere, and his mechanical arm fizzed and popped. He had been partially crushed by the pod. A muffled bang came from below as the pod impacted against the lower forest floor beyond the ledge. L'Arn grunted, grinding his beak together as he struggled to pull himself to the ledge with his unaltered arm. He felt like his body weighed ten tons as he dragged himself slowly through the snow. Sparks flew from his augmentations, and trace amounts of smoke began to pour from any open space in the machinery that made up his broken body.

L'Arn peered over the cliff ledge in time to see the man drag the woman from the pod. *Are his eyes glowing blue?* L'Arn's vision was entirely glitched. He coughed. With immense effort, he pulled himself onto his knees and kneeled in the snow. He let out a loud, shrieking birdcall as his hostages fled into the forest.

Mission failed.

He was ready to give up. L'Arn considered curling up in the snow and allowing death to overtake him. Instead, he breathed deeply and checked his augmented arm. His vision flickered as the damage began to affect the mechanisms in his eyes. His mechanical arm was a dead weight, and he couldn't move it. Indeed, he would die.

"What have you . . . *L'Arn!* . . . Can you hear—Idiot!" Auden's voice came through a fragmented speaker in L'Arn's ear. "Device! Use the . . . *Damn it!*" Auden shouted.

L'Arn huffed weakly and swung his hand over to the compartment on the bicep of his mechanical arm. He opened it, and his last device jumped out and landed in his lap. The device began to hum loudly. L'Arn felt like he might pass out. His vision became blurry. He felt a sharp pain in his flesh and feathered arm, and suddenly, his vision cleared up. He looked down at the puck and noticed it was cracked in half. Long tentacles were protruding from it, each end barbed with a different tool. One of the tentacles had injected L'Arn with something, while the others began work on his mechanical parts. Sparks flew as one tentacle welded. Another wrenched pieces together. A third tentacle removed broken useless bits and brought them into the device as if eating them.

"What . . ." L'Arn was still too weak to form complete sentences. One of the tentacles came up to L'Arn's face and began repairing his eyes and head.

"Hold . . . still . . . *idiot* . . ." Auden's voice became more precise over time. L'Arn heard something click into place, then his vision went black for a moment before slowly coming back.

"It's not perfect . . . It will do," Auden said.

"What is this?" L'Arn asked, his voice quiet and labored.

"I'm cannibalizing this unit to fix you. It will have to be enough until you come back."

L'Arn felt his arm twitch, and then it twisted and flexed, testing its limits. As the device traded L'Arn's broken pieces for its own internal hardware, it began to twitch and fidget with errors.

Eventually, L'Arn was able to stand, with nearly complete control of his arm. His vision still flickered and popped, but it was workable.

"Leave the device. It's useless now," Auden said.

L'Arn turned to the east and took a step forward.

"What are you doing?" Auden asked.

"Coming back—*back*—back so you can fix me," L'Arn answered, his voice fragmented as his head twitched and sparked.

"Not without those humans, you aren't! Get out there and find them." Auden's voice was laced with acrimony.

L'Arn looked out over the Ember-Lit Forest. He wanted to be done with this errand. He had no business with John Veston or his grandchildren. He didn't know Auden's friends and didn't care if they rotted in the ocean. L'Arn wanted to go back to his nest and sit in the trees.

Yet, L'Arn obeyed. He used his mechanical claw as a grappling hook and lowered himself from the ledge. From there, he followed the humans as best he could. His strength was returning with each step, and although he couldn't fly, he could still track them on foot.

L'Arn began to hunt.

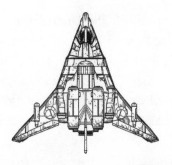

TWENTY-THREE

PRESENT DAY

ELIANA EMERGED FROM YET another cave in the Ember-Lit Forest without her children. The longer they trudged around, the more snow concealed the fate of Nella and Cade. It had been four days since they went missing. Although the team had covered a wide area around the admiral's stasis pod, they were no closer to figuring out where their missing people had gone.

What are we even looking for at this point? Eliana thought with a dread that raced through her heart. *Was it too late for Nella and Cade? Had the thing that kidnapped them found them once more and brought them back to wherever it was going? And the Undriel devices we keep finding, what does this mean for Kamaria?*

She had to keep her hope alive that she would find her children. Eliana remembered the deep despair she felt after her father was murdered and Roelin fled the colony. It was a mystery that haunted her for four years. She refused the feel that way again. If they could find Roelin when all the odds were against them, then they could find her children.

They had to.

The other problem—if the Undriel had made their way to Kamaria, there would be no escaping them this time. The *Telemachus* had been their only life raft in the past, and it now lay as a wreck in the Unforgotten Garden. The *Odysseus* spacecraft was sent away shortly after, with Nhymn inside. The *Infinite Aria* was still years away from completion. This paradise planet suddenly felt inescapable.

Faye Raike's voice piped in over the comm channel, "Everyone, meet back at the *Rogers*. Homer found something." Eliana moved through the snow back to the pod, hoping that this time, finally, they would find Cade and Nella.

A small disc-shaped platform was hovering above the snow near the pod, with Denton standing next to it. Eliana looked him in the eyes and shook her head. Denton shook his head too. This was how they reported that they hadn't found any clues. The longer this search continued, the less they spoke to each other. It was too hard to pretend it was going to be okay. It was too hard to look each other in the eye and not break into tears. It was too hard to not see the visage of their missing children in each other's faces.

They silently stood side by side on the disc, and it floated upward toward the access ramp of the *Rogers*. The ship hovered just above the trees. Eliana and Denton stepped off the disc and walked into the ship to see everyone waiting in the cargo bay.

Jess nodded to them as they walked in. Faye was sitting on the hood of the *Tiger* rover, tapping her hand against its frame. Talulo held the feathers Eliana wanted him to study, eyeing them closely. Homer had a holographic display hovering above a table. The jumping Undriel disc had a small metallic tentacle protruding from its side. Instead of jumping with errors, it was now spinning in circles like a canoe with one paddle.

Homer said, "We have studied the clues we found here. And we may have come up with a lead." They gestured to Talulo, who stepped forward and held the feathers up for everyone to see.

"Talulo can hear the song in these feathers. It is quiet but familiar. Talulo knew the one who had these," the auk'nai said. "These belonged to one called L'Arn. L'Arn abandoned the Song of Apusticus just before the final battle with the Siren to become an auk'gnell of the wild. L'Arn knew Nock'lu."

"We believe L'Arn may be responsible for the kidnapping and the murder of the Daunoren. These feathers were found near the admiral's pod, which was stolen from the *Telemachus*—where we found slices that matched the same unique blade density that killed the Daunoren. All link L'Arn to these events. His connection to Nock'lu also does not seem coincidental," Homer said flatly.

"Did L'Arn kill the Daunoren to stop us from being able to past-track him?" Faye asked. "Without the Daunoren, the auk'nai lose some of their powers, right?"

Talulo cooed, "It is possible. Talulo cannot think of a different motive for L'Arn. Whatever L'Arn is doing, L'Arn can do it far easier without our Daunoren." Talulo hung his head, remembering the sight of his decapitated god.

"I've never heard of L'Arn before," Eliana said. "Does any of this help us find Cade and Nella?" she asked, with pain in her voice, knowing the answer was *no*.

Denton put a hand on her shoulder, and she gripped it.

"That is not all we have found," Homer said. They gestured to the mysterious puck device on the table. "I have been examining this object. It is unlike anything I have previously detected on many levels. Still, I can conclude that this object has at least originated with Undriel technology."

Jess stepped forward, her eyes on the puck-shaped device. "Then we need to get it off the ship."

"I don't believe it can harm us. I have taken precautions—" Homer was interrupted when Jess grabbed the puck's tentacle and began to walk back toward the access ramp.

"Sergeant!" Faye tried to stop Jess but was shoved aside.

Jess hurled the puck out the access ramp and into the trees, watching it descend to make sure it didn't fly back up somehow.

"It is alright," Homer said, "I have created a digital replica of the device in my database by combining the scan data with the device we found on the *Telemachus*. I have had enough time with it to pull all the information I need."

"You all don't seem to understand," Jess said, turning back toward the others as the access ramp closed behind her. "The Undriel always have a hidden trick. Nothing they do is ever just on the surface. That thing could have been siphoning data from the ship, or worse, from Homer."

Denton looked to Homer. "Ah shit, is that true?"

Homer looked at Jess and said, "Sergeant, my programming allows me to recognize if I had been compromised. In the event of an external connection—whether wireless or hardline—I would automatically shut down and purge my databases."

"You said it yourself," Faye said. "Although this thing may have been based on Undriel tech, it still is nothing like previous objects found. Maybe this is an auk'gnell thing. Maybe L'Arn could have gotten a hold of some Undriel data or something."

"There is *always* a trick," Jess reiterated, ignoring the attempts to deflect the truth about the device's Undriel origins.

"Luckily, we can see who made this for ourselves," Homer said. "The device had trace elements of rare algae that can only be found on the Howling Shore on the eastern edge of this continent. Which lines up with the path L'Arn was taking from the city. If we go to the Howling Shore, we may be able to find Nella and Cade."

Eliana felt her heart surge with warmth, and her skin tickled up her back to the base of her hairline. She inhaled and looked to Denton, who was beginning to form a smile. *See, there is hope.*

Talulo added, "The *Rogers* has probes. Talulo can leave one here in case Cade and Nella return. Cade and Nella can even talk to the probe directly if they see it."

She turned to the group and said, "Okay, we'll leave a probe and head to the Howling Shore. It's the best lead we have."

———◆———

After a few hours of flying, the *Rogers* landed on the grassy hills near the Howling Shore. A small cliff covered in tall, wavy orange grass led to a beach with interspersed black rocks and crashing ruby waves. The water was tinted a pinkish red, filled with the rare algae that had led the scouts to this place. The coast was long, and the red waves spanned its entirety, providing an immense search area.

We have to be getting close, Denton told himself. *If they went beyond the coastline, there would be no way to track them across the ocean. Please let them be here.*

Eliana had withdrawn into herself during the search. In their shared pain, they had somewhat grown apart, like injured animals hiding to conceal their wounds. Denton had wanted to make Eliana's life happier, and for a long time, he'd been successful. They had their son, Cade, and he so full of love and energy. There was a little sadness when they discovered their newborn daughter, Nella. would never hear their voices. Still, the Castus family was strong and intelligent. *Always keep an open mind* was one of the Scout Program mottos. They learned Sol-Sign. By adapting, they discovered a beautiful language and found happiness once more.

Denton and Eliana watched their children grow into adults. Although Cade had left Kid Scouts behind, he'd pursued an important and exciting career in space. With their son working toward a job on the *Infinite Aria,* Denton and Eliana were filled with nostalgic pride. Cade was furthering the dreams of John Veston while also pursuing his own path, as Denton had. When Cade announced he was getting a promotion to crew leader, it felt just like the moment Denton heard he'd be an official scout. Cade was on his own bright path, and with good friends to be there with him when his family couldn't. Zephyr had become an asset in this search for their children. With friends like her, Cade was in good company.

Nella had found a life of peace, beauty, and brilliance as a botanist working with Marie Viray. Denton looked up to his daughter. She never let the world hold her back. She had this super-analytical mind, and Denton believed that any problem she came across, she'd overcome. She was still young, but already he knew she was destined for extraordinary things. Nella cared for people, much the way her mother did. Where Eliana used medical assets to help people, Nella helped her community. She organized programs for the Deaf Community of Odysseus City and taught Sol-Sign to children and their families through classes held at the archives. Denton imagined that one day she might even pursue a career in political leadership. Maybe Nella would be running Odysseus City at some point. Her future could branch into any path she chose, and he'd be proud of any choice she made.

But now, their children were missing. Cade and Nella's safety was in limbo. Every day that passed had eaten away at the hope Eliana and Denton shared at the beginning of the search. They clutched the last remaining straws they had left.

They had to find them here on the shore. They had to.

"Are we ready to head out?" Jess asked the crew. She was strapped to her teeth in Tvashtar combat gear and double-checking all of her weapons before leaving, prepared to meet the old enemy in battle once more if they should show themselves.

The team had buckled into their seats in the *Tiger* rover. Denton turned to the others and checked to make sure they were prepared. Faye, Jess, Homer, and Eliana nodded back to him. No one knew how long they would be searching the shore. It was a big continent. They only knew the mysterious Undriel puck had been here at some point. Whether it was during its creation or maybe passing by, they couldn't be sure. With a lack of other leads, this was all they had left.

"Alright, let's head out," Eliana said.

Denton started the collider engine of the *Tiger* and drove down the ramp of the *Rogers*. It was windy outside, and a light rain buffeted against the windscreen. The *Tiger* was equipped with scanners similar to those on the *Rogers*, and Homer could tap into their readings remotely. Talulo remained on the *Rogers*, scanning the coast in the opposite direction.

It was quiet in the rover as they moved across the grassy orange hills, keeping the ocean on their left side. They could see Kamarian seabirds flying in the rain through their windscreen, some diving into the red sea for food.

"Homer, you seeing anything yet?" Eliana asked.

"So far nothing I would consider unusual," Homer said. "If our rover suddenly ceased functioning, that would be a clear sign of an Undriel presence. The *Tiger* was not designed to combat Undriel electronic chaffing effects."

"Well, when I helped build the damn thing, I never expected them to show back up," Denton said. He'd used his scouting and mechanical engineering knowledge to bring the *Tiger* to the Scout Program. "Same goes for you, Homer. I think your body will shut down if we get too close. Regardless of your network being hacked or not."

"That might be a good thing," Jess said.

"Sounds like you're our canary, Homer," Faye said with a worried smile.

Hours had passed, without any signs of the origin of the Undriel puck device. Eliana put a hand on Denton's shoulder. "How about we get out and search on foot for a little bit."

"Yeah, it'll be good to stretch my legs," Faye said.

Denton brought the rover to a stop and placed it in park. They opened the doors and stepped out into the misty rain. The sound of the waves crashing against the rocks and sand beyond the grassy cliff filled the air. The wind pushed at them, like a bully looking for a fight. Homer began scanning the area with various tools built into their robotic human frame while the others took a breather.

Jess was on high alert in full combat gear. On a standard scout, she would keep her assault rifle slung to her back, referring only to her collider pistol as a deterrent if there were any dangerous beasts brave enough to get too close. Since the battle with Nhymn, Jess had seldom fired either weapon. The incident on the *Telemachus* wreck had been the first time in years. Today, she kept her assault rifle in her hands. The Undriel could be around, and her old enemy was not going to sneak up on her this time. She had lost dear ones to the nightmare machines back in the Sol System, and she would do her best to make sure there would be no other victims.

Faye had also fought the Undriel in the past, alongside her husband, Roelin Raike. They had flown an Undertaker-class warfighter called the *Astraeus* into many sorties and had been rare survivors of an encounter with an Undriel Reaper. She had been through a lot since the days of the Undriel War. Her husband had been possessed by Nhymn and forced to commit atrocities. She had thought he died in the wilderness, but then Roelin eventually returned to Faye years later, only to die again on a battlefield in the Siren's mind. His last actions had stopped Nhymn from annihilating humanity. Faye had fought in that battle as well, from the pilot's seat of a Matador starfighter. But ever since that day, the fight had left her. She felt invincible in a way that a person who had gone through so much trauma could only feel. In some ways, Faye had already died, so nothing could hurt her ever again. The thought of the Undriel coming back to haunt them once more was just another horrible thing she'd have to deal with.

Eliana stood in the rain and eyed the coast, her back to the rest of the team. Denton approached her side but gave her some space. He knew she didn't want to be coddled, or hugged, or given sweet empty words of hope. She stood there and watched the red waves crash against the rocks below.

"It keeps happening," Eliana said. "The second we get comfortable, there's another curveball thrown at us. We're cursed."

Denton lowered his head. He didn't know what to say.

"I don't know where we go from here," Eliana said. Her eyes hadn't moved from the waves. "If the kids aren't here . . ."

"It's like Kamaria swallowed them up," Denton said. It was similar to something he heard Eliana say about finding Roelin Raike.

"I remember, a long time ago, you said I didn't know how you felt. How there was nothing I could say to make you feel better. You felt hopeless, searching for Roelin in a world full of mysteries. And here we are again, searching."

Eliana looked at Denton, her eyes glossy, threatening tears.

"This planet doesn't care about us. It ignores our wills and hopes. Kamaria still revolves whether we live or die. The solution isn't going to come from the planet. It's going to come from us." Denton met her eyes. "When we searched for Roelin, it took auk'nai past tracking and a lot of luck to stumble on a good lead. But we still found him, four years after he had gone missing, surviving in the woods like some sort of prisoner hermit. We got lucky, and we had to cheat, but we found him."

"We might *not* find our kids," Eliana said. A tear rolled down her cheek and mixed with the salty air from the ocean. The truth she never wanted to admit had found its way out into the open.

Denton looked back at the ground. He was stabbed in the heart by her words, the blade sharpened with truth. The reality that they might not ever find Cade and Nella was now spoken out loud. And worst of all, she might be right.

They watched the waves. The ocean relentlessly crashed against the coast. Again and again, the waves hit. No matter how many times the sea hit the beach, the coast remained. It may have corroded over time, shrunk against itself in places, but the shore always remained.

Denton didn't feel as strong as the shore. He felt like the wind could knock him onto his back, and he wouldn't have the strength to ever stand again.

"Hey . . ." A voice came through on both of their soothreaders. It was George Tanaka, calling from Telemachus Outpost. "Hey, can you hear me?"

Denton turned away from the ocean while Eliana remained still. Denton swallowed back the impending panic attack to handle the call. "Yeah, what's up?"

"We picked up something strange. I'm not sure if it's related to

Cade and Nella, but it might be worth checking out," George said, his voice crackled slightly.

"We're open to ideas," Denton replied, looking over his shoulder at Eliana.

"In the Starving Sands, there was some sort of anomalous event," George said. "It's where Sympha's underground palace was. Our satellites show the ground shifted somehow. We compared it to the last time we imaged the area, and there is a large difference."

George sent the satellite images to Denton's soothreader, and it verified his statement. The before picture looked like a flat desert, the pit that Nhymn had emerged from decades ago filled in with sand. In the after photo, there was an apparent radius of debris around a gaping hole.

"That can't be good," Denton whispered. "Wait a minute, let me check something."

He gestured over his soothreader, pulling the afterimage of the exploded pit to the side and bringing up a map of the continent next to it. He marked where the hole was and where the admiral's pod had been found—Cade and Nella's last known location. He created a line between the pit and the pod and noticed it was a relatively straight path. There were some mountainous regions in the way. It would have been strenuous, but it was a possible hike for healthy people—in theory. Denton then traced the line from the pit to Odysseus City, and sure enough, it continued to be a relatively straight path.

"Can you see this, George?" Denton asked and pushed the map he made back to George with a gesture.

"Yes, I got it here. That looks pretty solid!" George said with enthusiasm.

"It might be worth checking out. We're having no joy over here on the shore. Let me run this data past the team and come up with a plan," Denton said.

"Let us know what you are thinking. I have some marines back here at the outpost. If you need them, I will ask them nicely," George said.

Denton thought of Private Ken Simmons. During the *Telemachus* search, the young marine had been killed, and Denton was unsure if he could risk more lives to find his children. At the same time, the thought of the Undriel lurking around, and maybe another Siren rearing its head, made Denton think it would be foolish not to bring more firepower.

"Elly—" Denton said.

"I heard," Eliana sighed and brushed her palm against her eye. She turned to him finally, but Denton still didn't see any hope on her face. She shook her head. "I don't know. It might be nothing. We didn't find anything suggesting they went that way."

"We also didn't find anything saying they *didn't*," Denton said.

"I just don't think it's reliable enough to go back west to investigate. We might be close here."

Denton thought for a moment. She was right—this could be something completely different. Either way, anomalies on Kamaria usually led to planet-changing events. If the Undriel were out there, maybe they found a way to reactivate whatever project Sympha had been working on in the underground palace. Simultaneously, the possibility of his children heading west toward Odysseus City instead of being taken farther east toward the Howling Shore was tantalizing. One theory suggested they had successfully escaped their pursuer and were heading home. The other theory suggested their pursuer found them again and brought them to its destination. Denton was an optimist by nature, and he wanted to run with the former theory instead of the latter.

"We can split up the team," Denton suggested. "You keep the *Tiger* here and stay with Homer, Faye, and Jess. Talulo and I will take the *Rogers* and check out the Siren Pit in the Starving Sands. We'll get a few marines from the Telemachus Outpost to help us. If we end up finding nothing, we'll come back and keep searching here."

Eliana winced. Denton knew what he was suggesting meant he would be leaving her side. Although they had grown distant, they were still physically close during the entire search. Taking that last element away meant they would have to face reality alone. But they had to change tactics. The current strategies weren't working.

"You might be right." She sighed, then nodded. "Alright, check it out. We'll keep scanning the shore. If the Siren Pit turns out to be nothing, bring the marines back here with you. They can make this search easier if you don't find Nella and Cade there."

"I will," Denton said.

Eliana frowned at him and nodded. She moved toward him and hugged him tightly. He returned her embrace equally. They held each other as if being pulled apart by a fierce and greedy dragon.

"We're going to find them. We will. We can't give up hope," Denton whispered into Eliana's ear.

She inhaled sharply through her nose and nodded silently. Eventually, Eliana released Denton and brought her soothreader up to her face. "Okay, everyone, listen up. We have a new plan."

TWENTY-FOUR

ONE DAY AGO

L'ARN HAD DONE IT again. Before him, lying on the beach, was another dead auk'gnell. He could hear the Song of the Dead filling the air with its haunting tune. This one had come from the North to live in the eastern regions of the continent. L'Arn knew a life like that once, living off the fruits of the land—freedom unlike any other.

The colossal timbermen paraded across the vast lake, away from the beach. They would march through the water for kilometers until they reached the shore on the other side, where they could then change direction and head north, bypassing the Starving Sands beyond.

"You lost them again!" Auden scolded, like an annoying insect buzzing around L'Arn's ear. The monster auk'gnell searched but couldn't find the humans. He was alone with a corpse, with the Song of the Dead in the air. But he did find something.

L'Arn's augmented eyes could see it sticking out from the sashes on the dead auk'gnell before him. He moved forward toward the body, trying to ignore her broken, bloody face and feeling the pain of his injuries with every step. He realized his luck. This auk'gnell was carrying a quickening salve and healing elixirs. She had been treating injuries not too different than the wounds L'Arn had endured. They wouldn't do her much good now.

L'Arn's mechanical hand flicked down into the sashes and retrieved the vials of salve. He opened them and rubbed them on his injured wings, feeling the rush of relief that followed the initial sting. He fell to his knees, facing the lake.

"They got away." Auden spat the words out.

"The humans—*HUMANS*—humans . . ." L'Arn slapped his mechanical hand against the back of his head and felt something click into place. He flexed his beak and began speaking again. This time his voice remained steady. He whispered, "The humans will be heading back to their city. They had help from this auk'gnell. Her Dead Song sings a tale of aid. She tells me now where they will go," L'Arn said, breathing deeply, allowing the salve to cycle through his blood.

"I'm surprised she doesn't keep it a secret. You killed her," Auden said.

"Auk'gnell do not lie, in life or death. The dead have no allegiances," L'Arn said.

"Well, what are you waiting for? Go get them and bring them back."

"I need time to heal."

"Stupid, imperfect thing," Auden hissed. "Fine, take all the time you need. We only have *all the other humans* to worry about! They will be knocking on our door any minute."

L'Arn hated Auden, but strangely, he still wanted to please him. It was as if fetching the lost prey for Auden would prove that he was more perfect than Auden gave him credit for. His spite made him want to succeed if only to throw it in Auden's face. It was a challenge, and it was a hunt. L'Arn liked hunting.

"I will leave as soon as I am able," L'Arn said.

TWENTY-FIVE

PRESENT DAY

NELLA SLOWLY REGAINED CONSCIOUSNESS. She was riding on the back of the loamalon, Cade guiding the beast. Their pace was a casual, slow walk. She felt tingles running through her body as if a door was opened in her heart and the air was rushing inside. *Where are we?*

The area was mainly desolate crimson rock, with plateaus and deep, winding canyons. *Right, we're in the Starving Sands.* In the distance, there was a cliff wall with waterfalls flowing from above. The jungle that contained the Sharp Top Mountain was on the higher ledge. *The Tangle Maze.* It was a place she remembered from stories her parents had told her about the days of Nhymn.

Nella tugged on Cade's sleeve, and he looked over his shoulder at her. He brought the loamalon to a halt and hopped off her sturdy flank to help Nella down. *"Are you okay?"* Cade signed, then handed her the flask of water.

After a big gulp from the flask, she felt a dull ache in her head and tested her jaw. She signed, *"I feel like I had my head ripped off."*

Cade inspected her and nodded. *"Nope, still on."*

She smiled and laughed weakly.

It was late afternoon, and within the next hour or so, the sun would be setting. Cade was petting the loamalon, and the beast enjoyed it, purring with delight as he ran his fingers through its short, fine hair. He removed the bit from its mouth and fed a sunpear to it. *"Penelope was getting hungry,"* Cade signed.

"Is that her name?" Nella reached out to pet the loamalon.

Cade nodded. *"What do you remember?"*

Nella thought for a moment. She remembered seeing the floating rocks from the back of the loamalon. And as they got closer, her memory seemed to get hazy. *There was something that happened, but what was it?*

"Floating rocks?" Nella signed, and shrugged, her face taut with deep thinking.

She took a seat on a boulder. Cade sat facing her as he explained the explosion and the lights in the pit. Then he signed, *"Your eyes were glowing green."*

Glowing green? Nella's eyes were naturally green like her father's—but *glowing*?

Then she remembered. *"Your eyes were glowing blue before."*

Cade looked puzzled. He scrunched his eyebrows together and frowned as he tried to process it. His lips implied that he said a few things to himself out loud that Nella couldn't hear. Cade had naturally blue eyes, so whatever the glow was, it only amplified their natural iris color.

"Hrun'dah said we were more special than we know," Cade signed. *"There's something we don't understand yet. Something we are missing."*

Nella somberly remembered their auk'gnell companion and played with the bracelet Hrun'dah had given her. It contained a concealed skinning knife, and at the moment, it was their only weapon. Nella tried to remember what happened right before she passed out. Whatever it was, it sat right on the edge of her memory. It was infuriatingly close, but just out of reach.

Cade stood up and walked over to a grouping of trees nearby. Two of the trees blossomed with desert flowers that Nella knew only opened at night. The third tree was dead—probably had been for a long time. Its bark was white, almost like stone. Cade grabbed a branch on one of the healthy trees and broke it off.

Nella clapped to get Cade's attention. *"What are you doing?"*

Cade plunked the branch into the ground and signed to Nella, *"We can make a torch and ride by night. Should make it to the cliffside soon. Don't want to be out in the open anymore."* He pulled the flowers off the branch and knelt to pick up a sharp rock.

Nella nodded. *Good plan.* She was about to stand up and help when Cade put a hand forward and smiled. *"I got this."*

Nella agreed, with her sign of endearment, and sat back down to soothe her headache.

Cade sat at the base of the dead tree. With the sharp-edged rock in hand, he split the branch's top, creating a four-pronged claw. Then he stripped the dead tree of its bark and placed each thin piece into the stick's pronged claw. He lifted it and shook it, making sure the bark tinder held firmly.

Nella snapped her finger to get Cade to look over. *"Where did you learn that?"*

"Kid Scouts," Cade signed with a smile.

"You would make a good scout."

Cade crunched his face as if saying, *Sure, maybe,* then sat in front of Nella and watched the sunset. He signed, *"It's weird."*

"What?" Nella shook both of her hands from side to side, her palms facing Cade. Her eyebrows scrunched up in curiosity.

"I loved working in space. It felt like I had my own little world each time I stepped out onto an asteroid. There was a quiet up there that you can't find planetside."

"Sounds pretty quiet down here to me." Nella smiled. Cade let out a quick laugh.

"I'm not so sure I want to keep working in space anymore," he signed, looking away from Nella toward the sunset.

Nella got his attention again. *"What do you mean? You were going to be crew leader for the* Infinite Aria. *Aren't you excited?"*

"Yeah," Cade signed, then, *"Kind of . . . I don't know anymore."*

Nella cocked her head.

"Being out here, I feel different. Something feels right about where we are. Like I've been here before."

Nella pumped her fist. *"Yes. I feel that too."*

Cade reflexively widened his eyes and scrunched his eyebrows up. *"So, it's not just me? You can sense it too?"*

Nella tried to understand what he meant, but she certainly felt something. When they got closer to the pit with the floating rocks, she remembered a strange sensation running through her body. The feeling you get when you return home after a long journey. What didn't make sense was that they were still very far from home, in the middle of a journey.

"I do sense something," Nella signed. *"What do you think it is?"*

"The Song of Kamaria," Cade signed. He flicked a finger toward his ear. *"I can even hear it sometimes when I listen really closely."*

Nella couldn't hear the song, naturally. But maybe that wasn't how the Song of Kamaria worked. Perhaps the auk'nai only interpreted the way the planet made you feel at home as a Song, but it was more than that. It certainly was beautiful, and it had a way of filling the soul. Nella interpreted the Song of Kamaria as something more tangible, more wonderful, and warm.

It wasn't a song at all. It was a hug.

"I sound crazy." Cade made his hand into a claw and waved it in a circle near his head. *"Humans can't hear the Song of Kamaria. We are songless."*

Nella remembered what Hrun'dah had said about the Song of Kamaria and the way the world worked. Auk'nai were filled with the shared empathy of their city. Their minds were full. They worked great as a team, but they seemed tone-deaf when it came to things outside their shared city. Hrun'dah had heard a powerful song within Cade and Nella, like there were two singers for each of them.

"I don't think Kamaria cares where you come from. Anyone can be part of the Song. They just have to know how to feel it," Nella signed.

As if a confirmation, the laser stones were beginning to sprinkle the desert with spots of red light, and the trees nearby bloomed with radiant desert flowers. The sun was dipped low, and the stars were revealing themselves. Insects buzzed, pleased with the approaching night. Cade and Nella shared a smile and watched the stars twinkle in the sky. Penelope grunted and lay down, resting her head on Nella's lap. They listened to the breeze and felt its coolness refresh their bodies after a long, hot day.

A creature climbed its way out of a burrow and observed Cade and Nella in confusion. It was a small thing with tentacles for a mouth, two large dark eyes, and two long arms it used to pull itself around. It had no hind legs, but it did have fleshy wings on its back. After a moment of observing the human invaders near its burrow, it took off into the night. The Castus family knew these creatures well—bully blokes.

Nella laughed and tapped Cade's shoulder. She signed, *"Remember when we were kids, playing hide and seek in Uncle Tyler's machine shop?"*

Cade let his teeth show as he smiled. *"Yeah, you're talking about the bully bloke incident."*

Bully blokes had plagued the Castus machine shop ever since they colonized Kamaria. Multiple generations of the strange, flying octopoid had lived in various hidden places in the shop, uncovered randomly throughout the years.

Nella scrunched her face together and let out a little giggle. *"Yes. I came looking for you, and I found the bully bloke instead."*

"It was mad. It was going to jump on you."

"You stopped it, though, remember? How did you stop it?" Nella signed.

"I shouted at it." Cade laughed. *"I said, you stay away from my sister, you bully!"* He formed horns on his right hand with his fingers and crunched his face into a stern, serious look.

Nella nodded, and her grin got wider. *"Then it jumped on your face!"*

"It did. It scratched me up good. Uncle Tyler had to whack it with a shop broom to get it off. The bloke had a nest near where I was hiding." Cade rubbed the side of his head, laughing.

After Uncle Tyler had separated the bloke from Cade's face, it had set up a permanent nesting area on one of the garage's higher shelves. The war between the Castus family and the bully blokes had finally come to an end. The creatures became a sort of shop mascot. Some of the new marketing even incorporated it.

"We better get going—running low on sunlight," Cade signed, then smiled.

Nella nodded.

Cade stood and mounted Penelope, then held a hand down to help Nella up. She grabbed his hand, then noticed something in the fading light. It was a spot in the sky, darker than the rest. There were no clouds over the desert, and the insects were scarce. The dot began to grow rapidly, and its shape began to form.

Nella gasped. Then she was pulled onto the back of Penelope. Cade had seen the shape too and kicked the sides of the loamalon. Penelope sprang into motion, running at full tilt. Nella looked over her shoulder and could see wings flapping and three glowing yellow eyes.

Their monster had finally found them.

Penelope rushed toward the cliffside, trying to get out of the open; they were an easy target with the monster in the air. The loamalon had no trouble with the uneven, rocky terrain, bounding over it like a large jungle cat. They pushed through glowing red stones and desert plant life.

The monster launched its mechanical claw, and Nella jerked Cade's left arm reflexively. Cade accidentally pulled Penelope left, dodging the claw as it impacted the dusty rocks where they had been. The claw retracted, and the monster grew closer.

The Starving Sands were beginning to bloom with light. The

dead-looking trees emitted a soft white glow, mixing with the red from the laser stones. In the distance, the cliff wall was speckled with green-glowing plants and rocks. Their monster became almost invisible in the darkening sky. Nella strained her eyes and spotted the bright-yellow eyes off to their right. It flanked them and grew closer.

Nella flicked her braceleted arm, and the skinning knife projected from it. The monster raised its arm and launched its claw at them once more. Nella swung her arm as hard as she could, slapping the side of the claw and knocking it behind them.

The claw smashed into the rocks, kicking up sand and dirt. The momentum pulled the monster behind them once more and gave them a little distance. The cliff wall was getting closer, and the canyon on their right side was beginning to thin out. Nella could see a river ahead. Slits of rainbow-colored light flickered in the dark. The river spilled from some of the waterfalls on the cliffside and trailed its way into the canyon below.

The monster came closer, staying low to the ground behind them, sailing just above the sand and rocks. Nella reached into the satchel near her leg and brought out a fist-sized sunpear fruit. She took aim and hurled the fruit, striking the monster in the eyes. It stalled itself to wipe its augmented vision clean.

<Come back to us.>

Nella *heard* a voice.

She almost fell off the loamalon. It was so alien to her, so clear. She had never heard sound before in her life, yet somehow, this voice had come to her, and she *understood* it.

<This way.> The voice came again.

Is it in my mind? Nella thought. She couldn't tell. Now that she had heard it again, she noticed the voice wasn't something audible. It came to her as sensations and images that her mind translated into words.

Up ahead, part of the cliff wall began to glow brighter with pulsing green lights.

<Come back to us,> the voice repeated. *<We need you.>*

Nella tapped on Cade's shoulder and pointed. He nodded, then steered Penelope toward the glowing spot on the cliff. The monster smashed into the ground ahead of Penelope, blocking their path. Cade held Nella's arm against his torso and then kicked his legs into Penelope's side, urging her to go faster.

Nella held on tightly. The monster launched its claw once more. Cade yanked Penelope to the right, and the claw sailed past, but the monster auk'gnell was still ahead. Cade steered the loamalon directly toward it, beating the retracting claw in a race to the auk'gnell.

The monster auk'gnell flicked out its sword, but before it could slash, Penelope trampled over it. The loamalon stumbled after hitting the monster but gracefully recovered at full speed. The auk'gnell tumbled on the ground, still rolling from the impact. Its claw swung wildly in the air as it flailed with the momentum. As Penelope gained some distance, Nella saw the yellow eyes glowing once more before vanishing in the dark.

Now that they were closer to the cliff wall, Nella could see an immense cave tunnel. Water spilled out of the tunnel like a pipe, creating the river that must have carved out the canyon.

<We are waiting for you.> The voice came to Nella again.

Who are you? Nella asked in her thoughts. There was no answer.

Cade guided Penelope into the cave, splashing into the water. The river was shallow here, coming up only to mid-shin on Penelope's long legs. Her progress was more labored now, but with hope, the cave would conceal them from the auk'gnell.

<We have waited for so long,> the voice said.

Cade lit his torch, and they proceeded deeper into the dark, wet cave.

"Can't you do *anything* right?" Auden shouted into L'Arn's ear. "They are getting away again!"

L'Arn pulled himself onto his feet and retracted his claw. He shook off the pain of being trampled by the loamalon and slung his sword back into its sheath. His augmented vision gave him perfect sight, even in darkness. He would have blinded them as they approached, but the sunpear the female had thrown at his face hindered his ability to do so. The fruit debris clouded his mechanical eyes. L'Arn wiped away the remnants of the fruit from his face and flexed his wings.

"I see them," L'Arn said. The loamalon hopped into the shallow river and walked into a vast cave tunnel. A light shined, possibly a torch. The humans didn't have night vision, and he'd use that disability against them. The flame would be an easy target to follow. L'Arn sprinted forward, then flapped his mighty wings, throwing himself into the sky. Although his prey had traveled into the cave and away from sight, he was confident he could follow.

L'Arn landed in the water at the mouth of the cave and began to trudge through the river, just as the others had done. The stalactites on the tunnel ceiling were too dense to risk flying and reinjuring his wings. His targets were close, and his hunt was almost over. He focused only on following the humans and catching them. It didn't bother him that the walls began to twitch and slither. The sound of crackling bones didn't deter his hunt.

L'Arn had come in a hunter and was blind to discover that he had become prey in the process.

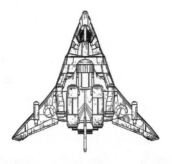

TWENTY-SIX

THE SIREN PIT WAS reopened in the heart of the Starving Sands. This was not Denton's first time here. During the days of Nhymn; Denton, Eliana, Talulo, George, and Captain Roelin Raike had visited this place as hostages. Nhymn took them all on a wild ride through the canyons in the warship named the *Astraeus*, only to crash it into the underground cave system below. They'd followed Roelin through a mysterious underground palace made of alabaster, where they discovered that Nhymn had taken control of Sympha's gigantic body. They could only watch as Nhymn clawed her way to the surface, caving in the entire structure in the process.

Scouts had been back to this place a handful of times since then, but nothing had come of it. Sand and rock had filled the palace. Attempts to excavate the site had led to disaster; the Pit would work against crews and bury itself. The council deemed it unsafe, and it had been forgotten about. Kamaria had concealed Sympha's plans, and years passed.

Until now.

Denton stepped out of the *Rogers* with Talulo at his side. Rocks and debris lined the radius around the hole where Nhymn had once clawed her way out, almost the same as when she emerged that day. *Did Nhymn somehow return here?* Denton wondered as he stood at the edge of the pit and looked down to see small glowing lights in the darkness below.

"What the Hells happened here?" Denton mumbled to himself.

"The marines have arrived," Talulo cooed.

A military transport shuttle came in and landed near the *Rogers*. Lance Corporal Rafa Ghanem and three Tvashtar marines stepped out with full kits and combat armor. After what Rafa had been through in the *Telemachus* wreck, he wasn't about to come to this mission unarmed.

"What are you up to now, Castus? Haven't caused enough trouble yet?" Rafa said as he approached. There was no humor in his voice.

"Thanks for coming," Denton said. He couldn't help but feel guilty dragging the marines with him. After what had happened to Private Simmons, he couldn't guarantee their safety.

"The old man sent us," Rafa said, referring to George, "and honestly, sitting around without Simmons feels wrong. We want to see this thing through. For him."

The other three marines nodded in agreement. They had lost a brother to this mystery, and they didn't want to wait for answers. If there was a way they could avenge the private, they'd do it.

"Sadly, I think we only have more questions here. Last time we checked, there wasn't a giant hole in the ground," Denton said.

"Want us to go in and look around?" Rafa asked.

"Not yet. We don't know what's down there," Denton said. If he was being honest with himself, he wanted to take Rafa up on his offer, but Denton also didn't want to risk any more lives if he could avoid it. He turned to Talulo. "We have another probe on the *Rogers*, don't we?"

Talulo cooed and gestured over his soothreader. A piece of the *Rogers* popped off and floated toward them. It was similar in appearance and function to the probe they had left in the Ember-Lit Forest. The main body was ball shaped, with four big camera-lens eyes—two in front, two in back. Robotic arms protruded from a rotating piece on the bottom near the auk'nai hover tech that allowed it to float silently in the air.

"Talulo can pilot the probe into the pit," Talulo stated. With a few more flicks of his hand, a holographic display appeared over his wrist, and the probe lowered itself into the pit. Through the display, they could see out of all four eyes on the probe.

Rafa gestured to his men to spread out and scan the area for anything that might be dangerous. He stood next to Denton and Talulo, watching the display with them. "Do you think your son and daughter are in there?"

Denton wasn't sure how to respond. This felt like a long shot. Things on Kamaria had been absolutely crazy since the Daunoren of the Spirit Song Mountain was found dead. A murdered god, people kidnapped, an old wreck vandalized, and now the rapid excavation of an ancient mysterious Siren palace. So sure, there was a possibility that maybe—*just maybe*—Cade and Nella were here.

"It's possible," Denton said.

Talulo piloted the probe into the pit. A thick haze filled the display screen, like a cloud layer when entering atmosphere. The probe lowered itself deeper and deeper into the abyss.

Memories of Nhymn stirred in Denton's mind. It was hard not to be nostalgic and also horrified. Over twenty years ago, Denton had stood in this underground palace. His mind had had a hitchhiker along for the experience—Karx.

Karx was sort of a half-brother to Nhymn and Sympha. He resembled them in some ways, made of gnarled bones and writhing wormskin tentacles, but Karx's frame was shaped like a centaur's. His bull-shaped skull had one cyclopean eye and two long horns. Sympha had pulled him into the physical realm to protect herself from her sister, Nhymn. He had both succeeded and failed in this task.

Karx's success came when he had destroyed Nhymn the first time. When she went berserk and tried to seize control of Sympha. Karx stomped Nhymn's skull in, and her body died. Sympha and Karx brought Nhymn's corpse to a cave and laid her to rest.

Karx's failure came when Nhymn reemerged from the cave centuries later, wearing Captain Roelin Raike as a life vest. Karx had calcified into stone and couldn't react in time to stop the humans from carrying Nhymn away from her resting place. By the time Karx had broken through his calcification, the humans were gone.

Denton was personally aware of all this. He had witnessed it himself.

After Nhymn had escaped from her tomb, Karx found Denton and jumped into his mind. Denton unknowingly gave Karx a piggyback ride to the alabaster palace—the Siren Pit, as it was now called. Through Karx's influence, Denton traveled across a mental tether in his sleep. He thought the visions were only dreams at first, strange and elusive. It was in the Siren Pit that it became clear to Denton that he had been traveling through time as a shade, something born when a Siren and a human mixed. He watched Nhymn, Sympha, and Karx play out their lives, sometimes zipping through eons in an instant. The Sirens were aware of him like they were aware of a cloudy day. From the Siren perspective, Denton was just always part of their world—ignorable.

Talulo's probe made it to the floor of the pit. In this room, Nhymn discovered Karx's presence in Denton's mind and bolted him with electricity. The bolt had killed Karx but spared Denton. Denton rubbed his hand over his spiral-shaped scar, remembering how it felt—such immense pain.

The probe saw none of the memories rushing through Denton's mind. Here it only found alabaster walls and floor. Questions remained about this place, hidden over time as the palace was consumed by the Starving Sands. No one knew what its purpose was. During his first exploration, Denton had noticed similarities in its design to that of a combustion engine. If the palace was actually some sort of machine, it was still unclear what it was designed to do.

"George, are you seeing this?" Denton asked his soothreader. Talulo was transmitting the data to the Telemachus Outpost for George and Marie. This would be the first time anyone had been inside since Nhymn had emerged from it. The mysteries of the Palace might finally reveal themselves.

"We got it here. Never thought I'd see this place again," George said over the comm channel.

"I was hoping we wouldn't," Denton said, and scratched his scar.

Talulo cooed in agreement.

The probe entered a giant's hallway, with tall ceilings shaped like a spear point. A haze filled the top of the hall like clouds. The smooth stone walls curved away from the probe in the distance.

"Strange," George said. "There is virtually no debris in this hallway."

"Someone's been cleaning," Denton said.

The probe came to a massive door and proceeded through it. It entered the cylindrical room in the center of the palace. In the past, a destructive battle had been fought here, leaving most of this central chamber a total mess. Presently, it looked brand new. The spiral stone ramp that led to the floor below was fully intact. Shelves lining the sides of the walls were all lined up beautifully. At the bottom of the room was a hole that led to a swirling pool of electrified water. In the past, lights pulsed from the swirling pool below toward the ceiling. Now, the water swirled, but no lights pulsed. The probe activated a searchlight to investigate the room.

"What is this?" Rafa asked.

"My theory was that the whole structure uses the raw power of the planet itself to power whatever it was intended to do. But we still have no idea what it was for," Denton said.

"The more complex the being, the more complex the motives," George said. "We may never understand what this place was intended to do. But that's not going to stop me from giving it a try."

Talulo whistled. The searchlight spotted an inert nezzarform. They were bulky things, made of boulders and stones. Each one took on a slightly different form, but most were like the one before them—two massive arms, a sizeable-shouldered torso with three legs, and a head with one cyclopean eye. It faced the probe, its arms lowered to the floor, its head staring emptily into the pit below.

As the probe panned around the room, more inert nezzarforms were revealed. They were all staring into the abyss. It almost looked like they were performing some sort of arcane ritual. They were waiting for something.

"Some of these were here last time. Maybe they cleaned up after Nhymn left?" George theorized.

"It's possible. But I'm pretty sure Nhymn converted all the nezzarforms into soldiers. I don't see why she'd leave these ones behind to tidy the house," Denton said.

"Nhymn was missing for one month after leaving this place," Talulo reminded them. "Auk'nai and humans do not know what Nhymn was doing in that time."

"True, but we sent scouts back here to search for her," George said. "This place had been completely cut off from the surface."

"I wouldn't know. I sat in quarantine for that *whole month*," Denton grumbled.

"I said I was sorry about that," George said.

Rafa pointed at the live feed footage. "Was that thing here last time?"

"What thing?" Denton, George, and Talulo asked in unison.

Rafa wiggled his hand to the left. "Ah shit, it's moving. Pan left."

Talulo nudged the probe, and it rotated left. As Rafa stated, something was moving around in the darkness. Something big. Every time the searchlight got to it, it slithered away.

"It is avoiding the probe," Talulo said. "Probe doesn't need visible light. Talulo will switch to night vision." He gestured over his soothreader, and the display shut off. It needed only a brief moment to switch from searchlight to night vision, but the moment seemed to hang in the air. The night vision kicked on, and the display flashed white, then began to settle into various gray tones as the cameras adjusted to the infrared light the probe was projecting to amplify.

Before the night vision adjusted completely, the probe was

smacked sideways. Alerts flashed on the display, and the viewscreen became corrupted. The video was jagged and failing to buffer in large areas, but they could tell that the probe had been hurled into one of the side walls. It landed on the floor and flickered with errors.

"What just happened?" Denton asked.

Talulo shook his beak and cooed. The parts of the display that were still active filled with what appeared to be a taloned claw. Then the video cut off completely.

There was silence. Rafa broke the stunned hush. "Someone's home."

"Any idea what that was?" George asked.

"It could have been the auk'gnell that kidnapped Nella and Cade," Denton said, but deep inside, he knew it wasn't an auk'gnell. He had seen claws like that before. Denton couldn't bring himself to admit the reality.

Talulo cooed, having read Denton's empathic wavelengths. He said, "Denton knows that was not an auk'gnell claw."

"What else could it have been?" Denton asked the question he knew the answer to. "We need to get in there and find out."

Talulo made a low caw, his brow furrowed at Denton.

"I'll get my guys ready," Rafa said, then walked off and summoned the other three Tvashtar marines.

Denton walked back toward the *Rogers* to get a full kit for the mission into the Siren Pit. Talulo hurried next to him. "Denton cannot lie to Talulo. Denton knows what that was."

Denton shook his head and stopped. He focused on the horizon. He could see the glowing cliffside that led to the jungle under the Sharp Top Mountain in the distance. All of this felt like reliving a nightmare. He knew that claw looked nothing like an auk'gnell's. Denton had watched claws like that cut through the throat of a friend.

It was the claw of a Siren.

"We don't know what it is," Denton said and winced. He turned to Talulo. "Look, even if it's not L'Arn, maybe he is working for whatever that thing is. Or maybe the kids fell into the pit on their way back to the city. I don't know. All I know is something weird is going on down there, and it might involve my kids. I'm going in."

Talulo eyed Denton with a stern, piercing gaze.

You can't lie to an auk'nai. They will call you out on it every time. Denton huffed and was about to continue the walk back to the *Rogers*, but he stopped. He turned to Talulo and admitted, "Fine. It's a Siren! The thought of my kids being down there with it terrifies me. Hells, the thought of my kids being on the same planet as a Siren scares me to death. So, even if Nella and Cade aren't down there, I'm going down there to stop it anyway. If we kill it there and seal the pit, its phantom can't escape."

Sirens were immortal. Their bodies could die, even decay over time. But their phantoms were still dangerous. Karx had killed Nhymn, and her ghost haunted the cave where they left her body for centuries until the scout team entered. It had possessed Roelin and almost eradicated humanity from the universe. They'd killed Nhymn again with the *Telemachus*, and she came back three years later, possessing the body of a creature called a nightsnare. The only reason Nhymn wasn't still around was because they launched her into space.

Denton remembered the day they got rid of her.

Nhymn was *scared* of something. She was so scared that she wanted to live for eternity in space rather than be on Kamaria with whatever it was. The thought of what possibly could have terrified Nhymn so badly haunted Denton. The cruelest thing the Siren had ever done was not tell anyone what made her want to leave the planet.

"That song is true," Talulo said.

Denton nodded. "Keep an eye on the ship. If anything happens to us, you need to get Eliana and the others and figure out how to handle this thing."

They went into the *Rogers* and prepared for what might happen next.

TWENTY-SEVEN

CADE HELD HIS TORCH high as Penelope trudged through the rushing cave water. The rocky tunnel traveled into the side of the cliff on a steady upward slope. Its ceiling was covered in hanging plants and sharp, dimly glowing stalactites. The light given off the stalactites seemed to be swallowed by the darkness. They were walking into the maw of a vicious beast. As Cade moved the torch around, things skittered away from the light. He couldn't help but feel as if he was being watched by a crowded auditorium. A strange tune was humming in the darkness. Cade wasn't sure if it was the rushing water playing tricks on him or something lurking in the cave.

Nella gasped.

Cade shifted the torchlight to their right and saw a pile of auk'nai bones on a flat rock surface next to the water, picked clean. Penelope almost plodded past when Cade noticed the daunoren hook staffs still attached to the old bones. He brought Penelope to a stop and signed to Nella, *"One second."*

Nella shook her head, but Cade ignored her and hopped off the loamalon. Penelope whinnied, and Nella patted her neck to soothe her as she kept her eye on the water behind them. Cade moved toward the bones. The water went nearly up to his waist. He shuffled his way to the rock with the bones and held the torch up to investigate.

Multiple broken daunoren hooks were scattered among the bones, most decayed or rusted with age, but one caught his eye. It looked untouched by time. The staff had a handle made of black metal with interspersed void stones, much like the one Cade had in his jacket-turned-saddle. The end of the staff had a sharp blade, flat like a sword, with the tip widened out, creating a T-shape. The humming was louder as Cade stood near the daunoren blade.

He grabbed the staff and yanked it free from the bones. Dust blasted Cade, and he coughed. The walls chittered and clattered. The humming stopped, and suddenly it was eerily quiet except for the rushing water. Cade decided he'd gotten what he needed and waded back over to Penelope.

A birdcall rang through the cave tunnel, echoing off the walls. The sound of splashing and metal clanging against rock followed it. Cade hoisted himself up onto Penelope and kicked her sides. The loamalon plodded through the water as fast as she could.

Cade knew the monster had followed them, and it was only a matter of time before it caught up. His new daunoren staff would be a useful weapon, and he still had the flare gun with one shot left. Nella had the braceleted skinning knife that Hrun'dah gave her, and perhaps the torch could be used as a weapon if all else failed. This was their arsenal.

Will it be enough to stop the monster? Cade wondered.

Nella pointed over Cade's shoulder to the tunnel ahead. Green lights on the walls lit up and created a guide, then subsided. Something was helping them, but the brief light also revealed a hidden danger.

Cade strained his eyes in the darkness, holding the torch forward in one hand. As they moved through the water, the torchlight began to reveal what the green lights had briefly shown them. Something was moving.

It was a creature. It had a gnarled, bone-white carapace and violet worm-skinned arms. The thing turned to face them, and both Cade and Nella gasped. Its head looked like a hollowed-out bird's skull with a single, long horn protruding from just above the beak. They had both seen this thing before, in their history books and in their nightmares. It was the bogeyman from their childhood, the cautionary tale of traveling to distant stars, the violent past they had roots in.

"Nhymn!" Cade gasped.

The Siren that nearly eradicated humanity. It twitched and shuffled through the water toward Penelope. Cade could see that there was something off about the thing as it stepped closer to the light. It looked broken, slightly mutated from the images he remembered.

There was a chittering. The light revealed another Siren, shaped much like the one shuffling toward them, but with its own unique mutations. Then another one. The cave was brimming with mutant Sirens, each shaped like a twisted version of Nhymn.

Cade waved the torch, and the Sirens shrieked and moved away from the light. They didn't seem like the powerful beings that their parents had fought years ago. These were mindless cave creatures.

Behind them, the monster auk'gnell let out a shrill birdcall that echoed off the cave walls. Cade decided they needed to push through if they were ever going to make it. He hoped with the combination of the torchlight and the strong forward momentum of Penelope, they could move their way to the end of the cave.

"Yah!" Cade shouted and kicked Penelope's sides. The loamalon roared and surged through the water toward the mutant Sirens. The Sirens reached toward them, but the light acted as a good deterrent. They shied away at the last moment and shrieked. One of the Sirens didn't move away, standing firmly before the loamalon and screaming in a shrill, otherworldly tone. Penelope used her powerful hind legs to push herself up, then slammed down on the Siren, stomping it into the water. Although it had been defeated, its bravery motivated the other Sirens.

Cade swung the T-bladed daunoren staff, slicing the head off of one of the cave Sirens that ventured too close to Penelope's side. Nella struck another with her braceleted skinning knife, shoving it back into the shadows where it came from and protecting their backs.

The green lights flittered through the cave walls again, highlighting their path. They pushed through, hacking and slashing their way through the crowd of cave Sirens until the water began to get more shallow. A wider area of flat rocks was before them. Penelope maneuvered her way onto it and was able to go full sprint through the amassing mutants, sometimes using the cave walls to bound off and smash into a group of the creatures.

Cade could see moonlight spilling into the cave ahead, and he felt a rush of hope that they would be done with the horrible tunnel soon. As they grew closer, part of the cave spilled water out into the desert valley below, and the whole left side of the wall was exposed to the open air. The cave tunnel continued onward beyond this point for an unknown length. Penelope whinnied and skidded to a stop in the moonlight, then spun in a circle and shook her head.

"*Whoa!* Whoa now," Cade said, almost out of breath from swinging the staff around. They stood in the open area on a flat rock. The water rushing through the cave split in two directions—some traveling down the way they came from, the rest spilling out into a waterfall into the open air.

Standing at the edge of the moonlight was a wall of mutant Sirens. Cade looked behind them and saw that the creatures had filled the tunnel there as well. They were trapped in the moonlit area.

Cade and Nella dismounted Penelope and watched the creatures to make sure none of them got too brave and attacked. They slowly swayed from side to side, haunting the shadows around them. Cade looked out over the waterfall to see if there would be a way out. They were close to the top of the cliff now, and there was no escape to be had by looking down. The water rushed into the open air and deposited into the valley below. Other waterfalls joined it, and each spilled into the canyon.

Cade noticed something near the end of the canyon in the Starving Sands desert below. *Lights?* He strained his eyes, begging for his vision to adjust to the moonlight. The canyon lights didn't resemble the laser stones in the rocky plateaus or the glow from the night-blooming desert trees. These were flat, organized, unnatural. *Man-made?*

He gasped. *Scout ship lights!*

It was a grouping of ships lighting an area for exploration. In the valley below, near the Siren Pit, were humans! Cade felt his blood pumping like a piston engine, and he hopped around in excitement. For a brief moment, he forgot about the mutant cave Sirens and the monster auk'gnell pursuing them. For a moment, he felt like they might make it back home. Cade grabbed Nella and pointed to the lights. Her horrified expression shifted to immense joy, and her smile was so wide her teeth were brightening up the moonlit cave area.

"Hey!" Cade shouted out to the valley. "Hey! Over here! Hey!"

It was useless. The scouts were too far off to hear anything, and the waterfall made it hard for Cade to even hear himself. A clattering of metal against stone and another shrill birdcall came from the tunnel behind them. Their monster was slicing through the mutants and would soon find them.

Hope switched to panic.

What can we do? Cade rushed through ideas in his head. He had the torch, but it wasn't bright enough, and there was no dry wood to make a signal fire. Shouting wasn't going to work, and he didn't have anything that made loud noises. *Wait, we have that!* He felt foolish not thinking of it sooner. Cade rushed over to Penelope, reached inside his scout jacket saddle, and brought out the flare gun. Cade checked the cartridge and clicked it into place, then pointed it toward the twin moons of Kamaria. In an ideal situation, he'd wait until they got to the surface to send out the flare, but Cade had no way of knowing how long the scouts would be around or how long it would take to breach the surface. He closed his eyes, then squeezed the trigger.

The flare launched with a bang. Its red light filled the cave and scared off the cave Sirens on each side. Cade and Nella watched as the flare arched into the sky toward the moons, then slowly hovered downward.

Cade hopped onto Penelope's back and hoisted Nella on behind him. The tunnel at their backs began to glow yellow, and they knew the monster was hot on their heels. "Yah!" Cade shouted, and propelled Penelope farther into the cave, bounding off the rock ledges on each side of the rushing river. The flare had created an opening in the barricade of cave Sirens, and Penelope rushed through before it could close.

They raced deeper into the cave tunnel.

———— • ————

The cave Sirens found L'Arn. The augmented auk'gnell had seen them skittering along the walls in his near-perfect night vision. These creatures did not scare him. Nothing did. He battled them one at a time, hacking through most with his daunoren sword and morphing its shape to dispatch them as efficiently as possible. The Sirens that approached him on the left were crushed by his mechanical arm. He used his retractable claw like a long whip, allowing it to hang loosely from the tether that bound it to his wrist.

L'Arn was slowed by the attacking Sirens, but he was not stopped. It wasn't until he felt something slither around his legs that his progress ground to a halt. There was a sharp pain in his thigh, and he almost dropped under the water. He plunged his claw into the river and pulled up a mutated Siren. Its horn had been lodged in his skin. L'Arn crushed the Siren's head like a sunpear, hearing it crunch in his metal claw. He tossed the body backward, where it floated face down out into the valley behind him.

The swarm came at L'Arn too fast, and he began to struggle to keep the Sirens off of him. The monster auk'gnell let out a shrill birdcall and flashed the creatures with his eyes. There was a deafening shriek from the crowd of mutants, and they backed off for a breath.

L'Arn flapped his wings and launched himself into the air. The tunnel wasn't a good place to fly, due to the many stalactites that clung from odd angles. Any one of them could slice through L'Arn's recently healed wings. He had to keep low to the water, but he could travel faster this way.

The plodding sound of the loamalon stomping through the water was close. L'Arn pushed ahead, dodging the Sirens that strayed into his path. He felt their claws on his chest as he flew through them. The mutated cave Sirens began to jump into his flight path. L'Arn was brought down into the water once more. The Sirens held his head underwater, piling on top of him and clawing into him. L'Arn surged with anger, the bloodlust filling him. His arm began to glow red hot, and the water around him began to boil. The Sirens squirmed away, but before they could all escape, L'Arn unleashed a berserker's fury upon them. He tore one in half from the torso with his metal claw and foot. He morphed his sword into a long katana and sliced through three more on his right. He kicked out with his leg and launched two more into the far wall of the cave. L'Arn was relentless.

When the cave grew quiet and the Sirens kept their distance, he let out another birdcall, daring them to attack once more. L'Arn was about to jump into the crowd of Sirens before him when he saw a bright-red flash of light up ahead, filling the cave. His prey was close. L'Arn flashed the Sirens and pushed through.

He came to an area exposed to the outside valley, but it was empty when he got there. The Sirens behind him filled the tunnel's width, watching him from the safety of their shadows. L'Arn looked out into the desert and saw the flare slowly drift downward and fade out. In the far distance, spaceships were glowing.

"That's them—the humans," Auden said in L'Arn's ear. "There's no time to waste. They will be on us shortly."

"I know what to do," L'Arn said. He flapped his wings and launched himself outward into the night sky. The sound of the rushing cave water was replaced by the whipping air that welcomed him so thoroughly. He was in his element, away from the mutant things in the cave. L'Arn knew the tunnel must have an exit at the cliff's top; the river was funneling water into it from the jungle above. He brought himself to the top and searched for an opening.

He would be waiting for his prey when they exited the tunnel, and then his hunt would end.

TWENTY-EIGHT

DENTON PREPARED HIMSELF FOR war inside the staging room of the *Rogers*. He pulled a thick undersuit over his bare skin and zipped it up from groin to just under the beard on his chin. Shin guards and jump-jets clipped onto the undersuit. The various belts, pouches, and holsters adhered to pieces of armor that protected his lower body. A chest piece slid over his head and clicked into place, with shoulder pads fastened on by the suit-donning station. Gauntlets locked onto his forearms. Denton tested the triggers built into his palm, listening for the flaps to open and close on the jump-jets throughout the Tvashtar marine combat suit.

Denton had never been a marine. He used to dislike the Tvashtar colony on Io for being direct competition to his family's machine shop. Still, after the final battle with Nhymn, he decided to get training in a combat suit. Denton Castus would fight his own battles.

His collider pistol slid into the hip holster, and the particle assault rifle magnetically attached to his back. Denton looked in the mirror near the lockers in the staging room. A man who had lost his children looked back at him. The man in the mirror had a thick, bushy brown beard and dark-green eyes. A scar on his right cheek went from near his nostril all the way back to his earlobe. Eliana had stitched the wound shut for him in the past, but she was not here to heal his wounds this time.

Memories of Captain Roelin Raike flitted through Denton's mind as he observed the mirror. Roelin had lost everything—his wife, his friends, and worst yet, his soul.

"Is Denton ready?" Talulo asked from the doorway. "Talulo put spotlights over the pit. They will sync to your suits and follow you into the underground palace."

"Thanks," Denton said with a sigh. "Are Rafa and the others ready?"

Talulo cooed.

Denton walked to the cargo bay, where the access ramp was already lowered. He felt the cold night air breeze over his face. Light poured in from outside from the spotlights that hovered over the pit. Rafa and the others stood around rope lines that had been secured in place by a rivet gun. The ropes dangled into the hole, seeming to vanish into the thick haze.

"Are you sure you want to do this?" Rafa asked. "We can go in and handle it."

"I'm the only one here who has had up-close contact with a Siren before. I'm ready to handle this one too," Denton reminded the Tvashtar marines.

"Alright, just stick close and let us lead. We'll take it nice and slow," Rafa said.

Denton nodded and walked over to the dangling ropes. He secured it through the harness built into the suit.

"Sir." One of the marines tapped Rafa on the shoulder and pointed into the distance.

Denton ignored it. Rafa gestured over his soothreader and called to Talulo over the comm channel, "Hey, can you kill the spotlights for a second." There was a brief pause, and then the spotlights went dark. Denton looked around as his eyes adjusted to the darkness.

"What's going—" Before he could finish, he spotted what the marines saw.

"There! See?" The marine pointed again.

They looked toward the cliffside in the distance, where the jungle loomed over the desert. Denton blinked and strained his eyes, then it came into focus. There was a thin line of flickering red light descending from the top of the cliff toward the valley below. Many of the glowing plants in the desert reflected a reddish hue, but this stood out from the others. It was falling too slowly, and it was too bright to look natural.

"Is that a—" Rafa began.

"It's a flare," Denton said in a faraway voice. He remembered that Cade had pulled the flare gun from the admiral's stasis pod before hurrying Nella away into the Ember-Lit Forest. Denton's eyes widened, and he shouted, "It's a flare!"

"Is that them?" Rafa asked.

"It has to be!" Denton shouted, and quickly removed the rope from his harness. "We have to move. They could be in trouble."

"What about the Siren?" one of the marines asked.

"It waited for over twenty years. It can wait a little longer. Cade and Nella are right there!" Denton hurried over to the *Rogers*. In all honesty, Denton was elated to not have to meet the Siren in the pit to save his kids. He was unsure what trouble they might be in, but nothing felt as dangerous as the Sirens—nothing except maybe the Undriel.

Denton thought of Eliana on the distant shore. He flicked his soothreader comm channel over to her and said, "Elly, I think I found the kids."

It took a few heartbeats for her to respond. "Please tell me it's true. We haven't found anything here. Do you have them with you? Are they safe?" Eliana asked.

"We saw Cade's flare and are heading to it now. It has to be them this time." Denton thought for a moment, then added, "I'm going to send some of Rafa's men over to you to pick you up. The flight here only took a few hours, so they should be there soon."

"Keep . . . inform . . ." Eliana said through garbled static.

"I'm losing you," Denton said. "I'll let you know when I have the kids."

"Dent . . . Ge . . ." Eliana's feed cut out.

"Damn it," Denton shook his wrist, but the feed was dead. He turned to Rafa and asked, "Can you send one of your men to these coordinates? On the Howling Shore. You'll see the *Tiger* rover there." He flicked the information over to Rafa, who passed it to one of his men.

The marine nodded and hurried over to their transport ship.

"The rest of you come with me. We don't know if the auk'gnell who took Cade and Nella is following them or not."

Rafa nodded, "Alright, everyone, move it!" Rafa said and twirled his finger in the air. Denton, Rafa, and two marines entered the *Rogers*. Denton ran all the way to the cockpit and sat in the copilot seat next to Talulo. They watched as the flare faded out.

"Alright, you got the positioning?" Denton asked, flicking switches to activate the preflight sequence.

Talulo cooed. "Talulo hears the song."

"Let's get Cade and Nella back," Denton said.

———— ◆ ————

"I'm los . . . you . . ." Denton's voice came through Eliana's soothreader in broken fragments.

"Denton!" Eliana said into the soothreader. "Denton, get our kids! Please," she begged the channel as it died in static. What wretched luck—of all the times for a comm failure. Faye drove the *Tiger* rover along the cliffside of the shore while Eliana, Jess, and Homer sat in the back and watched their scan data.

"He found them?" Faye asked. She parked the *Tiger* and turned around in the driver's seat to face Eliana. Her eyes were as wide as her smile.

"I hope so. We've had so many false leads, it's hard to tell. But he sounded so sure this time." Eliana smiled for the first time in days.

Jess said, "We'll know soon. I'll try and get in contact with the marines he's with and see if we can get a working comm feed."

"Good plan," Faye said. She turned to their robotic companion. "Homer, is there a way we can boost our signal—"

The lights in the rover shut off.

"Shit," Jess said and reached for her assault rifle. The rover's entire left side was ripped off and flung into the ocean. Homer's eyes went dark as they automatically shut down. The robot was ripped from their seat so violently that their mechanical legs were left twitching under the seatbelt.

The rover was hit with something huge and heavy. It rolled sideways, flinging everyone out into the darkness, into the long grass. Eliana hit the ground and heard something snap in her leg, followed by a sharp pain. She fought back the darkness that tried to overtake her vision, just barely preventing herself from passing out. Faye was screaming in agony.

"In all my days, I never thought I'd see one of these," a clear, calm, kind voice said. Eliana could barely hear the voice. It came from closer to the cliff ledge, where waves were crashing below. The voice continued, "Oh, please don't try and shut down, my dear friend."

Eliana grunted and pushed herself up. She peeked over the tall grass toward the source of the voice. Her lungs vented, and her heart sank.

Near the cliff ledge, standing at about two and a half meters tall, was an android made of jet-black metal. It was mostly obscured in the darkness of night, but the fire from the rover's destruction illuminated it. It had the metallic face of a spider, with an array of white-colored eyes and sharp, sinister teeth. Its torso was like the thorax of a bulky wasp, and its long cloak glinted with reflected light from the twin moons. Shoulder pauldrons vented heat into the air, with red-hot energy spewing steam. The android had four arms; the one that held Homer's half-body up was a curved blade, and the others were long and thin and terminated in sharp claws. On its back seemed to be a smaller version of itself, hanging on like a conjoined twin. The android had the lower half of a centipede, with long, thin legs that ended in sharp spears. The Undriel had been known to take the form of various old Earth insects, and seeing one here on Kamaria gave it an incredibly alien feeling. It was a nightmare.

"It's—It's . . ." Eliana whimpered.

"An Undriel augmentor." Jess stealthily approached Eliana from the side and readied her rifle. She kept her eye on the machine. "Get as far away from here as you can. If you find Faye, take her with you."

There was a scream from the tall grass between their position and the Undriel's position. Faye shouted, "Oh God—oh, Hells! Help! *Help!*"

The Undriel turned toward Faye's cries and let out a laugh. "I'll be with you shortly." It turned its attention on Homer once more. "Let's get you online again, eh?"

The Undriel rotated one of its arms, and a puck flipped out and slapped onto Homer's chest. Steel tentacles writhed out of the puck and slammed into Homer at all angles. Homer's eyes began to glow, and their body began to convulse.

"Eliana, run," Jess said.

"No, Faye needs—" Eliana began.

"Run!" Jess said, then stood and opened fire with her assault rifle.

The Undriel was struck with some of the shots, but it maneuvered away to avoid the full attack. Blazing particle holes pocked its cloak. The Undriel's eyes morphed from white to red, and it focused on Jess. Its white-fanged maw roared with anger, and steam seeped through its teeth. Eliana tried to turn and run, but her leg gave out, and pain shot through her body when she stood. She looked down and saw her leg hanging limply at mid-shin, having been broken in the tumbling rover. Eliana began to crawl inland, away from the fighting.

Faye screamed in the night as the battle raged around her. The Undriel rotated its two lower arms, and rifles appeared. It sprayed particle blasts into the grass, trying to track Jess's jet-jump-propelled movements.

"Damn Tvashtar marine!" the Undriel seethed, its voice augmented with a low bass undertone. Jess sprayed another volley of bullets into the Undriel's flank. In a heartbeat, the robot altered its lower half into a grasshopper's form and flung itself high into the night sky. Before Jess could track it, two mechanical claws smashed into the ground at both her sides, attached to long metal tethers connected the Undriel's wrists. It retracted its claws, propelling itself back toward the ground with incredible speed.

Jess rolled forward and turned in time to see the Undriel smash into the ground where she had been standing. Without missing a beat, the upper half of the Undriel rotated to face her, and its upper two arms morphed into curved blades. Jess ducked the first blade, but the second slammed into her left arm and flung her toward the cliff ledge. Jess counteracted her sideways movement toward the shore with a well-timed jump-jet. Instantly, her right hand was holding her rifle and spraying white-hot particles toward the nightmarish machine.

She struck the Undriel twice; one shot glanced its head, and another hit somewhere in its cloaked region. It roared and vented energy, then spun its torso independently of its legs and head while loosening its tethered claws. The top claw rotated clockwise, the lower counterclockwise. Jess dodged the first but was struck in the side of the head and knocked unconscious by the bottom claw. Her body tumbled off the side of the cliff and into the water below.

Eliana watched in horror as Jess vanished over the cliff. "Oh *shit!*" she whimpered. Her breaths became ragged with panic and her brow thick with sweat.

Faye shrieked in agony.

The Undriel finished venting and altered its form. It was standing on two long, locust-like legs and tucked its extra two arms back into its abdomen. The cloak concealed more of the machine's body this way, and it would have almost looked like a hooded man carrying junk on its back if it weren't for the glowing white eyes and shining razor teeth.

"Oh my dear, you look awful," the Undriel said as it approached Faye. Her lower half had been crushed as the rover rolled over her. Faye pulled out her collider pistol and let loose one shot into the cloaked region of the Undriel. The android grabbed Faye's hand and twisted so fast that her forearm was removed. Faye shrieked in pain and sobbed.

"I am only here to help you," the Undriel said with a smooth, calm voice.

"Stay away from her!" Eliana called out. She was unarmed, her leg broken. She could do nothing but distract and hope it was enough.

"I'll get to you next. I'm afraid you have caught me unprepared. I only have enough parts to make one of you perfect right now, and your friend here is not long on time."

"Don't you *fucking* touch her!" Eliana screamed, sobbing at the futility of it.

Faye let out one more agonized shriek as the Undriel collapsed on top of her. There was a shuffling under the cloak, the sounds of tearing and crunching. The Undriel was devouring her. Smaller, insectoid arms reached out from the cloak and into the pile of parts on the Undriel's back and brought them to Faye's body. After a few seconds, all the pieces on the machine's back had been used.

The Undriel stood, arching its spider head backward and laughing into the moonlight, the fire adding to its menace. Blood covered its fangs and chest. It took a few steps back. "I haven't done that in *ages*."

Eliana cried as she watched a second android rise from the grass. It was shaped like the Undriel that had remade her—spider-bot head, long spindly arms, locust legs all jet black. It lacked a cloak, and its full frame was exposed to the fire and twin moonlight.

Faye Raike had been fully absorbed by the Undriel.

Eliana cried out in horror. Faye had been like an aunt to her— family. Eliana felt like her heart would give out, and her brain was on fire. Rage, fear, immense sadness, and dark hopelessness engulfed her all at once. It was as if she were watching her father's murder all over again in real time. Faye had been with her at that moment as a fellow observer. Now, Eliana was all alone, watching Faye become an agent of humanity's shared nightmare.

"It will take some time to truly be perfect, but you are on your way to great things, Faye."

"Don't say her name!" Eliana shouted.

The remade Faye turned its head to Eliana and began to rush forward. Eliana closed her eyes and let out a strangled sob. The Undriel augmentor stopped Faye and said, "I know you're excited to help your friend, but you are not ready for something so intricate yet. We would let you jump right in with gusto in the past, but we are not in a warzone anymore. Not yet at least."

Eliana stared into the Undriel's array of white glowing eyes with ferocity. It looked over her and flicked out the curved blade. The Undriel rotated the edge so that it was under Eliana's chin. Then it pulled upward to tilt her head to get a better look. "Well, isn't that something. I didn't need L'Arn after all. *You* came to *me*."

Eliana's eyes widened. She recognized the name from Talulo's analysis of the feathers they found. L'Arn had kidnapped her kids and murdered the Daunoren.

He was an Undriel puppet this whole time?

"New plan." The Undriel turned to Faye and nodded. Their eyes flashed as some secret message was delivered between them. Then Faye ignited rockets on her feet and back. A second later, she was in the air and then rocketed off to the west with a sonic boom following her launch. Eliana watched the streak of light cut through the sky faster than anything she had ever seen before.

"Where—where is she going?" Eliana asked.

"That's not your concern, Dr. Eliana *Veston*."

TWENTY-NINE

ZEPHYR GALE SAT ON the seat of her rushcycle and watched the sunrise. She was perched atop an empty parking garage, alone with her thoughts. Her helmet rested in her hands, with the early light from the sun, Delta Octantis, reflecting off its visor. The glow of her tattoos faded as the world became brighter. The last snowflakes of the season melted away on the sleeves of her jacket. The city of white skyscrapers and floating platforms was sprawled out before her. Light spilled into the streets, killing shadows as the day stepped forward.

It had been days since Zephyr and Cade had gone to the Nightsnare. Her investigation had led to the discovery of a strange device, but Cade was still nowhere to be found. She didn't even know what the device's existence meant. Zephyr wiped away the wetness from her eyes and huffed a ragged sigh. She wanted to see Cade and Nella. She wanted to make sure they were safe.

Zephyr was out of ways to help. This was the end of the line for her effort. In a few days, she would return to the spaceport and head back Up to the *Infinite Aria*. Alone. It would be the first time since her very first trip into space that Cade would not be with her.

Her helmet's visor reflected her tired, sad visage. "I wish there was more I could do," she whispered to herself. "You're out there somewhere, and there's just nothing I can do about it."

She wished Cade would surprise her now. Wished he'd walk up beside her, take his earbuds out, and say, *You wouldn't believe where I've been!*

Zephyr sighed, and then her ears caught a sound.

It was a faint sound, like a gospel song being sung from a church a few blocks away. She looked up and saw hundreds of auk'nai flying overhead, all heading in the same direction. They were leaving the city and traveling to the east.

"The Hells?" Zephyr mumbled to herself.

It had been silent since she told Eliana about the strange device she found in the Kamarian archive with Jun. There were no more leads, no more anomalies to chase, no more devices to be found. There had been nothing strange going on until this. This mass exodus of auk'nai didn't seem connected to Cade's disappearance, but maybe if she followed it, she'd find something that did connect.

Zephyr put her helmet on and revved the rushcycle.

THIRTY

<We have waited so long for you to return.> The voice came to Nella's mind again. She rode on the back of Penelope, holding on to her brother as they raced through the dark cave tunnel. Nella kept her bladed bracelet at the ready to swat away more of the mutated Sirens that inhabited the cave system. Here the flowing water had carved out ledges on each side of the river, making it easier for the loamalon to gallop at top speed.

Nella wanted to ask who was speaking to her—*how* were they talking to her—and what they meant about "returning." But she had no way of signing into the darkness of the cave, and thinking her questions had produced no responses so far.

They were jerked forward as Penelope came to a stop in front of a large cave opening. Nella peeked over Cade's shoulder and gasped.

The dome-shaped area of the cave was massive, with glowing stalactites peering through slimy black walls. The dark ooze seemed to drip from every crevice. The ground and walls were littered with half-formed mutant Sirens, each resembling Nhymn in some twisted way. They twitched and gurgled up more ooze. The river pushed into the area from the far end and rushed through the cave's center, with some swirling into a pit below. Water that didn't spill into the central hole escaped back down the tunnel from where Cade and Nella had come from.

Electricity flickered from the hole in the center of the cave. Nella was reminded of the alabaster palace her parents had explored before she was born. In the days of the Nhymn, there had been a month where the Siren had been unaccounted for. Nella began to realize this whole cave system, and this nesting area—or whatever it was—could have been where she was hiding and planning.

Cade tapped his heels against Penelope's sides, and they began to saunter slowly into the nesting room. Nella pulled Cade's sleeve and shook her head.

Cade nodded firmly.

He was right. They needed to make it through the area. The monster auk'gnell could be right behind them, and then they would be stuck between the Sirens and the monster. Cade guided Penelope carefully through the mucky floor, stepping around the half-formed Sirens protruding from the ooze. The river flowed and swirled just off to their right side. One of the Sirens twitched, and Nella was sure it would grab Penelope's leg and pull them all into the mire, but it only lurched and gurgled up more of the black bile through its hollow eye sockets.

Nella noticed there was no smell in the room. Whatever this stuff was on the walls, it didn't emit any sort of odor. She had the same faint taste of the river moisture and general dankness of the cave atmosphere as before they entered. She could feel a low vibration throughout her whole body.

Ahead, three mutated Sirens lay in their path. One was formed all the way to its mid-shins, protruding on an odd angle from the muck. To each of Penelope's sides, more Sirens in various stages of formation were blocking their routes. Cade used his T-bladed daunoren staff to push the right shoulder of the one ahead. It twitched upon contact, but it didn't attack. He eased the thing over to the side, and the Siren's leg snapped as it toppled over into its half-formed sisters.

The room vibrated. Nella could even *see* it chattering. Each of the half-formed Sirens shuddered with the impact as if they all had been affected. With their path clear, Penelope moved forward.

<Come back to us,> the voice said to Nella. Green lights pulsed through the water on the edge of the room and up to the tunnel ahead. The Sirens chattered again.

Nella wanted to tell the voice to shut up. Now was not the time to have a conversation. She looked over her shoulder. The mutant Sirens that had chased them through the caves before were beginning to enter the room. The first ones to enter flopped mindlessly into the ooze, with the others stepping over them.

Nella tugged on Cade's sleeve, her eyebrows raised in worry and her mouth agape. He turned to see the pursuers as well, rapidly approaching. Cade kicked the loamalon's sides, and they propelled forward. The muck was slowing their progress, and the Sirens were gaining.

One mutated Siren got within claw's reach. Nella slammed her bracelet blade into its birdlike skull. It writhed and fell into the half-formed Sirens of the ooze. The ooze began to bubble and roll as the Sirens inside became aware of Cade and Nella's presence. Claws emerged and began to drag at their backs and pull them in. One grabbed Nella's arm. She shrieked as it tried to pull her from Penelope's back. The ooze was up to the loamalon's belly now. They were sinking. A wave of darkness flowed around them, grasping and pulling.

Cade held Nella's other arm, keeping her from being pulled entirely into the darkness. She felt helpless. All she could see was black.

Then she saw a blue light.

Nella felt a rush of heat pass over her. It was as if the air had grown superhot and exploded but didn't bring fire with it. The muck was thrown aside, freeing Penelope's legs. The Sirens were flung away like discarded toys. Some fell into the electrical whirlpool, others into the roiling river around them. Penelope bucked and scrambled to get her footing. When the loamalon could feel the floor again, it sprang forward, darting across the room at full speed.

Cade's eyes ebbed a bright blue light. His dark skin flickered with energy. He held Penelope's reins in one hand, and he swung the T-bladed daunoren staff in the other. Sirens were sliced in half with each wild arc Cade made with his blade.

<*The Decider brought him back too,*> the voice said to Nella. <*We missed our brother.*>

Nella paid no attention to the strange things the mysterious voice was saying. She watched Cade surge with energy and clear their path. As they reached the end of the ooze-filled area, Penelope leaped onto the adjacent stone platform. Behind them, the chasing Sirens poured into the raging river, but they were unable to cross. The current was strong enough to pull them away faster than they could pile in and cross over.

Up ahead was daylight. Nella had to strain her eyes as they grew closer to the end of the cave. They emerged into the early morning sun, surrounded by dense jungle and rock formations. Penelope reared back on her hind legs in victory. She roared a loud, rolling bellow, then slammed her two-toed hooves on the ground, kicking up dust and dirt.

Cade hunched over on the saddle. Nella patted Penelope on the neck, and the loamalon halted its victory dance. Nella dismounted Penelope and pulled Cade onto the ground, where she checked him over. He was breathing, but he was weak. She looked back into the cave tunnel to make sure nothing was following them, and when nothing emerged, she scrambled for Cade's scout jacket saddle. She found the flask of water and went back to her brother's side.

Nella lifted the back of Cade's head and gently poured water into his open mouth. He drank, and his eyes opened. He mouthed something out loud that Nella couldn't hear. She laughed at his mistake, and he smiled.

"*Thank you,*" he signed, and nodded.

"*You saved us,*" Nella signed back.

Cade looked confused. He sat up. "*Didn't you do something to the ooze?*"

She shook her head. *"That was you,"* she signed.

Cade looked around, then slowly brought himself to his feet. He flexed his hands as he peered at his fingers in confusion. Cade's face suddenly flashed into a smile, and he rushed toward the cliff ledge. Nella followed him over and looked out over the vast desert plains. Cade waved his hands wildly and was shouting something.

In the distance, the *Rogers* was floating toward the trees. It must have been responding to Cade's flare. Hope instantly filled them, and Nella joined Cade's side, shouting and waving.

Nella felt a cold embrace her. Metal and inhuman.

A vise wrapped itself around Nella, pinning her arms to her sides. Before she could figure out what it was, she was ripped backward so fast she almost blacked out. The jungle floor punched at her as she bounced along the ground, then was flung back into the air. Nella whipped past Penelope, scaring the loamalon. The faithful beast stomped its feet and shrieked. The air was knocked out of Nella's lungs when her movement halted abruptly.

Nella gasped for air and looked up to see three glowing yellow eyes. With her arms pinned to her sides, she couldn't slash at it with her bladed bracelet. It pulled Nella close to its beak. There was a white flash that followed, and then darkness.

Before unconsciousness overtook her, she could hear the mysterious voice say, *<You must come back to us. Don't leave us again.>*

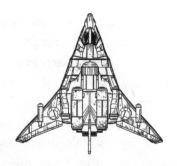

THIRTY-ONE

"YOU HAVE BEEN A tough human to find," the Undriel augmentor said to Eliana. "If I knew you'd come to me, I wouldn't have sent L'Arn out to fetch you."

Eliana lay in the grass, her leg broken. Tears ran down her cheek in a mixture of horror and sadness. Faye had been absorbed right before Eliana's eyes. She wanted the machine to kill her, get it over with. Undriel weren't known to waste time taunting, so what made this one do so now?

"Ironically, I may not even need you anymore. You've delivered me this unexpected gift," the Undriel said and walked past the burning rover. Its left arm detached and began to disassemble the vehicle. At the same time, the rest of its body approached the upper half of Homer. The Undriel considered the robot for a moment. The two were like half-siblings. The Undriel didn't bend to pick up Homer. Instead, its arm lashed out like a whip and grabbed the android.

The mysterious puck device had planted itself in Homer's chest and dug into their body with tendrils made of metal. It hummed with energy. Eliana had never seen collider cylinders like that before this investigation began. The Undriel's spiderlike head spun and faced her, and then the rest of its body turned. "Perhaps you remember me? I worked for your father a long time ago."

The Undriel augmentor walked back through the grass toward Eliana. Its arm had finished absorbing material from the downed rover and rejoined the rest of its mechanical body. It slung a pile of parts onto the Undriel's back. It could absorb again now, make Eliana into a machine just like itself, as it had done to Faye moments ago. This was what made fighting the Undriel in space stations so hard. Surrounded by metal and machinery, they could absorb more humans by disassembling the station around them for spare parts.

"You look like all the other Undriel soldiers." Eliana spat the words. "Why would I remember you?"

"Oh, where are my manners?" The Undriel laughed. It leaned forward, and its head split in half and pulled back to reveal a human face adorned in a crown of metal tubes and machinery. It was a male in his late fifties, possibly. Eliana recognized the face instantly, although the black marble in his right eye had not been there when she had met him in the past.

"Dr. Auden Nouls," Eliana gasped. The man who had brought the crown technology to Tibor Undriel. The man who had started the chain reaction that eventually led to humanity being chased from the Sol System—the man who had initiated the apocalypse.

"You *do* remember me!" Auden said with a smile.

Dr. Nouls was part of the original *Telemachus* project, working alongside John and George in the early days. Eliana remembered the day her father had removed Auden from the project. Dr. Nouls had wanted to use technology to evolve humanity, but his methods made his subjects nonhuman in the process.

"Your father didn't see artificial intelligence the way I did. He saw it as a partner." Auden held the half body of Homer and inspected it with disdain. "I saw it as much more than that. I saw it as a ladder." A thin rod protruded from Auden's wrist, and he plunged it into the smooth surface of the puck device on Homer's chest. The rod breached the disc's flat surface as if he had slipped it into a puddle without disturbing the water around it. "That's why I quit when I did. I had other interested parties who wanted to do things the right way."

Eliana knew that was a lie; she was there when her father fired him. It wasn't hard to guess where he took his business after that day.

"Tibor Undriel," Eliana said flatly.

"My good friend Tibor is waiting for me right now."

"What do you want with me?" Eliana asked.

Auden stood over her, and for a moment, she thought he'd absorb her right there. Eliana thought of her children, remembering them as toddlers laughing and playing together. She saw Denton and his smile. She braced herself for destruction.

But destruction didn't come.

"I hate to admit it. I don't need *you*, Eliana. I needed your father. But this machine you brought me might be even better than the man himself."

Eliana looked toward the dirt. "Then kill me and get it over with."

"Maybe I will. I don't remember how I left things with John. It was a very long time ago. Should I be *angry*? Should I vent my anger on you?" Auden's wrist lashed out and grabbed Eliana, lifting her into the air. He closed his spider-bot head and said, "No, no. I may still need you. If this Homer unit fails, you're my contingency plan. I hope you can hold your breath long enough to be of use." Auden turned toward the cliff ledge and said, "When my work is done, perhaps I will make you perfect. Or perhaps I will kill you. You Vestons are slippery fish. It might not be worth keeping you around."

Eliana grunted and grasped at the strong metal claw holding her up.

Rockets on Auden's locust-like legs ignited. They rose into the air above the grass, then flew over the side of the cliff. The Undriel was a graceful flier. Eliana almost felt like they were simply walking through the air. They lowered toward the water. Before they breached the waves, Auden's rocket feet changed their propulsion type to something Eliana had never seen before. Auden walked across the ocean's surface, creating strange, orange, glowing ripples of energy with each step.

They approached a cave. Auden stepped from the water and onto the rocky shore, and the ripples of light stopped, but his stride remained the same. The walls of the cave ahead were covered in Undriel technology. Black metal, machinery, and pipes lined the walls.

Eliana almost threw up from the smell of decay that filled the air. The center of the cave had a flat surface with Nock'lu's dissected body on display. On the wall behind the corpse was something new—a robotic frame. It had similarities to Auden, but with an auk'gnell spin to it. Instead of insects, the frame looked like various birds of prey. It had a sharp metal beak, long-bladed wings, four arms, and a tentacle that held something akin to a daunoren staff.

Auden pushed Eliana against the wall, and mechanical arms clasped around her, pinning her in place. Her leg had a dull pain to it, but her horror pushed that pain to the back of her mind.

Auden planted Homer on top of Nock'lu's body and retracted the metal rod from the puck on their chest. Homer's eyes lit up, and Auden patted them on the head. The Undriel augmentor moved toward the entrance of the cave and looked out over the crimson waves. "My friends are trapped out there, just under the waves. Do you know how long they have been waiting for me to rescue them?" Auden said. "Close to two hundred and seventy years, Sol-standard. I hope they brought something to read."

Eliana thought for a moment—that didn't make sense. If what Auden was saying was true, that meant the Undriel had been on Kamaria for almost 230 years *longer* than humanity had been.

"How is that possible?" Eliana asked. "It takes three hundred years of travel to get from Sol to Delta Octantis."

"Maybe for *you* it did." Auden laughed.

The Undriel had been on Kamaria the entire time, trapped in their ship under the sea. This was what Nhymn had stumbled upon. This was the reason she wanted to leave the planet so badly. Nhymn knew they were here, and she abandoned the planet.

There has to be more to this than he's admitting. The physics are impossible.

"I'll admit, I took long naps in stasis." Auden said, turning back to Homer and plunging his wrist-rod into various parts of the robot. "I told my body to wake me up in certain situations. Although my form is perfect, a mind can rot with nothing to do."

"You stayed *here* the whole time? In this cave?" Eliana asked.

Auden stopped, hesitating in his work. He retracted his wrist-rod and said, "I don't need to explain myself. I had my reasons." Homer's head jerked sideways. "There's no rush to do anything when you can live forever."

Auden was nothing like any of the stories of Undriel that Eliana had heard over the years. He was chatty and sophisticated. How an Undriel couldn't fix a ship in almost three hundred years made no sense. Eliana was sure that Auden could have traveled to an auk'nai city and found any resources he needed. Suddenly, there was a theory that made all these things make sense.

"You were *scared*." Eliana smiled.

Auden looked up at her.

"If you left this cave and something destroyed you out in the wild, then the Undriel would be trapped in their ship forever. Everything you accomplished would not have mattered if they just rotted in the ship for all eternity. You were *afraid* to die alone," Eliana said. "Apparently, you're more human than you realized."

Auden hesitated, then said, "If this little trick I'm about to perform doesn't work, then I'm going to need you to swim down there and free my friends. If you can't, then I will kill you and find someone else who can. I'm sure your son or daughter is up for the task." The Undriel picked up Homer's body and slithered out of the cave toward the water, using his centipede-form legs to move seamlessly toward the shore. His legs morphed into a bipedal form, and he took a few steps out over the waves, then slipped into the water without making a splash.

"Coward," Eliana muttered after Auden had left. She tried to free herself from the metal arms and escape, but they held her firmly against the wall. She hoped Homer couldn't fix whatever was wrong with the Undriel ship. *What does Homer have to do with it? What exactly is going on under the waves? There has to be more to this.* Auden may have believed Eliana could help as a backup, but she didn't know the first thing about fixing interstellar starships. Where her father had studied engineering, she'd studied medicine. If Homer failed, Auden and the Undriel would quite literally be dead in the water.

———◆———

Sergeant Jess Combs pulled herself ashore and coughed up a lungful of water. Her suit alerted her that she had been cut with an Undriel blade and administered a healing salve, stopping the localized hemophilia caused by Undriel metal lacerations. Although it was common three hundred years ago during the old war in the Sol System, Jess had never thought she'd hear that alert come from her suit on Kamaria.

She pulled herself over to a nearby boulder and leaned her back against it as she regained her senses. The Undriel augmentor had flung her from the cliffside, away from Faye, Homer, and Eliana. Jess had failed to protect them.

A roar of jet fire filled the sky. Jess peered over the boulder and watched as the Undriel augmentor floated down toward the water, carrying Eliana and Homer in its arms. Its cloak flapped in the wind as it moved gracefully into a cave.

Where's Faye? Jess wondered, but she knew the probable answer. She had been half crushed by the *Tiger* rover during its wreck, and she was either absorbed after Jess's failure or killed by her injuries. *Shit.*

Maybe she would get lucky and still have time to save Faye later. Jess tried to keep her hopes up, but she had fought this enemy before, in a war that was so hopeless, they ran across the stars to escape it.

Jess checked her equipment. Her particle rifle remained with her, magnetically attached to the armor on her back. The collider pistol was still slung in its holster on her hip. Two stun grenades were on her chest plate and a combat knife on her right shoulder.

Thoughts of the old tricks filled her mind—old battles, trials and errors made by plenty of brave men and women who were absorbed along the way. Every strategy they used against the Undriel was bought with human lives.

Silently, Jess moved across the shore. She used boulders to keep out of direct eyesight, should the Undriel emerge looking for her. Her suit could still help. Jess had a panel on her wrist that affected the way it used power. She toggled "cold" mode, which would hide her from other sensors the Undriel used to find humans. In this mode, she would have to work harder to move, and her jump-jet would be inaccessible, but stealth would be her advantage.

When she reached the cave mouth, she crammed herself against the wall and kept low to the ground. She could hear talking from inside. *Chatty bastard, isn't he?* Jess thought. All of her previous encounters with the Undriel had been silent affairs.

"If this little trick I'm about to perform doesn't work, then I'm going to need you to swim down there and free my friends. If you can't, then I will kill you and find someone else who can. I'm sure your son or daughter is up for the task," the Undriel said, and a heartbeat later, it emerged from the cave carrying Homer's limp robotic half-body.

Jess held her breath and kept her suit toggled in cold mode. She watched as the machine slipped under the waves and out of sight— *time to move.*

Favoring her pistol, she whirled into the mouth of the cave. She didn't let the horror of the dissected auk'nai on the table distract her. With her focus on Eliana's safety, Jess blasted the two mechanical arms holding the woman against the wall.

Eliana looked relieved to see Jess. She cried, "I thought you were dead."

Jess said nothing, her focus on mechanisms in the room.

Eyes emerged from the metal walls, with particle guns close

behind. Eliana dropped to the floor and began to crawl toward Jess. The eyes went into alert mode, and the guns started to hum with energy. These were Undriel defense drones, automated things with basic functions, no human interior.

In one movement, Jess slid her pistol across the floor to Eliana and palmed her assault rifle. She set the gun to spread shot and sprayed the room with buckshot particle blasts as she moved toward Eliana. Drones were ripped apart, with some breaking away from the wall to rush them with knifelike appendages.

"Shoot the ones that get close!" Jess shouted.

With one hand, Jess grabbed Eliana's jacket near her shoulder and began to pull her from the cave. Particle blasts cracked against the cave's floor where Eliana's feet had been. Eliana picked off drones with the pistol as they raced toward her with their knives outstretched.

"Is Faye here?" Jess asked, shouting over the destruction while blasting away at the drones.

"She's been—" Eliana couldn't say it. She cracked the skulls of a few more drones with some well-placed shots.

"Shit," Jess said. They made it outside, the sea at their backs. Jess shot the last drone, and Eliana picked off the final knife-wielder as it approached her. There was a deep bass noise mixed with an intense vibration as the sea burst with foam. They turned to see lights under the surface of the boiling sea. A rock formation crumbled into the water.

A leviathan was coming to life.

"Oh, God. It worked," Eliana whispered in horror.

"We can't stay here," Jess said. She pulled Eliana onto her back and shouted, "Hold on tight!" Jess shut off cold mode and used the jump-jets on her legs and free arm to propel them into the side of the cliff and scramble upward. They bounded off a few hanging boulders until they were eventually at the top of the grassy cliff ledge.

They didn't stop to watch. Jess continued her breakneck pace, getting as much distance from the Undriel cave as possible. She ran across the grassy cliffside, breaking into the tree line of the forest nearby. Eventually, Jess's legs gave out, and they tumbled to the ground. They lay there for a moment, catching their breath. Eliana sat up and looked at her soothreader. She had power again, now that they were away from the disruptive technology of the Undriel machines.

"Dr. Castus—" a voice came in over the comm channel, slightly fuzzy. "Are you out here, Dr. Castus?"

"Yes!" Eliana shouted into her soothreader. "I am pinging you our coordinates. We need immediate evac."

Jess stood and watched the horizon through the trees. The clouds blotted out the rising sun, and the threat of rain loomed in the air. The old enemy was back. *Hells, how could this happen?*

The transport ship circled in and landed in the grass at the edge of the forest. The access ramp lowered, and a marine beckoned them to get inside. Jess helped Eliana to her feet and noticed her shin hanging at an irregular angle. During all the chaos, Jess had not seen exactly how injured Eliana was until now. Jess hurried her to the ship's medical bay to repair her broken leg.

Eliana sat down in the auto-surgeon's seat and cursed. "How could this go so wrong?" she asked as she prepped the machine.

"I told you the Undriel always have a trick." Jess reminded her. Eliana nodded and lay back in the seat to begin her treatment. When she was secure, Jess moved to the cockpit with the other marine.

"Sir, what happened out there?" the marine asked as he got back in the pilot's seat. "I found the *Tiger* all smashed up. Weren't there more of you?"

Jess sat in the copilot's seat. "I need a secure line to Odysseus Command."

"Roger that," the marine said, asking no more questions. He toggled a few controls to give her access to the comm. Within a few heartbeats, she received an answer.

"This is Odysseus Command, reading you."

Jess leaned into the microphone and said, "Odysseus Command, we have a situation."

THIRTY-TWO

IT HAPPENED SO FAST Cade barely registered it at first. Nella was ripped away from his side. He managed to turn quick enough to see her vanish into the jungle, followed by a bright flash in the trees.

The monster had somehow gotten ahead of them. And now Nella was taken.

"Nella!" Cade ran to Penelope and mounted the loamalon in one smooth movement. "Yah!" With a kick to the sides, the loamalon sprang into the jungle, racing through the dense foliage. Bushes and low-hanging branches assaulted them along the way. Cade didn't care. The only thing that mattered was finding Nella.

The sun was rising. But even with the light filling the jungle, the pursuit had gone cold quickly. Cade followed the path that should have led to Nella and found himself surrounded by boulders and trees. He steered Penelope in a circle as he looked for any clues.

<*OVER HERE,*> a booming voice came to Cade.

"What the—" he whispered through ragged breaths.

<*FOLLOW THE LIGHTS,*> the voice said again. This time, Cade turned to see a path glowing in the bushes and trees. They were so bright that even the approaching daylight could not blot it out.

There wasn't any time to question. Cade followed the path. Penelope pounded through the jungle, grunting and heaving with the strain of all the running. Ahead, the monster was preparing to take off into the sky. Cade kicked Penelope, and she bolted it forward. As the auk'gnell left the ground, Penelope leaped into the air.

The loamalon collided with the auk'gnell with a resounding crash. All four bodies tumbled to the ground and rolled down a slope in the jungle. Cade couldn't stop his tumbling or make sense of where he was falling. The whole world felt like a spin cycle in a washing machine. Color and light blurred together—the shrieking birdcall of the auk'gnell mixed with the roaring of the loamalon. Nella tumbled silently.

Cade hit a hard, flat area facedown. He felt every bump and bruise from the violence of the tumble. There was a loud clattering as his T-bladed daunoren staff fell near him. He looked up and watched as Nella rolled into the open area ahead of him. The auk'gnell and the loamalon came to a stop near her. Penelope recovered the fastest of the group, kicked her long legs out, and scrambled to her feet to back away from the auk'gnell.

They found themselves in an area open to the sky, with rock ledges and vines. Inert nezzarform statues stood in a circle around the site on a higher ledge, peering down like stone judges. Defunct remnants of Nhymn's twisted nezzarform army. These had moss growing on them, and some even had small bird nests within their cracks and crevices.

Nella remained motionless. Cade's heart sank. He couldn't tell if she was breathing from this range. The monster auk'gnell rose to its feet, its mechanical arm venting steam and its head shooting sparks in violent spurts.

"Enough!" the monster said through technical glitches and sparks. It flicked its nonaugmented hand, and its sword morphed into the shape of a long katana. The monster began to approach Nella and raise its sword.

Cade grabbed his T-bladed daunoren staff and rushed toward the auk'gnell. As the monster brought its sword crashing down, Cade slid on his knees and intercepted it with his daunoren blade. A loud clang echoed off the boulders. Cade pushed sideways, parrying the monster's sword. The morphing blade ricocheted toward the stone floor and sliced away rock as if it were melted butter.

Cade stood over Nella's body and kept his daunoren blade ready. He had never fought with a weapon like this before, but it felt natural in his hands. Somewhere, riding the wind that sighed through the jungle trees, a song came to Cade. It filled him with a rhythm like a drumbeat, pounding with his heart. He took in a deep breath and let the song fill him.

The monster auk'gnell roared and rushed forward. It swung its morphed katana horizontally at Cade. He ducked under it in time, then brought his daunoren blade up fast enough to deflect the metal arm that followed the sword swipe. Cade flicked his wrist and brought his blade around in an arc, slicing the mechanical claw away from the monster's wrist. The claw crashed to the ground with a heavy thud, where it twitched and sparked.

Cade smashed the back end of his daunoren staff into the monster's augmented eyes. He heard glass shatter, and the beast shrieked. The auk'gnell slapped its wing into Cade's side and sent him rolling across the mossy stone floor.

Cade recovered and crashed his blade into the auk'gnell's sword, pressing into his defense. Penelope whistled and stamped her feet in confused terror. The loamalon was scared but remained in the arena. The auk'gnell parried Cade's blade then flapped its wings, propelling itself forward into Cade—shoulder first. It smashed him against the wall. One of the nezzarform statues above crumbled, sending large rocks cascading onto the monster. The auk'gnell was struck by some of the falling debris and took a step back to avoid further injury.

It was a small opening, but Cade took advantage of it. He thrust his blade forward and struck the monster auk'gnell in the shoulder area between feathers and mechanical arm. The monster roared and pulled Cade's blade from its skin, releasing a torrent of blood. Steam vented from the augmented arm. Small robotic needles emerged from the monster's pauldron and began to stitch the arm back onto the monster's flesh.

The auk'gnell twisted its sword, and it morphed into a curved blade. It swung the scythe, not at Cade's body, but at his weapon.

The curved blade wrapped around Cade's daunoren staff and wrenched it free, flinging it over to Penelope's feet. The loamalon whinnied in surprise and stamped its feet, but it stayed in place.

Unarmed, Cade watched as the monster swung its blade around again. He dodged to his right in a sloppy maneuver that caused him to roll against the stone wall. The auk'gnell followed him only a heartbeat behind, swinging and morphing its scythe into various different blades in an attempt to cut Cade in half.

Cade scrambled along the rim of the rock wall and rushed toward Penelope, just missing the blade with every swing. In one movement, he grabbed the daunoren blade in his left hand and Penelope's makeshift saddle in his right. The loamalon began to run. The auk'gnell got one good slash at Cade's leg, spraying blood onto the stones.

Cade ignored the pain and lifted himself onto Penelope's saddle. He pulled hard on her reins and spun to face the monster. The auk'gnell was flying straight at them, gaining the distance rapidly. Nella lay unconscious on the floor behind Penelope. Cade was the last line of defense.

He had to protect her. <*WE WILL NOT FAIL AGAIN!*> the voice boomed.

Cade felt heat rise within him, filling in his lungs and surging through his arms. The monster arched its sword back, ready to strike. As the auk'gnell brought its sword down, a wave of blue energy exploded from within Cade. The auk'gnell was knocked backward and smashed into the rock wall. Its mechanical arm and augmented head began to violently spurt electricity. Its wings had been broken from the impact. The monster was a bloody mess of feathers and broken machinery.

Cade marched Penelope toward the monster slowly, feeling the immense energy within him spill into the air.

———◆———

L'Arn was scared for the first time in his life.

He had lived in the wild for a long time, where he had encountered many things, but never anything like the horror that paced toward him. The sun was beating into his damaged, augmented eyes, filling them with a blinding white light. The human he faced fought like a titanovore, and its Song was as loud and intense as an entire chorus. The man stepped toward L'Arn, a shadow against the bright sun.

His silhouette didn't look human.

L'Arn could see a behemoth before him that had the top half of a man and the bottom half of a loamalon. The shadow was all one shape. Its eyes were glowing an intense blue, so brightly that they almost merged together in their luminosity like one cyclopean eye. Energy spilled from the thing before him and raced up the rock walls to the null nezzarforms. They began to glow, and then they began to chant.

<*Karx! Karx! Karx!*> The voices repeated the strange word.

L'Arn lifted his Undriel blade to shield himself from the nightmare shadow before him, but it sputtered and flopped in his hand. The blast of energy had caused all of his augmentations to malfunction. All of Auden's "perfect gifts" were reduced to garbage.

The blood rage filled L'Arn, and he muscled through his injuries to ready for a pounce. The four-legged shadow stepped toward him slowly. L'Arn's mechanical arm dangled loosely from his shoulder, but his auk'gnell hand still had sharp claws. He thought of everything he had done for Auden—murdered the Daunoren, killed Nock'lu, slain a fellow auk'gnell on the shore of the far lake, and kidnapped people he didn't have any attachment to. The thought that it all might have been for nothing caused him to seethe with hate for himself.

L'Arn remembered freedom. He remembered living in the wilderness alone, cultivating the land, forging his own path. Since the day Auden saved him, he had been like a caged animal—a dog. Whatever that was. He wanted to be free again. L'Arn knew he could never return to his life of solitude after what he had done to the world. The Song would not allow him to rest. He thought of his nest in the far shore and the gentle sway of the trees there—the calmness of nature and the freedom that came with every new day. He could never have it back. L'Arn lowered his beak and stared down the approaching shadow.

L'Arn vaulted toward the human.

———◆———

<*Karx! Karx! Karx!*> the mysterious voices chanted.

Cade's mind was clear. This was no blackout episode of power. He had been aware of all of his actions and understood everything that was happening to him now. When the auk'gnell launched, he was ready.

The monster raced toward him at incredible speed. Cade swung downward with his daunoren blade, catching the monster auk'gnell directly in the neck. The blade sank into the monster's body diagonally, cutting all the way to its mid-chest. Cade released the blade and allowed the auk'gnell to stumble back a few paces. The daunoren staff remained firmly lodged in place.

The chanting stopped.

The monster coughed raggedly. Blood spilled from its beak as it shuffled past Cade. The auk'gnell stood and wobbled for a moment but didn't turn to face him. It pulled the blade from its neck and dropped it to the ground with a loud clang. It looked up to the sky for a long moment and exhaled its last breath, then slumped onto the stone facedown.

The monster auk'gnell had been slain.

Cade took a few deep breaths as the energy that had filled him began to wane. He heard something mixed with the light jungle breeze. It was a different song—a deep humming. It was somber, yet also filled with happiness.

"The Song of the Dead," Cade whispered to himself, remembering something Hrun'dah had told him. He listened to the song, hearing its sweet tune mix with the world around him. At once,

Cade could feel Kamaria in his blood. It felt warm like a hug, soft like a blanket, brisk like a breeze, and it tickled like a lover. It also felt very familiar, but Cade couldn't explain how.

Cade looked at the daunoren staff on the ground near the monster auk'gnell's dead body. Cade had been to the Spirit Song Mountain, where the dead Daunoren laid. He had plucked a stone from the cave there and brought it back to the colony with him. He even found a daunoren staff of his own later, reclaimed from the body of a deceased auk'gnell.

Did that count as a pilgrimage? Cade wondered. He had been the only human to take anything from the mountain. The Song of Kamaria was not science. It was not organized in the way societies were. It was nature. It didn't accept resumés or care about qualifications. The Song of Kamaria had accepted Cade's accidental pilgrimage.

Humans were not so songless, after all.

Cade dismounted Penelope and patted her fur. The loamalon had become a dear friend during the short time they had come to know each other. With the monster auk'gnell dead, they were free. Penelope could leave whenever she wanted. For now, she remained at Cade's side.

Nella groaned and lifted herself up from the floor. Cade went to her side and helped her into a sitting position. She saw the monster's body, and her eyes went wide. Cade patted her shoulder and signed, *"Dead,"* flopping both hands, palms facing each other, from left to right.

Her face relaxed with relief.

The siblings stared at their monster's corpse, wondering what it was all about. Why was it so crucial for this auk'gnell to chase them across the continent, and what had happened to it to make it half machine? Cade listened to the Song of the Dead as it faded away with the breeze. He pictured the auk'gnell free of its augmentations, no longer an abomination. The auk'gnell whistled, bowed its beak in appreciation, and walked away into the unknown. Somehow, Cade thought he understood the monster right at the end.

Nella shook her head and rubbed her face. She stood and looked around at the nezzarforms statues. They were pulsing with a dim green light.

Cade stood and tapped her shoulder. *"What is it?"* he signed.

"I can hear them," Nella signed, her movements slow and her face scrunched in confusion.

Cade's eyes widened. He knew the voices she spoke of—he had heard them call him Karx. Currently, he couldn't hear the voices, but perhaps they had nothing to say to him now. He remembered the booming voice that guided him through the jungle to find the monster and Nella. It all led them here, to the inert nezzarforms, maybe not as inert as once thought. The nezzarforms wanted them here. For what purpose, Cade didn't know.

The roar of starship engines came from above the trees. Cade covered his eyes against the bright sun. A shadow came over them, shaped something like an arrow. It was a scout ship—more specifically, it was the Pilgrim-class explorer called the *Rogers*. Cade was so excited to see it he waved both arms in the air and felt every injury he had sustained during the fight. Nella stood next to him and began waving too. The scout ship lowered its landing gear and began to bring itself toward the ground between the trees.

Something moved so fast Cade could barely tell if he imagined it. There was an explosion. The *Rogers* took on a mad tilt. Cade's eyes widened in horror as the ship caught fire and smashed into the ground near them. Cade and Nella were flung backward from the explosion that followed.

THIRTY-THREE

THE SUN WAS RISING, and hope was filling Denton's heart. He sat in the copilot's chair of the *Rogers* as Talulo began the flight sequence. In the main cabin behind them were Lance Corporal Rafa Ghanem and two other Tvashtar marines. They were on their way to finally find Cade and Nella.

Denton was about to save his children.

The flare had long extinguished, but they had committed its approximate location to memory. The flare was like the light at the end of a long, dark tunnel. Denton had never given up hope, and now he saw that hope fulfilled. He thought of the other problems he would have to one day face. The Siren in the pit was a nightmare, and it would have to be taken care of, but it could wait. This moment was about rescuing his kids and nothing else.

"Liftoff," Talulo whistled. The *Rogers* took to the sky, and it would only be a matter of minutes until it arrived at the location on the cliff. Denton felt the rhythm of a drum beating in his chest, and his face felt hotter the closer they got to the cliff ledge. Once they arrived, they searched the area for any signs of Cade and Nella. With only a rough idea of where the flare had come from, they had a general radius to search through. Denton shifted back and forth like waves on the shore, dread and excitement stirring in the swirling waters of his mind. Close to an hour passed, with no noticeable movement. A buzz on the comm interrupted their search.

"*Rogers*, this is Telemachus Outpost. Can you hear me?" George Tanaka asked over the comm channel.

"We hear you, George. We're tracking Cade and Nella right now. Hopefully, we'll have some good news soon," Denton said.

"That's excellent!" Marie Viray cut in.

"Yes, yes, quite. I have a question for Talulo if you have a moment," George asked.

Talulo whistled, "Yes?"

"We are seeing a lot of auk'nai approaching the *Telemachus* crash site. Do you know anything about this?"

Talulo turned to Denton and cooed, "Yes, Talulo is aware. Talulo sent auk'nai to the crash site. Talulo surveyed the site when the others were inside investigating the admiral's quarters. It is perfect."

Denton eyed his auk'nai friend with confused wonder and asked, "Perfect for what?"

Talulo cooed again, pleased with himself. Before he could answer, Denton saw his children standing in a stone circle below. Talulo traced his gaze and whistled with joy.

"It's them! We *found* them!" Denton felt tears in his eyes. "It's actually them!"

"Well, hurry! We can discuss this auk'nai . . . *bus* . . . *late*—" George's channel cut out. The lights in the cockpit shut off, and the engines reverted to backup power to keep the *Rogers* from falling. Denton looked around, and before he could register the object rapidly approaching the *Rogers*, they were struck. The ship was pierced through its hull and began to spin. It fell to the ground. Denton was jerked sideways so fast that the Tvashtar marine suit he wore went into recovery mode to keep his spine from snapping. The *Rogers* smashed into the ground below and cracked in half with a blast.

———◆———

Nella pushed herself off the ground and looked toward the crash. *Were Mom and Dad inside?* she frantically thought to herself. She coughed, trying to get the air back into her lungs. Cade was slowly getting to his feet, and Penelope ran into the tree line of the jungle in fear.

Shapes emerged from the fire and smoke of the *Rogers* crash. They stumbled about in confusion until they found each other, then inspected for injuries. Some were in worse condition than others, but they were all standing, which was a good sign. It looked like four Tvashtar marines and a wingless auk'nai—safe to assume it was the pilot, Talulo. He was most likely in the cockpit, away from the thing that passed through the center of the ship. The auk'nai pilot was beaten and bruised, but alive. The marines spread out from the crash, searching for whatever took the ship down. It wasn't until one marine ran toward her with his arms open that she recognized her father in a combat suit.

Denton hugged Nella so hard that she thought she might snap in half, but she didn't care. She hugged him back and matched his intensity, as if any slight separation might tear them apart and throw them across the world. When the hug ended, he held her at arm's length and checked her for injuries, then looked over her shoulder for Cade. Cade surprised them from the side and embraced them both. Tears began to run down their cheeks as they smiled with immense joy.

The family was back together again.

Denton used Sol-Sign while speaking so both his children could understand him. *"Are you injured?"*

They shook their heads. Cade asked a question vocally and pointed to the ship. Nella read his lips. "What happened? What do we do now?"

Denton shook his head, unsure. Talulo approached them and pushed his head against Nella's chest. She could feel the vibrations in his neck and feathers as he cooed with delight.

<The shade—the shade—the shade.> The voices came to Nella's mind. They seemed to grow frantic, and their sounds overlapped each other in panic. The words came to Nella like an echo in a cave. <Danger—danger—DANGER!>

Something dropped from the sky—long and black—and impacted with the *Rogers's* wreck. The twisted metal began to rip itself apart and repurpose its shape. Nella could hardly see the insectoid metal arm and the razor-sharp blades that swirled around in the fire. After some reconfiguring, the metal arm shot off into the sky, bringing with it a large amount of the ship's hull.

The Tvashtar marines began firing at something in the trees.

A figure had zipped around the jungle canopy and stopped to allow the metal arm to fly back to its shoulder. It was a metal monstrosity, something Nella had only seen in history books. Its head a robotic spider, its body metal a wasp, its legs an iron locust, its arms mantis scythes. Nella was looking at an Undriel foot soldier.

The Undriel came into view for only a moment, then darted into one of the marines and dragged him into the forest. A heartbeat later, its mechanical arm flew out from the trees and crashed into the remaining wreck to gather more material.

Denton grabbed Nella by the arm and shouted something to Cade and Talulo. They hurried into the jungle as the Undriel smashed into another marine and began absorbing him on the spot. Nella could see the machine devouring the marine, ripping his body to pieces and replacing his flesh with metal.

In her mind, Nella could hear the voices screaming, <Don't leave—DON'T leave—DON'T LEAVE!>

———◆———

Cade could hear the marines screaming, metal whirring, and the awful low bass tone the Undriel emitted. It was a nightmare enemy that made their monster auk'gnell seem like a baby arcophant. Denton handed Cade his assault rifle. His father urged Cade to follow him into the jungle with Talulo and Nella. Cade winced as the mysterious voice came to him once more. *<Karx! Stop! Come back! Bring her back!>*

Are you kidding me? Do you see that thing? Cade thought to himself. He followed the others into the jungle. After running for some time, they pressed up against a mossy rock and caught their breath. Talulo kept an eye on the jungle behind them, gun raised.

"Was that—" Cade tried to ask between breaths.

"An Undriel footsoldier. I only saw video feeds of those, but that's definitely one of them," Denton answered.

"How the Hells—" Cade began but was cut off when a rustling came from the nearby foliage. Denton lifted his collider pistol. Penelope burst through the bushes and stomped around in fear and excitement.

"Hold your fire!" Cade shouted. "That loamalon is with us."

Penelope shook her long snout toward Cade and approached them. She nuzzled against Nella's chest and accepted some reassuring petting.

"It's *with* you? How the . . . you tamed it?" Denton asked, impressed.

"Sort of. Nella did something to it," Cade said. "A lot has happened. I'm not sure how to explain it. I've heard these voices recently. I don't know what it is or why it's happening."

Denton thought for a moment and shook his head. "Are you sure you hear voices? You guys have been out here for a long time. You might be exhausted—or maybe it's shock."

"I *heard* them, Dad. Nella said she could somehow too." Denton looked like he had been slapped with shock. Cade continued, "They helped me find Nella in the jungle when I lost her. The monster took her and ran off, and without the voice's guidance, he would have taken her away."

"*Monster?* Cade means L'Arn," Talulo said. "Where is L'Arn?"

"Was that his name?" Cade now knew the name of their nemesis. He remembered the Song of the Dead and the bittersweet tune L'Arn had sung as he left this world for another, far stranger one. Cade sighed. "I had to kill him. He gave me no choice."

Talulo nodded somberly. He lowered his pistol. "Talulo knew L'Arn while in the Song of Apusticus. Finest hunter to the city. But L'Arn sought freedom. L'Arn did not fight with Apusticus against the Siren Nhymn. What happened to L'Arn after going auk'gnell, Talulo did not know."

"It sounds like he ran into an Undriel, by the looks of it," Cade explained. "He had a robotic arm and eyes."

"We have been searching for you for days," Denton said. "In that time, we have been tracing L'Arn's actions. We found some Undriel devices, and we couldn't believe it. It all ties back to the murder of the Daunoren. Looks like the Undriel finally found Kamaria."

Talulo sneered, "Humans were so sure they had left Undriel behind."

"Hey, what's that supposed to mean?" Denton asked.

Talulo shook his beak and turned away.

"Regardless," Cade interrupted, "these voices have to be something important."

"Let's figure it out when we get back to the city," Denton said. "Right now, we need to focus on contacting the other marine transport ship and getting the Hells out of here." He gestured over his soothreader and noticed it was offline.

Cade turned to Nella. She was holding her ears and kneeling on the ground. He went to her side and put his arm around her. As soon as he touched her, Cade could hear the voices screaming, *<COME BACK—COME BACK—COME BACK!>*

A machine roared. It was like a spaceship being shredded into fragments. Cade, Denton, and Talulo turned in the direction of the sound. An Undriel foot soldier covered in orange and black metal rushed toward them, slicing through trees with its sharp-bladed arms. It was one of the marines, absorbed using the orange metal hull of the *Rogers*.

"Shit—shoot it!" Denton shouted, and there was an eruption of gunfire. Cade, Denton, and Talulo sent a barrage of particle blasts into the approaching machine. One of the Undriel's arms fell off and wreathed on the jungle floor while the rest of it dodged behind a boulder. Denton turned to Cade. "Get you and your sister out of here."

"Screw that! We're not leaving you," Cade shouted. "We'll fight this thing together."

The Undriel emerged from behind the boulder and leaped into the air. It morphed its arms into a sort of helicopter blade and smashed into the ground ahead of their group.

Penelope ran off, hustling into the jungle at high speed. The rest of the group split up and continued firing on the machine. The Undriel whirled its blade at Denton, who jump-jetted backward to a higher ledge. Cade unleashed a burst of particle blasts at the machine. It turned toward him and took a step forward.

Denton jump-jetted onto the Undriel's back. He let loose a few shots into the back of the machine's spider-bot head and watched as blood splattered onto the rocks below. The machine's body writhed with multiple errors, and then it collapsed onto the ground and split into various parts. Although the human head within had been destroyed, the rest of the body reassembled itself behind Denton.

The helicopter blade reactivated and whirled violently. The Undriel pulled its elbow back, ready to push forward and shred him into pieces. It jolted as something collided with its arm, separating the forearm from the wrist. The rotating blade smashed into the ground and flung itself off into the jungle, embedding itself into a thick tree.

Talulo's daunoren staff remained lodged in the body of the machine. The auk'nai deftly leaped onto the machine's body, removed his staff from its side, and slammed it into the Undriel's other arm. Denton jump-jetted forward into the Undriel's torso. The machine broke into pieces again. Denton smashed into the dirt and kneeled over a headless torso, while Talulo fell to the ground with the severed metal arm blade. The Undriel's legs rushed toward Cade.

Cade let the assault rifle rip and tore the legs into scrap metal. Denton flicked his hands, bringing out the knuckle blades in his gauntlets and repeatedly smashing them into the Undriel's torso. Talulo twirled his daunoren staff, flung the severed bladed arm into the air, and then used the collider pistol to shoot the arm into fragments before it hit the ground.

Each of the Undriel's separate pieces sputtered and died. Everyone took a moment to catch their breath. Denton broke the silence. "*Hells*, that was just one of those things?"

Denton's soothreader came back online. The comm channel was signaling him. With a quick gesture, Denton opened the comm and heard Sergeant Jess Combs's voice, "I repeat, we have discovered the presence of the Undriel on Kamaria."

"Jess, this is Denton. Can you hear me?" Denton interrupted. "Are you guys safe?"

A side-channel opened—Eliana's tag. Denton accepted it.

"Denny, is that you? Did you find them?" Eliana asked.

"I have them here with me," Denton said. "But it's bad here. We've been attacked by—"

"The Undriel. I know," Eliana said. She seemed to gulp in sadness and added, "That was Faye."

Denton and Talulo shared a horrified look. Finally, the reality was sinking in. A longtime friend had become an enemy through absorption, and just like that, the old nightmares had returned. Denton muttered, "Hells . . . what happened?"

Eliana continued, "We were attacked on the shore. One ambushed us and absorbed Faye. After she was converted, she took off in your direction. We couldn't contact you because of the Undriel interference."

Denton looked at Cade. Coming to Kamaria was supposed to be freedom from the tyranny of the machines that had driven them from the Sol System. Memories of watching news reports for fifteen years filled Denton's head. He remembered the aching dread he felt every day the Undriel got closer to Ganymede. Denton hoped his children would never have to live with that dread.

"Shit," Denton said. "Faye took out the *Rogers* and absorbed some of the marines I was with. We just destroyed one of them, I think. There could be two or three more depending on how many she absorbed."

"Oh God," Eliana said. "They are really back. It's all happening again."

Denton didn't respond.

"We will come to get you. Ping me your coordinates," Eliana said.

"It's not safe here—"

"*We are coming.* Ping me," Eliana insisted.

Denton sighed and swiped his hand over the soothreader.

"Coordinates received—we'll be there in a few hours. "Denny . . ."

"I love you too," Denton said.

"Stay safe," Eliana said. "Keep our children safe."

"I will."

The call ended. Denton sighed and turned toward the group. Talulo had his daunoren staff in one hand and his pistol in the other. Cade checked his assault rifle to make sure the collider cylinder had not been jammed up.

Wait, hold on. Denton counted only two heads.

"Where's Nella?" Denton asked.

Cade turned. He'd thought she was right behind him, but now she was nowhere to be seen. Penelope was also missing. Cade's eyes were wide with realization. "Shit! I think she went back to where the voice was calling us."

"Hells!" Denton shouted, and took off, racing back the way they had come. Cade and Talulo followed close behind.

THIRTY-FOUR

<Come back—COME back—COME BACK!> the voice called to Nella. *<We need you.>*

I'm on my way, Nella thought, hoping her thoughts would reach the mysterious beings that craved her attention so badly. She held on tightly to Penelope and did her best to steer the loamalon through the dense jungle. The wilderness seemed to want to help her. All the bioluminescent elements of the jungle around Nella created a bright-green path for her to follow. The colors for these varieties of plants were all wrong, but this day was full of wrongness. The voices wanted her to come to them, and even stranger, Nella felt compelled to join them. The planet was rooting for this reunion. Nothing else mattered except reaching the stone circle. Nella was uncertain what she would do when she arrived at that place.

A shadow stepped into the tunnel of green light, and Nella pulled back hard on Penelope's reins. The loamalon skidded to a halt, tearing up shrubs and other low jungle plants to not trample the shadow. When Penelope was stopped, Nella could finally see who it was.

It was one of the Tvashtar marines that had arrived on the *Rogers* with her father. His nametag read *R. Ghanem.* He was saying something, unaware that Nella could not hear him. She put her hands near her ears to tell the wounded marine she was deaf. He didn't seem to notice, or maybe he was too hurt and desperate to care. His suit had been damaged, and blood was seeping out from his chest plate. The marine had been fighting the Undriel, and it looked like he may have escaped, but his wound would kill him.

R. Ghanem fell to his knees.

Nella dismounted the loamalon and knelt in front of the marine. She could feel something inside of her chest. Her blood felt like a cold, babbling brook in a temperate forest.

<We want to see you again.>

<You can help him.>

<We missed you.> The voices echoed in her mind. It was as if there was a crowd waiting at the end of a finish line, and only one witness could see her clearly enough to tell her what she needed to know. She focused on the smallest voice that had said, *You can help him.*

But how? Nella wondered. She saw the look on the marine's face. It was a mixture of horror and confusion, with a layer of pain from his wounds. He looked like he wanted to run away from Nella but couldn't. She shook her head, then signed, *"I will help you,"* with her left hand crunched into a fist, thumb up, planted on top of her flat open palm on her right hand. She pushed this sign from her chest toward R. Ghanem. He didn't seem to understand, so she reached out to touch his shoulder, hoping to calm him down, and noticed something strange about her hands.

A green mist seeped out of her skin. It drifted onto the jungle floor, where small plants began to bud and grow. She pulled her hand back to her face and watched the strange thing—a residual glow was reflecting off her dark-brown skin. Something was emitting from her face. Cade had said her eyes were glowing green before. They must have been now too. That explained the marine's confusion and horror.

<You can help him,> said the small voice from within the crowd

of loud voices. *<It is easy. You already know how.>*

Nella reached for the marine's chest plate. At first, R. Ghanem recoiled like a scared animal. She nodded and smiled. The marine's eyes darted from Nella's hands to her eyes. He winced in pain, then nodded. Nella pressed her hand against his wound, allowing the mist to flow into him. R. Ghanem's eyes widened, and he coughed. Then it looked as though the air had been pulled out of his lungs. He blinked rapidly, then crooked his eyebrow and looked down.

Nella removed her hand and noticed it was covered in blood. She wiped it on the closest plant, but the sticky stuff wouldn't completely come off. There was a sharp pain in her head, and she pushed her clean palm against her forehead in an attempt to ease the sting. Ghanem inspected his wound, and together they noticed the deep laceration that had threatened his life was gone now.

Nella stood and mounted Penelope. She kicked the loamalon's sides and rushed toward the stone circle once more. The marine stood in the jungle, urging her not to go that way.

<We missed you. You are close. Come back.>

Nella could see the stone circle ahead, with the scattered remains of the *Rogers* still burning near it. The Undriel that had taken down the scout ship stood in the center. It lifted the limp body of the monster auk'gnell. The Undriel attempted to pulse energy into the dead monster, but there was no reaction from the corpse.

Nella slowed Penelope down and dismounted the loamalon in the dense jungle foliage just outside the circle. She patted Penelope's fur and thought, *You may want to get out of here.*

The loamalon exhaled a grunt and backed itself into the bushes. Nella wasn't sure if it understood her thoughts or if she had made her intentions clear enough with her body language. Still, she was glad Penelope would stay hidden. Nella crept forward through the bushes, uncertain of how much sound she was making.

<She's back—YOU'RE HERE—WE missed YOU.>

Shh! Quiet please! Nella shouted in her mind. The Undriel had not noticed her yet, or it simply didn't care. There wasn't anything

Nella could do that could be more threatening than the marines it fought earlier. Nella did a headcount. In front of her was the Undriel that had taken down the *Rogers*; another one was far behind her now, fighting with her father and brother, and Nella had helped R. Ghanem. That left one marine—or Undriel—unaccounted for.

What am I supposed to do now? Nella thought. She could walk into the circle and hope something would happen, but that meant risking a speedy death. Or worse, a swift absorption. She couldn't just ask out loud. Nella had never spoken words before; she had no idea how they even sounded. Regret crept over her, and she felt paralyzed as she crouched in the bushes near the stone circle.

The Undriel holding the monster auk'gnell's body tried pulsing energy into it one more time. The red light flicked out from the crevices in the machinery that made up the robot's body and lapped over the auk'gnell's feathers, roasting anything that wasn't bone or metal. It looked like she was trying to reactivate the monster, but something wasn't going right. *What did Cade do to that thing?*

Something in the corner of Nella's eye caught her attention. It was an array of white lights that was slowly moving toward her in a serpentine fashion. It raised its head as it grew closer, revealing a centipede made of orange and black metal. The final marine was accounted for now. He must have been absorbed with whatever was left of the *Rogers* and therefore took on a strange, unfinished form.

The Undriel centipede lunged at Nella. She jumped forward just in time to avoid the impact and turned to see it coil up for another strike. Nella scrambled forward, and she sloppily brought herself to her feet and rushed into the stone circle.

The tall Undriel dropped the monster auk'gnell's body and faced Nella. It took a step closer to her and opened its spider-bot head, revealing a familiar face. Nella recognized Faye Raike in the tangled mess of the Undriel machinery. Her eyes looked kind, inviting almost. On Faye's head was a crown of metal and wires. Nella froze and shivered at the gruesome sight. Faye looked like she was saying something, but Nella wouldn't know for sure. She was happy she couldn't hear what Faye was saying; she was afraid it would have haunted all her nightmares going forward.

This is a distraction. Nella thought, as horrifying of a disturbance as it was.

The Undriel centipede lunged again, this time from behind. Nella threw herself to the side, rolling into the remains of the burning spacecraft and scratching her back on some sharp metal. The robots bashed into each other. Faye violently ripped the centipede away from herself and threw it against the rock wall. She closed her spider-bot head and moved toward Nella.

Nella pushed herself deeper into the wreck of the *Rogers*. There wasn't much cover left. The wreckage had been stripped into a skeleton by Faye to absorb the other marines. Faye ripped away anything that blocked her path to Nella, moving quickly through tangled metal. It wasn't much, but it did slow Faye down ever so slightly.

Nella crawled out through the other side of the *Rogers* and faced the stone wall. Nezzarform statues looked down at her from above, and suddenly Nella understood who was calling to her.

<YES—YOU ARE HERE—WE MISSED YOU.>

The centipede coiled itself again, and little insectoid arms twitched with anticipation.

What do I do? Nella thought with panic.

<You recognize your creations. What will you have us do?>

Help me! Nella shouted with her mind.

The centipede lunged.

A crackle of lightning—the world filled with a green light.

Nella fell onto her back, unsure if she was hit with a missile or killed by the centipede. When the light dimmed, Nella watched the metal centipede disintegrate into ash.

Faye rushed toward Nella, using jets on her back to cover the distance with alarming speed. Nella covered her face with her arms.

The ground shook like a mountain had fallen from the sky. Something immense jumped from the upper ledge and landed in front of Nella. An arm made of stone and lightning swung so fast that Nella almost didn't see it happen. There was a loud crash. Faye was knocked across the stone circle and into the jungle beyond. A few of her parts sprang free and scattered on the ground.

A nezzarform turned to face Nella. *<We missed you, Sympha.>*

It was a creature made of boulders, moss, jungle plants, and green electricity. It was a thing made by the Sirens long ago, and it was *speaking* to Nella's mind. She had received their messages directly, in a format she understood but didn't understand how. It was a mixture of images and sensations that gave the appearance of words when combined. As crazy as it all was, Nella also felt like she was seeing an old friend after a long time apart.

Another nezzarform climbed down from their rock ledge and joined the first one's side. Their electricity lit up the jungle. They bowed before her, and the first one said, *<I am Oolith, and this is Lahar.>*

Can you hear my thoughts? Nella asked with her mind.

<Only when you speak directly to us,> Oolith said.

Suddenly, Nella felt as strong as an army.

THIRTY-FIVE

DENTON RACED THROUGH THE jungle. He felt stupid losing Nella so quickly after just reuniting with her. He didn't have time to wonder what she was thinking—running *toward* an Undriel foot soldier—his mind was focused on getting back to the crash site as fast as he could.

Please, let her be safe, Denton thought to himself as low-hanging jungle vines and shrubs assaulted him in his mad pursuit.

"Dad!" The shout came from behind him. "Dad, wait up!"

Denton stopped and turned to see Cade struggling behind him. His leg had been injured the entire time, and now the injury was starting to take its toll. Cade stumbled to the ground. Before Denton could rush to him, Talulo kneeled and helped Cade to his feet.

"Thanks," Cade said, trying to catch his breath.

Talulo cooed. Before they could start running again, there was a thunderous crackle and a bright-green light in the distance through the trees. The clap of thunder was so loud, Denton almost fell to his knees in shock. "Was that a nezzarform blast?" Talulo asked. The auk'nai looked at Denton with worry in his eyes.

"The statues, right?" Cade asked. "I think those are the voices I'm hearing."

"Nezzarforms don't talk," Denton stated.

"You just can't hear them," Cade said, his voice laced with frustration.

"You're tired. You don't know what you're saying," Denton said. "Come on, let's—"

"I know what I'm saying, and I know what I'm hearing," Cade shouted, his voice vibrating with another speaker's tone. *You think you know the Sirens, but you're just a shade. You never understood us.*

"What did you just call me?" Denton asked. His skin felt cold.

"A *shade*. A nothing. An insect on the wall," Cade said. The distortion in his voice sounded familiar to Denton. Cade's eyes were glowing hot blue. Talulo let Cade go and stepped back a few paces. Denton remembered the footage from the admiral's stasis pod, how Cade's eyes were glowing when he pulled Nella from the wreck and took her to safety.

What the Hells is going on? Denton thought.

Cade moved toward his father. His leg seemed to not bother him at all anymore. When Cade spoke, it sounded like two voices talking. One was his own, the other a profoundly alien thing. "I trusted you to save Sympha. Instead, you brought Nhymn to her, and she killed her. *I* failed her, but *you* failed *me*. I was wrong about Nhymn bringing oblivion. It was *YOU* who brought Armageddon to this planet."

"Ca—" Denton whimpered half the name, then corrected himself. "*Karx?*"

Cade didn't respond. His brow was furrowed, his nose bunched up, and his teeth were showing in a snarl. This was not Denton's son. Denton whispered, "How is this possible?"

"Denton!" The voice of Lance Corporal Rafa Ghanem shouted to them from the thick of the trees. "Watch out!"

Cade blinked, and his eyes returned to their normal state. They looked into the trees and found a dark shape moving ultrafast toward them. Denton shoved Cade into the bushes and was struck by the shape. He was thrown into a tree, then ricocheted off and rolled on the ground.

Denton strained to look up. He saw the Undriel that had taken down the *Rogers*, Faye Raike. She turned toward him, revealing massive damage she'd recently received from some unknown combatant. Parts of her armor had been removed entirely, one arm was missing, and her spider-bot head had been cracked open.

"Faye!" Denton shouted.

She didn't react in any way to Denton's shouts. There was a loud crash and an eruption of gunfire as Lance Corporal Rafa Ghanem stormed toward the Undriel. Faye jumped and shifted into ultrafast mode once more. Her movement was so quick that it sliced a tree in half. Denton rolled away from the falling jungle tree and curled into the fetal position to avoid being smashed.

Talulo let out a shriek. Denton scrambled to his feet in time to watch Faye bash into his auk'nai friend and lunge toward his son. Cade fired off a few rounds from his assault rifle, striking Faye directly in the torso, but it didn't stop her movement. The Undriel slammed into Cade and pinned him to the ground. Denton's heart sank, thinking he was about to watch his son become absorbed by the Undriel machine. He shouted at the top of his lungs and rushed toward them, using his jump-jet to cover the distance as quickly as possible.

Faye slung Cade's limp body over her metallic shoulder, then launched into the sky. Within a few heartbeats, Faye and Cade were only a dot on the horizon.

"Cade!" Denton shouted into the air. He slunk to his knees as the Undriel and his son vanished from view. It was quiet. It had all happened so fast, the slow creep of realization began to fill Denton's body. *No. No. Oh God, no!*

Cade was lost a second time.

Rafa pulled Talulo to his feet, then went to Denton's side. "She didn't absorb him. There's still—"

"What—*a chance?*" Denton stood and sneered. "You saw what that thing did to your men. You think it's going just let my son just sit around? Oh, God." Denton began to sob. His dread, regret, and sorrow mixed in his chest. He felt cold, yet his heart was on fire. Denton wanted to vomit.

"Nella is still up ahead. We have to make sure she's alright," Rafa said. "Your kids are different. Nella, she—well, look." Rafa lifted his chest plate and showed Denton his healed wound. It looked smooth, not even a hint of a scar. "About twenty minutes ago, I was cut right through, but your daughter stopped the bleeding. She saved my life. I don't know how she did it, but she has some sort of power."

"Nella," Denton said, and rushed toward the stone circle. Rafa put one of Talulo's arms around his shoulders and followed behind. They ran the remainder of the way to the stone circle.

Denton burst through the tree line and landed in the circle, ready for anything except what he discovered there. He lowered his weapon and observed the odd sight. Nella and her nezzarforms turned to face him. They were standing around L'Arn's corpse, near the remnants of the downed *Rogers*.

Nella signed, *"It's okay. These are friends."* She gestured to the glowing stone statues that surrounded her. The last time Denton had seen these golem-like creatures, they were attacking people in one of the bloodiest battles humans had ever fought.

Denton ignored the nezzarforms and walked toward Nella. He signed, *"Your brother . . ."* and held his hands still, unsure of how to complete the signs.

Her eyes went wide, and her breathing became erratic.

"He was taken. The Undriel," Denton finished with tears in his eyes. He couldn't bring himself to sign more—his hands were shaking, and his face looked lost in the sadness.

Nella gripped her hands into knuckles and looked at the ground. They had come so far, only for Cade to be taken right back to the start. She began to shake with anger. Denton noticed Nella's skin was seething green mist. Her eyes glowed green.

Nella exploded with a wave of green energy. The emerald light passed through everyone in the stone circle. After it had passed, she fell to her knees. Rafa and Talulo looked around and patted themselves to make sure they weren't hurt by the energy. Denton didn't react to the explosion. He had seen it once before, in a dream that was more than a dream.

A dream about Sirens.

"I failed," Denton said out loud, knowing his daughter couldn't hear his confession. "I was right where I needed to be, and I failed. It should have been me. They could take me and cut me to pieces and rip out my bones, and it still wouldn't hurt as much as this does. I'm so sorry, Nella. Your brother is gone, and it's my fault."

Nella read his lips and cried.

Denton sank to the floor and hugged his daughter. Nella sobbed quietly in his arms, and the two stayed on the ground while the nezzarforms watched over them. They had no way of chasing Faye to save Cade. There was only the wreck of the *Rogers*, the hum of the nezzarforms, and the survivors of the fight with the Undriel.

THIRTY-SIX

ELIANA STROKED HER DAUGHTER'S hair with slow, gentle movements. The marine transport cargo bay was quiet. They sat together on the upper balcony catwalk, looking out the long window at the stars. In the main cargo area below, two nezzarforms stood near a sleeping loamalon. L'Arn's broken, burnt form lay in a body bag in the corner. Jess and Rafa watched over them and discussed the Undriel situation in whispers.

Nella had cried herself to sleep. Eliana felt so weak, so paralyzed by the thought of her son being taken a second time. Eliana knew her daughter couldn't hear her, but regardless, she whispered a Martian lullaby her mother used to sing. It was something that calmed her during the bad days—when the ocean of sadness overtook her, and she needed a breath of air.

"Follow the wind, that blows the dust
To a place I found, just for us
So far away, yet also near
You'll know it then, 'cuz I'll be here . . ."

The vibrations in Eliana's throat echoed into Nella's skin. Eliana wished she could sing this song to Cade, like she had when he was just her little baby boy. She came to the end of the lullaby and thought of him.

"If dreams are true (I know they are)
We'll travel to this bright new star.
So far away, yet also near
You know it now, 'cuz you are . . ."

Here. Eliana thought. But Cade was not here. No one knew what had happened to him. She had no closure. Her son was lost.

Eliana had tried to force herself to be strong ever since she opened the access ramp and discovered her son had been taken a second time. She held back her tears with a dam built of the previous losses of her parents. She wanted to cry—to allow the dam to break and let the emotions flow. But this dam was impenetrable. She had built it too strong. Her son might be dead, and she could do nothing about it, and so *nothing* was the punishment for her failure. Raw nothingness, as if her heart had suddenly vanished. If it had been ripped out, there would have been a sharp pain followed by screaming. Eliana had not even a dull ache in her chest, only a void in her heart and mind.

She had gone inert.

Footsteps echoed off the catwalk as Denton approached. Eliana didn't turn to face him. She couldn't. She hated him for his failure, whether she wanted to or not—it was involuntary. Eliana had known Denton long enough to understand that he knew about her feelings toward him. Still, he was always going to be near her side. Her hate didn't scare him away. In this sweet irony, her hatred was also mixed with love.

Denton sat next to Eliana and Nella and looked out the long, rectangular window, his eyes red and glossy. He had been sobbing privately. Denton looked like Hells. He had not removed the combat suit, perhaps because he needed armor now more than ever.

The military was already mobilizing against the Undriel, and Denton was planning on being there with them when they stormed the beach. The hope was that Cade could somehow avoid being absorbed until they could arrive, but it was a long shot. The more significant problem for the world right now was the fact that the Undriel were on Kamaria. One abducted person was not a priority for humanity as a whole, even if it meant the world to Denton and Eliana Castus.

The nightmarish machines had pushed humanity into deep space before. The survivors had come so far and adapted to a strange world with toxic air and monsters, only to meet the very thing that had driven them from their home. There was no escape plan this time. They couldn't just hop back onto the *Telemachus* and ride it to the next habitable planet. The *Infinite Aria* was going to be their exploratory vessel to continue John Veston's mission, but it was a long way from being completed.

"We have to stop them this time," Denton said, finally breaking the silence, "We ran last time, and they just followed us here. If we run again, they will follow us again. We need to annihilate them here on Kamaria."

Eliana didn't say anything.

"You know, I thought when we shipped Nhymn away, we were through worrying about the future of the human race. I should have forced her to tell us what she saw—tell us why she wanted to leave so bad."

"She saw the Undriel," Eliana said, her voice hoarse from swallowing back her emotions. Her silence had strained her more than a night of screaming.

"She must have. She predicted the Undriel would follow us to Kamaria. You mentioned Auden claimed they have been here longer than us. Nhymn was wandering around as a nightsnare and found him."

Eliana sighed. Nhymn knew what danger lurked here and just abandoned the planet instead of warning anyone. Her final blow to humanity and the creatures of Kamaria.

Denton hesitated, then said, "We found something in the underground palace."

Eliana stopped stroking Nella's hair and turned to him.

"The probe we sent down was attacked by something. A thing with claws like a Siren."

"Do you think it's Nhymn?" Eliana asked in a hushed whisper, as if to hide it from the world and keep it from coming to fruition.

"I don't know. I don't see how that would be possible," Denton said. "But shit, it seems like anything is possible now."

Eliana looked down at Nella, then over to the two nezzarforms in the cargo bay below. Her children had found something on their journey home.

Denton huffed with torment. "I think Sympha and Karx have regenerated. Sirens don't die like we do. They continue on. Before he was taken, Cade said some things to me, implying he was with me during my visions of the Sirens. I think he is some sort of vessel for Karx."

"And Nella is a vessel for Sympha," Eliana whispered and stroked her daughter's hair once more as she winced with pain. *What has happened to our children?*

"Yeah," Denton said, "Sympha must have tethered herself to me during that battle with Nhymn years ago. And Karx would have still been with me, just dormant. So, they must have regenerated and used our kids as an escape pod from me."

It made sense in its weird way. Tethering was something that only happened between humans and Sirens. The exact methods were still a mystery. The only two people previously known to experience tethering were Captain Roelin Raike—now deceased—and Denton Castus. Denton had been under the assumption his tethers snapped when Roelin was killed. Apparently, Cade and Nella had proved otherwise.

"I thought they were gone for good. Looks like I was wrong. Cade even told me that I knew nothing about the Sirens. I was just a stupid insect on the wall." Denton quoted his son, "A *shade*. A *nothing*."

Eliana sighed. "So, there's potentially a Siren in the underground palace. Nezzarforms are now reawakening. Our son is a vessel for Karx and our daughter a vessel for Sympha. And the Undriel have not only been on Kamaria this whole time, but now they are also a threat to us again." They shared silence. The odds were against them once more. It didn't feel like they could survive against so many threats.

"But how did the Undriel end up trapped underwater on the Howling Shore?" Eliana asked. "It doesn't make any sense. They had such advanced technology and end up messing up the landing? And Auden somehow couldn't bring the Undriel ship back online, and that Homer was the perfect tool to do so." She thought about her encounter with Dr. Nouls for a moment. "Everything I saw in Auden goes against what we know about the Undriel. He was chatty and even showed signs of fear."

"Fear? What could an Undriel be scared of?" Denton asked.

"He was scared of the ultimate end—death. If Auden was destroyed before freeing the other Undriel, everything they had accomplished would have been sealed underwater for eternity." Eliana wished that had been the way things went. "But now they are free. I don't think we understand the Undriel at all. There's more going on than we know."

Denton rubbed the back of his hand against his nose and looked out the window at the stars. "Karx might be able to save Cade."

Eliana turned to Denton and felt the tears well up in her eyes. "You think there's hope?"

"Just maybe. The Undriel don't know anything about the Sirens, right? Hells, we barely do, apparently."

Eliana didn't know. If Nhymn had found Auden, there was a chance the Undriel had figured out how Sirens work. But if Nhymn was scared enough to leave the planet behind and Auden was scared of leaving his cave, there was a chance she saw Auden and took off running before he had an opportunity to know what was going on. Their fears were their disadvantage. She hoped the Undriel didn't understand the Sirens.

If they were working together, they'd be invincible.

THIRTY-SEVEN

CADE'S EYES OPENED, BUT he couldn't see anything. He lifted his hands and could barely see his dark skin faintly in the null black void around him.

<WE ARE IN GREAT DANGER . . .> The deep voice echoed in his mind.

"Who's there?" Cade asked, feeling small in the darkness. He heard the clop of a hoof and turned around to see a monster step out of the shadows. It had a bull-skull head with two long horns and a cyclopean eye. Its neck was a series of pale-blue tentacles connected to a torso made of white bone carapace. The monster had two bulky, muscular arms, with immense fists that terminated in talons. Its lower half was much like a loamalon's, with four long legs and hooves made of bone and wormskin. Cade had seen this figure before in some drawing his father had sketched. Maybe a dream once too—it was hard to recall.

It was Karx.

<YOU KNOW WHO I AM. WE ARE ONE . . .> Karx said in his slow, booming drawl.

"The voices in the jungle. I heard them say your name," Cade said. He thought about the events of the past few days—his glowing blue eyes, the power he felt when fighting the auk'gnell, and the energy he pulsed in the nest of the mutant Sirens. Yes, Karx had been with him this whole time—his entire life, in fact.

<WE ARE IN GREAT DANGER . . .>

"What is happening?" Cade asked.

<THE MACHINES HAVE TAKEN US . . .>

"The Undriel." Cade rubbed his shoulder. The thing had hit him so fast he went unconscious. If he was taken by the Undriel, then absorption was soon to follow. "They'll kill us. Or worse, absorb us."

<THEY WILL TRY . . . THEY MAY SUCCEED . . .> Karx said. *<BUT THERE IS A WAY WE CAN ENDURE . . .>*

"What, stop the absorption?" Cade looked away. "I don't think you understand the Undriel."

<WE CAN ENDURE . . . BUT NOT COMPLETELY . . .>

Cade allowed that to sink in. What Karx was suggesting wasn't a cure-all for his situation. It was only a chance to remain intact instead of becoming a full-fledged Undriel-*and-loving-it*. Cade knew this meant his body might be destroyed, but his mind would be his own—shared with Karx.

"How?" Cade asked.

<YOU MUST DO EVERYTHING I SAY . . . EXACTLY . . .>

———◆———

Cade's eyes snapped open. He was face down on something wet and hard. He blinked away his confusion and pushed himself up onto his knees, noticing he was on the Howling Shore, the boiling crimson sea before him. Lights were glowing under the waves, and the water was rolling and bubbling with chaos.

An Undriel rose from the water. Its spiderlike head broke the surface first, followed by its wasp torso and long, metallic arms. In one claw, it clutched the half-body of Homer. As its feet broke the surface of the waves, ripples of orange light flicked out. The machine walked across the water toward Cade.

"That is not L'Arn," the Undriel said. "But he is certainly a catch. You've done us proud, Faye."

Cade turned to his right and saw the damaged Undriel that had taken down the *Rogers*. Her facemask was half-open, revealing the visage of an old family friend, Faye Raike. Cade was so horrified he wanted to vomit.

The Undriel on the water tossed Homer's body onto the rocks like discarded trash and approached Cade. It leaned in to inspect his face. "I've seen some of the things you can do through L'Arn's eyes. You're not like any human I've encountered before. How *strange*."

"What do you want with me?" Cade asked, fighting through his terror.

The Undriel stood straight and shook its spider-bot head, a human gesture. "Honestly, this is sort of a clerical error. I already got everything I wanted. That Homer did the trick. I was too busy to tell Faye I didn't need you anymore, so she fetched you regardless. Nevertheless, you still deserve *perfection*."

"Are you going to absorb me?"

"In time. So *eager*." The Undriel laughed and looked toward the water.

A white metal skull rose from the waves, its eyes like abyssal marbles, its bottom jaw void-black. Shoulders spread out wide from the mechanical neck, and long arms flowed from the sea like a tower being erected. Pieces of coral and other sea life clung to the metal frame of the tall mechanical figure. Its legs were still as it rose, not walking like the other had. It slid over the water silently. Ghostlike.

"Welcome back, Tibor," the Undriel said, pleased. Tibor planted his metallic feet on the wet rock in front of Cade. Tibor Undriel was the trillionaire who had brought the evil artificial intelligence to life and thus consumed the Sol System—the nightmarish machines' namesake.

This was the King of the Old Star.

"Auden." Tibor's voice sounded like gravel being dragged over a grave. He barely moved his head to acknowledge the Undriel who had risen from the waves before him. Tibor looked at Cade with his void-like eyes. Cade couldn't speak. His breathing became ragged, and his eyes widened.

"Extraordinary, yet imperfect. Don't you agree?" Auden said in a quiet, measured tone. "This is John Veston's grandson."

Tibor's eyes flashed yellow, then faded back to black. The machine looked down at the wet rocks. *Is it sad?* Cade wondered. There was a strange emptiness in Tibor's mechanical visage that Cade couldn't place.

"John is dead," Auden stated flatly. "He was flawed anyway. No amount of absorption could have made John see the truth of what we were doing."

Tibor looked at Auden with no noticeable expression. *Agreement? Regret?* It was unclear what Tibor was feeling or thinking.

"We came to elevate the universe," Auden said to Cade.

Tibor nodded to Faye. She grabbed Cade's arm and lifted him to his feet. Without saying another word, they dragged him into the cave. Cade struggled to get away from Faye's tight grip but soon became paralyzed in horror. More Undriel walked out from the water, enough to fill the beach with coral-covered machines. An enormous metal ship rose from the waves and bellowed out a loud bass roar—the *Devourer*.

This was an invasion.

Auden had finally reunited with his friends.

THIRTY-EIGHT

FAR ACROSS THE CONTINENT, past the crimson shores, through the mountains, and beyond the desert and the jungle, the auk'nai were flocking to the *Telemachus* wreckage. Zephyr Gale had followed them on her rushcycle. The trip had taken hours. When she reached the entrance to the valley, she stopped to take in the view.

There were thousands of auk'nai, and more on the way. They brought tools and weapons. They spent hours inside the *Telemachus*, torching out the dangerous creatures within. When they had made it safe, they began reconfiguring the ship for some purpose, taking large pieces of it away and breaking the massive wreck down.

They began converting the ship into something beautiful. Intricate jewels were fused to the outside, reflecting light onto the inert nezzarform statues surrounding it. Others draped the foundation with vines and foliage, blending it in with the nature of the valley.

"George, Marie?" The crackled voice of an auk'nai came in over Zephyr's wave transmitter. It was an illegal device used to hack into private comm channels. She had one built into her rushcycle to monitor police transmissions from back when she thought being a street racer would be her career. Back before she started working in space with Cade Castus.

"Yes, Talulo, we can hear you," Marie Viray said. "What is happening with all these auk'nai?"

"Auk'nai are bringing a new Daunoren into the world. The nest must be perfect, and the resources for pilgrimage must be present. Talulo scouted this place when others were inside. It is perfect for the new Song."

"I see. Amazing," George Tanaka said. "Can we help?"

"Humans will not be allowed in the new Song," Talulo said firmly.

There was silence for a moment.

"What are you saying?" George asked, hurt.

"The new Song is built despite the pain humans have caused to the auk'nai. It is a Song sung only by auk'nai, for auk'nai alone to hear. The world is shared, but the Song of Kamaria is for the auk'nai alone," Talulo said.

Zephyr watched the structure being built, now with a pain in her heart. She had lived in a world where everything was everyone's, where humans and auk'nai lived in harmony. Apparently, the balance wasn't equal. These auk'nai had lost everything after the humans arrived. In a way, humans were much like the Undriel. Good intentions didn't stop things from being taken away. If humanity had never arrived on Kamaria, Nhymn would have never destroyed the city of Apusticus. The Daunoren of the Spirit Song Mountain might still be alive.

"I understand," George said. "We will not interfere with your work."

Talulo cooed, and the comm winked out.

A group of auk'nai flew in, harnessing a large egg in an intricately designed ceremonial sash. They brought it over to the pedestal and placed it in the center. Elite auk'nai protectors, with peck rifles strapped to their faces and wearing deep-black armor and sashes, stood near the egg platform. They would protect the egg and ward off any humans who grew curious enough to get too close.

Zephyr put her helmet on and revved her rushcycle's engine. She'd heard what the auk'nai wanted and decided to honor it herself. The rushcycle turned around and then thrust back toward the city of Odysseus.

———— ◦ ————

The Song of Kamaria played the tune of new life, and the Song of the Dead hummed along with it. In the cargo bay of the marine transport, a family mourned the loss of a loved one. On the far shore, the King of the Old Star reunited with his flock.

In the crimson desert, an old mechanism came back to life. Large boulders began to float above a colossal pit. Dark ooze from the tunnel of mutated Sirens began to flow downriver and into the canyon, where it would eventually find the alabaster palace. There was only one creature on Kamaria that understood this mechanism's intent.

It flexed its claws as it waited.

ACKNOWLEDGMENTS

To my wife, Carrie, who continues to support and inspire me every day. Since the release of *In the Orbit of Sirens*, she has been pivotal in helping me become an efficient bookseller. I love you, babe.

To my brother, Danny. My greatest teacher.

To my parents, thank you for being so supportive with these novels. I have been fortunate in my life to never feel like anyone thought I was bluffing when it came to writing. With your belief in me, I can create worlds. Thank you.

To Treva, who helped me make Nella as authentic as possible. Your notes were excellent and thorough. If I made any mistakes, they are my own. You were a fantastic help, and I appreciate the time and care you put into this. Thank you.

To the people who helped me with notes about Deaf Culture. Kim R., A. Walker, and Kim B. Your notes not only opened the door to a beautiful community to me, but they also brought a level of legitimacy to this novel. I wanted to do this justice, and with your help, I hope I did. Thank you for being patient with me.

To my team of freelancers, job well done! Beautiful work as always, and I know you may even be editing these words here. I hope they bring you a smile and do not disappoint. Thank you for helping me with this work.

To Daniel Schmelling, who has not only delivered some fantastic cover art but has become a new friend in the process. I'm glad to have crossed paths with you, and I look forward to continuing working with you.

To Jason Michael Hall, who brings my world to life with so many excellent illustrations. I am always blown away by your work, and I miss working with you in our day jobs. It's a small world, and I'm sure we'll work side by side again, but until then, the work you've been doing with these novels has been a dream. I cannot thank you enough.

To my readers—yes, you! Especially if you came here from *In the Orbit of Sirens*. When I released the first novel, I had no idea how the world would react. Since *Sirens* launched, readers from all around the world have shown their support. I am floored by the response, and I hope this second entry in the Song of Kamaria was equally satisfying.

Thank you for joining me on this journey, and I hope to bring you along for the conclusion to this trilogy.

ABOUT THE AUTHOR

T. A. Bruno grew up in a suburb south of Chicago and moved to Los Angeles to pursue a career in the film industry. Since then, he has brought stories to life for over a decade as a previsualization artist. At home, he is the proud father of two boys and a husband to a wonderful wife. T. A. released his debut novel, *In the Orbit of Sirens*, amid a global pandemic in 2020, and it has won multiple awards.

FOR MORE ABOUT THIS BOOK AND AUTHOR, VISIT

TABruno.com

Follow the adventure

Facebook.com/TABrunoAuthor
Instagram.com/TABrunoAuthor
Twitter.com/TABrunoAuthor
Goodreads.com/TABrunoAuthor

PLEASE CONSIDER LEAVING A REVIEW.

CPSIA information can be obtained
at www.ICGtesting.com
Printed in the USA
FSHW010829170921
84817FS